UNDER *this* SAME *Sky*

Prairie Skies Series ~ Book One

CYNTHIA ROEMER

Scrivenings PRESS
Quench your thirst for story.
www.ScriveningsPress.com

2020© Cynthia Roemer

Published by Scrivenings Press LLC
15 Lucky Lane
Morrilton, Arkansas 72110
https://ScriveningsPress.com

Printed in the United States of America

Paperback ISBN 978-1-64917-034-7
eBook ISBN 978-1-64917-035-4

Library of Congress Control Number: 2020940027

Cover by Diane Turpin, www.dianeturpindesigns.com

(Note: This book was previously published by Mantle Rock Publishing LLC and was re-published when MRP was acquired by Scrivenings Press LLC in 2020.)

All characters are fictional, and any resemblance to real people, either factional or historical, is purely coincidental.

Unless otherwise noted, all scripture is quoted from the King James Version of the Bible.

"To the Maker of Heaven and earth
Who makes all things possible.
I love you, Lord, my Rock and my Salvation."
Psalm 62:7

And to my family whom
I love so very much.

May you be blessed
by Becky's story.

Cynthia
Roemer

Acknowledgments

I want to thank you readers for investing your valuable time into Becky and Matthew's story. I pray their journey touched your hearts in some small way. This novel has experienced many changes along the way, but I am most grateful for each stage of growth the Lord walked me and my characters through. It is by God's grace and power alone that I have come to this point in my writing career. And I am humbled and grateful for His love and blessings.

There are many others I need to thank for spurring me along in my writing journey. First, I wish to thank my husband, Marvin, for his patience and understanding as I spent countless hours at the computer writing, editing, and figuring out this whole book publishing process. I am so grateful for your love and support. May our next twenty-three years together be even more special than our first.

Thanks to my sons, Glenn and Evan, for all of your technical support and helping me make sense of things when I didn't know what I was doing. Thanks for peeking over my shoulder, teasing me about being a #1 best-selling mom, and making me laugh. I love you both dearly!

I'm so grateful for my loving Christian parents, Alvin and Florence Smith, who have always been supportive of my writing. Thank you for being there for me and cheering me on as I pursued my dream of becoming a published author! Thanks also to my sisters, Lisa Cannon and Renae Ernst and their families for their love and support through the years.

Special thanks to my sweet Skype partners and beta-readers Savanna Kaiser and Cara Grandle for all your wonderful counsel, support, and much needed pep-talks. You two are truly a gift from the Lord. When we connected at the ACFW three years ago, who would have guessed what a special bond the Lord had in store for us? God bless you both as we continue on our writing journeys together.

I wish to thank my wonderful critique partners Misty Beller, Hannah Conway, and Linda Cushman for helping to refine my writing skills. Thank you for your honesty, your candor, and your wonderful encouragement. God bless you!

Thanks to the staff at Mantle Rock Publishing: Kathy Cretsinger for giving me this opportunity to fulfill a life-long dream and all her helpful advice and encouragement, Diane Cretsinger Turpin for her beautiful cover art and typesetting, and Pam Harris for helping weed out unnecessary words and punctuation.

Finally, I again thank you dear readers for taking a chance on a new author. I pray you'll join me for the next installment in my Prairie Sky Series: *Under Prairie Skies* set to release in 2018. I would love to connect with you on my website: http://cynthiaroemer.com/connect/ any time. If you enjoyed reading *Under This Same Sky*, I would appreciate you posting a review on www.amazon.com/ or www.goodreads.com/ . Thank you so much.

God bless you all!

"For I know the plans I have for you," declares the LORD, *"plans to prosper you and not to harm you, plans to give you hope and a future."* *(Jeremiah 29:11) NIV*

Chapter One

PART ONE: SEPARATION

Illinois – May 8, 1854

NOTHING COULD HAVE PREPARED her for this.

Nothing.

Becky Hollister gripped her horse's mane, pressing her heels into his flanks. Samson raced along the muddy path, the sound of his hooves echoing in the stillness. The vast prairie loomed ahead of her like an endless sea. Miles from the nearest neighbor or town, she had no choice but to keep going.

Would she make it in time?

The sun sank lower in the western sky, illuminating the line of thunderheads to the east. Becky shifted her gaze from the remnants of the devastating storm, her attempts at prayer skewed by images of her fallen family and shattered home. *Why didn't You help them, Lord?*

Tears stung her eyes. She alone could save Pa now.

Sweat streamed down the horse's neck and withers. His pace slowed.

"Come on, boy. Pa's depending on us." The memory of her father lying face-down on the ground, spattered with blood and dirt, flashed through Becky's mind. She smacked the reins across Samson's neck, and he surged forward, giving her all his strength.

A piercing howl of a wolf sounded in the nearby timber. Samson lurched sideways, almost causing Becky to tumble. She tightened her hold on his neck, struggling to regain balance.

A dark figure appeared on the path ahead, half hidden behind a fallen branch. Becky pulled back on the reins, straining to distinguish the shadowy horse and rider. The dim light of evening toyed with her eyes. Treacherous men sometimes roamed the area. She hadn't considered her own threat of danger when she'd left their only gun with Pa.

As the rider edged closer, Becky's heart pounded in her ears. Should she turn aside or press forward?

With each breath, Samson's sides heaved under her. He was too fatigued to outrun the stranger. She'd have to risk it. Clicking her tongue in her cheek, she dug her heels into Samson's flanks. She could only pray the person was friend, not foe.

MATTHEW BRODY PUSHED his broad-brimmed hat further back on his head, keeping his eyes trained on the horse and rider approaching at break-neck speed. He urged his mount forward, craning his neck to determine who it could be. The brunt of the storm had passed to the south, in the direction of the Hollister farm. Had someone been injured?

He swerved his horse to dodge a splintered branch in his path. Young leaves and twigs littered the prairie, evidence of a strong wind. Having taken refuge in an abandoned shack during the storm, he'd determined then and there to swing by to check on the Hollisters.

Perhaps he'd done right in coming.

Hunched low about the horse's neck, the rider looked too

slight to be Joseph. Surely Meg or one of the girls would have better sense than to ride out alone as night approached.

Or had there been no choice?

A peek of evening sun shone through a break in the clouds, revealing a bonnet atop the rider's head. Matthew winced. There was something amiss.

He urged his horse into a canter. The thunder of hooves grew louder as the rider sped toward him. She certainly was in an all-fired hurry. As she neared, the woman straightened and tugged at the reins. One glimpse of her tanned face and wheat-blonde braid confirmed his suspicions.

Becky.

Bringing his horse up beside her, he scanned her unkempt hair and smudged face. Were those blood stains on her dress? "What is it? What's happened?"

Tears welled in her eyes as she met his gaze. She swallowed hard, seeming to struggle for words. "A tornado hit our farm. Ma and Melissa are...dead."

The alarming words weighed on his chest. Just weeks ago, he'd shared a meal with them at their cabin. Among his most devoted patrons, the Hollisters were ever willing to provide food and shelter when he rode this area of his circuit. Head bowed, he heaved a quiet sigh. "I'm sorry."

Becky swayed in her saddle, and Matthew placed a steadying hand on her arm. Was she overcome with grief or merely exhausted? "You all right?"

She gave a hurried nod, mouth trembling. The pained look in her eyes intensified. "Pa's injured. Please, he needs help."

Her desperate plea seared Matthew's heart. Veering back in his saddle, he slackened his hold on the reins. "Show me where."

Becky wheeled her horse around, then took off toward the Hollister farm. Matthew chased after her, the acres of prairie passing in a haze. Each endless stride wedged the tragic news deeper. Was Joseph's injury life-threatening? If he died, where would that leave Becky?

Lifting his eyes heavenward, he peered into the thinning line of clouds. *Lord, see him through—for Becky's sake.*

When the wind-struck farm came into view, he slowed his pace to avoid the clutter of debris. Worse than he'd even imagined, the devastation sliced through him like a sword. Bits of clothing, furniture, and broken shingles littered the ground. Of the buildings, only the barn remained intact. The cabin site lay in total ruin, recognizable only by the fireplace and stone chimney. Not one log remained atop the other.

He shuddered. Were Meg and Melissa buried beneath the rubble? It was a miracle Becky had escaped unharmed.

There was something solemn, almost holy, in the quietness as he followed Becky to the barren field. The rich soil was glazed over now, black as tar. An abandoned harrow lay twisted beside it. Had Becky been helping her father when the storm hit? More than once, he'd witnessed her laboring alongside him. Within the confines of the cabin, she'd have been lost.

The Lord be praised for his mercies.

A low bark echoed in the stillness. Spurring her horse forward, Becky led Matthew to a grassy area beyond the field where the land sloped downward toward the creek. Their old dog, Nugget, rose to his feet, his thick, yellow fur ruffled and smudged. Clearly, he'd held vigil over his master in Becky's absence.

"He's over here." She reined her horse to a stop and hopped down. Kneeling beside her father, she struggled for breath. "I'm here, Pa. Pastor Brody's gonna help you."

At Joseph's lack of response, she gave him a gentle shake, the color draining from her cheeks. "Pa?"

Matthew squatted beside them. He placed a hand on Joseph's scarcely rising chest, breathing a sigh of relief as warmth coursed through his fingertips.

Becky's voice strained. "Is he...?"

"He's unconscious."

She brushed a tear from her cheek. Her gaze trailed to the bloody rag around Joseph's head. "He's lost so much blood. I tried to stop it."

"You did fine." Matthew loosened the make-shift bandage and gently shifted Joseph's head to the side, cringing at sight of the open wound. "Mighty bad gash." He tossed aside the bloodied rag and replaced it with his bandanna.

"What can I do?" Worry lined Becky's sapphire eyes.

With a sigh, Matthew sat back on his haunches. "Not much can be done till we get him to town. Let's see what sort of shape your wagon's in."

Standing, he offered Becky a hand up. She slid her fingers into his, and he pulled her to her feet. Her drawn expression and weary eyes charted a map to her aching heart. Yet even in her frazzled state, she'd kept her head, showing a depth of maturity beyond her years.

Or was it faith that held her together?

Tethering his horse, Gabriel, to a nearby tree, Matthew took up Becky's horse's reins. Heavy silence hung between them as they strode closer to the demolished homestead. With a soft whimper, Becky averted her gaze from the cabin remains, concealing her face beneath her bonnet.

Matthew placed a hand on the small of her back and steered her toward the barn. What could he say to this distraught young lady? As her pastor, it was his duty to offer comfort. But he had no words to alleviate such a crushing blow. He could only offer up prayers for strength and for her father's well-being.

The overturned wagon lay wedged on its side, beneath the collapsed lean-to. Together they cleared away broken timbers that had fallen. Matthew weaved his way around the wagon, assessing the damage and then pushed his hat back with his thumb. "Well, the axle's a bit bent, but at least it's still in one piece." He gripped the wagon's front edge, gesturing Becky to the back. "Help me turn it."

She strained to lift her end, but with each attempt, the wagon fell back on its side.

He shot her a weak smile, his voice soft. "Try again. Put all your weight into it."

With a nod, she tightened her hold, arms shaking under the strain. The wagon gave just a little, then a few inches more.

"Keep pulling." Matthew ground his teeth, tugging with all his strength. At last, a final heave sent all four wheels jostling to the ground with a thud. He rubbed dirt from his hands, a corner of his mouth lifting. Clearly, Becky wasn't afraid of hard work. She'd been but a girl three years ago when he'd begun ministering in this region. He hadn't been much over twenty at the time himself.

He glanced her way, stirred by the hurt emanating in her eyes. How he longed for words to comfort her. And yet, none came. He touched a hand to her elbow, his voice catching. "I'll need you to find what you can to cushion your pa's ride, while I hitch the team."

"We've plenty of straw in the barn."

He gave a reassuring nod. "How 'bout your harnesses? Are they about?"

"Inside, by the stalls."

Together, they strode into the barn. Matthew found the harnesses hanging untouched on their pegs. While he worked at hitching the team, Becky carried out several armloads of straw and spread them in the wagon bed. More than once, he caught her staring in the direction of her father. She should be with him. Matthew placed a hand on her arm. "Go see to your father. I'll finish here."

Appreciation settled in her blue eyes, then she turned and dashed away. Matthew watched her go, amazed at her stamina. What was she now, seventeen? Somehow, today, she seemed much older. She'd managed well for one so young. Most people would buckle under such circumstances.

He buckled the harness, brow raised. When had Becky become a woman?

BECKY TRAMPED over the fallen grass, eyes moist as she stared into the darkening sky. Shades of purple and pink cloaked the western horizon, its beauty only mocking her pain. Were Ma and Melissa looking down on her even now? Did they sense the longing in her soul, the loss she felt at not having the chance to even say goodbye?

Worse yet, would she lose Pa too?

She tugged on a stubborn grass stem and tossed it aside. Nothing would ever be the same.

Kneeling beside her father, she clasped his hand, his fingers lacking their usual warmth. Fear strangled her heart. How would she survive on her own if she lost him? She pushed the thought from her mind.

Nugget grunted and sat up beside her. His heavy tail thumped the ground as she leaned against him. They were a family now. The three of them. A tear trickled down her cheek, fueled by an overwhelming hollowness inside her. The image of Ma and Melissa lying intertwined on the cabin floor remained seared in her mind. She'd watched desperately for some sign of life in their limp forms. Yet their sunken chests hadn't stirred. It had all happened so fast.

The creak of a wagon curtailed her thoughts. She dried her eyes on her sleeve as Pastor Brody brought the team to a halt beside her. What would she have done without him? His calming presence had given her renewed strength.

He hopped down and knelt next to her father.

Looping his arms through Pa's, he hauled him to the edge of

the wagon and climbed in. Becky took a firm hold on Pa's legs, her eyes never leaving his face as she helped slide him into the wagon bed. The kind pastor pillowed Pa's head with a blanket and gathered straw around him to cushion his ride.

A cooling breeze caressed Becky's cheeks as she moved to the side of the wagon. Pa's ashen complexion stirred unwanted angst within her. He looked so weak. Would he survive the trip?

Pastor Brody hopped from the wagon bed and helped her onto the seat. "Take it slow and easy. A rough ride would do more harm than the time it'd spare you."

He slid Pa's muzzleloader onto the floorboard, locking his eyes onto hers. "Be careful."

"You're not coming?"

"I'll be along, once I tend to things here." He lifted his hat and raked a hand through his chestnut hair, shifting his dark eyes to the cabin remains. Understanding washed over Becky. Of course. He intended to lay their loved ones to rest. No telling what would become of their bodies if left unattended, even for a night. A proper burial would have to wait.

"Thank you." She reached a hand down, moisture pooling in her eyes.

With a slow nod, he wrapped her hand in his. "God be with you."

Turning, she released the brake, a lump rising in her throat. Fatigue tore at her muscles. Could she manage the five-mile trip alone?

Nugget's raspy bark sounded below. Doubtless, he didn't want to be left behind. Pastor Brody lifted the old dog onto the wagon seat, and Becky stroked his rough coat. Somehow, having him at her side offered her a sense of security. She gave Pastor Brody a gentle nod. If there was one redeeming element in this appalling day, it was the chance meeting with the pastor. Strange he'd happened by so soon after the storm. At one time, she would have credited it to the Lord.

But not now. Not after He'd abandoned them.

The western sky turned fiery red as the sun dipped low on the horizon. She would need every stitch of daylight for the long trek to town. Taking a firm grip on the reins, she struck them across the horses' rumps. As she guided them onto the muddy path, the memory of Pastor Brody's warning to take it slow squelched her urge to press them faster.

A glance back at Pa's motionless form sent a wave of unease rippling through her. Everything in her longed to cry out to the Lord. But why should she? He'd failed her.

She squared her shoulders, tightening her hold on the reins. From now on, she'd trust only herself.

Chapter Two

WOULD THE TRIP NEVER END?

The last trace of twilight had fled the western sky, leaving only the crescent moon and stars to light the horses' way. Becky kept them under tight rein as they plodded along the rutted path, her tired muscles aching under the constant strain. The darkness only seemed to magnify her already sullied spirit. Would she be able to rid herself of the awful images plaguing her mind?

At last, the village of Miller Creek came into view, with only a few lights shining from within the settlement. Becky guided the team into town and stopped them before Doc Pruitt's large frame house. Through the windowpane, she could see him reading by the glow of lantern light. Thank goodness he hadn't been called away for some other crisis.

Securing the brake, she looped the reins over the seat, then climbed from the wagon. The door creaked open, and the elderly doctor peeled off his spectacles. He held the lantern out in front of him, staring at her from the doorway. "Why, Becky. What's happened?"

Tortured memories laced their way through her, robbing her

of words. She pointed to the wagon bed, eyes glossing over with tears.

Doc Pruitt swept past her, his short legs taking quick strides to the wagon. Becky hesitated before peering over the sideboard. Had her father succumbed to his injuries? She held her breath as the doctor lowered the lantern to Pa's face, lifting first one eyelid then the other.

Doc Pruitt's expression grew taut. "Go get Anna."

Heart pounding, Becky fled toward the door. Moonlight streamed through the windows, guiding her way through the dim house. Nugget traipsed after her, his sharp toenails clicking against the wooden floorboards. Becky made her way to the back bedroom and called to Mrs. Pruitt from the doorway. The woman's heavy breathing remained steady. Stepping closer, Becky called louder. "Mrs. Pruitt. Come quick."

The older woman popped up, one side of her silvery hair flattened against her head. "Land sakes, child. What's the matter?"

"It's Pa. He's been injured."

Slipping from the bed, Mrs. Pruitt draped a shawl over her shoulders. Heavy footsteps padded after Becky as she wound her way to the front door.

"Come take hold of his legs," the doctor called to his wife. "Becky, you steady his middle."

Pa's boots now rested at the wagon's edge. Taking a firm hold under his lower back, Becky helped lift him from the wagon and carry him toward the building. In the dim moonlight, it was hard to tell just how pale he'd become. But the warmth radiating from his clothing revived her hope. If he'd made it this far, perhaps he had a chance.

They carried him to the room directly across from where Mrs. Pruitt had been sleeping. A stale, musty smell poured from within as they entered and laid Pa on the bed. The doctor lit a lantern, illuminating the tiny sickroom. It was a part of the house Becky had never seen, for its door always remained closed.

Rumor had it that those who were confined to it rarely left on foot.

She shuddered. Would the same prove true of Pa?

Doc Pruitt took a half-filled bottle of iodine and a handful of gauze from the glass-door cabinet against the far wall. He pulled a chair up beside the bed, brow creased. More accustomed to tending the sick and setting broken bones, would he know how to treat such a severe injury? Gently, he turned Pa's head to the side and with a pair of scissors, snipped away the bandana and clumps of bloodied hair from around the wound.

Mrs. Pruitt placed an arm around Becky. "Come, child. Let's leave Charles to his work."

Becky stiffened. She couldn't leave. What if Pa woke and she wasn't there? Worse yet, what if he didn't pull through? "Please. I wanna stay."

Mrs. Pruitt's gaze met the doctor's. Some unknown communication seemed to pass between them. A moment later, she placed an arm around Becky's waist. "Rest easy, dear. If there's any change, Charles will let us know."

The older woman's comforting touch and warm smile weakened Becky's resolve. She turned and followed Mrs. Pruitt to the door, her feet like dead weight beneath her. As Mrs. Pruitt attempted to pull the door shut behind them, Becky braced her hand against it. The wooden door seemed an unsurpassable barrier between life and death. "Couldn't it be left open?"

"No need to worry, child. Your father's in good hands."

Becky's eyes moistened. "Please?"

The doctor's wife pressed her chin to her neck, understanding in her eyes. "All right. Just a crack."

Drawing her hand away, Becky stole a final glance at Pa. That he lay unconscious seemed almost a blessing. For now, she alone would shoulder the anguish of their loss.

Mrs. Pruitt pursed her lips. "By the looks of things, your father will rest easier than you tonight."

Becky hung her head. With all that had happened, how could she rest? To close her eyes meant reliving the awful scenes she'd witnessed.

Mrs. Pruitt gave Becky's arm a soft tug. "Come. Let's slip these damp clothes off and get you to bed."

Giving in to the woman's pull, Becky followed her to the bedroom. The strange surroundings wedged an emptiness inside her. The fine dresser and mirror. The white-washed walls. The decorative, wooden headboard and wide mattress. All foreign to her. She should be in her own cabin, snug and safe with her family.

A lump rose in her throat. How many times had she wished for her younger sister to stop crowding her on their narrow, straw-filled bed? Now, staring down at the large mattress, she only wished her sister were there to share it.

Mrs. Pruitt turned up the lantern, then poured fresh water into a wash basin. "Sit down, and we'll see about getting you cleaned up."

The bed creaked under Becky as she sat, gaze fixed on the smooth, puncheon floorboards. Her tired muscles begged for rest. Yet she dared not give in. Not with such vivid images churning in her head, nor with Pa teetering between life and death. She pried her eyes wider and peered toward the door. Why could she not stay with him? He needed her.

Or was it more that she needed him?

Mrs. Pruitt took a seat beside her. "That was quite a storm that blew through. Are your ma and Melissa all right?"

The question tore through Becky like a dreaded disease. By now, Pastor Brody had laid their bodies to rest beneath the quiet earth. Would she ever see them again? Whole and happy?

Was there indeed a Heaven? She'd always thought so. But, if God were as loving as she'd been told, would He have snatched Ma and Melissa away so young? So violently?

With a shake of her head, she stared down at her mud-crusted feet. "They're gone."

An audible gasp escaped Mrs. Pruitt. "Oh, dear."

Becky drew an uneven breath, her chin quivering. "I can't bear to lose Pa too."

Mrs. Pruitt draped an arm around Becky's shoulders. "Don't fret, child. Your pa's not one to give up without a fight."

With a nod, Becky straightened. Mrs. Pruitt was right. The Hollisters were fighters. Pa would do all he could to pull through —for her sake, if not for his own.

"Poor dear. You're plumb tuckered. You need a good night's rest." Rising, Mrs. Pruitt wiped moisture from the corner of her eye. She opened the trunk at the foot of the bed and pulled out a linen nightdress. Holding it out in front of her, she shook her head. "I'm afraid it's a bit large for your needs."

Becky reached to unfasten her frock. Stiff with dried blood and dirt, her fingers fumbled to unlatch the buttons.

"Here, let me help." Mrs. Pruitt laid the nightshirt on the bed and pushed Becky's tousled braid to one side.

Becky pulled away. "I can do it."

The pained look on Mrs. Pruitt's face hinted Becky had spoken too harshly. She dropped her hands to her sides with a sigh. "I'm sorry. It's just…"

"That's all right, child. Take your time." With an understanding smile, Mrs. Pruitt gave her a soft pat on the leg. "You can rinse in the basin when you're finished."

The woman's gracious manner was soothing balm to Becky's soul. A corrective word would surely have brought her to tears. She finished unbuttoning her frock then walked in her shift to the wash stand. One glimpse at her unruly blonde hair and smudged complexion in the dresser mirror convinced her she looked nearly as awful as she felt.

She dipped the cloth in the bowl of water, then wrung it out, her sullen mood deepening. Would this ache inside fade in time? Or deepen?

She winced as she touched the damp cloth to her skin. Glancing in the mirror, she spied several small cuts on her neck and shoulders. She'd hardly noticed them until the sting of the water. Where had they come from? Her mind churned up unwanted memories. Vaguely she recalled straw and splintered wood swirling about her, pricking her skin like steel blades as she huddled beside their cow, Tess, in the barn. The wind had grown to a deafening roar. The horses stomped and whinnied in their stalls. And then…

Silence. Not a bird or insect uttered song. Only the animals' heavy breaths broke the stillness.

"Now for something a bit drier and cleaner." Mrs. Pruitt's words cut through Becky's thoughts.

Shaking off her troubled demeanor, Becky took the towel the older woman offered. She dried her hands, then donned the loose-fitting nightshirt. Her lean figure became lost in the bulky gown as she tugged it into place.

"It's plain there's a lot more of me than you, child." Mrs. Pruitt pressed her hands to her cheeks. "Well, it'll have to do. You can sleep here. I imagine Charles will be in with your father the remainder of the night."

Tightening the drawstrings around her neck, Becky haphazardly tied them in a bow.

Mrs. Pruitt drew back the covers on the far side the bed. "Hop in and try to get some rest, dear. Charles and the good Lord are looking after your pa."

With a hesitant sigh, Becky slid into bed, face to the wall. Silent tears trailed along the bridge of her nose and onto the sheet as she blinked her eyes shut. In the stillness, a scratching noise sounded at the front of the house, followed by a high-pitched whine. Becky raised her head, recognizing Nugget's pleading whimper.

Mrs. Pruitt coaxed her onto her pillow. "Lie still. I'll see to him."

The bed jostled as the elderly woman rose and started toward the dining room. Moments later the front door creaked open and shut, and toenails tapped the wooden floorboards. Nugget traipsed into the room, sounding a contented bark at sight of Becky. She leaned down and scratched him behind the ears, feeling the warmth of his tongue on her cheek. The old dog plopped dirty front paws on the bed just as Mrs. Pruitt returned. With a shove from Becky, he sat back, his heavy tail thudding against the floor.

The older woman shook her head and smiled. "That's all right. Let him be. He'll be a comfort to you tonight."

With a relieved grin, Becky coaxed him up and nudged him to the foot of the bed. She stroked his head as he settled into place, then lay back with a sigh. How drastically her life had changed in one short day. If only they'd known the deadly storm was coming. If only the day could be erased. If only…

Mrs. Pruitt dimmed the lantern, and the room fell silent.

A tear trickled onto Becky's pillow as she attempted to pray. Her family made it a practice to gather for prayer each night before bed, but tonight no words would come. She longed for the warmth of her parents' touch as they knelt together in their small cabin and the comfort of her sister climbing into their own straw bed. The dark night seemed lonesome and empty without them.

A cry rang out from across the hall, sending her heart aflutter. What was happening in there? Propping herself up on her elbow, she fought the urge to go to him.

A gentle hand touched her shoulder. "Rest, child. Charles will see to him."

Laying her head back on the pillow, she stared into the darkened room, praying the morrow would not bring further heartache.

Chapter Three

Ominous clouds churned in the distant sky, beckoning.

A strong hand clutched Becky's arm, and she pulled her gaze from the pitch-black clouds. She squinted up at her father, a swirl of dust engulfing them in the barren field.

He leaned closer, voice raised above the angry squall. "See to the horses. I'll finish planting."

A gust of wind caught Becky's bonnet, and she held it in place, peering into the billowing sky overhead. Thickening clouds blocked the sun's rays. "It's coming too fast. You'll never finish in time."

Gathering her skirt in one hand, she started to rake a layer of soil over the row of corn seed with her feet.

Pa gripped her shoulders, his dark eyes tinged with urgency. "I said go."

With a reluctant nod, she handed him her seed pouch. She drew a shallow breath, stealing another glance at the western horizon. A shiver coursed through her. Never had she seen such a menacing sky.

Sprinkles of rain dampened her skin as she jogged to the far end of the field. With a firm yank, she unhitched the team from the harrow. Thunder rumbled in the distance. The horses tugged at their leads, threatening to bolt. Becky tightened her grip on the reins and trotted with them toward the yard. In the dust-filled air, she could just make out the outline of their cabin nestled in the clearing. The swelling breeze thrashed Becky's long, thick braid as she gazed out over the swaying grass.

In the yard, her younger sister, Melissa, scrambled to rally flustered chickens into the coop. Ma flapped her apron at them, then stood with hands on hips, shaking her head as the hens cackled and fluttered past. She cast a worried glance at the darkened sky and motioned to Melissa. "Forget the chickens. Get to the cellar!"

Melissa hugged her bonnet to her face, her slight frame struggling against the forceful wind.

Ma cupped her hands to her mouth, shouting to Becky above the roar. "Where's your pa?"

"Still planting."

The sudden slump of Ma's shoulders and brief silence betrayed her angst. She pointed toward the cabin. "Hurry in!"

Nodding, Becky quickened her pace. Their Jersey cow, Tess, stood outside the barn, eager to escape the approaching storm. Becky struggled to pry open the barn door against the thrust of the wind. Lightning flashed, followed by a tremendous clap of thunder. The horses pressed into her, their high-pitched whinnies cutting through the humid air.

At last, the wind lost its grip, and the door flung open. Tess nosed her way to the front, and Becky smacked her on the rump. With a loud bellow, the cow trotted inside. Becky rushed the flighty horses to their stalls. They nickered and pranced about while she unbuckled their harnesses.

With a smack, the barn door slammed shut, and an eerie darkness overshadowed the interior.

Samson reared, white showing in his eyes. Becky patted his dampened neck. "Easy, boy."

Stepping from his stall, she slid the wooden bars into place. The clapboard shingles rattled against the howling wind. Becky lifted her gaze to the dim rafters. If she tarried any longer, Ma would be sick with worry.

She hung the harnesses on wooden pegs outside the stalls, then strode to the door. Hail and heavy rain pelted the barn roof and oak sideboards. She pushed against the door, but it held tight against the surging gale. Again and again she pressed her shoulder into the stubborn door. Each time, it refused to budge. Finally, she smacked her fist against it in defeat.

Trapped.

The vicious storm had barricaded her in the barn like a tomb. She backed away, heart hammering in her chest. The powerful wind whistled through cracks in the hewn log walls, soiling the air with a dusty haze. Becky shielded her face with her sleeve and crouched in the corner of Tess's stall. A pang of uneasiness ripped through her. She had no choice now but to hunker down and wait out the storm. Drawing a shallow breath, she forced herself to relax. The Lord would protect them. He always had.

A loud clattering sounded overhead, followed by a blast of moist air. With a shriek, she squinted up at the roof. A gush of wind sucked the air from her lungs as she peered through the opening where a patch of cedar shingles had torn free. Furious clouds loomed overhead, casting a strange, greenish glow. She tensed, shielding her face from the gust.

Becky startled and opened her eyes. The terrible darkness of the barn faded, and in its stead, came the furnishings of the strange bedroom. When had she fallen asleep?

She swiped a hand over her sweat-drenched brow. Just a dream.

No, a nightmare. Every gut-wrenching moment relived. If only that's all any of this had been—a dream.

She wiped a wet spot from her cheek with the back of her hand. Nugget peered at her, his moist nose close to her face. She sank back on the feather pillow and gave him a soft pat. Sometime in the night, he had inched his way up beside her.

Early morning light filtered into the room, and her eyes scanned the unfamiliar quilt and bedframe. She sat up, glancing at the closed door. Had Pa survived the night? He'd lost so much blood.

The smell of coffee and freshly baked bread hinted her hostess had been up for some time. Becky's stomach rumbled, reminding her she'd had nothing to eat since noon the previous day. Nugget hopped from the bed and stared back at her, as if to say it was time to go. No need to coax further. She was as eager to leave as he was.

Swinging her legs over the side of the bed, she shivered in the coolness. The oversized nightshirt sagged off her shoulder as she stood, and she tugged it into place.

A tap sounded outside the bedroom door. "Becky?" Mrs. Pruitt peeked in, her silvery hair swirled in a loose bun. A smile lit her wrinkled face. "Ah, you're up." She gestured toward the trunk at the foot of the bed. "I laid out an old dress of mine for you to wear till your own is mended. Once you've changed, come have some breakfast."

Becky's shoulders drooped, disappointment tugging at her heart. "Couldn't I see Pa first?"

The older woman cocked her head and pursed her lips. "Perhaps you should wait a bit. Charles will be out shortly." Her eyes were kind, yet grave. Was she hiding something? Had Pa worsened in the night? "Is he all right?"

Mrs. Pruitt flashed a reassuring grin. "Patience, child. Charles will answer your questions as soon as he comes out."

With a reluctant nod, Becky gave a soft sigh. Without another word, Mrs. Pruitt backed from the room and closed the door. Why was she so secretive? Did she truly not know? Surely they'd have told her if something had gone wrong.

Becky squatted and rubbed Nugget behind the ears. His caramel eyes locked onto hers as if sharing her discontent. She sunk her hands into his fur, leaning her head against him, moisture pooling in her eyes. "You don't like being away from Pa any more than I do, do ya, boy?"

He gave a soft whine and licked her arm. The old dog seemed almost human at times. Standing, Becky drew a jagged breath. All this waiting was unnerving. She had no choice but to believe the best.

She slipped out of the nightshirt, eyeing the gingham dress atop the trunk. Though not as bulky as the nightshirt, it appeared ample big. Putting it on, she surveyed herself in the dresser mirror. With a sigh, she tugged at the sides of the saggy tan and white checkered dress. At least it was dry and clean. She pinched her colorless cheeks to detract from the dark shadows under her eyes. What little rest she'd gotten had done nothing to improve her appearance.

A brush and blue hair-ribbon lay atop the mahogany dresser. Loosening her braid, she ran the bristles through her tangled hair. With each stroke, her stomach tightened. What would this day hold? She had no home, no mother and no sister, nothing to look forward to.

Nothing—save the hope that Pa would get well.

Nugget whined and pawed at the door.

"All right, boy. I'm comin'." Quickly, she braided her hair and tied it with the ribbon then went to open the door. Nugget trotted out ahead of her and positioned himself outside the sick-room door, knowing full well Pa was on the other side. And like a hound with a treed coon, he had no intention of moving. Becky paused beside him. Surely, a few moments with Pa wouldn't hurt.

The doctor's muffled voice sounded within. She listened for her father's response. When none came, Becky squared her shoulders. No more waiting.

As she reached for the door handle, Mrs. Pruitt beckoned to her from the dining area. "Becky? Come, dear."

Becky tensed, her hand still clutching the door latch. Another moment and she'd have been at Pa's side. She hesitated, the thought of food holding no enticement. Yet, Pa wouldn't want her to go against the doctor's wife's wishes. Turning, she grabbed Nugget by the scruff of the neck and tugged him toward the front room. "Come on, boy."

With a whine, Nugget stood and begrudgingly followed Becky down the hallway. She knew just how he felt. Her patience was wearing thin too. How much longer would she have to wait?

Mrs. Pruitt flashed a reassuring grin and motioned toward the oak table. "Have a seat, dear. I'll bring you some breakfast."

Becky dropped onto a chair and motioned Nugget to lie down beside her. Her torn frock lay draped over the back of a chair near the fireplace, looking much cleaner than when she'd arrived. Spacious compared to their small cabin, the Pruitt home seemed drafty and a bit void of life. She'd heard tell the elderly doctor and his wife had once had a house full of children. But they'd grown and ventured out into the world, rarely returning. Becky could recall only meeting the youngest child, a daughter who'd married a well-to-do easterner. Sad the couple had no grandchildren nearby to enjoy. No wonder Mrs. Pruitt seemed so attentive.

The aroma of fresh biscuits filled the room as the doctor's wife lifted the lid to the Dutch oven resting on the hearth. She scooped a couple onto a plate and doused them with sausage gravy. A wide smile touched her lips as she set the plate of biscuits in front of Becky. "Well now, other than being a mite large, that dress suits you fine. Your frock will soon be dry enough to mend…that is if it can be."

Nugget stood, nosing his way toward the biscuits. Seeing Mrs. Pruitt's distraught expression, Becky nudged him away. When he refused to be deterred, she stood and edged toward the front door. Opening it, she slapped her thigh. "Come, Nugget."

Like a scolded pup, the old dog took a final sniff, then lowered his head and trotted outside.

"Poor fella. Here, give him these." Mrs. Pruitt handed her a wedge of sausage and a couple of warm biscuits.

Taking them from her, Becky smiled her thanks. The instant she set them on the walkway, the hungry dog snatched them up. As Becky closed the door behind her, Doc Pruitt emerged from the sickroom, toting a partially-eaten plate of biscuits. His slumped shoulders and tired eyes hinted of fatigue. As he neared, his lips sprouted a weak grin.

"Seems your dog's the only one with an appetite." Mrs. Pruitt took the plate of food from her husband and set it aside.

Becky searched the doctor's face for some inkling of Pa's condition, but gleaned only a weary sigh. Doc Pruitt took a seat beside her, folding his hands on the table in front of him. He peered at Becky's untouched plate. "Even your father managed a few bites."

Becky straightened. "He's awake?"

"And eager for your company."

Becky's lips spread in a grin. "May I see him?

Mrs. Pruitt brought over the remaining biscuits and took a seat beside her husband. "The poor child has worried herself sick over him."

At the doctor's careful nod, Becky scooted her chair from the table and rose to her feet.

He caught her by the arm, brow furrowed. "He's suffered quite a blow. Healing will take time."

"But he will get well." Becky's words were more statement than question.

The doctor loosened his hold on her arm and poured himself a cup of coffee. "Lord willing, yes. But he'll need a great deal of quiet and rest."

Something in the doctor's demeanor stymied Becky's enthusiasm. Was he being overly cautious? Or was he preparing her for what was to come? Her stomach lurched as she turned toward the sickroom.

Apparently, Pa wasn't out of the woods just yet.

JOSEPH LEANED his bandaged head back on the pillow, squinting against the light filtering through the windowpane opposite his bed. He squeezed his eyes shut and rubbed his temples. How his head throbbed. The pain was excruciating—though nothing compared to the agony from his loss of Meg and Melissa. He opened his eyes and groaned inwardly at the blurred, shadowy objects around him. Would his eyesight improve given time? Or was he destined to live out his days in this fog?

If anything, his eyes had worsened. He could still envision Becky leaning over him, her wheat-blonde hair glowing like a halo about her face. Even then, he could barely make out her sky-blue eyes and gentle features. Was it the dimness of the room or his eyes that made it so bleak?

A sound at the door drew his attention. With a slight turn of his head, he strained to make out the approaching visitor. The patterned material swaying to and fro lent to the trappings of a woman.

A gentle hand touched his arm. "You all right, Pa?"

He reached out his hand, warmth washing over him at the sound of his daughter's voice. At some point, his blood-stained shirt had been replaced with a loose-fitting, cotton over-shirt.

"Better, now that you're here." He clasped his hand atop hers as she bent to kiss his cheek.

The mattress shifted downward as she took a seat beside him on the bed. "When we found you unconscious, I feared the worst."

"We?"

"I met Pastor Brody on the way into town. He hitched the team and helped load you in the wagon." She paused, her tone softening. "He stayed behind to... tend to things for us."

Joseph tensed his jaw, turning his face to the wall. Was that it then—his lovely wife of twenty years and his beautiful daughter stolen away from him, never to be seen again? How could he have known the noon meal they'd shared would be their last? "Be sure to thank him for his kindness."

He heard a sniffle and felt a gentle hand brush hair from his forehead. "For a while, I thought I might lose you too."

The quiver in Becky's voice seared his heart. He squeezed her hand, shifting toward her. "By the grace of God, I'll not leave you alone."

A gentle rap on the door pulled their attention. The faint image of the balding doctor came into view. "Someone's here to see you."

A tall, slender figure stepped inside. "I hope I'm not intruding." Matthew Brody's familiar voice sounded from the doorway.

"Come on in." Joseph slid his hand from Becky's and extended it to the pastor. "Becky tells me I've you to thank for helping get me here last night."

"Glad to help." Matthew scooted a chair up beside the bed and straddled it. "I took your horses and wagon to the livery stable. Jethro said he'd keep 'em there as long as you need, at no charge."

"'Preciate that. Thank him for me, will ya?"

"Sure thing." Matthew cleared his throat. "I hope you don't

mind, but I let a few of your neighbors know of your hardships. I figure the more prayers the better."

With a sigh, Joseph scratched at the stubble on his chin. "We'll take all the prayers we can get."

Squinting, Joseph faintly saw the preacher reach inside his vest pocket. "I...uh, thought you might want this."

Matthew placed a small object in Joseph's open palm. The light-weight trinket settled in Joseph's hand like a tiny treasure. He ran his fingers over the smooth, round surface, his eyes widening as recognition washed over him.

Meg's wedding ring.

With a shaky hand, Joseph raised the gold band to his lips and gave it a gentle kiss. Never had it left Meg's finger. Now, the token of love was all he had of her. He closed his eyes, a sob catching in his throat as he recalled a phrase from their vows.

Till death do them part.

"THANK you for all you've done." Becky walked with Pastor Brody to the door.

"If there's anything else I can do, don't hesitate to call on me." He met her gaze, offering a weak smile. His dark eyes oozed compassion. What would they have done without him? His timely visit may very well have spared Pa's life.

Muffled voices sounded from the front of the house. Waving her goodbyes to the pastor, Becky followed him outside the room, easing the door shut behind her. A lump caught in her throat at sight of Uncle Jed and Aunt Clara conversing with the Pruitts. Aunt Clara's gaze locked onto Becky, and her eyes filled with tears. Her aunt covered her mouth with a kerchief, starting forward. "Oh, Becky."

Becky's stomach clenched. Though a few years older, never

had Aunt Clara's resemblance to Ma been so striking. Same deep blue eyes, blonde hair, and high cheek bones.

Tears dampened Becky's neck as she melted into her aunt's outstretched arms. No doubt, she too was deeply grieved. With Ma's passing, Aunt Clara had lost not only her sister, but her dearest friend. At last, she released her hold, face streaked with tears. "Pastor Brody told us what happened. How's your father?"

"Weak, but better."

"Is he up to visitors?" Uncle Jed removed his hat, combing his fingers through his wavy red hair.

The doctor peered over-top his spectacles, calling to them from the front room. "Not too long, folks. The man needs his rest."

Uncle Jed nodded, his bulky frame belying his gentleness. With a soft tap on the door, he followed Becky and Aunt Clara into the room. "Hello, Joseph."

Pa turned toward the voice, eyes searching. "That you, Jed?"

Sharing a puzzled look, Uncle Jed and Aunt Clara stepped closer. "Sure is. Clara too."

"Eyesight's still a bit fuzzy."

Becky made her way to the bed and eased down onto it. "Doc Pruitt says you'll heal in time."

"Sure, he will." Uncle Jed flashed Becky a reassuring smile.

Aunt Clara's chin quivered, and she let out a wail. "Oh, Joseph!" She buried her face in Uncle Jed's shirt, dampening it with her tears.

He reached in his pocket for a handkerchief and turned to Pa. "What Clara means to say is we're awful sorry for your loss, an' we'll do whatever we can to help."

"Tis a tough blow to us all." A shadow fell across Pa's face as he tightened his grip on Ma's wedding band.

Becky placed her hand atop his, tears threatening to spill from her eyes. She alone could truly share the depth of his loss.

"Our prayers are with you both." Uncle Jed's cheek flinched as he placed an arm around Aunt Clara.

"Reckon that's what we need most—that and getting our place back in shape."

"Now don't you fret none about that. I'll tend to things, till you're up an' about."

"Much obliged." Pa's eyelids flickered shut, then opened slightly.

"We'd best go and let you rest." Uncle Jed nodded to Aunt Clara.

With a sniffle, she dabbed her reddened eyes with the hand-kerchief. "If there's anything you need, anything at all…"

"There is one thing."

"Name it." Uncle Jed stepped forward, his expression earnest.

Pa's jaw tensed, and he hesitated as though warring within. At last, he seemed to will himself to speak. "Look after Becky for me till I'm well."

The words sliced through Becky like a death sentence. "But, Pa. Why can't I stay with--"

He raised a hand to silence her. "I'll not have you sitting here pining away for me night and day. Could be weeks before I'm up and about. You'd be better off with Jed and Clara than camped out here."

Becky pursed her lips, tossing his words around in her head. There was truth in what he said. Still, her place was with him. If anyone could help him recuperate, she could.

"We'd be pleased to have you, Becky." Aunt Clara swept a hand over her tear-stained cheek, her vivid blue eyes so like Ma's it pained Becky to look at them.

Palming his hat in one hand, Uncle Jed gestured toward Pa. "I'd see to it you come visit as often as you like."

Becky squelched the urge to protest. Balking would only cause Pa more grief. She peered at her uncle. "Every day?"

"If need be."

Her gaze shifted from her aunt and uncle to her father. Finally, she gave a slight nod.

Aunt Clara stepped to the bedside, fastening an arm around Becky's shoulders. "Come dear, we'll take you home."

Becky stiffened. Home? She had no home. And until she and Pa were together, no place would ever be home.

Chapter Four

THE LEATHER SADDLE creaked under Matthew as his horse strode along the trail. He breathed a sigh, his mind wandering. It seemed he spent more time in the saddle than out of it. He was due in the Scottsdale's region soon, then three weeks later, he'd head for Palmer. It would be a full six weeks before he'd be back at Miller Creek. Normally that wouldn't bother him, but somehow, with Joseph injured and Becky hurting as she was, it seemed his place was here for now. Perhaps others had suffered when the storm moved through as well. Would the neighboring towns understand if he prolonged his stay here?

At times, he wanted to stem his circuit riding and settle to one place. Of the three areas, the people of Miller Creek held a soft spot in his heart. No doubt the town could support its own full-time pastor. It had nearly doubled in size within the three years he'd ministered. But if he concentrated his efforts here, where would that leave the rest of his circuit? And what reason would he have for settling down? At twenty-four, he had no family, not even a sweetheart to call his own.

Not anymore.

His thoughts turned to Becky. The look of gratitude in her

eyes still lingered on his heart. If he'd done one service worthy of his calling, it had been in aiding her and Joseph. And though burying Meg and Melissa had been anything but pleasant, he'd do it again for the satisfaction in knowing the act had brought them a sense of peace.

He turned his eyes heavenward. "Lord, I don't pretend to understand Your ways, but I pray, trusting in Your wisdom and grace, that You might shower blessings on Joseph and Becky. Empower them to let go of their hurt and embrace Your love."

Coming to a fork in the road, he tugged Gabriel to a stop and rested his hands atop the saddle horn. To the right lay the path toward Scottsdale, while the road to the left led to the Hollister farm. He drew a long breath. The images of Becky thanking him in the doorway and Joseph's emotional response to his wife's wedding band remained etched in his mind. How could he leave with his dear friends in need? He clamped his jaw. The Scottsdale congregation would simply have to understand.

With a click of his cheek, he reined Gabriel to the left. He'd wire one of the elders explaining the reason for his delay. They might disapprove of his actions, but his obligation was first and foremost to God. Right now, the Lord was urging him to stay.

And that's what he intended to do.

BECKY CLIMBED FROM THE WAGON, clutching her tattered dress along with a small bundle of items Mrs. Pruitt had given her. Her cousins, Charlotte and Esther, stepped from inside their cabin, stopping short at sight of her. Did they know all she'd been through?

"Hey, Becky." Charlotte toyed with the tip of her red braid, taking in Becky from head to toe. By the distasteful look on her cousin's face, the oversized dress didn't meet with her approval.

Though only three months Becky's elder, Charlotte seemed years more refined and self-assured.

Becky merely stared back, indifferent to her cousin's scrutiny. She had no wish to be here and saw no cause to pretend as though she did.

Esther edged back in her older sister's shadow, hazel eyes filled with tears. She and Melissa had been inseparable when they were together. Her obvious grief stood in stark contrast to Charlotte's flippant manner. "Where's Uncle Joseph?"

Aunt Clara stepped up beside them. "Your questions can wait. Let's get Becky settled in."

Charlotte flicked her braid over her shoulder. "She's staying?"

"Till your Uncle Joseph is back on his feet and they have a roof over their heads."

Aunt Clara's words churned inside Becky like soured milk. Though grateful for her relatives' kindness, the only place that could satisfy was at Pa's side.

Uncle Jed tugged on the leather latch-cord, and the cabin door swung open. Following the family inside, Becky scanned the one room cabin, so like her own. Centered on the north, the huge stone fireplace housed a Dutch oven suspended over hot coals. Long-handled spoons, ladles, and other cooking utensils dangled from metal hooks across the front of the fireplace.

A loom and spinning wheel rested in the far corner, and at the cabin's center, sat a sturdy oak table and chairs where her family had shared many a meal. Reminders of Ma were everywhere, in the intricately woven quilt overlaying her aunt and uncle's bed, at the fireplace hearth where she'd knelt to help prepare meals, and in Aunt Clara's familiar blue eyes.

A gentle nudge from her aunt shook away the bittersweet memories. "Why don't you take your things on up to the loft? Just set them on the bed for now."

With a nod, Becky placed her foot on the ladder that

stretched upward into a cozy loft. She climbed to the top and set her small bundle of things on her cousins' bed. An odd feeling permeated her as she gazed around the tiny garret. What had once been a welcome place to visit now seemed strange and life-less to her, like a confining prison separating her from all she held dear. Her own cabin remained only a memory to her now. She only hoped Pa would recover soon and together they could regain some sense of normality and purpose. Slowly, she climbed back down, hopeful her stay would not be long.

Uncle Jed set his hat on his head "I reckon there's enough time to show you our new calf b'fore lunch. Dandy little heifer, just two days old." He motioned for Becky to follow, then turned to her cousins. "You girls help your ma get lunch on. We'll be in shortly."

Charlotte's eyes locked onto Becky's briefly before she lowered them and turned away. Was she irritated at Uncle Jed for making her stay behind? Or annoyed at Becky's intrusion on her family? With her fiery locks and jade green eyes, Charlotte was the spitting image of Uncle Jed in every way but temperament. While her uncle was as gentle and pleasant as a spring breeze, Charlotte's moodiness was more akin to a summer storm. Her older cousin had been the apple of her father's eye for as long as Becky could remember. Spoiled was more like it. Uncle Jed alone could reel Charlotte in when she drifted out of sorts.

Becky followed her uncle outside, grateful to escape the confines of the cabin. She took quick strides to match his pace, as she had so many times with Pa. She twisted her mouth to one side to stymie quivering lips. If only it were Pa at her side now.

The barn door creaked open, and Becky breathed in the familiar scent of hay and livestock. Sunlight shone a dusty beam through the barn's interior as they stepped inside. With the other animals having been released to spring pasture, all was peaceful within for the mother cow and calf.

Uncle Jed leaned against the stall, staring at the newborn calf curled up next to its mother. "A dandy, ain't she?"

"She's beautiful." Becky stepped toward the tan and white Jersey calf, its spindly legs tucked beneath it. The momma cow gave a low "moo" and turned her head, causing Becky to pull back.

Her uncle stroked the cow's neck. "Go on. Ol' Nell won't mind."

Kneeling beside the newborn, Becky rubbed her hand across its soft coat. The calf lifted its head, but lay still, indifferent to her touch.

Her uncle smiled, his red hair a shade darker in the dim light. "Aren't afraid of much at this age."

"I remember when Tess was a calf. Melissa an' I..." Becky paused, voice fading to a whisper. The reality of her sister no longer being there had yet to fully sink in. "Well...we had a lot of fun with her."

Uncle Jed cleared his throat, breaking the abrupt silence. "Did I tell you the calf had a twin?"

Becky shook her head, still trying to squelch her swelling emotions.

She sensed her uncle's eyes on her as he squatted beside her. "We lost the little bull calf. He wasn't as strong as the heifer here. Only lived a few hours."

"Poor thing." Becky stroked the calf's face. Did animals feel loss same as people?

Her uncle placed a hand on her shoulder. "Life's a mixture of joys an' sorrows, Becky. Reckon we have to learn to accept the bad along with the good."

She sniffled, fighting tears as he turned her toward him, his round eyes full of compassion. "The Lord's dealt you a rough hand, but He's promised never to give more than we can handle."

She shook her head, tears spilling onto her cheeks. "I've always trusted He'd take care of us. But, now..."

He put a hand under her chin. "Give it time. The Lord'll help you sort through things. You'll see."

With a nod, she dropped her gaze. The Lord had deserted them when they needed Him most. How could she ever trust Him again?

"SURE YOU WON'T COME? It's a mite early, but if we're lucky, we may scare up enough gooseberries for a pie." Aunt Clara slipped off her apron, glancing at Becky.

So accustomed to Ma's earthy tone, Aunt Clara's higher pitched voice sounded strange in Becky's ears. She gripped the ladder rung. "No, thank you. I'd just as soon stay here and rest."

Her aunt cocked her head, disappointment lining her eyes. "If that's what you want." She batted the air with her hand. "You go on up and rest. The girls can help."

Relief flooded over Becky as she climbed the loft ladder, her mind still bludgeoned with images of the storm. Shaking off the painful memories, she tumbled onto the bed and stared up at the log rafters. How could she think about picking berries, or anything for that matter, with all that'd happened? Tears welled in her eyes, and she heaved a quiet sigh. Did Pa miss her as much as she missed him?

Lacing her hands together behind her head, she turned her face to the tiny loft window where a cottony cloud drifted by on a sea of blue. Could this really be the same sky that had only two days ago wielded such vengeance? How could a God who created such beauty spawn such devastation?

She closed her eyes, sending teardrops trailing down her temples. *I don't understand, Lord. Why'd You spare Pa and me, but not Ma and Melissa?*

"We're leaving now." Aunt Clara's words cut through Becky's prayer. "Won't be gone more than an hour or two."

Becky craned her neck to the side, willing her voice to steady. "All right."

As the door closed, Becky rolled onto her stomach and buried her face in the worn quilt. How she'd longed for solitude to give vent to her grief. Alone at last, she let her tears flow freely.

A creak of the ladder silenced her cries. She sat up, eyes searching.

A head of golden hair topped the loft ladder. Esther peered up at her, pigtails draped over her shoulders. The fourteen-year-old's rosy cheeks and quiet nature were reminiscent of Melissa. "I... I heard you crying. You all right?"

"I'm fine." Becky turned away, drying her cheeks with her palms. She just wanted to be left alone.

Esther's presence drew closer, and the bed jostled. "I know you're hurtin' real bad inside. You've every right to cry." Her voice trailed to a whisper. "I miss 'em too."

At the genuineness in her cousin's words, something gave way inside of Becky. How she longed for someone to share in her grief. Someone who understood. Turning, she reached out her arms, and Esther latched onto her, their sobs intermingling. Esther was everything her sister, Charlotte, wasn't. Kindhearted, compassionate, gentle. No wonder Melissa had loved her. As Becky melted into her embrace, she sensed their souls knitting together, like a sturdy cord that couldn't be broken.

With a sniffle, Esther leaned close to Becky's ear. "The Lord knows you're hurtin'. He'll see you through."

Becky tensed, wanting to dispute Esther's faith-filled words. But how could she, when taking in her cousin's healing embrace?

"Come on, Esther," Charlotte called from outside the cabin. "What's keeping you?"

Becky loosened her hold, blinking back tears. "You'd better go."

"I wish you'd come with us."

"I need some time to myself."

With a nod, Esther stood and edged toward the ladder.

Gratitude welled inside Becky. "Esther?"

Her cousin paused, pivoting toward her.

"Thank you."

Esther's lips parted in a grin as she started down the ladder.

From the loft window, Becky watched her aunt and cousins leave, then lay back on the quilt, dampened now with tears. Esther's words raced through her mind. "The Lord knows you're hurting. He'll see you through." How she wanted to believe that. But what sort of God allowed such a cruel, senseless end to His people?

Becky's only hope now was for Pa to be well again and for them to be together. Closing her eyes, she breathed a quiet sigh. *Lord, if You're listening, and You give any thought to us at all, watch over Pa.*

MATTHEW TUGGED off his boots and rubbed the balls of his feet before the campfire. He must have hit every homestead in the countryside, spreading word of the Hollisters' hardships. He stretched out his legs. A soft bed would feel good about now. But he'd roamed too late to impose on anyone's hospitality. Besides, with no one around, he wanted to keep an eye on things here at the Hollister farm.

The setting sun glowed fiery red in the west, illuminating the wide birth of destruction left from the storm. Joseph and Becky wouldn't see it in this shape again. Not if he could help it. He'd get an early start on it in the morning. It would take a lot of doing, but prayerfully, tomorrow this place would be teeming with willing workers. Many hands made for light work, so they said.

He took out the bundle of food he'd accumulated throughout the day and peeled back the cloth he'd wrapped it in. His mouth watered at sight of the savory smoked ham, cornbread, and sugar-coated donuts. At least he'd not have to worry about filling his belly. He'd been loaded down with food to spare. The people of Miller Creek were a giving lot. God bless 'em.

Biting off a chunk of meat, he leaned back, propping himself up with his arm. The velvety sky began to fade, replaced by a canvas of deep blue and a sprinkle of starlight. What a spectacular view. He felt a bit like Abraham in the Bible, sleeping under the stars, leading the life of a nomad. It got old at times not having a place to hang his hat, but it did have its moments.

He finished off the ham with a sigh. If only he'd someone to share such wondrous sights with. He'd come close once. But it wasn't to be.

Someday, when the Lord gave the word, he'd settle in one place and minister to a single community. Then he could concentrate on finding that special someone to share life with. Someone who'd capture his heart in a way no other had.

Becky's delicate features invaded his thoughts. She'd grown into such a lovely young lady. His chest tightened. He should've stopped by today to see how she was faring. But if he had, he'd not have made the rounds. Perhaps he'd see her here tomorrow. If not, he'd make a point to stop by Jed and Clara's soon.

Chapter Five

ANOTHER SLEEPLESS NIGHT. With a yawn, Becky pried her eyes wider. How could she rest? Her whole world had been torn asunder.

She climbed atop her uncle's wagon, eager for him to make good on his promise. Nugget whined, thumping his matted tail on the ground. Uncle Jed scooped him up in his burly arms and heaved him into the wagon bed. Sliding the backboard into place, he turned to Aunt Clara. "We'll be home come suppertime."

"Give Joseph my regards." She waved to them, squinting into the rising sun.

Becky lifted her hand in return, then scooted to make room for Uncle Jed. As he took up the reins, her cousins emerged from the cabin. Charlotte leaned against the door frame, arms crossed, glaring at her. Becky winced, her cousin's rejection stinging her already fragile spirit. Not a word had passed between them throughout the evening hours. Nor at breakfast. What had she done?

The two of them had never been close. Not like Esther and Melissa. Yet they'd managed to be polite and cordial. Now tension hung like a fog whenever Charlotte was around. Not one word of sympathy had passed from her cousin's lips.

None too soon, Uncle Jed smacked the reins across the horses' rumps, and the wagon jolted forward. He leaned forward, resting his arms on his knees, a rein in each gloved hand. "We'll stop by and visit your pa, then head out to your place. May just be some things out there you can salvage."

"All right." Becky gazed out over the wide prairie. Every broken twig and downed tree limb along the worn path stirred unwanted memories. Could she handle fronting their demolished homestead again or bear seeing earth heaped atop her loved ones?

The mile-and-a-half trip to Miller Creek seemed an eternity —but nothing compared to the five-mile trek into town two nights before. Becky's heart warmed. Thank goodness for Pastor Brody. Would she have the chance to thank him again before he left the area?

At last, Miller Creek appeared in the distance, serene and peaceful, as though nothing out of the ordinary had taken place. Becky's stomach clenched. What she wouldn't give to believe just that.

Uncle Jed halted the team outside Doc Pruitt's house and set the brake, then offered Becky a hand down. "You head on in. I need to stop in the mercantile a minute."

With a nod, Becky climbed from the wagon, relishing the idea of a few precious moments alone with Pa. Hopefully he would be much more alert and able to visit this morning. She hurried to the door, her gentle knock generating footsteps within.

Mrs. Pruitt beamed as she swung the door open, her silver hair pulled back in a loose braid. "I'm not at all surprised to see you this mornin'. Come on in."

Mustering a weak grin, Becky stepped inside. How different the house looked to her now. No longer did it seem the dark, foreboding place it had the night of the storm. Instead, it exuded warmth and welcome. Would her father show such a marked improvement? "May I see Pa?"

The older woman shooed her down the hall. "Give a knock and go right on in. He'll be pleased you're here."

She tapped her knuckles on the sickroom door, renewed hope in her heart.

"Come," Doc Pruitt called from within.

Pushing the door open, she stepped inside. Instantly, something like icy fingers gripped her throat. She'd envisioned Pa seated upright, smiling as she entered. Instead, he lay motionless on the bed, eyes closed, a blood-stained bandage wrapped around his head. It didn't seem right, her strong, able father lying helpless and weak. And yet, Doc Pruitt had warned her such a blow to the head would take time to heal.

Like the wound in her soul.

The doctor paused from his work, peering over-top his spectacles. "Well now, you didn't waste any time gettin' back here. I 'spect you're just the remedy he needs about now." He tamped powdered medicine into a glass bottle and screwed down the lid.

Becky moved closer, gaze fixed on Pa's face. "Is he all right?"

The doctor brushed his hands together. "As good as can be expected."

"He's still so pale."

At the sound of her voice, Pa's eyelids flickered open.

Rising, Doc Pruitt stepped toward the door. "I'll let you two visit a while."

Nodding her thanks, Becky sat on the edge of the bed. She gripped Pa's hand, its coolness sending a wave of unease through her. "How are you, Pa?"

"Been better." He blinked, his voice raspy.

The same dazed look clouded his eyes. "Is your eyesight improving?"

"Not yet, but give it time."

45

Becky tucked her foot up under her leg with a sigh. "Wish I could stay here and help look after you."

"Don't you fret. Doc's takin' good care of me. Besides, I'm asleep more than I'm awake." He strained to look past her. "You alone?"

"Uncle Jed'll be along shortly. He's gonna run me by our place. Thought I might be able to salvage some things."

Pa's brow creased. "You sure that's such a good idea?"

Tightness gripped Becky's chest. She wasn't certain she was ready to face the downed homestead again so soon. She squeezed his hand, trying to sound convincing. "I'll be fine."

Pa hesitated before reaching in his pocket. When he drew out his hand, Ma's wedding band lay clasped between his fingertips. "Here. Your ma would want you to have this. For when you marry."

Unspoken anguish stirred inside Becky. The ring was a token of Pa's love for her mother. It belonged with him. "No, Pa. You keep it."

"Go on. Take it." He pushed it into her palm. "Put it somewhere safe till you have need for it."

Tears welled in her eyes as she clung to the tiny gold band. She loosened the ribbon from her hair and looped it through the ring. Tying together the ends, she slipped the ribbon around her neck, where it would stay until the day she wed. "I'll keep it always."

The muscles in Pa's jaw tensed. He swallowed hard, staring up at the ceiling. "Do you know what happened? Why they didn't make it to the cellar?"

Becky dropped her gaze, her eyes glossing over. "A branch barred the cellar door. At first I didn't know whether they were trapped inside or if the limb had blocked them from entering. I kept calling and calling."

The image of their ravaged homestead drudged across her mind, bringing it all back.

"Ma? Melissa?" Again and again she'd called, pounding on the cellar door. But her endless pleas had met with silence.

Heart thumping, she turned to face the cabin. Had they been forced to wait out the storm there? She sifted through piles of broken timbers, tossing aside shattered pieces of what had been her home. The oak table Pa had fashioned for them lay over-turned at the cabin's center. A bit of cloth beneath it caught Becky's eye. The soiled fabric's familiar pattern choked off her breath. There was no mistaking it. The remnant of cloth belonged to Ma's calico dress.

Becky edged forward, hand clutched to her chest. Bits of stoneware tumbled to the floor as she strained to push the table aside. With a gasp, she fell back at sight of her loved ones lying intertwined on the floor, Ma's arms draped limply about Melissa.

Becky's voice wavered as her thoughts returned to the present. "But they weren't there. They were in the cabin." She bit her lip, tempering the urge to cry.

A single tear slid to Pa's temple, though any emotion had fled from his face. He reached for her, and she melted into his embrace. Would he ever be the same?

Becky shuddered. Would she?

FROM HER UNCLE'S WAGON, Becky canvassed the wind-swept homestead, for the first time realizing that, even when Pa recov-ered, they had no home to return to. Sitting taller on the wagon seat, she squinted against the cresting sun. Her heart sank at the cluster of wagons and people milling about the property. With precious little time alone to lament her loss, here she'd hoped to find solitude. "What are all these people doing here?"

Uncle Jed slowed the horses, swerving to dodge a stray beam from their cabin. He bobbed his chin. "Reckon we're about to find out. Here comes the preacher."

Pastor Brody waved as he strode toward them, his winsome smile eroding Becky's disappointment. By now he should have moved onto another area. She'd never known him to delay riding his circuit. What was holding him here? Had he felt obligated to stay?

The kindness in his eyes silenced her questions. Whatever his reason, she was glad for it.

"Mornin'." Matthew tipped his hat and brushed off his soiled clothes as Jed brought the team to a halt beside him. His gaze settled on Becky. "Thought you could use some help getting this place back into shape."

"That's very kind." With a wide glance, she scanned the dozens of hardworking neighbors piling debris and sifting out salvageable items. A group of children scuttled about in an attempt to capture the handful of flustered chickens.

Matthew offered her a hand down. It had been a long while since he'd held a woman's hand. Yet Becky's delicate fingers felt strangely at home in his. "Come. I want to show you something."

She walked with him toward the creek, leaving Jed to join the others. Nugget traipsed alongside in the tall grass that had sprung up anew. The swollen brook had receded to its normal level, its water once again clear and sparkling in the sun. A rhythmic hacking sound echoed in the distance, drawing Becky's attention downstream.

Matthew watched her expression as she took in the group of men standing along the timberline. Their sharpened pole axes and two-man saws cut into the trees, flinging wood chips about them. A loud crack sounded as a tree fell with a vibrating thud.

Becky turned to him, blue eyes filled with question. He stared down at her, the corners of his mouth tipping upward. It was difficult to discern her thoughts, but the wonderment in her eyes lifted his spirit. Removing his broad-brimmed hat, he raked a hand through his hair. "When this mess is cleared out, those who can spare the time will be back to build you a new cabin."

Her eyes moistened. "I-I don't know what to say. How can we ever repay you all?"

"The Good Lord placed it on our hearts to help, else we wouldn't be here."

"Is that why you stayed?"

He stared down at his boots. Why had he stayed? Was it a sense of duty? A pastor's concern for his flock? What was this sudden need to oversee Becky and Joseph's well-being? He squinted over at her. "Let's just say I sensed the Lord nudging me to stay."

Her expression softened. "I'm grateful to you. For everything."

He smiled down at her. "That's reward enough for me." Donning his hat, he offered her his arm. "Shall we go back? There are those who'd like to express their sympathies."

With a deep breath, she linked her arm through his.

As she strolled with him, something melted inside him. If he had doubted he'd made the right choice in staying, this moment had erased it.

BECKY CAST PASTOR BRODY a sideways glance. How different he seemed from the devoted preacher who frequented their home and community with stirring messages from God's Word. Of the three to four times a year she saw him, she'd never thought of him as anything but a minister fulfilling his duty. Yet the warmth of his touch somehow made him more real. More...manly. Was he viewing her differently as well? He'd certainly been attentive. But then, he'd probably have done the same for anyone under such dire circumstances.

At sight of her, neighbors dropped what they were doing and gathered around. Jesse Albrecht handed Becky a satchel, his feathery, white beard tossing in the breeze. "We've gathered up what we could salvage of your things. Our prayers go out for you and your pa."

Becky blinked back tears. "Thank you, Mr. Albrecht."

His wife Pearl, stooped and hunched in the shoulders, raised shaky arms out to her. "God bless you, child."

Becky closed her eyes, touched by the woman's heartfelt embrace. "Thank you for coming."

The couple moved on to make room for Hank and Ida Brimmer. Tears filled Ida's oval eyes as she clasped Becky's hand in hers. "Tis an awful thing that's happened. Couldn't rightly believe it, till I saw the graves over yonder." The slender, dark-haired woman pointed toward the newly planted field, tears trailing down her hollow cheeks.

Becky turned, a lump rising in her throat at sight of two crude, wooden crosses staked at the edge of the field. Not the place they would have chosen for a grave site. But the kind pastor had done what he could in the little time he had.

She pried her hand from Ida's and glanced up at Pastor Brody. Try as she may, her mouth refused to form words. She only hoped he could glean from her expression how grateful she was.

He met her gaze, the sorrow in his dark eyes mirroring her own. "Would you like me to go with you?"

She shook her head. This was something she herself had to front. "If you don't mind, I'd rather go alone."

With a nod, he stepped aside to let her pass. "Take all the time you need."

Leaving behind the satchel, she trekked to the edge of the field, her legs threatening to give way. The heaps of earth loomed ahead of her like the burdens mounted in her soul. How would she and Pa carry on without them? Somehow, they'd manage.

But it wouldn't be the same.

The wooden crosses at the head of the graves loomed ahead of her—the very image of the cross Jesus had died on. A sudden notion caught in her chest. Had God suffered the same loss and heartache when Jesus died?

Her foot kicked against something hard, and she cringed. Not solid enough to be a rock, whatever it was slid forward when she hit against it. Curious, she bent over, peeling back the layers of prairie grass. The momentary pain in her toes forgotten, sight of the familiar, cherry case made her eyes go wide.

Pa's fiddle. Could it have survived the storm in one piece?

She picked it up and ran her fingers over the smooth surface. Though a bit water-stained, it otherwise appeared undamaged. Loosening the lid, she held her breath. At first glimpse of the instrument, the muscles in her face relaxed. It was perfect. Not so much as a scratch or broken string. Amazing!

She closed the lid and then stood, clutching the wooden case to her chest. What a gift to have found it. How often Pa had strummed a tune before the fireplace on cold wintry nights. Their cozy cabin would vibrate with song, shutting out the chill and ushering in warmth and cheer. Ma would hum and tap her foot as she mended clothes, while Becky and Melissa sang along.

Pa would be overjoyed to know it survived the storm.

But no. With his injuries, it might sadden him not to be able to play it.

A tearful smile pulled at the corner of her mouth. She'd tuck it away until he was well and could play once again.

Kneeling beside the graves, she plucked a handful of violets and, one by one, placed them atop. With a soft whine, Nugget trotted past and lay between the mounds of earth. Somehow he knew, sensed the loss.

Tears stung Becky's eyes as she leaned over the heaps of soil.

Which grave housed who? The cross markers gave no hint. But what did it matter? In her heart, she knew her loved ones weren't held captive beneath. Yet somehow the graves made final their absence. They were forever gone from this life.

And from her and Pa.

Chapter Six

LAUGHTER from the far side of the barn pulled Becky's attention. She stopped milking and watched her cousins chase after Nell's young calf. Belle, as they called her, kicked up her heals and traipsed around the roomy stall as if playing a game. The little Jersey calf grew stronger and livelier each day. Looking on, Uncle Jed leaned on his pitchfork and gave a loud chuckle.

Becky sank her forehead against Tess's flank and resumed milking. Try as she may, she couldn't help but let the happy scene fester inside her. With half of her family stolen away, would she ever know such joy again?

In the two weeks since the storm, life had fallen into some semblance of normality. Given the tasks of gathering eggs and milking Tess, Becky's allotted duties helped fill her mornings. Yet, the days crept on, her only enjoyment being the daily visits with Pa. Each afternoon, Uncle Jed drew his work to a halt early to accompany her into town. Though the short time with her father made the days more tolerable, she longed for when he would be well and they could make a fresh start.

But while his wounds appeared to be mending, his eyesight waned. Whenever she asked about it, he would mumble a reply, assuring her, that in time, it would get better. But each day, his gaze grew more strained and distant.

Coming up beside Becky, Uncle Jed stabbed his pitchfork into a heap of straw. "You about to make it?"

"Almost."

He gave Tess a pat on the rump. "Your cow here's come in real handy, what with Nell nursin' her calf."

Becky nodded but didn't look up. At least something good had come of their troubles. Yet it was of small consolation.

Uncle Jed placed a hand on her shoulder, and she glanced up at him. A slight smile crossed his lips as he seemed to read the discouragement in her soul. "I've nothing pressing this afternoon, what say we head for town a bit early today and give you a little more time with your pa?"

"I'd like that." Warmth surged through her. "Love" was more like it.

"We'll head out right after lunch." With a wink, he turned and headed outside.

No more had he stepped through the doorway when Charlotte sidled over to Becky, her hands behind her back. "How much longer you figure on being here?"

Becky worked to keep her voice agreeable, despite her cousin's obvious ill intent. "Till Pa's well, I reckon. Why?"

"I don't know. I just hope it's soon."

Becky paused, hands still resting on the cow's udder. Heat flamed in her cheeks. Something in her cousin's tone hinted she spoke more of Becky leaving than Pa's recovery. She aimed one of the teats in Charlotte's direction, fighting the urge to give her cousin's fiery-red hair a coat of white. Instead, she clenched her jaw and sprayed a stream of milk into the bucket. She pulled a bit too hard, causing Tess to bellow and twist her head around. Easing her grip, Becky patted the cow's shoulder. "Sorry girl."

With a smirk, Charlotte swiveled toward the door. Apparently, she'd accomplished what she'd set out to do—get under Becky's skin.

Esther gave Belle a final scratch on the chin and then stood, brushing straw from her frock. "Comin', Becky?"

"In a minute." Somehow, she'd let Charlotte's rudeness etch its way into her own voice. Yet her shortness only succeeded in luring her young cousin closer.

"Don't let her get to you."

Becky kept up her cadenced milking, mumbling under her breath. "She hasn't wanted me here since the day I arrived."

Esther leaned over Tess, resting her chin on her arm. "It's not that."

"What then?"

Lowering her gaze, Esther pushed straw along the barn floor with her toes. "She's jealous."

"Jealous?" Becky sat back on the three-legged stool, brushing a strand of hair from her cheek. In light of all she'd been through, could Charlotte be so trivial? She had her family intact, a cabin, food, provisions, everything Becky lacked. "Jealous of what?

Esther hesitated, as though what she had to say pained her to speak. At last, she blew out a breath. "Of the attention Ma and Pa have been giving you. Especially Pa. She and Pa have always shared a special bond of sorts. Guess she's feeling a bit...slighted."

Her words coiled around Becky's heart, squeezing her chest. Was what her cousin said true? Was her being here bringing discord to the family? And if so, did Esther feel the same? Becky's mind retraced the past couple of weeks. How many times had Uncle Jed stopped what he was doing to escort her into town or asked her to go somewhere with him while leaving his own girls behind? Aunt Clara, too, often catered to Becky, giving her easier tasks compared to Charlotte and Esther.

"Do you feel that way too?" The words spilled out slow and

choppy. She'd come to look upon her young cousin as her dearest friend. The thought of causing her to feel slighted settled heavy on Becky's heart.

Esther's foot again toyed with the straw beneath Tess. "N-No."

The uncertainty in her cousin's voice belied her words. Though she would never admit it, Esther's inability to meet Becky's gaze spoke all too clearly.

Becky clenched her jaw. Then she had no business staying. In fact, she refused to stay where she wasn't wanted. That left but one choice.

To leave.

JOSEPH SQUEEZED HIS EYES SHUT, blocking out the shadows. The blurred shapes and images he'd seen in the beginning had faded to light and darkness. He'd been fooling himself thinking his eyesight would improve. Becky too. How could he tell her it wasn't to be?

He cleared his throat, elbowing his way to a sitting position. "I've always been straight with you, darlin', and I'm gonna be straight with you now."

Becky wedged the pillow in behind him. "What is it, Pa?"

Her query sliced through him like a knife. He could no longer hide the truth. Bowing his head, he pulled at the bed sheets. "Doc says the worst is over, and my head is healing, but…"

She clutched his arm, a slight quiver in her voice. "Tell me."

He swallowed, the muscles in his neck tightening. "I…I'm goin' blind."

Heavy silence followed Becky's harried breath. She pressed her fingers deeper into his arm. "Given more time, maybe…"

"No! No more pretending." He turned toward the light of the

window, jaw clenched. "Shadows is all I see now, an' Doc says that's as good as it's gonna get."

"Even so, we'll manage. Somehow. I'll look after you."

His lips grew taut. He refused to live like an invalid. "I won't be a burden to you."

"You could never be a burden to me. What matters is that we're together."

He scrubbed a hand over his face. "Don't ya see? I'll have to learn the simplest things all over again."

"I'll help you."

The strain in her voice made him wince. "That's just it. I don't want everything done for me. A man's got his pride."

Silence fell between them, and he heard a faint whimper. Reaching for her hand, he gave it a gentle squeeze, softening his voice. "I've got to learn to do things for myself. To do that, I'll need special training."

Becky sniffled. "What sort of training?"

"Doc knows of a school for the blind, where I could learn to fend for myself more. Even learn some sort of trade."

"But where? There's no place like that around here."

He hesitated, his throat tightening. The last thing he wanted was to be uprooted from the familiar. But there seemed little choice. "It's in St. Louis."

She drew in a breath. "But that's so far away. How would we even get there?"

"Matthew has offered to take me as soon as I'm well enough. In a couple of weeks maybe. My sister Ellen lives there. I've asked Doc to wire her I'm comin'."

"For how long?"

He shrugged. "A few months. Maybe a year."

"A year? But who'd look after our place while we were away? They're building us a new cabin, you know. It wouldn't be right to let it sit idle for squatters to overtake."

"Jed 'll look after things." Joseph hesitated. What he had to say was as hard for him to stomach as it would be for her. "But, Becky. You'll not be goin' with me."

"What?" The word squeaked out in a whisper.

He gritted his teeth, choking down the angst inside him. "I don't know what's in store for me there. St. Louis is no place for a young country gal. You'd be better off here."

"I'd be better off with you." Her quivering voice raised a notch.

He turned away, moisture pooling in his eyes. He didn't mean to hurt her. Only protect her. "My mind's made up. Jed an' Clara will look after you till I get back."

She slid her fingers from his arm. "But, Pa..."

"No arguments." With a sigh, he lowered his head. "It's how it has to be."

MATTHEW PULLED the telegraph office door closed behind him. He'd hated to send for a replacement preacher, but he couldn't leave now. Not when he was needed here, with several families affected by the tornado. Not least of all, Joseph and Becky. It wouldn't serve anyone well for him to leave when he felt he should stay. He'd promised Joseph he'd get him where he needed to go. He couldn't renege on it now.

Nor did he want to.

Out of the corner of his eye, Matthew caught a glimpse of Becky Hollister stepping from Doc Pruitt's house. She dabbed at her eyes with a hankie.

Was she crying?

His muscles tensed as he ventured closer. Had Joseph worsened? Or had he simply shared his plans to leave?

"Becky," he called to her, quickening his stride.

She glanced his way, eyes red with tears.

Coming up beside her, he tipped his hat. "Is everything well?"

She drew in a breath and knit her brows. "How could you promise to take Pa to St. Louis?"

"I was simply trying...."

"He belongs here. Not in some strange, unknown place. He'll be helpless without..." The tremor in her voice cut off her words.

Dryness cleaved to Matthew's throat. When he'd agreed to take Joseph, he'd not given thought to whether Becky would approve. He placed a hand on her arm. "I only meant to help."

She lowered her gaze, her expression softening. "Forgive me. It's just...I need him. If he must go, could you convince him to take me with him?"

Matthew arched a brow. "I'm afraid that's between the two of you."

She gazed up at him, eyes blue as starlight. "He has such respect for you. Couldn't you at least try?"

Something within him longed to brush a hand over her cheek. How could he resist such a heartfelt request? A corner of his mouth lifted. "I'll see what I can do."

Becky's lips hinged upward in a smile—one that nearly brought Matthew to his knees. "Thank you."

As she walked away, his stomach quavered. The hand-me-down dress couldn't hide her soft curves. What was this strange, new awareness he had of Becky? Concern? Compassion?

Or something more?

TWO MORE WEEKS. Was that all the time she and Pa were to have together?

Becky sat dazed atop her uncle's wagon as it jostled along the rutted trail. News of Pa's blindness had notched a raw spot on her heart. Hadn't she sensed it in each hollow stare? Not once since the storm had his eyes glowed with warmth or connection.

Even worse was his decision to travel to St. Louis without her. She lowered her gaze, wedging her feet against the floorboard. Here she'd every intention of convincing him to let her stay with him until he recovered, and instead she'd learned he planned to leave her with her aunt and uncle indefinitely. How could she bear it? How could she abide to live under the same roof with her spiteful cousin an entire year?

Becky pressed her lips together, squelching the anguish inside her. She couldn't do it. She just couldn't.

But leave the prairie? It was unthinkable, even for a short while.

Pastor Brody's reassuring smile resurrected in her mind. Could he persuade Pa to stay, or at least to take her with him? Would he even try?

Of course he would. She could still envision the sincerity in his rich brown eyes. She'd never realized how caring and thoughtful he was.

Or how handsome. Had he truly stayed here on account of her and Pa?

Uncle Jed's elbow nudged her arm, jarring her from her reverie. "Awful quiet. Everything all right?"

"Just mulling things over in my mind."

He clicked his tongue in his cheek. "Reckon your whole world seems a bit topsy-turvy about now. But don't you fret. Things'll work out."

Would they? Ever the optimist, her uncle's words fell flat in Becky's ears. Pa seemed determined to make things worse by striking off to some unknown place and leaving her behind.

She gripped the edge of the wagon seat. Only one thing could make her leave the prairie...and she'd do it too.

If that's what it took to be with Pa.

Chapter Seven

June, 1854

BECKY SMOOTHED the thickened mortar with her hands. The mixture of clay, lime, and straw clung to her fingers, leaving them dry and tight. She raked her hands together to shed the excess and glanced around the new log cabin. Sunlight shone through gaps in the log walls. Would this replica of her old place ever feel like home?

Esther and Aunt Clara worked to chink the far side of the wall, while half a dozen others daubed the notched timbers from the outside. Becky rose from her knees, a jumble of emotions welling inside her. So much work only to have it sit empty.

Every attempt to persuade Pa to change his plans had failed. He would have none of it. Even Pastor Brody's influence had fallen on deaf ears. If only she could make Pa understand. All she wanted now was to be with him. Wherever it may be.

Regardless of his stubbornness, her heart was knit with his much as Ruth's was tied to Naomi in the Bible. This cabin would wait, and the prairie would always be here. But nothing could replace time with her father. To separate just wouldn't be right.

She gripped the handle of her empty mortar bucket and started toward the doorway.

Esther scurried up beside her, bucket in hand. "I'll go with you."

Becky leaned toward her cousin. "How'd Charlotte get out of helping chink?"

"She sweet-talked Pa into letting her gather sand and moss for the mortar."

Becky smirked. Softer than feather down, that's what Charlotte was. Not one to get her hands dirty, she'd nabbed the easier job of gathering materials to mix with the mud and clay.

As they rounded the corner of the cabin, Mrs. Bradshaw loomed before them, face knotted in an unwelcome scowl. The heavy-set woman lowered her buckets of mud and clay, then pointed to the line of empty containers bearing remnants of moss and sand. She glared at Esther. "Where's that sister of yours? We're plumb out of fillers for the mortar."

Esther stumbled back, eyes round as silver dollars. "I-I don't know, ma'am, but we'll find her."

With a shake of her head, the woman snatched up two of the empty pails and lumbered past, muttering under her breath something about doing things herself.

Esther scanned the timberline. "Where could Charlotte be?"

"I don't know, but we may as well go help." Taking up an empty bucket, Becky started after Mrs. Bradshaw.

Esther's firm grip on Becky's arm locked her in place. "Look. Over there."

She followed Esther's gaze to where two bare feet extended from the far side of a hickory tree near the creek. Sharing a look of exasperation, they stormed toward her missing cousin.

Charlotte sat leaned against the tree, head bowed, arms in her lap. She made no move as they neared. Had she fallen asleep?

Stepping up beside her, Esther nudged Charlotte with her

foot, a calloused look on her face. Had she finally had her fill of her older sister's shenanigans?

With a start, Charlotte squinted up at them, her long, auburn braid draped over her shoulder. "What was that for?"

Esther cocked her head, hands on hips. "You've not done your job, that's what."

With a complacent yawn, Charlotte stretched out her arms. "What of it?"

"You'd best get a move on. Mrs. Bradshaw is fit to be tied."

Rising to her feet, Charlotte smoothed the creases in her frock. Her green eyes flashed, and she nodded toward the bucket in Becky's hand. "It's your cabin. You do it."

Edging closer, Becky let the container fall to the ground. She'd had just about enough of her cousin's sassiness.

Esther wedged herself between them. "That's enough, Charlotte. I've put up with your bad-tempered ways all these years, but I won't stand by and let you treat Becky so. She's suffered more than you'll ever know, and you won't so much as lift a finger to help."

"Why should I?"

Heat burned Becky's cheeks. She could only take so much. Grabbing up the pail, she plunged it in the mucky water along the edge of the creek. Edging closer, she aimed the half-filled bucket toward Charlotte.

Eyes wide, Charlotte took a step back. "You wouldn't dare."

"Wouldn't I?" Becky cocked her arm back further.

Cowering, Charlotte shielded herself with her hands.

Becky slackened her hold. What was she doing? Here she was nearly eighteen and acting like a child. As she started to lower the bucket, a force from behind shoved her arm forward, spraying the mixture of muddy water onto Charlotte's face and down her dress. Esther's girlish giggle from behind sealed her guilt.

Stretching out her arms, Charlotte stood wide-eyed, nose

flared. Her loud squeals brought some of the neighbors scurrying. Mrs. Bradshaw hurried over, mouth agape. "What goes on here?"

Rushing at Becky, Charlotte knocked her to the ground. Sharp fingernails dug into Becky's neck and shoulder, cutting into her skin. She tugged at Charlotte's bonnet and pulled it off, jerking her head back with it. Locked in a tight coil, they rolled over the grass until strong hands pried them apart.

Charlotte squirmed in her father's arms, her face pinched. What a sight she was, plastered with mud, hair askew. Becky dare not look at Esther, lest she give into the urge to chuckle. Her young cousin's courage had surprised her. She'd done what Becky had longed to do but couldn't.

The grip on Becky's arms loosened, and she turned to see Mrs. Bradshaw scowling down at her. Heat flamed in Becky's cheeks. Though no words passed between them, she could sense the woman's thoughts—that Ma would be ashamed. Averting her gaze, Becky brushed bits of grass from her dress. Those who'd gathered around began to disperse, leaving them to their fate.

Aunt Clara shouldered her way to them, her penetrating gaze shifting from Becky to Charlotte. "What's this all about?"

Charlotte pulled her arm free from her father, pointing at her soiled front. "Jus' look what she did."

Aunt Clara's blue eyes probed Becky's. "Why would you do such a thing?"

There were a hundred reasons why she could have done it. But the truth stood in her way of answering. She refused to incriminate Esther for doing what she herself had wanted to do. After all, Scripture said that as a man thinketh, so he is. She would willingly accept whatever punishment Aunt Clara rendered.

"Becky didn't do it... I did." Esther's timid voice startled Becky. She tried to catch her young cousin's eye as she stepped forward, but Esther's gaze remained fixed on her shoeless feet.

Aunt Clara's eyes widened. "What?"

"Becky only threatened to. It was me that flung the mud at her."

Aunt Clara shook her head as though having as difficult of time believing it as Becky. "But why?"

"Because she's a traitor." Charlotte answered for her, brushing bits of mud from her soiled frock.

"Am not." Esther flashed Charlotte a wounded stare, then turned to face Aunt Clara. "Just to spite Becky, Charlotte didn't do her part with the mortar. She's been nothing but mean since Becky came to stay with us."

Unwilling to allow Esther to take all the blame, Becky stepped to her side. "I'm as guilty as she is. I shouldn't have lost my temper." Turning, she met Charlotte's embattled green eyes. "Sorry, Charlotte."

Aunt Clara's eyebrows lifted. "Well, Charlotte? Haven't you anything to say?"

She tossed her braid over her shoulder. "Why should I be sorry? She's the one who's brought on the trouble. She's turned you all against me. First you and Pa, and now Esther.

Her glare tore into Becky. "Just 'cause you lost your family is no cause to steal mine."

"Charlotte!" Aunt Clara scolded.

Steal her family? Tears welled in Becky's eyes. Is that how Charlotte viewed her, as divisive and conniving?

Uncle Jed placed a hand on both of their shoulders. "I'm not sure what this is all about, but no one's turned anyone against anybody. You girls may as well make the best of things, 'cause it sounds like you'll be together for some time."

Becky lowered her gaze, a knot tightening in the pit of her stomach. The last thing she wanted was another family to be torn apart. She couldn't bear it. Turning, she freed herself from her uncle's grasp and fled toward the open field, tears streaming down her cheeks. Drawn to her loved ones' graves, she knelt beside them. With a sob, she sank her fingers into the powdery soil. "I wish you were here, Ma. You'd talk sense into Pa and make him change his mind about leaving. He belongs here with me, not at some ol' school for the blind."

A gentle breeze caressed her cheeks, and a meadowlark's sweet song sounded in the distance. Tossing aside the wilted violets from days prior, she plucked a handful of golden butter-cups and placed them atop the graves. She swiped away a tear and sat back, mustering a slight grin. "You'd have been proud of Esther, Melissa, the way she stuck up for me. She's so much like you."

An overwhelming presence spilled over her, easing the burden in her soul as she smoothed down the unsettled earth. Pastor Brody often spoke of the calming presence of the Lord during troubled times. Did she dare to hope He cared or even took note of her sorrow? Or was it her own tender thoughts that made her loved ones seem near?

She reached to straighten the rickety crosses, shoving them further into the soil. "Someday you'll have more sturdy markers with dates and names."

Boot steps swished in the grass, stopping just behind her. "I'm afraid it's the best I could do at the time."

She straightened, brushing dampened hair from her face. There was no need to turn. She knew at once the voice belonged to Pastor Brody. Had he just arrived? Or had he witnessed her disgraceful actions? If so, he must think her such a child.

She hung her head, keeping her face hidden beneath her bonnet. "Promise me. When Pa's able, we'll give 'em a proper burial."

"How 'bout now?"

Her breath caught in her throat at the familiar tone of her father's voice. Turning, she saw him beside Pastor Brody, his hand fastened on a sturdy walking stick. She rushed toward him and clasped her arms around his waist, her troubles melting away like spring snow.

He chuckled, trying to regain his footing. "Careful now. I'm not so steady on my feet yet."

Easing back, she drank in his every feature. Weeks of bedrest had faded his tanned skin, and his gaunt face paled against the bright sunlight. A thin band of gauze remained wrapped around his head. His skin was pink beneath stubble surrounding the wound where his hair had been shaven. "I can't believe you came. Are you up to it?"

He gave her shoulders a squeeze, resting his chin on her head. "Doc wanted to see how I'd do traveling."

The words left Becky cold. Was he so near to leaving?

Pastor Brody grinned and folded his arms across his front. "Truth is, he pestered the doc till he gave in an' let him come. That and I promised I'd soon bring him back."

"I've had enough lyin' around. I know what I can stand better than the doc."

Becky warmed at the resilience in her father's words. It was that dogged determination that would see him through. "I'm just glad you're here."

Pa twisted his stick in the dirt, his expression sobering. "Go rally the others, preacher. It's time we said our goodbyes."

A wave of sorrow washed through Becky. This day marked a full month since the storm that had taken their loved ones. It seemed both a moment and an eternity. Even now, if she allowed, her mind could relive every terrifying image, each grueling detail of the destructive windstorm. Yet she refused to let it. Today, she would lay the memories to rest alongside her mother and sister.

Taking her father's arm, Becky guided him to the graves. How she'd longed for the day he would again be at her side. At last, he was here. But for how long? With his recovery came his plans to leave for St. Louis. As yet, she'd not devised a plan to go with him.

She only knew she must.

"MUST YOU LEAVE SO SOON?"

The strain in Becky's voice pierced Matthew's soul. How she clung to her father's arm, as if he were being snatched away, never to return.

Joseph cradled her against him. "Promised Doc Pruitt I wouldn't overdo."

She stretched to give him a peck on the cheek. The dread of their parting, not only for the day but for long months over many miles, told on both their faces.

Matthew faltered. Could he live with himself helping bring about such a separation? Still, he'd given his word. Hopefully Becky wouldn't hold it against him.

He helped Joseph onto the wagon seat, then swiveled toward Becky. She'd grown to be quite a beauty, even with her mortar smudged face and misfit dress. How he longed to erase the anguish that shrouded her face. "Why don't you ride along? I'd be happy to take you back to the Stantons after I drop off your father."

It was the least he could do.

"Why don't you, darlin'? It would give us more time together."

Her lips tipped upward at her father's words. "All right. I'll just let Uncle Jed and Aunt Clara know."

Hiking her skirt, she jogged toward the cabin. The smile on her face told Matthew he'd done well in asking.

If only, somehow, that joy could last.

"THANKS AGAIN FOR ALL YOUR TROUBLE."

The lilt in Becky's voice spilled over Matthew like summer rain. He flashed a wide grin. "Glad to help."

Silence settled over them, the space on the wagon bench seeming to carve a wedge between them. Matthew loosened his grip on the reins, venturing a sideways glance. He'd never felt awkward with Becky before. But then, he'd never been alone with her. Why was it he had to keep reminding himself she was merely a member of his flock in need of encouragement? Almost overnight it seemed she'd changed into a young woman.

A beautiful one at that.

The churning of the wheels sounded loud against the stillness. At last, she turned toward him. "How will you manage the time off to go to St. Louis?"

Matthew drank in the blueness of her eyes. "I've asked for a short leave of absence from my duties and have someone covering my ministry for a time."

With a nod, she laced her fingers together in her lap. "Do you ever tire of wandering the countryside? I mean, do you ever wish to stay in one place?"

Matthew sensed himself relax, a corner of his mouth lifting. "The thought has crossed my mind."

More often of late.

"If you do, I hope it's here." His gaze locked onto hers for a moment before she turned away, a hint of red flashing in her cheeks.

He stole a sideways glance in her direction, his chest warming. He'd not felt so vibrant and alive since...since he'd courted Sarah. Was he falling for Becky?

He couldn't be. She was so young and vulnerable. Still, he couldn't deny the swelling tide of emotions surging within him.

Surely what he was experiencing was a deep sense of compassion.

Or was it?

He pursed his lips, tapping the reins down on the horses' rumps. This was no time to fall in love.

Chapter Eight

BECKY HELD the sopping dress up and pinned it into place on the clothesline. Had she been too bold? What was she thinking, telling Pastor Brody she wished he'd stay? What must he think of her? She brushed a wayward strand of hair from her face. Well, it was true. He'd been not only a devoted pastor, but a good friend to her and Pa. They'd have been lost without him these past few weeks.

Glancing down the row of dripping clothes, Charlotte's steady gaze thrust Becky back into reality. Stuck was what she was—doing penance for her foolish behavior, with no real hope of resolving the situation.

Esther lugged over another heavy basket, filled to overflowing with wet bed linens. With a loud huff, she set it on the ground beside Becky. "Here's the last of it."

The hot sun soaked through Becky's frock, warming her to perspiration. She swiped a hand over her damp forehead. "I'd rather chink than wash and hang clothes."

Nodding, Esther spread a pillowcase on the line. "I thought at least Ma would let you go back and help with the cabin."

"Guess she didn't want to be accused of playing favorites." Becky gestured toward Charlotte. "I've never seen Aunt Clara so upset."

"She was pretty angry all right, angry enough to keep us saddled with work till nightfall."

Becky pulled one of the linen sheets from the pile, her cousin's words penetrating deep. Was Aunt Clara so vexed she would deny Becky the chance to see her father?

She shook out the wrinkles in the bedsheet and pinned it to the rope line, blood draining from her cheeks. Surely her aunt wouldn't go so far as that.

Would she?

Her basket empty, Charlotte strolled over to them, her stare locked on Becky. "Don't forget we've wood to carry in."

Becky squared her shoulders, meeting her cousin's steady gaze. "I haven't forgotten."

No doubt Charlotte blamed her for their punishment. Yet it seemed more Charlotte's fault than anyone's. If she'd done what was expected, there would have been no cause for quarreling.

Becky bit her lip. Then again, if she hadn't raised the bucket of sludge to throw, they'd not have tussled. Perhaps if they at least attempted to get along, Aunt Clara would be more inclined to slacken their load.

Her cousin's emerald eyes flickered downward as she pivoted toward the woodshed. Was she, too, feeling a pang of remorse?

Becky snagged her by the sleeve. "Uncle Jed's right. There's no reason we can't get along."

"So long as you remember who your pa is." Averting her gaze, Charlotte tugged her arm loose and hurried on.

Becky fell into stride with her. "Listen. It wasn't my idea to come here. I needed a place to stay, and your ma and pa were kind enough to take me in. I never meant to cause any grief."

Charlotte paused, opening her mouth as if to speak. Instead, she gave a slow nod, the fire in her eyes extinguished.

Nugget barked and wagged his tail, pulling Becky's attention westward. A swirl of dust trailed behind a wagon as it jostled along the worn path toward the homestead. That it was her uncle's wagon and team was plain, but why did it come by way of Miller Creek, rather than the shortcut across the prairie from her place? Was he truly so sore at her for yesterday that he went to see Pa without her?

Shielding her eyes against the midday sun, she strained for a better look. There appeared to be two men atop the wagon seat. Most certainly the burly driver was her uncle. But who was the smaller-framed man beside him, head bowed, hat low over his face?

As the wagon neared, her heartbeat quickened, and a smile stretched over her lips. It was Pa. Hiking her skirt, she ran to meet them, Nugget leading the way. Uncle Jed halted the team outside the barn, his steady grin upon her. "Thought we'd surprise you."

"You did that," she called back. As her gaze shifted to Pa, the smile on her lips faded. Instead of the jubilant expression she'd expected, his face bore a blend of emotions she couldn't quite place. Her stomach knotted. There was more to this visit than a pleasant surprise.

Uncle Jed hopped from the wagon, then gave Pa a hand down. His ready arms encircled Becky, and he planted a kiss atop her bonnet. "The sunshine feels nice, but this is better."

Becky leaned her head on his shoulder, fixing her eyes on his face. Though he'd regained some of the color in his cheeks, his gaze remained clouded.

Nugget whined and pawed at his leg. The poor old dog had been deprived of his master far too long. Bending over, Pa rubbed the dog's back, and Nugget leaned into his pant leg. "How are ya, ol' fella?"

"He's lonesome for you, same as me." Even as the words left her mouth, she could sense their devastating effect on her father.

With an audible sigh, he hugged her to him, giving Nugget a scratch behind the ear.

Uncle Jed took hold of the horses' bridles and tugged the team toward the barn. "Fool dog hardly eats. Don't know how he'll take it when you leave."

Becky tensed. Was that what this was all about? Just like that, was Pa up and leaving? Had his sightlessness blinded him of her need for him? She choked down the angst threatening to cut off her words. "How soon will you go?"

Pa hung his head. "I expect Matthew here first thing in the mornin'."

"So soon?" Here she'd spent the better part of yesterday with the two of them and neither had breathed a word of it.

Pa's brow furrowed. "That's why I came, to spend what time I have left with you."

"But you're not fully healed. You can't…"

He held a hand up to silence her. "Don't make this harder than it already is. Doc gave the okay, and I'm goin'. The sooner I leave, the sooner I'll be back."

She gnawed at her lip, blinking back tears. Pleas were useless and would only ruin their final evening together. Yet his stubborn resolve only deepened her willful determination to go with him. Somehow there had to be a way.

BECKY SQUINTED against the early morning light seeping through the loft windowpane. Long hours of sleeplessness left her fatigued and dreading, more than ever, the day ahead. She closed her eyes, mustering what faith she had left. *Lord, please, if there's a way, let me go with him.*

Boot steps below, followed by the door opening and shutting, indicated Uncle Jed had gone to chore. The faint smell of smoke rose to the loft as Aunt Clara stoked the smoldering coals in the fireplace. Pa's muffled voice wafted upward, sending a wave of contentment through Becky. Then a tormenting thought crept in to steal her joy. He was leaving today, and there was no way to stop it.

She and her cousins dressed in the cramped confines of the loft, not a word passing between them. Esther glanced her way, offering a weak smile as Becky finished buttoning her frock. The friendship she and her young cousin had forged was the one positive that had come of her stay. Yet even that couldn't muster a grin from her this morning.

Hurrying down the loft ladder, she joined Pa at the table and greeted him with a peck on the cheek. "Morning."

He reached for her, a cavalcade of emotions running through his features. At last, a faint smile touched his lips. "It's a treat to hear your voice greet me of a morning instead of Doc's."

Too bad the pleasure would be short-lived. Becky took a seat beside him, taking in his every detail. The shaven hair around the gauze bandage had grown back specked with gray, looking distinguished against his natural brown. His clothes sagged about his frame. "You've grown thin."

"Haven't had much of an appetite, I reckon."

Aunt Clara took a pitcher from the corner cupboard and filled it with gravy. "You do look a mite frail. I'll send you with a batch of biscuits and a slab of smoked ham for your journey."

The comment revived the ache inside Becky. There was no getting around it. Pa was leaving.

Her cousins climbed from the loft and headed out to do their chores, reminding her of her own duties. Rising to her feet, she tugged at Pa's hand. "Come with me to milk Tess."

He hesitated, then shook his head. "I'd only be in the way."

"Come on. It'll do you good."

Aunt Clara gave him a gentle nudge on the back. "Joseph Hollister, I've never known you to stay indoors when there's outdoor work to be done. Now get yourself out there."

With a groan, he gave in to Becky's pull.

Taking his arm, Becky handed him his walking stick. As they stepped outside, Nugget nuzzled his head under Pa's hand for a pet. He rustled the old dog's fur, the bond between them unhampered by long weeks apart. "How ya doin', ol' boy?"

Nugget let out a soft whine, staring up at Pa with moist, brown eyes. A hint of sadness lined Pa's face as he rubbed his hand repeatedly along Nugget's back. White hair had replaced the yellow strands around the old dog's eyes and muzzle. Nearly ten years had passed since they'd taken him in as a pup. Was Pa, like her, wondering if his old friend would be here to greet him when he returned?

Becky guided him toward the barn. Sunlight beamed through the open barn door, casting a trail of light through its center. Pa took a deep breath as they entered. "No mistaking the earthy smell of a barn. I've missed that."

Tess let out a low "moo", and Pa's face brightened. "Seems someone else is glad to see me."

Becky warmed at her father's softened expression. A dash of the familiar might be just what he needed. Bracing him against the stall beam, she placed his hand on the cow's neck. He stroked her as Becky took up the three-legged stool and started to milk.

He rubbed the cow's face, and she bobbed her head up and down. "Good ol' Tess." There was longing in his voice.

Becky paused from milking. "You wanna try?"

He gave a soft snicker. "You know I can't see anything but shadows."

"You always said you could milk blindfolded. Now's your chance to try."

Standing, Becky latched onto his arm. With reluctance, he gave into her promptings. Gently, she guided him onto the stool and positioned his hands on the cow's udder. She stood back, hope rising in her heart. "The bucket's just beneath you."

"I'll never hit it." He hesitated, and Tess turned her head for a look.

"Just try."

He squeezed, spraying milk into the straw bedding below him.

Becky centered the bucket under the stream, catching the next spurt. She smiled as he gained rhythm, renewed confidence telling on his face. Squatting beside him, she placed a hand on his knee. "See? I knew you could do it."

His lips turned upward. "Reckon I'm not completely useless."

"I could teach you all sorts of things, if you'd only stay around long enough to let me."

He sat back, his hands falling free of the cow's udder. "Maybe you could teach me a few simple things. Maybe we'd manage an' get by. But I want more than that for us...for myself. I'd die inside knowing you were shouldering the burden to provide for us."

"I wouldn't mind. Not if it meant we were together."

"And we will be...in time. But this school can teach me a trade, a way to help provide for us." He breathed a sigh, furrowing his brow. "Don't ya see? I've gotta go, so I can feel useful again."

Heavy silence pierced the still air. She'd given it her best try and gotten nowhere once again. Well, she could be just as bull-headed as him. Not once had she ever questioned her father's authority. Never had he given her cause to doubt the wisdom of his decisions. But this time, he was wrong.

Her hands grew clammy, and she wiped them on her frock.

For the first time in her life, she felt the need to go against his wishes.

MATTHEW LEANED FORWARD on the wagon seat, stomach churning as he neared the Stanton homestead. This day had come all too soon. Not that he minded the trip to St. Louis. He enjoyed traveling and meeting new people. It was the circumstances that didn't sit right.

Much as he wanted to help, he didn't relish being the catalyst that would tear father and daughter apart. Would Becky forgive him? Last time he'd seen her, she'd seemed at peace with things. Still, he had an uneasy feeling about it all. He tipped his hat back on his forehead, an odd sensation ripping through him. Why was her impression of him suddenly so important?

He arched a brow, tightening his hold on the reins. If he could, he'd take her with them. A little female companionship along the way would do them both good. But the return home alone with her would be sure to raise some eyebrows.

The canvas top swayed with each bump in the trail. It would be his first trip by covered wagon. A much different feel than horseback. Jethro had been more than generous in offering to loan the livery's canvas and rig.

Matthew's gaze settled on Joseph and Becky, standing together outside the Stanton cabin, faces drawn. Already he could read the anguish in Becky's expression. His chest tightened. He hadn't realized the hardship the separation would cause her. He had to keep reminding himself it was for Joseph's good.

Matthew heaved a sigh. He'd make it up to Becky. When he returned, he'd spend as much time as he could with her. The thought stirred an unexpected eagerness within him. It wouldn't take much of a nudge from the Lord to forfeit his riding circuit and settle here at Miller Creek. A corner of his mouth lifted. To do so would give him more opportunity to look in on Becky.

"Mornin', folks." He tipped his broad-brimmed hat and set the brake, pasting on a smile.

Striding over to him, Jed hooked his fingers under his suspenders. "The Lord's blessed you with a good day for travel."

"More a mixed blessing from where I stand." Moisture pooled in Becky's eyes at her father's words.

Matthew's chest clenched. This obviously wasn't easy for either of them.

"Have you time for a cup of sassafras tea before you go, pastor?" Clara called from the doorway. The singled-out invitation seemed more than a mere polite gesture. Clara's nod in Joseph and Becky's direction hinted she meant to give them a few moments alone to voice their farewells.

"All right by me." Matthew hopped from the wagon.

Like a frightened fawn, Becky's gaze darted to and fro. What was going on inside that pretty head of hers? She helped Joseph to the wagon and fastened his hands on the wheel rim. "I'll be back, Pa."

Joseph gave a slight nod. "Bring my satchel when you come."

Aunt Clara edged toward the cabin. "I'll fetch it, along with a bundle of food, soon as Pastor Brody's had his tea."

Out of the corner of his eye, Matthew caught a glimpse of Becky whispering to Esther. Whatever Becky said produced a noticeable look of shock on young Esther's face. With a nod, she took a tentative step back, then started toward the cabin along with the rest of them.

Matthew held the door open for the others to enter, keeping a watchful eye on Becky. Her cheeks pinked, and she turned her attention to her father. With a final glance, Matthew followed the others inside. He pulled the door shut behind him, turning just in time to see Esther scurry up the loft ladder.

No doubt about it. The two were up to something. Just what he couldn't say, but something inside pleaded with him not to interfere.

DRYNESS TORE at Becky's throat. At last, she'd hatched a plan. But why must she plot to give her and Pa what they wanted most —to be together?

"It's not forever." Pa draped an arm around her, his quivering voice belying his words.

She leaned into him, the agony on his face almost more than she could bear. He looked so torn at the thought of leaving. A year apart would certainly feel like forever.

What if her plan went awry? What then?

A soft thud sounded outside the cabin, drawing Becky's attention. At sight of the small bundle, a flurry of excitement washed over her. Esther had come through for her, tossing down her things. Becky caught a glimpse of her cousin at the loft window and smiled. She would miss her dear friend.

Pa pressed his cheek against her head. "Mind Jed and Clara while I'm gone."

"Yes, Pa." Even as she spoke, the deceptive words evoked a bitter taste in her mouth. Was she wrong to mislead him? If by chance her plan succeeded, would he forgive her for disobeying? Would God?

Could she even forgive herself?

She clasped her arms around his middle. "I love you, Pa."

"Love you too, darlin'." He pulled her closer and kissed her forehead.

Becky closed her eyes, locked in his firm embrace. He didn't want to be apart from her any more than she did him. She could feel it in his touch.

With a sniffle, he loosened his hold. "Putting off leaving won't make it any easier. Go tell Matthew I'm ready."

"Yes, sir." Becky worked to steady trembling hands. She had but one chance to make this work. And so little time.

Keeping a watchful eye on the closed cabin door, she hurried to retrieve her bundle of things. At any moment, the door might swing open, putting an end to her deception. A nervous twinge seared her abdomen as she doubled back to the wagon bed.

Nugget's playful bark sounded behind her, bringing her to a sudden stop. She'd not thought of him. He padded up to her, and she shooed him away. The slightest sound might arouse Pa's suspicions. The old dog stopped and stared, head cocked and tail wagging.

Pa stood, face downcast, at the front of the wagon, waiting for Becky to return with the others. Casting a wary glance at the cabin, she set her bundle in the wagon and climbed up on the rear-wheel axle. The wagon's thick canvas-covering, fastened down by two coarse ropes crossed over each other, formed a tear-shaped hole just large enough for Becky to fit through. A few more seconds and she would drop to the wooden planks within, unnoticed.

But Nugget was at her feet now, his inquisitive caramel eyes gazing up at her. Breathless, she slipped through the opening, her bare feet landing silently on the oak planks. She hunkered down out of sight, praying he wouldn't give her away. His front paws scraped against the end-gate, and she cringed. With Aunt Clara already on edge, things were certain to go from bad to worse if Becky were found out.

Among the provisions for the journey, she spied a wool blanket and quickly unrolled it. Darkness enveloped her as she pulled it over her.

"Nugget!" Uncle Jed's voice bellowed in the distance.

Becky lay paralyzed, heart pounding in her ears. They were

sure to miss her. She could only pray Esther would think of some sort of excuse.

"Get down from there. Come here." Her uncle's voice was closer now, just outside the end-gate. Becky dared not even breathe.

Nugget's high-pitched whimper tore at Becky. Poor ol' fella. If there was a way to sneak him aboard, she would. But he'd be certain to give her away—if he hadn't already.

"What's wrong with him?" Pa questioned from the front of the wagon.

"Must be in the notion to go along."

Becky breathed a quiet sigh as the dog lowered himself and trotted away.

Boot steps sounded outside the wagon. "Thanks for the tea, Clara." Pastor Brody's voice held a deep, brisk tone.

"My pleasure," Aunt Clara called back. "Here are Joseph's things and the food I promised. Safe journey to you. And Joseph, don't worry about Becky. We'll take good care of her."

Becky clenched her jaw, a nervous pang gripping her middle. Aunt Clara would be beside herself with worry. Becky would write to explain once she and Pa got settled. To be sure, her aunt and uncle were fond of her, but she'd never be more than a guest in their home, an extra pair of hands and a mouth to feed. Pa needed her, and she needed him. As dearly as she loved the prairie, it wouldn't be the same without him.

The wagon joggled to one side, and the creak of the seat ensured Pastor Brody had helped Pa up. Something knocked against Becky, grazing her arm, and she tensed. No doubt Pastor Brody had tossed back Pa's satchel. She strained to see beyond the blanket, but glimpsed only faint bits of light. Was this what it was like for Pa?

A drop of sweat trickled down her nose. She was sweltering beneath the thick wool blanket.

"Where's Becky?" Pastor Brody sounded close enough to touch.

She held her breath, scrunching lower in her hiding place.

"Didn't she come to the cabin?" Pa's voice was sated with concern.

"Saw she was gone, so we came on out." It was Uncle Jed's voice now, just outside the canvas.

"The poor dear probably needs some time alone is all." A wave of relief washed over Becky at her aunt's words. If she could, she'd have run out and kissed her.

"Do you want me to look for her?" Though Becky warmed at the note of compassion in the pastor's tone, her heart hammered as she awaited his reply.

"Let her be. We've said our goodbyes."

Whether from the intense heat or sheer relief, Becky's entire body fell limp. Had she heard him right? Had she succeeded? Bittersweet victory flooded over her. To leave her home and the people she knew to live in a strange place against her father's wishes seemed almost too great a sacrifice. Yet something deep inside compelled her to go.

With a click of his tongue, Pastor Brody smacked the reins down. The wagon jostled forward, shattering Becky's doubts. She'd made her choice. There was no turning back.

Nugget's raspy bark rang out behind them. Uncle Jed's stern command to stay halted the barking and, instead, yielded a high-pitched whine. How Becky hated to leave the old dog behind, but deep down she knew it was best he stay. He'd be miserable in the city.

An odd feeling surged through her. Funny. That's what Pa had said of her.

Lying still beneath the blanket, she waited until she was certain they'd traveled a safe distance from the cabin. At last, she slid from under her wool cocoon and ventured a look out the opening in back. Esther alone remained watching after them, bent down with arms clasped about Nugget's neck. How Becky longed to show herself and assure her young friend all was well. But she dare not.

No doubt Aunt Clara had returned to the cabin and Uncle Jed to his work. They would soon grow anxious about her. But Esther would keep quiet as long as she could. With the mood her aunt was in, Becky could only pray it would go well for her young cousin when she made their secret known.

Becky caught site of Charlotte making her way inside the cabin, and a tinge of sadness coursed through her. She'd begun to hope the two of them could resolve their differences. Now, she'd never know. At least not for some time.

As they angled onto the worn path, her uncle's farm disappeared from view. She sat up, without fear of detection, watching the boundless prairie pass behind her. There was something soothing in the rhythm of the wheels turning over the ground, not unlike the beating of her heart. She rested her chin on her arm, wondering how this had all come about. She had no desire to leave the prairie. Her only wish was to be with Pa.

The jostle of the wagon over the rugged terrain left her stomach a bit queasy. Or was it the worry of what Pa would say when she was discovered? She draped an arm across her middle. As determined as he'd been to make her stay, it might take well over a day's journey to convince him not to send her back.

She startled at the sound of Pa's voice at the front of the wagon. Though there was no danger of him seeing her, hearing his muffled tone so near both comforted and disturbed her. One backward glance from Pastor Brody, and she'd be undone. She snugged herself into the corner, resting her head against one of the hickory bows that held the canvas. She hated to think what Pa would say when he found her out. Would he be lenient with her or adamant she return?

The shrill cry of a hawk sounded overhead, soaring against the indigo sky. Acres of lush prairie grass swayed in the breeze, carrying the cadence of insects. Groves of trees lining the creek pulsed with the songs of robins, bluebirds, and meadowlarks. Such pleasures would be scarce where they were headed. Why was it, now that she was leaving, each sight and sound seemed more endearing? If only she could capture them in her mind's eye.

In that moment, she whispered a pledge—a promise to return.

Chapter Nine

PART TWO: THE JOURNEY

A COOL BREEZE swept through the tunnel-shaped canvas, sending a chill through Becky and waking her from a light sleep. She stretched, rubbing a kink from her neck. How long had she slept leaned against the hard, hickory rib? An hour? Two?

Dusk had fallen, and the sky was a fiery pink as she looked out, the setting sun reflecting off a line of rippled clouds to the north. In the distance, trees appeared black against the brilliant sky. Crickets and katydids sang out their raspy chants, bringing the darkening prairie to life.

The horses no longer followed path or road, but trod over unbroken terrain. The tall grass raked against the floorboards of the wagon, only to spring up behind it, scattering seed.

Pastor Brody urged the team to a halt beside a narrow stream. "We'll put up here for the night. You sit tight while I set up camp."

Becky reached for the wool blanket, her stomach knotting. A few moments more and he would come in search of supplies— and find her as well. Would a day's journey be enough to convince Pa to let her stay?

Perhaps, given the dim light inside the canvas, she could conceal herself beneath the blanket until daybreak. But then, what would it gain her? She'd be found come morning. Her gaze fled to the lantern hanging on a peg near the back of the wagon. Even her small frame couldn't hide from its light. She had no choice but to let herself be found and pray her deceit hadn't all been for nothing.

The wagon joggled as Pastor Brody climbed down. His soothing voice mingled with the clank of metal as he removed the harnesses. The sound of the horses snorting and shaking hinted they were happy to be free of their burden for the night. Boot steps skimmed past the side of the canvas. He was coming. Becky drew a shallow breath, bracing herself. Would Pa be cross with her? She could withstand his anger, but not his disappointment.

Pastor Brody loosened the rope cords and drew back the canvas flaps, letting in the last bit of brightness from the setting sun. He reached in an arm and grasped the lantern without venturing a look around. Becky gripped the blanket, warring within herself. How she longed to duck beneath its protective shelter. Yet to be found hiding seemed such a coward's way.

Chin lifted, she raised herself to a full sitting position, letting the blanket fall to her lap. She much preferred owning up to her choice, whatever the consequences.

The lantern's flame glowed outside the canvas, causing Pastor Brody's shadow to dance along it. Becky's heart hammered in her chest as he hung the lantern back on its peg. Long seconds ticked by while he rummaged through supplies without noticing her. She held her breath, each moment teetering between agony and anticipation.

At last, his gaze skimmed over her, then darted back. Like a bandit uncovering loot, his eyes widened. "Sufferin' polecats! How'd you get in here?"

Becky forced a grin, wanting to fade into the rough grain of the wood. What must he think of her stowing away like a frightened mouse?

"Somethin' wrong?" Pa's familiar tone broke the uncomfortable silence.

Pastor Brody seemed to battle within, his brown eyes searching Becky's. He leaned against the end-gate, as though not knowing how to respond. She'd put him in quite a predicament —either to betray her or her father. They both knew what he had to do. He tilted his hat back, a touch of a grin lining his lips. "Let's just say there's a bit more back here than I reckoned on."

"What is it?"

Becky held her index finger to her lips to silence him. It was her job to right things with Pa. It would only anger him further hearing the news secondhand.

Pastor Brody gave a slow nod, seeming to understand. Offering her a hand down, he helped her from the wagon.

With a deep breath, Becky smoothed her dress, making her way to the front. She cringed to think what Pa would have to say about her little ruse.

At the sound of her footsteps, Pa cocked his head to the side. "Matthew?"

Becky paused, staring at his silhouette against the soft glow of the evening sky. Then, with a reluctant sigh, she pulled herself up beside him. "It's me, Pa."

"Becky?" It was difficult to read his expression, but his tone was one of utter disbelief.

"Please don't be angry with me, Pa."

"What are you doin' here, girl? I told you to stay behind."

"I know you said I shouldn't come, but don't you see? My place is with you, wherever that may be."

He raked a hand through his hair. "Clara and Jed will be half out of their minds looking for you."

"Esther knows where I am. She'll tell 'em not to fret."

He released a frustrated huff, running a hand over his face. "If you were younger I'd take a switch to you."

Her face warmed. "I'm sorry."

Pastor Brody stepped around the side of the wagon, arms laden with supplies. "Don't be too rough on her, Joseph. The Lord works in mysterious ways. There may just be a reason in her being here."

His kind eyes found Becky's, and she smiled. Could it be true? Could there be a deeper purpose in her coming? Regardless, the pastor's words were like sweet balm for her soul. At least she had him pulling for her. She gripped her father's arm, her throat tightening. "Please let me stay."

His cheek flinched, then he shook his head. "No. You'd get homesick for the prairie and come to resent me."

"My home's with you."

He released a jagged breath, cupping his hand over hers. "There'd be no turning back. You'd be stuck till I'm ready to come home."

Hope rose within her. Was he weakening? "I don't care. I just want to be with you."

Leaning forward, he bowed his head in long silence. At last, he straightened, a hint of agitation in his voice. "I still have half a mind to make Matthew turn around and head back first thing in the mornin'."

Becky squeezed his hand. "I need you, Pa."

With a sigh, he pulled her to him. Though he didn't say so in words, Becky sensed he, too, needed her. She clung to him, tears stinging her eyes, for the first time in weeks feeling as though she were home.

MATTHEW TOSSED another log on the fire and squatted beside it. The sun was just beginning to crest the horizon. His favorite time of morning. So peaceful and still and full of God's presence. He opened his Bible, its pages frayed from years of use. Starting the day with a chapter and Psalm always set things off right.

Joseph stirred on the bedroll beside him. His eyes flickered open, and a grim expression lined his face.

Matthew pursed his lips, heaviness tugging at his chest. His friend had been dealt a double blow. First the loss of home and loved ones, and then his blindness. What must it be like to awaken to shadows, unable to drink in a sunrise or your daughter's face?

He glanced toward the canvas-covered wagon where Becky still slept. A corner of his mouth lifted. Hers was a face one couldn't easily forget. Eyes blue as starlight. Rounded lips. Delicate nose. Beautiful inside and out.

They'd allotted Becky the privacy of the wagon bed. Though, no doubt, its stiff floorboards offered little more comfort than the ground. To Joseph's credit, he'd allowed her to stay. It'd been a tough call, but his heart had won out. Plainly, the tragedy had woven a bond between father and daughter that wouldn't be broken.

Still, Matthew couldn't help feeling a bit cheated. Just when he'd begun to relish the thought of spending more time with Becky, she was leaving. He'd so enjoyed their ride back to the Stantons'. Come to think of it, that had been the first time he'd been alone in her company. Lightness threaded through him. Given opportunity, might they gain a fondness for each other?

Or had they already?

With a yawn, Joseph raised himself up on his elbow. "Is that coffee I smell?"

Pulled from his reverie, Matthew eased his Bible closed. "Freshly made."

"Hand me a cup, will ya?" Joseph sat up, rubbing a hand over his face. His brow seemed creased with concern. Was it for himself or Becky?

Laying his Bible aside, Matthew moved toward the fire. With a handkerchief, he lifted the coffee pot from the embers at the fire's edge. He poured some into a tin cup and passed it to Joseph, guiding his fingers to the handle. "Careful. It's hot."

Joseph gave a nod of thanks, then took a sip. "Becky still sleeping?"

He kept his voice low, and Matthew followed suit. "It appears so."

Joseph leaned forward, cradling the tin mug in his hands. "You think it's right to let her stay?"

"Only you and the Lord can answer that. But I do know this. You need each other. Now more than ever."

"Even if it means she's miserable?"

Standing, Matthew clasped a hand on Joseph's shoulder. "I reckon, to her, being apart from you is more miserable."

Joseph's cheek flinched, hinting Matthew's words had found their mark.

Soft footsteps sounded behind him. Matthew turned toward the wagon to see Becky striding toward them, her warm smile edging out the tension in the air.

His lips hinged upward. One thing was certain. Her presence would make the trip a lot more pleasant.

BECKY KICKED a final spray of dirt onto the smoldering fire, then turned to Pa. "Ready?"

With a slight nod, he rose to his feet. He seemed no more eager to start the next leg of the journey than her. Did a part of him wish to turn back?

Placing a hand on his arm, Becky guided him toward the wagon. She ventured a sideways glance at Pastor Brody as he hitched the team. There was something different about him. Some endearing quality she couldn't quite put a name to. But whatever it was, it was most becoming.

The look on his face earlier that morning lay etched in her mind. When he'd turned toward her, his eyes had sparked. Almost as if seeing her for the first time.

Her heart drummed in her chest. Was he viewing her as...a woman?

Loading up the rest of their belongings, she dreaded the thought of again being confined to the wagon bed. She'd had enough of the incessant jolting yesterday. Today she'd walk alongside, at least until the sun grew hot.

Pastor Brody climbed into the driver's seat. With a glance her way, he steadied his hand on the brake lever. "You're welcome to ride."

For a moment, she was tempted to slide in beside him. Yet, the seat on this wagon seemed narrower. To sit so close to an unmarried man didn't seem proper—especially such a handsome one. "I don't mind walking."

He hesitated, then pulled back on the lever. Smacking the reins across the horses' backs, he goaded them forward. The leather straps tightened, raising the tongue of the wagon as the team strained to rouse the heavy wheels from their night's rest.

From early morning to mid-day, the horses trudged on. Becky struggled to keep pace, tiring as the sun rose higher in the sky. Rest came only when the creak of the wheels developed into an irritating screech.

"Better stop an' grease the axles." Pastor Brody guided the team to a shady spot near a grove of trees. He set the brake and secured the reins, then hopped from the wagon.

Becky wiped her brow with her sleeve, catching sight of Pa

trying to climb from the wagon on his own. She jogged toward him. "Wait. Let me help you."

"I can manage." He struggled to find a foothold.

Becky edged closer but paused when Pastor Brody clasped her arm. Would he really let Pa try it on his own? What if he fell?

Something in Pastor Brody's dark eyes and winsome smile reassured her. Turning her attention back to her father, she resisted the urge to go to him.

He placed his foot on the wheel, but lost his balance and clung to the wagon seat.

Becky hoisted herself onto the hub of the wheel and reached for his arm.

He pulled away. "I said I can do it."

His harsh tone pricked her. Was he angry at her for disobeying? Or was it his pride she'd tampered with?

He breathed a frustrated sigh, his foot probing for a fresh hold. Gradually, he lowered himself down the side of the wagon and stumbled to the ground, falling backward.

Clamping a hand to her mouth, Becky forced herself not to reach to steady him.

Pastor Brody stepped up beside her. He leaned in close, his deep voice a warm whisper in her ear. "Don't take his sternness to heart. His need for independence is a good thing."

With a nod, she lowered her gaze, trying to suppress the unexpected yearning his nearness set off inside her. "I suppose I'd best get used to watching him struggle."

Pastor Brody cupped a hand under her chin, lifting her face to meet his gaze. "It's the way he wants it."

His limpid brown eyes held hers. The warmth of his touch brought a smile to her lips. He seemed more man to her now than pastor. Did he merely view her as another soul in need of encouragement? Or a budding young woman?

A flurry of elation welled within her, the near seven years' difference in their ages seeming to melt away. If the way he looked at her was any indication, it was the latter.

MATTHEW FETCHED the bucket of tar and tallow from beneath the wagon. He leaned against the end-gate, a bit woozy. No denying it. Something intimate had passed between him and Becky back there. He'd sensed it. And so had she.

He blew out a hasty breath. What a time to fall in love. She was so young. What would Joseph think? Would he even allow Matthew to court her? Yet how could he, now that Becky was going away?

Bucket in hand, he rounded the corner of the wagon. As he bent to brush the greasy mixture on the wheel hub, he noticed Becky had unbuckled the head straps to let the team graze. Their withers damp with sweat, the horses nickered and lowered their heads, nibbling grass as Becky stroked their long necks. With such compassion for beasts of burden, her heart for people must be even greater.

A smile touched his lips. What a pastor's wife she would make.

She glanced his way, the breeze catching her bonnet. "The horses seem thirsty. Hope there's a creek nearby."

"Should reach one soon." Pushing aside his thoughts, he wiped his brow and moved to the front wheel. "I could use a swallow myself."

At that, Becky brushed her hands together and disappeared to the other side of the wagon. A moment later, she returned with the canteen. She held it out to him, a playful gleam in her eyes.

Setting his wire brush aside, Matthew stood, peering down at her. "Thanks." He took a long swig, then gave a refreshed sigh. With a tip of his hat, he held out the canteen, soaking in the warmth of her gaze. "Water never tasted so good."

Their fingers brushed, and a hint of color pinked her cheeks. Taking a step back, her mouth angled in a pleasant smile. "I'd best go see to Pa."

Matthew watched her go, a nervous churning in his middle. The more time spent with Becky, the more invigorating she became. But in a matter of days, she'd be in St. Louis, and he'd be headed back to the prairie. It seemed a cruel trick to gain someone's affections, only to lose her. But then, the Lord had His reasons for when and how things came about.

He stooped down, drawing the brush from the bucket of tallow with a sigh. Maybe it was for the best. Now wasn't the time for sparking. Not with her still grieving her loved ones. Courting would have to wait.

Regardless, returning home alone sounded more dismal all the time.

Becky plunged the canteens in the shallow creek, just upstream of where Pastor Brody watered the horses. A hint of warmth still clung to her cheeks. The way he'd looked at her when he handed her the canteen spoke more than mere gratitude.

Affection perhaps?

Her cheeks flamed anew. It was a silly notion. He was simply a kind and caring man. When this trip ended, he'd return to the prairie and to his ministry, more than likely forgetting any closeness they'd shared along the way.

Ripples fanned out from where the team dipped their noses in the crystal-clear stream. They pawed at the water with their hooves as though enjoying its coolness. The midday heat demanded frequent rests and keeping near a water source. Becky tried not to think about where their journey would end. Instead, she chose to relish the unexpected adventure of traveling the countryside. It had been a rare occurrence for her family to venture more than a few miles from home. An occasional trip to a larger town to visit relatives was all they'd managed. She found the journey itself rather enjoyable. It was the destination that bothered her.

The canteens filled, Becky climbed inside the wagon bed for the trip across. The wheels bogged in the muddy creek bottom, forcing the horses to strain under the load. Pastor Brody raised his voice, urging them forward, then praised them as they reached the other side.

Hour stretched into tedious hour, the humid air suffocating in the heat of the day. Having rolled up the sides of the canvas, Becky stared out at the vast terrain, the flatlands of the prairie gradually giving way to the slant of hills and trees. By late afternoon, wisps of clouds dulled the sun's rays. Weary of the jolting ride, she again trailed behind the wagon, fanning herself with her bonnet.

At last they came to a wide river, much larger than the stream they'd crossed earlier in the day. Pastor Brody halted the team along its bank, laced with hickory and elm trees and an array of wildflowers. Coming up beside him, Becky gazed out at the clear, flowing current. "Surely this isn't the Mississippi already?"

He climbed from the wagon, tipping his hat back with his thumb. "I'm afraid this doesn't compare to the Mighty Mississippi."

The Mighty Mississippi. Pa's sister, Ellen, had boasted of it in letters through the years, calling it majestic and grand. Becky sighed, a knot balling in her chest. More than anything, it would seem a barrier separating them from home.

Propping his foot on a log, Pastor Brody scanned the river's edge. "It's the Kickupau, and it feeds directly into the Mississippi."

"It looks deep. Can the horses manage it?"

"We'll soon find out." Loosening the neck straps to let the

fidgety horses drink, he waded into the water. At mid-stream, it hit just below his waist, a depth certain to test the team's endurance. Water streamed from his trousers as he traipsed back onto the bank. He arched a brow, giving the horses each a pat on the neck. "Reckon a few prayers wouldn't hurt."

Pa shifted in his seat. "Is it too much for them?"

"It could get a mite tricky, but Lord willing, we'll make it." Taking his place on the wagon seat, Pastor Brody held the reins taut in his gloved hands. "You'd best go back with Becky till we're across."

Pa tightened his grip on the bench. "Go ahead. I'll be all right."

"Better listen to him, Pa."

"I'll be fine," he countered, irritation again seeping into his voice.

Becky shared a concerned look with Pastor Brody, then climbed in the wagon bed. A nervous twinge pricked her abdomen as he smacked the reins down and the wagon jerked forward. She clutched the sideboard, keeping a watchful eye on Pa through the opening in the canvas. It was hard not to coddle him. When would he learn he couldn't do what he once did?

Her chest tightened. Pure stubborn's what he was.

And she loved him for it.

"Haw! Get up there." Pastor Brody's voice bellowed above the babbling current. The horses whinnied and paced side to side, then plunged in, spraying water on the sides of the canvas.

Becky braced herself against the corner of the wagon bed. She held her breath, her muscles tensing at the rocking of the wheels on the mucky floor of the river. The water sloshed against the bottom of the wagon, jostling it back and forth. Would it hold?

Again and again, Pastor Brody smacked the reins down with a shout, prodding the horses deeper into the stream. The wagon swayed as water smacked against the sideboards. Minutes seemed like hours as the team trudged their way across, their shrill whinnies cutting through the sound of the current. A splash of water sprayed in at Becky, and she drew her feet up, clutching the wooden rail. All at once the wagon jolted to a stop, causing Pa to lose his hold and slide forward. Bracing himself, he settled back on his seat. "What happened?"

"Must've hit something along the river bottom." Locking the brake in place, Pastor Brody, glanced over his shoulder at Becky. "Take the reins, and I'll go have a look."

Becky climbed out onto the wagon seat, heart pounding. She'd never handled a rig in deep water. What if the team bolted? The whole wagon would tip, and they'd lose everything.

With a reassuring nod, Pastor Brody handed her the reins. Tossing his hat onto the floorboard, he charged into the water. With a deep breath, he plunged beneath its surface to check the front wheel. A moment later, he stood and made his way to the back, where he again submerged himself beneath the flow.

Becky struggled to calm the jittery horses, losing sight of Pastor Brody as he rounded the corner of the wagon. Tightening her hold on the reins, she darted a look from side to side. What was taking so long? She couldn't hold them much longer.

At last, he trudged up beside her, a bit out of breath, water dripping from his hair and shirt. "The back right wheel is lodged on a rock. It's too heavy for me to move. You'll have to urge the team forward while I pry with a lever."

A ripple of unease washed through Becky. "The horses are pretty skittish. I'm not sure I can hold 'em."

"You'll do fine." Pastor Brody rolled up his sleeves. "Hold 'em steady while I find a log to use as a lever."

Squaring her shoulders, she gave a slight nod, his confidence giving her courage. She rested her hand atop the brake, watching Pastor Brody tramp toward the bank. The horses pawed at the water and tugged at the hitch. With each pull, there was the chance they could break loose of the wagon and run off. Then where would they be? Pa's white-knuckled grip on the seat displayed his growing concern.

At last, Pastor Brody returned with a sturdy shaft of wood. He paused beside her. "When I holler, release the brake and give 'em all you've got." Plunging deeper into the water, he disappeared around the corner of the wagon. Becky cocked her head, listening for his signal.

"Now, Becky."

"Yee-ah!" she yelled, slapping the reins across the horses' backs. The wagon jerked forward slightly, then settled back in its spot.

"Again."

Over and over she urged the team forward, but each time the wagon lurched and fell back into place. Tears stung her eyes as she relaxed the reins. "It won't budge."

Pa swung his legs over the side and, with raised voice, called over his shoulder. "You need another pair of hands, Matthew. Help me back there."

Drawing a shallow breath, Becky shoved the brake forward. "Pa, don't. It's too risky."

"You just keep listening for the preacher's signal. I know what I can do."

With a shake of her head, she slumped her shoulders. His stubbornness would be the death of her.

The slosh of water grew louder as Pastor Brody made his way toward them. His chestnut eyes found hers, speaking reassurance as he reached to help Pa down.

Becky gnawed at her lip. All she could do was trust. And pray. A seed of hope took root in her heart. God had answered her pleas for Pa's healing and for him to let her stay. Perhaps He would answer this prayer as well.

The horses' heads bobbed up and down as they paced and stirred in their spots. Becky tightened her hold on the reins. She clutched the brake, cocking her head to listen.

"Okay, Becky. Now!"

Releasing the brake, she smacked the reins across the horses' backs. "Yee-ah! Get up there." The harness straps grew taut as the team strained to pull the load free. A sudden bump jolted her forward, and she clung to her seat. Free of the rock, the team pulled with renewed vigor as if eager to escape the confines of the water.

At the river's edge, Becky tugged on the reins, breathing easier as the wagon wheels gripped solid ground. Securing the brake, she leaned forward, trying to still her trembling hands.

The two men slogged out of the river together and plopped down breathless on the bank. Becky climbed from the wagon and took a seat in the grass beside Pa. "You all right?"

He smiled, wringing water from his soggy clothes. "Just dandy."

Drawing in a jagged breath, she pushed back her bonnet. Why did men so enjoy taking risks? She herself felt completely spent by the endeavor. "Wish I could say the same."

"You done fine. Didn't she, preacher?" Becky warmed at his words. For the first time since the storm, there was vibrancy in his voice and demeanor.

Pastor Brody's mouth tipped in a sideways grin, his gaze falling to Becky. "She's her father's daughter."

Becky suppressed a smile, heat rising in her cheeks. Was it Pa's stubborn willfulness or his courage Pastor Brody attributed to her?

He stood, patting the weary, water-soaked horses. "Good place to dry out and make camp."

"How much further to St. Louie?" Pa's question sparked a myriad of emotions within Becky. Monotonous as these days of travel had been, they'd been her only enjoyable ones for many weeks. The thought of them coming to an end left her wanting.

"Another day I expect, if all goes well."

Becky wilted at the pastor's words. Soon buildings and

people would replace the vast prairie, and she'd be forced to rely on her memory to keep it alive. Her eyes canvassed the smooth grassland lined with trees. The sun beamed through the timber, low in the west, casting elongated shadows over the terrain, reminiscent of the shadow that cloaked her heart.

When would she see home again?

Chapter Ten

THE SOUND of men's voices awakened Becky. She stretched and opened her eyes. It took but a moment to regain her senses and recognize the voices belonged to Pastor Brody and her father. Daylight streamed through the canvas draped over the wagon bed. Despite the hard surface of the floorboards, she'd enjoyed the best night's rest she'd had in weeks. Her conscience clear at last, she was where she'd longed to be. With her father.

The air was crisp and sweet with the scent of wildflowers as she climbed from the wagon. The endless shades of lavender and yellow painted the hillsides with color. The prairie's beauty was one of many things she'd miss while away. Their neighbors and friends, too, would be ever in her thoughts. They'd shown such kindness in the wake of the storm. Despite its challenges, the prairie would forever hold her heart. Its people and ways were all she knew.

All she wanted to know.

A light breeze toyed with tender branches of oak and sycamore along the sparkling Kickupau River as she joined Pa and Pastor Brody by the fire.

Pastor Brody poured her a tin of coffee. "Nice of you to join us."

With a soft smile, she took it from him. Though cheerfulness lined his words, something in his expression carried a more sullen tone. Their time together was short. Was he, too, sorry to see it end?

Easing onto the log beside her father, she broke off a piece of pan bread. Pa's silence unsettled her. His hollowed cheeks and drawn expression hinted he was troubled about something. Was he still sore at her for coming? Or was he, like her, dreading what was to come?

She was thankful he couldn't read the concern mounting on her face—the one advantage to his blindness. Never could she let him know how hard it was for her to leave.

Pastor Brody stood and brushed crumbs from his trousers. "Reckon I'd best hitch the team so we can be on our way."

Dousing the fire with the remainder of his coffee, he started for the wagon.

No one spoke as they loaded their things for the final stretch of the journey. St. Louis. The very thought of it cast a shadow over Becky's heart. What unknown struggles awaited them there?

Would there be blessings as well? Pastor Brody would say so. The man seemed a tower of strength, holding to the premise that God had some unseen purpose in their suffering. Was he right?

As she helped her father to the wagon, he swayed forward, almost losing his balance.

Pastor Brody rushed to help steady him. "Whoa there. A bit unstable on your feet, aren't ya?"

Becky loosened her hold on Pa's arm. "What's wrong?"

"Tired's all." He squinted, squeezing the bridge of his nose.

A trace of drainage had seeped through his thin, gauze bandage. He was pushing himself too hard. She never should have let him help at the river crossing. But then they'd not have managed without him.

Pastor Brody clapped him on the shoulder. "Maybe you'd best lie down a spell."

With a reluctant nod, he gave into their promptings. They laid him on Becky's make-shift bed, cushioning his head with a rolled-up shirt.

Pastor Brody hopped from the wagon bed and extended a hand to Becky. "You may as well ride up front."

"Shouldn't I stay with Pa?"

Her father waved a hand at her. "Go on an' let me get some shut-eye."

With a steadying breath, she turned and clasped Pastor Brody's hand. The warmth of his touch dissolved any remaining doubts. She had to admit, the thought of riding alongside him was a pleasant one. This last leg of the journey would be a memory she would hold and cherish for a long while.

Pastor Brody helped her onto the wagon seat, then climbed up beside her. Tying on her bonnet, Becky canvassed the wide river stippled with flowering shrubs and trees. "Never saw such a grand site."

Taking up the reins, Pastor Brody grinned. "Wait till you see the Mississippi."

The Kickupau led to a well-traveled path. After some time, the road veered away from the river and slanted further south and west. Pastor Brody seemed to ride with renewed vigor, travel by road being much quicker and easier than that of the tall-grass prairie. As the river faded further into the distance, rolling hills, bluffs, and trees replaced the level plains. An unsettled twinge worked through Becky as she bid the last of her homeland goodbye.

Minutes lengthened into hours, and before long the sun was at its peak. Dividing her time between the changing scenery and keeping a watchful eye on her father, Becky couldn't help but wonder what lay ahead. There was something frightening in the unknown, and yet exhilarating.

Pastor Brody lifted his face to the wind, drawing in a deep breath. "We're getting close. I can smell the river."

Becky craned her neck for a look, but the hilltop blocked her view. Even now, it didn't seem real—the storm, the loss of Ma and Melissa, Pa's blindness, and now their journey into the unknown. Ma always said God had a purpose in everything. But what reason could He have for taking them so far from home, away from all they held dear?

The wagon eased to a stop as Pastor Brody halted the team at the crest of a bluff. Standing, Becky peered into the valley below. Spanning as far as the eye could see to the north and south, the huge river sparkled in the afternoon sun. She pushed a stray tuft of hair under her bonnet, holding a hand to her chest. "The Mississippi?"

"The one and only." The preacher tipped his hat back with his thumb, eyes fixed on the flowing river.

"Aunt Ellen was right. It's beautiful." Trees, as thick as molasses, bounded the water on both sides. Settling back on the wagon seat, a hint of awe and regret edged into her voice. "Wish Pa could see it."

"Your father sees with his heart."

Her lips turned upward as she met the pastor's gaze. "What a wonderful perspective."

He lifted his hat, raking a hand through his chestnut hair. "The Lord's ways sort of rub off on a person after a while."

Becky laced her fingers together in her lap, taking in his chiseled jaw and handsome profile. What a fine man he was. So Godly. Always thinking of others. What would he think of her if he knew of the dark spot on her soul, that she held God responsible for their hardships? She turned her gaze to the flowing river, certain if he did, he'd not look at her so charmingly again.

MATTHEW TAPPED the reins across the horses' rumps, urging them further down river. He sat a little taller in the seat. There was something stimulating about sitting alongside an attractive young woman. Ever since they'd been thrown together the day of the storm, he'd felt drawn to Becky. Not in an obliging sort of way, but in a manly one. Even now, he sensed the urge to close the gap between them. Yet she seemed suddenly quieter, withdrawn. Had he done or said something wrong?

Dust flung about them as they rounded a bend. Matthew nodded at a sign along the road. "Two miles to Illinoistown."

"How far to St. Louis?"

"If I remember, it's just across the river from there."

"You've been to St. Louis before?"

"It's been a while, but then it's not a place one soon forgets." He clicked his cheek, and the horses quickened their pace.

"What's it like?" She squinted against the afternoon sun, a hint of wonderment in her voice.

"Full of tall buildings an' every type of store you can imagine. Churches with towering steeples, fancy hotels, restaurants, factories, an' more people than you've seen in a lifetime."

Becky lowered her gaze, threading her fingers together in her lap. "Doesn't sound real. Not like anything I've seen anyway."

He leaned closer, narrowing the space between them. "Sometimes new ventures are the best sort."

Her attempt at a grin spoke well of her nature. The poor young lady must have so many emotions churning inside her. It was a wonder she wasn't constantly in tears. How he longed to wrap an arm around her and reassure her she wasn't alone. He sensed her doubts and uncertainties and prayed for her more than she knew. But only the Lord could heal her inner wounds and put her qualms to rest.

A noise inside the wagon drew their attention. Joseph poked his head through the opening, rubbing his neck. "Where are we?"

"A couple miles out." Matthew held tight to the reins, slowing the team for a rut in the path. "If we can catch a ferry across, we should be in St. Louis by nightfall."

They rounded a curve and met with a long hill, the road swerving upward in an unwelcome slant. Becky breathed an audible sigh. "It's so steep."

"We'll make it." Slowing the team, he weighed his options. The best thing seemed to be to gain momentum and go at it full force. Taking a firm grip on the reins, he hollered over his shoulder. "Hang on, Joseph, we've a heap of hill to climb." He whistled through his teeth, urging the team up the rise. Sweat frothed from beneath the leather harnesses as the horses strained under the heavy load. With labored breaths, they trekked on, heads arched downward.

Something banged against the end-gate. Had Joseph lost his grip?

Becky jerked her head around, peering through the opening in the canvas.

Keeping alert to the team, Matthew cast a sideways glance. "He all right?"

With a sigh, she swiveled back around. "Holding tight. Some of the supplies slid."

They hit a bump in the road, causing the wagon to shimmy. Gentle hands clutched Matthew's arm, only to fall away just as suddenly. If he hadn't been so preoccupied with the reins, he'd have done his best to keep them there. Becky widened the space between them and gripped the seat. Matthew kept his gaze fixed ahead of him, trying not to add to her embarrassment.

He lifted a brow. Perhaps he should seek out another rock or rut to hit along the way.

At last the ground leveled, and Matthew tugged the team to a halt beneath a shady elm at the side of the road. The river sprawled out ahead of them like a swollen ravine. Nestled in a clearing at the water's edge, a settlement much larger than Miller Creek stirred with activity. Yet it was the mass of buildings on the other side that held Becky's attention. By the wide-eyed look on her face, the sight was more striking and intimidating than she'd dreamed.

"There she is. St. Louie." Matthew shook his head and gestured to the other side of the river. "She's doubled in size since I last saw her. Must be a hundred steamboats lining the levee."

Becky's gaze drifted from the endless line of riverboats to the mass of buildings beyond. "It's huge. How will we ever find where we're goin'?"

Matthew leaned forward in the wagon seat. "We'll worry about that later. First we've gotta get there."

When the team was rested, he guided them down the slope, traveling at a slant rather than attempting the hill head-on. Several buggies and wagons met them along the way, few offering a tip of a hat or a neighborly smile in return.

With a scowl, Becky straightened her bonnet. "City dwellers aren't so friendly as folks back home."

"Then I reckon it's your job to teach 'em." Matthew's hurried wink garnered a slight grin from Becky.

She turned to face him. "Are you always so optimistic?"

"A tool of the trade, Miss Hollister. Wouldn't be much of a pastor looking at the downside of things, now would I?"

"I suppose not." Her words spilled out in an airy sort of way.

He sensed her eyes upon him for a time, as though trying to decipher his very soul. Pity they didn't have more time to delve deeper into each other. He had a feeling, where Becky was concerned, he'd barely scratched the surface.

As they ventured into Illinoistown, two-story buildings lined the busy street. Throngs of people strolled by, traipsing in one store and out the next. A group of boys darted in front of them, and Matthew pulled back on the reins just in time to avoid hitting them.

Becky heaved a sigh. "So many people. Where are they all going?"

"Many are headed west to the gold fields. River towns like this are bursting at the seams with people bent on finding their fortunes." His voice blended with the clopping of hooves and creak of wagons and buggies.

It became impossible to take in all the sights and sounds as they drove through town. Wooden barrels and crates filled with dried beans, fruits, and vegetables lined the storefronts. Piled high with animal pelts, weary horses hung their heads while fur trappers bartered with store owners.

As they neared the riverfront, Matthew gestured to a row of wagons. "Looks like this is where we need to see about crossing."

A group of rough-looking men stood at the water's edge, waiting for the flatboat ferry to dock. Pulling up beside the row of waiting wagons, Matthew secured the brake. "Wait here. I'll see about reserving a spot on the ferry."

Becky gave a stiff nod, her eyes darting to and fro, finally settling on Matthew.

He hesitated, drinking in the blueness of her eyes. Was she frightened? How he would hate leaving her and Joseph alone in a strange city. He placed a hand atop hers, giving it a gentle squeeze. "I won't be long."

With a reassuring smile, he climbed from the wagon.

BECKY WATCHED Pastor Brody weave his way through the horde of people, then gradually disappear. She scanned the crowd for his broad-brimmed hat, but it was lost to her. A terrifying thought seared her heart. What if they became separated? What would become of them?

She wrung her hands, unnerved by the wide array of people passing by. Shifty-eyed men in striped suits and tall hats, women in elegant dresses, sour-faced store owners, and short Chinese with coarse, black braids. The view from the bluff had been captivating, but here, amid the sea of people, it was overwhelming. Fearsome even. Heaviness weighed on her heart. St. Louis was bigger and more crowded still. How would they even find her aunt in such a place? They would be swallowed up in its vastness.

A deep bellow sounded upstream, and Becky whirled about, eyes searching.

Pa worked his way to the opening in the canvas. "That a riverboat?"

Three stories high, the magnificent boat floated downstream, its huge red paddle wheel propelling it forward. "Wish you could see it, Pa. Must be hundreds of people lining its decks."

Enormous smoke-stacks billowed black smoke as it glided effortlessly through the water. Its huge stern-wheel paddles slowed to a halt, and it docked at the levee on the St. Louis side of the river.

She caught sight of Pastor Brody making his way toward them. His face showed little expression as he climbed onto the wagon. "Let's get some grub. It'll be a couple of hours before we catch a ferry."

The horses plodded along the bustling street, heads bobbing with each step. The long line of buildings brimmed with people as they traveled deeper into town. How would they manage in such a place? Once they crossed the Mississippi into St. Louis, the crowd would be even worse.

Pastor Brody stopped the team in front of an establishment bearing the name Sally's Hotel and Restaurant. "This all right?"

Becky nodded. The place looked among the most respectable

of those they'd passed. Blue and white checkered curtains hung inside the windows, giving it a homey look.

Pastor Brody looped the reins around the hitching post then offered her a hand down. While he went to help Pa, Becky snugged close to the wagon to veer out of the way of those passing by. Everyone seemed in such a hurry. Gone were the quiet, unassuming ways of country life.

They maneuvered past a cluster of people at the front of the establishment. Though most paid them no attention, one or two stares lingered on her father's face. Muffled conversation poured from within as the restaurant door opened and a well-dressed couple emerged. At sight of them, the woman's face lost its smile, her discerning gaze trailing over Becky's homespun dress and worn shoes before she turned away. Becky squared her jaw, refusing to be intimidated by such arrogance. She tightened her grip on Pa's arm and guided him through the narrow entrance. Tables, decked with matching blue and white checkered cloth, decorated the dining area.

A fair-haired woman dressed in a satiny, indigo dress approached. Pastor Brody removed his hat and combed down his hair with his hand. "Good day, ma'am. We'd like a table."

With a nod of her head, she smiled, revealing a row of pearly-white teeth. "Follow me, please." She led them through a spattering of tables, occupied by chattering patrons, to an empty one by a window. A wilted bouquet of wildflowers adorned its center. As Becky guided Pa through the maze of tables, she sensed eyes upon them, at times catching a glimpse of someone's elusive glance or concealed whisper.

A slender woman approached, hair black as pitch. She set three water glasses on the table, seeming in too much of a hurry to care whom she was serving. "What can I serve you, young lady and gents? Biscuits and chicken fixings, or beef stew and corn bread." Her voice was dull and nasal, and she spoke without pausing for breath.

Pastor Brody brushed aside crumbs from the table. "Chicken sounds good."

"Makes little difference to me." Pa removed his hat, and with a twist of his hand sent the glass flower vase crashing to the floor.

The room quieted, and all eyes turned to them. Becky dropped her gaze to the checkered tablecloth. She and Pa had no business here. If only he'd been content to stay at home. Even now, it wasn't too late. They could still turn back.

The waitress stooped to gather the jagged bits of glass.

"Let me give you a hand." Pastor Brody leaned to help.

"Thanks, mister."

Pa set his hat in his lap, brow furrowed. "I'm awful sorry, ma'am."

"It won't take a minute to clean up." She smiled up at him, for the first time noting his bandaged head and hollow stare. Her grin faded as she returned her attention to the broken glass. "I-I'm sorry. I didn't realize he was..." Her voice trailed off, her countenance changing. Gathering the four corners of the napkin with the glass piled inside, she stood and started toward the kitchen.

"Warn me next time, will ya?" Pa shook his head, sounding cross.

"No harm done. It isn't the first time someone's broken something." Pastor Brody sipped at his water. He caught Becky's eye, tossing her an easy smile.

With an appreciative grin, Becky melted back in her chair. Not only had his comment seemingly settled Pa's angst, but also lightened the mood. What would they do without the pastor's calming, good-natured way? How she dreaded when he'd no longer be with them.

"Why don't you bring the man another vase?"

Becky turned toward the raucous voice. A scruffy-looking man had their waitress by the arm. Remnants of his meal clung to his unshaven face. He pointed in their direction, a wry grin lining his lips. "I'd like to see that again."

His laugh shattered Becky's moment of contentment. Why did people have to be so rude? Eating stale pan bread in the solace of the wagon was better than the best of food in such ill company.

The waitress shifted her feet, pulling free of his grasp. "Go home, Harley."

"Aaah, now, Ira. Not before Hank an' me has our pie."

Ira adjusted her dress, irritation in her voice. "I'll bring it in a minute. I've other customers, you know." With that, she blew a tuft of hair from her forehead and hurried on.

Becky glanced at her father, hoping he hadn't overheard the exchange. His face remained sullen, but gave no indication he'd been offended.

A hearty laugh sounded from across the room. Out of the corner of her eye, Becky saw the man named Harley whispering to his friend Hank, a sneer lining his lips. He tossed her a quick wink, and she looked away, heat flaming her cheeks.

A chair scooted, and she shot an uneasy look at Pastor Brody.

Yet he didn't seem to notice. His gaze was fixed on the man strolling toward them.

Chapter Eleven

THE BURLY MAN swaggered up beside them. Bushy eyebrows formed a line on his forehead, and thick sideburns trailed down to his jawline. The scar marring his upper lip hinted he was a man who'd seen trouble before. Drawing himself to full height, he spread his legs and rolled up his sleeves, revealing muscular arms fringed with curly hair.

Matthew smiled up at him. "What can we do for you?" He kept calm and composed, amid Becky's wide-eyed stare.

A smirk overspread Harley's face as he gestured toward Joseph. "Your friend here put on quite a show. Blind, is he?"

Joseph's jaw clenched, irritation telling on his face.

Leaning forward, Matthew circled his forefinger over the rim of his water glass. "He is. Is that a problem?"

Sobering, Harley leaned his knuckles on the table, steely gray eyes casting daggers at Matthew. "Yeah. He bothers me."

"You mean his blindness bothers you?" Matthew gestured toward the empty chair at their table. "Why not join us. I'm sure once you get acquainted you'll see he's no different than the rest of us."

The man's pungent breath assaulted the air as he leaned in

closer. "I don't know what your game is, mister, but why don't you take your blind friend and mosey on out of here while I get better acquainted with the young lady?" His eyes probed Becky, and she melted down in her chair.

"Why, you..." Joseph lunged forward, face flushed.

Matthew placed a restraining hand on Joseph's chest, eyes trained on the stranger. It took all Matthew's self-control not to go at the man himself. Instead he drew a calming breath. "Never mind, Joseph. Harley here was just leaving."

"Says who?" the man sneered.

Rising to his feet, Matthew wedged himself between Becky and the intruder. The man had gone too far, accosting her with his roving eyes. "I do."

With a snicker, Harley stepped closer, coming nose to nose with him. "I said, get!" Taking hold of Matthew's shirt collar, he gave him a shove.

Matthew staggered back, knocking against the table. A hush fell over the restaurant as all eyes pivoted toward them. No one made a move to interfere. Obviously nobody wanted any part of this.

Regaining his balance, Matthew balled his hands into fists. He drew back his arm, eyes narrowed.

Behind him, he heard Becky suck in a breath. "Pastor Brody, don't."

Harley's eyes widened as he took Matthew in head to boot. "Pastor?"

In his layman's clothes, Matthew looked like any other west-bound traveler. Relaxing his fists, he flashed a sideways grin. "Nearly forgot it myself for a moment."

Ira pointed toward them from across the room, whispering to a husky man at the front counter. He glanced their way, his massive frame dwarfing the waitress's as he stood. Would he come to their aid or throw them all out?

As he neared, his large hand gripped Harley's shoulder,

whirling him about. "That's enough, Harley." The bulky man had two inches and twenty pounds on his stunned patron.

"Ahh, Frank. I was jus' havin' a little fun. I didn't know he was no preacher."

"Fun's over." The man gave Harley a shove toward the door. "You can pay on your way out."

Harley stumbled over an empty chair and fell to the floor. Picking himself up, he motioned his companion to follow.

Frank clutched the front of his black, leather vest, his upper lip hidden beneath his mustache. "Sorry for the trouble, folks. I'll have Ira bring your vittles."

"Much obliged." Forcing a carefree nod, Matthew took a seat. What had come over him? He'd never struck a man in his life. If not for Becky, he'd more than likely be in a lot of pain about now. But whether the man gave him a thrashing or not, he'd still have fought to protect Becky.

Joseph let out a huff, tilting his drawn face in Becky's direction. "Now you see why I wanted you to stay home? I wished to spare you such goings on."

Becky's downcast face tugged at Matthew's heart. Was it the incident itself or her father's words that stung her so deeply?

He cleared his throat. "Well, I, for one, am grateful she's here. Her sensibleness saved me sore knuckles and a poke in the jaw."

Becky's face seemed to brighten as she scooted her chair back under the table. She met his gaze, a shy grin crossing her lips "Wouldn't know how you'd explain a shiner to folks back home."

He let out a chuckle. "Neither would I."

It was good to see her smile. Since the storm, it seemed as if the weight of the world were pressing down on her. Now, if only for a moment, a glimmer of hope shone in her sapphire eyes.

He raised a brow. And perhaps, a smidgen of affection?

BECKY LEANED BACK, steadying herself against the wagon, glad to leave the troublesome river town behind. The smell of fish and the constant rolling motion of the flat-boat ferry left her nauseous. She took a deep breath and gazed out over the river. Traveling over open water didn't agree with her. But it sure was pretty, bounded by trees and glistening in the late afternoon sun.

The constant drone of the steam engine waned as the ferry jarred to a near stand-still, lurching her forward. Pastor Brody attempted to calm the jittery horses, his low voice soothing them as he stood at their head.

Pa teetered, then slid back onto one of the heavy wooden blocks that secured their wagon in place. "What happened?"

Becky's eyes scanned the water below. "The river's shallower here. Must've snagged on something."

A loud scraping sounded beneath them as strong-armed men, stationed at each corner, leaned on sturdy poles, straining to free the raft. It edged forward, finally busting loose and floating forward.

Pa raised his hat, swiping a hand over his sweaty forehead. He appeared years older than the agile, outdoorsman he'd been little over a month ago. "How much further?"

"We're about halfway." To Becky, one shore looked as far as the other.

A cloud of gnats swarmed about her, and she waved them away, turning her focus to the five wide-eyed children just ahead of her, faces full of wonder. Much like a hen gathering chicks, their parents worked to keep the excited brood huddled close. The young couple to their left stood gazing over the water as though mesmerized. Slight of build, their yellowed skin and slanted eyes pegged them as foreigners. What had spurred them to traverse so far from their homeland? What dreams for the future were they envisioning? Or had they too suffered a loss that compelled them to leave?

At the rear of the ferry, four dusty horsemen stood beside their mounts, looking relaxed as though they had made the journey many times.

A shout erupted in the distance, and Pa straightened. "What's all the ruckus?"

Becky stood, craning her neck. "It's another ferry, headed for Illinoistown." Her voice trailed off soft and wistful.

The enthusiastic waves of the passengers on the east-bound ferry sparked a spontaneous response from their own vessel. She raised her hand in a half-hearted gesture, gnawing at her lip. Would that they were on it, headed back to Miller Creek.

Pa slumped forward on the wooden block, locking his fingers together. "You regret comin', don't ya?"

She breathed a quiet sigh. How could she deny the skirmish within her? One word from him and she'd turn for home, without a backward glance. Melting down beside him, she leaned her head on his shoulder. "My place is with you. Besides, it's only for a little while."

"Could be a year...maybe more."

With a squeeze of his arm, she willed herself to sound cheerful. "As clever as you are, we'll be home in no time." She leaned to kiss his cheek, relieved he couldn't see the moisture stinging her eyes.

Once the Illinois-bound ferry passed, the travelers quieted and returned to lulled conversation. Pastor Brody stood conversing with one of the workmen manning the ferry. How like him to make a friend of a stranger. Perhaps that's what made him such a good pastor. No. It was more than his love for people that set him apart. He seemed driven by an unshakable devotion to God. Did he never lose faith in the Lord's promises? Knowing what she and Pa had been through, how could he not doubt God's love for them?

How could she not?

The thought of him returning home left her hollow. He'd been at their side each step of the way, lending strength and encouragement. His absence would leave a gaping hole.

A twang of guilt rippled through her. Once, the Lord had held such a cherished place in her heart. Now, she clung only to a remnant of faith, to the one hope that God really did care.

As Illinoistown lapsed further into the distance, St. Louis loomed ahead of them. A huge riverboat finished unloading passengers and supplies, then moved on, leaving clear passage to shore. Along the bank, a sagging willow branch arched over the water, shading those who fished from boats and rafts at the river's edge. As the ferry approached land, the scent of tar and spices overpowered the fishy smell.

A gentle breeze carried the steady, low chants of muscular slaves down river as they lugged heavy barrels of supplies to awaiting wagons. The unfamiliar sight left Becky cold. How could one man own another? And yet, while she was in this place, she too would feel enslaved, shackled by its smothering restraints. Grand sights such as the towering buildings along the riverfront and the steamboats lining the cobblestone levee might thrill others, but to her, they were but a shadow of things to come, despairing times devoid of happiness.

The noisy steam engine quieted as the workers slowed the ferry for unloading. The men braced their poles deep in the murky water, and there was a slight jolt as the flatboat ferry ran aground. Men on shore secured it in place with thick ropes. Horses and passengers were allowed off first, followed by the wagons.

A foreboding mood enveloped Becky as she helped Pa to his feet and guided him to shore. He stumbled, and she tightened her grip on his arm, her own legs wobbly from the drifting feel of the ferry. He tired so easily. Hopefully her aunt's place wasn't far. They were all due for a good rest.

Once the blocks were removed, Pastor Brody drove the team off the ferry and onto the pavement. Shifting the reins to one hand, he reached to help Pa onto the wagon seat, then turned to Becky. "I could use a second set of eyes to help find where we're going."

"Is there room?"

He offered her his hand. "We'll make room."

With a gentle nod, she placed her fingers in his. Right now, she could think of no place she would rather be than seated with the two men she admired most. Warmth surged through her as she eased onto the seat, her shoulder brushing his. Was it fitting to sit so close to a man?

She ventured a glance in his direction, fearing he might find the nearness objectionable. But the smile playing on his lips didn't tend toward embarrassment, but pleasure.

The corners of Becky's mouth lifted. If Pastor Brody didn't mind the tight squeeze, neither did she.

MATTHEW TOOK UP THE REINS, struggling to focus. Surely, Becky must have some inkling he cared for her. The fact that she hadn't shied away gave him hope she returned his admiration. It had been years since he'd given thought to courting a woman. Until recently, Becky had seemed but a girl to him, the daughter of a friend, a young lamb in his flock. But now, having witnessed her residual spirit and the depth of devotion to her father, his outlook toward her had blossomed. Was it the Lord's doing?

Regaining his composure, he leaned forward on the seat. "Where to, Joseph?"

"Rosedale Street. The west edge of town. At least it used to be the west edge when we traveled through here in '39."

"Good enough." Releasing the brake, Matthew urged the

team into a slow walk. Their hooves clopped along the cobblestone pavement, taking them deeper into the bowels of the city.

Tall buildings, fashioned of brick or smooth frame, enveloped them as they traveled down Market Street. Shop windows displayed frilly dresses, rich foods, and items which he couldn't name.

The crowds began to thin as they drove further through town. He kept a watchful eye on the street signs, passing by Oak, Hickory, and Magnolia. Dillon, and Thrush. Nothing even close to Rosedale.

Joseph cocked his elbows on his knees. "Any luck?"

"Not yet."

"We could travel half the city and not find it."

"I'd best stop and ask." Matthew probed the street for someone to approach. To his right, a man with a broom struggled to maneuver around the spattering of shoppers as he swept the walkway outside of a dry goods store. His quick strokes, accompanied by his puckered brow, hinted of frustration. Halting the team beside the apron-clad man, Pastor Brody tipped his broadbrimmed hat. "Could you tell us where Rosedale Street might be?"

The man scowled up at him, pausing just long enough to point westward.

"Thank you and God bless you, sir." Matthew nodded his thanks, but his gesture went unnoticed as the worker returned to his sweeping.

Becky's hands fidgeted in her lap. She hadn't spoken since they'd left the waterfront. In the dim light of evening, it was difficult to read her expression. Was she uncomfortable? Dreading what was to come? How he wished he could ease the heaviness in her heart.

The row of buildings to the west hid the lowering sun. Twilight's shadows blanketed the street. Matthew slowed the horses, straining to read each street sign in turn. At last, he sat back, releasing a quiet sigh. "Rosedale. We've made it. Any recollection what her apartment looks like?"

"Ellen lives near a clothing factory. She rents from the man she works for. Billings is the name. If you can find it, I can guide you from there."

Veering the team to the right, Matthew scoured the street. "Not much daylight left. Keep your eyes peeled, Becky."

She pointed to a sign in front of a huge brick building up ahead. "There it is. Billings Clothing Factory."

Joseph straightened. "Good. A few blocks further down, you'll see three small houses side by side. Ellen lives in the furthest one."

With a nod, Matthew tapped the reins across the horses' backs. As dusk deepened and less people roamed the street, the clopping of the hooves on the cobblestone grew more pronounced. Matthew tugged the team to a halt in front of the trio of closely laid apartments. Small and quaint amid the larger buildings, the houses were still nearly twice the size of the log cabins back home. Soft lamplight shone through thin ivory curtains from the last house's windows, hinting of a woman's touch. "Looks like this might be it. And not a moment too soon. We're out of daylight."

Becky sat with head bowed. Was she nervous? Frightened?

Matthew helped her from the wagon, sharing her misgivings. Their journey was fast coming to an end. Something within him balked at the idea of leaving Becky behind. He longed to shield her from the challenges that were certain to come.

But wasn't that the Lord's responsibility? Matthew could only pray for her well-being—and for a quick and safe return.

Becky's eyes sparkled in the dim light of evening, searching. Matthew forced a grin. "Go meet your aunt. I'll stay with the team, till you're sure this is the place."

She hesitated, then gave a slight nod. Taking her father's arm, she started forward.

Matthew leaned against the wagon, watching them fade into the shadows. Becky's silhouette wedged its way deeper inside him. Would she come home the same person? Would his feelings for her deepen or lessen over the coming months?

At times, his failed relationship with Sarah still stung. He'd been so young then. He'd hardly known what true love was all about.

Was he ready to love again?

BECKY TIGHTENED her hold on her father's arm, her insides knotting. Until this moment, she'd given little thought to her spinster aunt. Was she the disagreeable sort? Is that why she'd never married? Becky had met her Aunt Ellen only once, when Ma and Pa had first traveled to Illinois. But she'd been little more than an infant and had only vague recollections of meeting her father's older sister.

She paused outside the door, setting Pa's satchel at her feet. Her father had sent a telegram regarding his own coming, but Aunt Ellen would not be expecting her. What would she think of Becky coming unannounced? Would she badger them with questions? Drudge up unwanted memories of the storm?

Lifting her hand, she brought it within inches of the door, then stopped. "Will she be upset I've come?"

Pa's face softened to a grin. "If I know your Aunt Ellen, she'll welcome you with open arms."

Becky glanced over her shoulder at Pastor Brody waiting by the rig. How she would miss his reassuring presence when he was no longer with them. With a deep breath, she tapped on the door, then took a step back.

A moment later, the latch lifted and the wooden door creaked open. A slender, brunette woman with her father's features stared out at them, her plaid dress fringed with ruffles and lace. A look of recognition lit the woman's eyes. "Joseph!" she chirped, throwing open the door.

With a jubilant cry, she sprang forward to embrace him. As they drew apart, her gaze shifted to Becky, and her hazel eyes widened. "Why, this can't be Becky."

"Hello, Aunt Ellen." Becky forced a grin. Her aunt's face was kind and genuine, not at all what she'd feared.

Aunt Ellen bent to kiss Becky's cheek. "What a wonderful surprise. But, Joseph, in your telegram you said—."

"I know," he interrupted, his tone a bit apologetic. "There's been a change of plans."

"It was my doing." Becky stared down at her cousin's hand-me-down shoes. She'd left home with Aunt Clara out of sorts. Was she going to start off on the wrong foot with Aunt Ellen as well?

"I'm glad." Taking Becky by the hands, Aunt Ellen surveyed her from head to toe. "Why, you're a young lady."

Becky sensed her muscles relax. Her aunt's warm welcome seemed the only bright spot in an otherwise dismal city.

Pa braced an arm around Becky's waist. "Hope it won't put you out, sis."

"Nonsense. You talk as though you're a burden. I'm more than pleased to have you both for as long as you need to stay." Aunt Ellen tugged at Pa's sleeve. "Come in. I'll fix you some hot tea and a bite to eat."

He hesitated, gesturing over his shoulder. "Our pastor was kind enough to accompany us. Is there a livery stable nearby for our horses?"

Aunt Ellen craned her neck, squinting out into the street. "Of course. At the end of the street."

"I'll tell him." Turning, Becky hurried toward Pastor Brody. He walked to meet her, his familiar stride now etched in her mind.

A pleasant smile lined his lips as he strode up beside her. "It appears you found her."

"Yes. She seems very nice. There's a livery at the end of the street." Becky pointed in the direction of the stable, then paused at sight of the handful of men with long poles dotting the street with light. "How...?"

"Amazing, isn't it? They're gas powered street lights. I've seen them once or twice, but never on such a grand scale."

She shook her head. Once the sun set on the prairie, darkness prevailed. Here, it seemed, they had the ability to turn night into day.

Pastor Brody turned to her, his dark eyes trained on hers. "And never in such lovely company."

Warmth flooded Becky's cheeks, the wonderment of the street lamps forgotten. Her heart pulsed in her chest, the dryness in her throat choking off her words. Had she heard him right? She'd never known Pastor Brody to pay a lady a personal compliment or even take interest in a woman. Could it be he truly cared for her?

She managed a shy grin, grateful the lamplighters hadn't lit this portion of the street.

Pastor Brody took a step back, the shadows of evening shrouding his expression. "Well, I best get the horses to the livery."

She watched him go, conscious of the hollowness his absence evoked inside her. Soon he would leave for good. That she was indebted to him went without saying. Yet it seemed the emptiness at the thought of him leaving had less to do with loneliness and more to do with a strange sort of fondness that had taken root inside her.

With a muddled heart, she made her way back to the house.

Aunt Ellen met her at the door. "Make yourself at home while I heat some water for tea."

Becky set their belongings down, hesitant to step on the

painted floorboards without checking her shoes. The room was spotless, not a speck of dust or item out of place. How would she ever feel at ease?

Her aunt must be wealthy to own such elegant furniture as the cherry wood table and chairs decorating the dining area and the glass-doored corner cabinet. Or was this how all city folk lived? With all its fine furnishings, the spacious room lacked the lived-in quality of their log cabin back home. Sad. Living alone as she did, her aunt had no one to consider but herself. No wonder her home was impeccable.

Pa sat in one of two upholstered chairs facing the fireplace. Tip-toeing across the floor, Becky pulled a cushioned chair up beside him. A metal contraption on a stand table in the far corner caught her eye. With all the fabric piled near it, it looked to be some sort of sewing mechanism. Becky was still taking it in when Aunt Ellen returned with a kettle of water.

"That's a sewing machine. If you like, sometime I'll show you how it works."

Becky gave a slow nod. A machine that sewed stitches? Evidently, she was in for a number of surprises in this strange place.

Her aunt set the kettle on the hearth then took a seat opposite Pa, eyes brightening. "So tell me, how was your trip?"

Pa rubbed his hands over the chair's abundant arm rests. "No complaints, though I will say we're glad to have it come to an end."

Aunt Ellen smiled, easing back in her upholstered chair. "I'm glad you arrived in the evening. Earlier I would have been at work."

Becky tried to hide her surprise. A woman working outside the home seemed so strange to her. Managing their homestead had been a full-time job for both Ma and Pa, not to mention her and Melissa. But then her aunt had no one to provide for her and no one to look after but herself. She had no need for livestock or homespun dresses. With everything ready-made in nearby shops, she only had need for money.

Becky crossed her arms in her lap. City dwellers were soft, with no chores to tend to and everything at their fingertips. She refused to fall into such idleness.

The clock on the mantel chimed eight. A framed, copper-plated photograph sat to its right, bearing the image of five children standing behind a seated, somber-faced couple. One of the younger boys resembled her father. The spindly girl beside him seemed a younger version of her aunt.

Conversation remained light as Pa recapped the events of their trip and filled Aunt Ellen in on happenings at Miller Creek. While no mention was made of the reason for their visit, Becky detected a hint of sadness in her aunt's oval eyes as she watched Pa. Was she pitying him for his blindness or simply grieved over their loss?

A light knock on the door brought Aunt Ellen to her feet. Her domed skirt rustled as she crossed the floor. She eased the door open. "Come in."

Pastor Brody removed his hat and smoothed down his hair, nodding toward Aunt Ellen. She held out her hand, bending in a slight curtsy. "I'm Joseph's sister, Ellen."

"Glad to meet you, ma'am. I'm Matthew Brody." With a nod, he brushed grain dust from his hands, then gripped her palm.

"I want to thank you for your kindness in bringing Joseph and Becky all this way."

"My pleasure." Tossing his hat aside, he scooted a chair closer to the fire. Perhaps it was his experience as a circuit rider, but he seemed at home in any setting, with any sort of people.

Aunt Ellen brought a tray of fine china and a plate of muffins, then retrieved the water for their tea. "It isn't often I have guests, so you'll excuse me if I'm not the most refined of hostesses."

As her aunt stooped to divvy out drinks, Becky begged to

disagree. Everything about Ellen seemed refined and proper. Even down to the delicate way she filled their teacups.

The room darkened as the last bit of lightened sky turned a deep blue. An amber glow radiated from the fireplace, casting shadows on the walls and ceiling. Aunt Ellen turned up the lanterns, brightening the room

"What do you know of this school for the blind, Ellen?" Pa's question shifted everyone's attention to her aunt.

Smoothing her ankle-length skirt under her, she sipped her tea. "Not much. Other than the students attend the church I go to. Tomorrow being Sunday, you'll waste no time making contact. The students always sit along the back bench."

Pa finished off his cup of tea. "The sooner the better."

Becky's insides churned in disagreement. It was all happening too fast. She'd hoped they'd take a few days to get accustomed to the place before settling in at the blind institute. Wilting back in her chair, Becky set her half-eaten muffin on her plate, her appetite gone. She shared an uneasy look with Pastor Brody, wondering if he too dreaded when they would part ways.

Chapter Twelve

BECKY SHIVERED and opened her eyes, cool morning air sifting through the cotton sheets that covered her. Aunt Ellen lay still beside her, strands of chestnut hair draped over her neck and cheek. Dim light filtered through the window as dawn awakened. Becky rolled onto her back, the soft bed soothing her weary muscles. So much nicer than the hard floor of the wagon bed. Or even her straw mattress back home.

A faint smoke smell drifted from the sitting room where Pa and Pastor Brody conversed in low tones. Sitting up, she stared down at her nightshirt. When had she changed out of her frock? She'd been so fatigued last night, her muddled mind held little memory of it.

The bed rustled, and with a wide yawn, Aunt Ellen stretched her arms over her head. Her hazel eyes squinted open. "Good morning. Did you sleep well?"

"Yes, ma'am."

Aunt Ellen cocked herself up on one elbow, a scowl lining her lips. "Ma'am. Why so formal? Please. Call me Aunt Ellen."

"Yes, M...Aunt Ellen." The words spilled out stiffly. It was hard to claim someone she barely knew as her aunt. Perhaps someday it would seem more suitable, but for now, kind or not, her newly acquainted aunt was little more than a stranger.

Aunt Ellen smiled. "That's better. I could get used to that." She swung her feet over the side of the bed and reached for her shawl, the tip of her long braid sweeping the mattress.

Boot steps thudded outside the bedroom, and Becky hugged the covers to her chest.

Her aunt smothered another yawn with her palm. "My, I'd forgotten what early risers country folk can be."

Becky twisted her mouth to one side. Just as she'd thought. Soft.

"Sounds like the gals are awake." Pa's voice sounded just beyond the open doorway.

Pastor Brody cleared his throat. "Think I'll go see to the horses." The door opened and closed, then silence cloaked the outer room, but for the crackle of the fire.

Aunt Ellen rose and traded her wrinkled nightgown for a petticoat and a satiny, emerald dress. The sleek bodice hugged her slender torso, while the hooped skirt flared out in a wide dome to her ankles. Becky tried not to stare as her aunt surveyed herself in the dresser mirror. What an elegant picture she made in her store-bought dress. So cultured and lady-like. Why had such a lovely lady never married?

She gathered her long braid into a loose bun, pinning it in place with ivory combs. Swiveling on her heels, she smiled back at Becky. "Take what time you need to get ready. There's a pitcher, basin and towel on the wash stand if you want to freshen up, and a comb and brush on the dresser. I'll start breakfast."

With a nod, Becky pulled back her covers. The water in the basin called to her. It had been a long journey with little opportunity to wash. She dipped the cloth in, then wrung it out. Dredging the dampened cloth over her face, neck, and down her arms, she thought it a wonder Pastor Brody had wished to sit so near her.

His leaving again pierced her thoughts. Perhaps he could stay on a few days, just to be certain things worked out for them here. Drying off with a towel, she chastened herself. No. He'd already sacrificed far too much of his time for them. He was needed back home. What a shame that just as they were getting acquainted it had to end.

She searched through her satchel and took out the wrinkled, lavender dress Ma had made for her sixteenth birthday. Much like Pa's fiddle, somehow the dress had miraculously survived the storm in one piece. The expensive fabric had been a sacrifice for both her parents to purchase. Worn only on special occasions, it had been kept in a chest instead of a drawer. More than likely the only reason it had survived.

Laying it on the bed, she smoothed out the creases and traced over its hand-sewn seams with her fingertips. Love lingered in each tiny stitch. Though much fancier, Aunt Ellen's store-bought dress lacked such a luxury. Becky fingered the wedding band that dangled on the ribbon around her neck. The dress and ring were the only tangible remembrances she had of her mother. She would wear them both with pride.

Donning the dress, she stood before the mirror. She pulled at the sleeves that seemed shorter than when she'd last worn it. The bodice too appeared a tad snug. Her heart sank. Would she outgrow it so quickly? No doubt the homespun dress would stand out among the city finery. But what did it matter. There was no one here she cared to impress.

Unless it be Pastor Brody.

Brushing the tangles from her wheat-blonde hair, she crinkled her nose at the faint line of freckles staring back at her in the mirror. They appeared each spring, the moment the warm sun kissed her cheeks. She swirled her long hair up behind her, twisting her head side to side. Ma had often chided her for not wearing her hair up on occasion. Somehow a chignon just didn't suit her.

Perhaps someday she'd be ready to shed her country-girl ways and become the lady Ma always hoped her to be.

But not now. Not yet.

Then again, Pastor Brody might think her more mature with her hair done up like a lady. With a sigh, she let it fall to her shoulders. She couldn't pretend to be someone she wasn't. Not even for him.

Sectioning off portions of hair, she weaved her locks into a loose braid. Then, with a final glance in the mirror, she went to join the others.

A BURNT SMELL accosted Matthew as he returned from the livery. If he'd had any thought to escape his mediocre campfire cooking, something told him this wasn't the place.

Aunt Ellen removed her apron and called everyone to the table. "I hope you like corn cakes and sausage." Her expression turned apologetic as she placed a steaming platter of rather charred food at its center. "I'm sorry, but I'm afraid I don't get much practice cooking on just myself."

Matthew surveyed the overcooked food. Perhaps it would taste better than it looked. "Shall we pray?" Bowing his head, Matthew closed his eyes. "Lord, we thank You for safe travels, for Miss Hollister's hospitality, and for this food. May Joseph and Becky's time here be fruitful, and Your hand be upon them. In Your Son's name, Amen."

He opened his eyes and jabbed at the overcooked sausage with his fork, then at the dry, crusty corn cake. "What time do church services start, Miss Hollister?"

"Ten o'clock. You needn't bother hitching up your team. It's only a short distance."

He nodded, beginning to saw at his shriveled piece of sausage. Popping a bite in his mouth, he struggled to chew the tough piece of meat. He might just have to visit Sally's restaurant again on the return trip and stock up on food supplies before leaving town.

"Is it a large church?" asked Joseph.

"I suppose it will seem big, when you aren't used to it." Ellen filled her plate and returned the tray to the center.

"You said some folks from the institute for the blind attend. Do you know who's in charge...who we need to talk to?" With Becky's help, Joseph managed a bite of corn cake.

"I'm afraid not. I've only viewed them from a distance. They generally sit in back and make a quick exit, to avoid the crowd, I assume. The school isn't far from here, though. Just a few blocks further west, on the outskirts of town."

Ellen took a bite of corn cake and cringed, her face turning crimson. "Salt. I knew I'd forgotten something. Cooking has never been my strong suit."

Matthew washed a bite of cornbread down with milk. He swallowed, his voice a tad dry. "It's the company that counts."

"You're very gracious." Ellen laced her fingers together, her gaze settling on Becky. "Perhaps Becky can give me a few pointers. I'm sure she's had her share of lessons."

Becky dredged a piece of corn cake through her syrup, color glowing in her cheeks. "I'm not much on cookin' either."

Having shared several meals with the Hollisters, Matthew could attest to that. With Becky, it seemed more a lack of interest than skill. He tried to catch her eye, but she kept them trained on her plate. She seemed rather subdued this morning. No sense trying to decipher why. With what she was facing, any number of things could be troubling her.

He himself had lain awake hours talking to the Lord and mulling the situation over in his head. The truth was, he didn't relish leaving Becky here anymore than she wanted to stay. Patience seemed the key. If God intended them to be together, no amount of time or space could interfere.

Joseph cleared his throat, seeming to sense Becky's angst. "Becky spent more time out helpin' me than in a kitchen. Truth is, I was hopin' you'd be able to give her some tips."

"As you can see, I won't be much help." Ellen gave a soft chuckle then turned to Becky. "Maybe we can learn together."

"I doubt Pa and I will be here long enough for that."

An uncomfortable silence permeated the room. Becky had fallen asleep prior to last night's conversation regarding her living arrangements. Matthew had a feeling she wouldn't be pleased with what had transpired.

Joseph leaned forward, rubbing his forehead. His thin, gauze bandage had been removed, revealing scaly, pink skin and a stubby patch of hair around the wound. "There'll be time."

Becky's expression begged an explanation. "What do you mean?"

"Ellen's agreed to let you stay with her for the time being."

Becky's fork clanged on her plate. "But why? She'll be at work much of the time. Can't I stay with you while she's away?"

The intensity in her voice seared Matthew's heart. She'd risked everything to be with her father. Now it seemed she'd come only to be separated again. The thought left his appetite waning.

Joseph's cheek flinched. "There'll be no arguments. You stay with Ellen."

Matthew slumped back in his chair at the injured look on Becky's face. As a pastor, he could see the wisdom in Joseph's decision. But as a man, who cared deeply for the young woman beside him, his heart ached. It was yet another loss she would have to bear.

BECKY STRAINED to see through the dispersing congregation. So many people. Would they miss their opportunity to meet the instructor from the school for the blind?

"There they are." Aunt Ellen pointed toward the back of the church building. "You'll have to hurry to catch them."

Pastor Brody nodded to those passing by and ambled his way down the aisle. He'd been quieter than usual following the discussion at breakfast. Did he, too, feel Pa was being unreasonable? Becky balked inwardly. She might just as well go home if she couldn't stay with him.

She watched Pastor Brody draw closer to the line of students holding hands. The tall, bearded man at their front helped maneuver them through the crowd. Becky's eyes widened as she caught a better glimpse of the students. "They're all children."

"There are adult students, aren't there, Ellen?" A hint of alarm marred Pa's voice.

"Why, I don't know. Come to think of it, the children are all I've seen." Her fluctuating tone hinted of concern.

Pa nudged Becky. "Well, let's go talk to 'em."

They pushed through the throng of people to the double doors. As they stepped outside, a peaceful lull replaced the endless chatter. Becky peered over the row of buggies and motioned toward the wagon at the far edge of the street. "Over there."

Aunt Ellen looped her arm through Pa's, opposite of Becky. "Careful. There are five steps down."

Becky gripped him tighter as he leaned into her with each downward movement. At last, they reached the bottom step and veered in the direction they'd seen the students. The farther they moved from the church building, the thinner the crowd became. Becky could see the blind children clearly now. She grinned, not a bit surprised to see Pastor Brody helping load them onto the wagon while conversing with the bearded man.

The stranger's expression showed a genuine interest in what

the pastor was saying. With the students aboard the wagon, he reached to shake Pastor Brody's hand. "I'm Peter Bennett, director of the school."

Pastor Brody seemed to sense them coming and turned for a look. "Ah. Here he is."

The man's brown-flecked eyes sparked with compassion as he sandwiched Pa's hand in his. Wisps of gray lined his wavy reddish-brown hair, but his face was marked with youthful vigor. "Happy to know you, Mister . . . Hollister, is it? Your friend tells me you're interested in attending our school."

"That's right. I hope to learn enough skills so I can make a livin' for me and my daughter back home in Illinois."

"Who is it, Mr. Bennett?" A child's voice called.

Becky's eyes were drawn to the inquisitive young boy in the wagon bed. He sat cross-legged, head cocked and brow knit. No more than five or six years of age, his full cheeks and rounded face melted her heart. The rest of the students, a mixture of boys and girls, ranged from very young to seventeen or eighteen. All bore calm, expressionless faces and downcast eyes.

"Just a minute, Amos." Mr. Bennett tugged at his beard, returning his attention to Pa. "We'd be breaking new ground, I'm afraid. You see, our program is geared for children. State funding doesn't allow us to house those over eighteen."

"You're sayin' you can't help me?" Pa's voice deepened.

His words set off a flurry of emotions inside Becky. Had they made the trip for nothing? Part of her longed to return home and forget the whole thing. Yet she knew how important it was to Pa. It wouldn't be fair to him to give up.

"Not necessarily." The man leaned against the wagon. "It may require you to fund yourself. Do you have means to do that?"

"Not to speak of." The truth was, any money they had had been a gift from their neighbors back home.

Pastor Brody clamped Pa on the shoulder. "I'm sure there'd

be those in our church willing to help. I'll do my best to see you get what you need."

"I'd be glad to help as well." Aunt Ellen stepped closer, hazel eyes shining.

Tension lined Pa's face. Not one to take charity, more than likely he was taking great effort to hold his tongue. "We'd work something out."

Becky bit at her lip. Perhaps she should try to find a position to help finance Pa's training. After all, it sounded as if she would have time to spare. Maybe Aunt Ellen would know of a place she could work. Pa would likely not approve. Yet, they would need to earn money somehow.

Mr. Bennett's mouth lifted in a satisfied grin. "Well then, we may have to make a few adjustments, but I don't see why we can't make it work. I'll have to check with Mr. Whelan, the school's founder, though, before deciding anything definite. Our biggest problem is space. We've been established only a couple years, but we've already about outgrown our facility."

Pa's expression lightened. "The floor would suit me just fine."

"There'll be no need of that. One more won't cause much grief."

The director's eyes shifted to Becky and Aunt Ellen. "Have you plans for your wife and daughter?"

"This is my sister, Ellen."

Aunt Ellen slid her arm around Becky's waist. "His daughter, Becky, will be staying with me."

Mr. Bennett tipped his hat to her, a hint of recognition in his eyes. "Have I seen you here before?"

Aunt Ellen flashed a warm smile. "More than likely. I'm here every week."

Mr. Bennett nodded, then turned to Becky. "Feel free to visit your father as often as you like."

"Thank you." The words rolled stiffly from her tongue. It

seemed Pa would have his way after all. Still, being only a few blocks away was better than many miles.

Mr. Bennett moved to the front of the wagon and bounded up onto the seat. "Come by tomorrow morning. If all goes well, we'll get you settled in."

Pa shifted his face in the direction of the man's voice. "We'll be there first thing. Ellen knows the way."

"We'll look for you in the morning then." With a tip of his hat, Mr. Bennett gathered the reins and tapped the horses into motion.

"Seems a right nice fellow," Pastor Brody commented, watching the wagon pull away. "You'll do well for yourself here, Joseph."

Becky tensed, looping her arm through her father's. She knew she should be grateful. At least here she would be close to him. At home, she would know nothing of his progress and be utterly lost without him.

Aunt Ellen fell into pace beside Pastor Brody as the four of them strolled down the street. "How long will you stay, pastor?"

"If Joseph gets settled, I reckon I'll leave tomorrow."

Becky jarred to a stop, the color draining from her cheeks. "So soon? Can't you stay a while longer?" The words flew from her lips before she could stop them. She clamped her mouth shut. Must she be so transparent? Still, if her words hadn't spoken the longing in her heart, her eyes would have.

Pastor Brody met her gaze. "Folks back home might start wondering what's become of me if I linger too long. But I'll stay longer, if need be."

Pa shook his head. "You've done enough already. See us to the school for the blind tomorrow, an' if all's well, you can be on your way."

Becky swallowed the dryness in her throat. What if things didn't work out for them here? They'd have no way home. Her chin quivered as she stared down at the pavement. Back at Miller

Creek, everything had seemed so clear. She'd not anticipated becoming so attached to Pastor Brody, or being separated from Pa.

Aunt Ellen stepped up beside her, placing a hand on her arm. "I know I'm not much more than a stranger to you, but I'll do my best to make you feel at home."

With a nod, Becky forced a smile. What else could she do? She'd made her choice. Now she would have to live with it.

Chapter Thirteen

PART THREE: CHANGES

AN EARLY MORNING mist gave the sky a hazy appearance as Pastor Brody guided the team westward. Becky crouched beside her father in the wagon bed, hugging her unsettled stomach. Perhaps the school founder wouldn't accept Pa, and they could leave this miserable place.

He cocked his head, seeming to wait in quiet expectation for news they had arrived. Becky chided herself for her selfish thoughts. Pa needed what all her wishful thinking couldn't give him—skilled training and the means to feel needed again. She couldn't deny him that.

The city was quieter now, but for the jingling of harnesses and the clap of hooves on the cobblestone pavement. A handful of shoppers began milling about, looking over the town's wares as businesses opened their doors. Buildings became more widely spread toward the outskirts of town. At least here, away from the heart of the city, maybe Pa could find some solace.

"That's it. There," Aunt Ellen announced from the wagon seat.

Becky peeked out the opening in the canvas as Pastor Brody halted the team in front of a two-story brick building. A bold-faced sign in the yard read: The Missouri Institution for the Education of the Blind.

Pa straightened, a slur of emotions rippling over his face. "What's it like?"

Rising to her knees, Becky gazed at the large structure, its two-acre yard framed by a rail fence. "A big building with a fenced in yard. Not much else."

His face puckered. "Don't suppose it matters, long as they'll take me in."

A pang of regret stabbed at Becky. She'd neglected to mention the sizable garden at the far corner of the property, or the towering oak and sycamore trees out back, or the pair of young apple trees blossoming at its front. Was her attitude so skewed by self-centered thoughts that she would intentionally taint his image of the place? Even if he couldn't see the finer points, it would have helped him to paint a truer image of the place in his mind. She shuddered at the coldness that had over-shadowed her heart.

Pastor Brody stepped around the corner of the wagon and removed the end gate for Pa to lower himself down. Becky gathered up their things, then took the hand Pastor Brody offered. His dark eyes bore an uncharacteristic melancholy hue. It seemed neither of them was eager to see this day come.

Aunt Ellen joined them at the back of the wagon, placing a gentle hand on Pa's arm. "Looks like your welcoming committee is on its way. Here comes Mr. Bennett."

Pa edged forward. "Take me to him." He seemed so eager, so certain this was what he needed to get back on his feet. Would this place really be all he hoped?

Mr. Bennett smiled as he approached. "Well, I see you made it."

Pa shifted toward the man's voice. "Did you get things squared with Mr. Whelan?"

"Yes. He's willing to give it a try. Come on in. I'll get you settled."

Heaviness shackled Becky in place, the man's words spilling out like a jail sentence. There was no turning back now. What would the coming months bring? She moved to her father's side, tightening her grip on the satchel.

Pa seemed to sense her uneasiness. "Would it be all right if my daughter stayed, just for the day?"

The director smiled through his beard. "Certainly."

Becky nodded her thanks. She would try to be content—for Pa's sake.

The man's gaze swept the others' faces. "You're all welcome to come have a look around."

Pastor Brody gestured toward Aunt Ellen. "I'd like that, but Miss Hollister is due at work shortly."

"Yes. I'd best be going." She leaned to embrace Pa. "Good-bye, Joseph. Don't worry. I'll take good care of Becky."

"I know you will. Come see me."

"I will." She turned and strode toward the wagon, dabbing moist eyes with a handkerchief.

Pastor Brody helped her onto the seat and then hurried back. "Would you like me to stop by afterward, Joseph?"

For a moment, hope swelled within Becky. She was no more ready to see him leave than for her and Pa to stay. But, at her father's words, her hopes died away.

"No need. You've done more than enough already." Pa extended his hand. "Sure appreciate all your help, Matthew."

"My pleasure." He gave Pa's hand a firm shake, his gaze falling to Becky.

Her breath caught in her throat, the intensity of his stare washing through her. She couldn't let him go. Not yet. Not until she got her bearings. He was so strong and sure. Without him, she was certain to crumble.

Pa eased his hand away. "Godspeed, my friend."

Pastor Brody's voice seemed to waver as he clasped Pa's shoulder. "Send word and I'll be back for you."

With a slight nod, Pa turned with Mr. Bennett toward the school. Hesitating, he shifted his head from side to side. "Becky?"

"Be right there, Pa. I...have something to give Pastor Brody."

Mr. Bennett placed a hand on Pa's arm, guiding him forward. Becky waited until they were at a distance, then turned to Pastor Brody. Reaching in her pocket, she removed the two short notes she'd penned earlier that morning and took a step toward him. "I've written to Uncle Jed and Aunt Clara, sort of explaining things. I figure I owe 'em that. There's one for Esther too. Would you see they get them?"

"Sure thing." He pressed his hands to hers, a gentle smile playing on his lips as he clasped the letters.

"Thank you." A hush fell over them as Becky attempted to slip her hands from his.

Yet, instead of releasing them, his grip intensified. "You take care now. I'll pray the time passes quickly."

She glanced up at him, his rich brown eyes seeming to penetrate her very soul. Did he sense her inner struggle, her unspoken doubts and fears? "I-I don't think I can do this."

His steady gaze washed over her like the first day of spring. "Alone, you can't. But, with the Lord's help, you will."

She wet her lips to still her quivering chin. How she wanted to believe him, to feel the Lord's presence once again. But how could she when He'd abandoned them in their time of need?

Loosening his hold on her hands, Pastor Brody tucked the letters in his vest pocket and pulled his frayed, leather Bible from his overcoat. "Here, I want you to have this."

"But it's your preaching Bible. I couldn't."

"Yours was ruined in the storm, wasn't it?"

Becky gave a slight nod, still hesitant. Everything had been ruined by the storm.

Everything.

"Well then, it's yours to keep. Besides, I have another at home just itching to be broken in."

Her gaze fell to the leather-bound Bible, and she reached for it, clutching it to her chest. It was a piece of him, and though she couldn't say so in words, she'd cherish it—always. "It'll never leave my side."

"It couldn't be in better hands."

She stepped toward him, moisture pooling in her eyes. Many months would pass before they'd see each other again. Knowing that gave her courage to speak what was in her heart. "I wish you didn't have to go. I don't know how we'll manage without you."

He gazed down at her, his voice soft and low. "Truth is I'll miss having you along."

His confession set off a thunderous beating of her heart. A corner of her mouth lifted. "You will?"

Her breath caught as he brushed a hand over her cheek. Tenderness lined his dark eyes. "But you were right in coming. Your father needs you. Remember, he can't be hurt by people's stares, but he can hear the coldness in their voices and sense their unease. More importantly, he can sense when you're upset."

Tears stung Becky' eyes. "I'll remember."

Cupping a hand under her chin, Pastor Brody lifted her face till her eyes met his. "Draw your strength from God, Becky. He won't fail you."

She searched his face. How was it he found such cause for hope? In the midst of so much bad, he seemed to glean only the good. She lowered her gaze. How could she look him in the eye when her heart was shadowed with doubt? God *had* failed her. How could she trust Him not to let her down again?

Bending over, Pastor Brody gave her hand a soft kiss. "God has great plans for you, Becky. Never lose sight of that."

Heat flamed in her cheeks. The tenderness in his gaze removed all doubt that he cared for her. How she longed to melt into his arms. His unshakable faith could almost persuade her to believe God did have a plan for her, that somehow, He would utilize the hurt to make a difference for someone else.

Pastor Brody nodded toward the Bible. "Put it to good use."

Becky mustered a grin. "I will."

With a squeeze of her hand, he edged toward the wagon. "I'd better go. Don't want to make your aunt late."

For one sweet moment, all but the two of them had disappeared. Now reality trickled back like a cold mist. Clutching the worn Bible to her chest, Becky called after him. "Let us hear from you."

"I'll be in touch," he assured as he disappeared around the corner of the wagon.

Aunt Ellen waved as they pulled away. "See you tonight. I'll come for you around six."

Becky watched until they rounded the curve and disappeared in the haze of buildings and people. A soft breeze dried her eyes as she turned toward the school. *Lord, help me believe as Pastor Brody does, that You've brought us here for a purpose. Give me strength, for Pa's sake.*

With a deep breath, she pressed forward. Their last tie with home was gone.

Along with her heart.

Chapter Fourteen

MILK-WHITE PETALS FLITTERED and fell about Becky, cushioning her path as she strode to join her father. The two-story building loomed ahead of her like a creature ready to devour. She topped the porch steps and then turned, stealing a final glance at the empty street. The wagon's absence wedged a hole in her heart. They had no choice but to forge ahead.

A gritty sound drew her attention to the far end of the porch. A curly-headed boy about her age sat stooped over an oak chair, weaving a strand of cane along the unfinished seat. As he pulled it tight, the irritating squeal sounded again.

Becky vaguely recalled seeing him among the students in the wagon at church. Eyes downcast, he cocked his head toward them as they passed. Becky slowed her pace, trying not to stare. Was he blind? If so, how could he follow the pattern of the cane?

Taking Pa's arm, she followed Mr. Bennett inside the building. A stale, closed-in smell emanated from the room. Becky took shallow breaths, wondering how Pa would manage living in such a confined area. For someone accustomed to the freedom of the outdoors, the closeness of the place seemed stifling.

A huge stone fireplace with iron netting across its front

greeted them in the sitting room. Chairs with caned seats, like the one the boy was working on, were situated in an arch around it. Two thinly-curtained windows filtered in light from the morning sun.

Becky followed Mr. Bennett to the base of a stairway. "We're a bit cramped for space, but you'll find the place clean and well-maintained." The instructor started up the narrow flight of stairs, pausing at the top.

"The second story is divided into two large bedrooms, the one on the left for the girls and one on the right for the boys." He placed Pa's hand on the door frame, letting him feel his way along. "This first door leads to my quarters. Mr. Whelan's room is directly across from here." He opened the door, revealing a tiny compartment containing a small desk, bookcase, and cot. "The next door down is the boys' room. Just remember to go to the second doorway on the right, and you'll do fine. The girls' room is across the hall. They'll soon let you know if you've made a wrong turn."

Pa paused along the wall, brows raised. "I'll try my best not to make that mistake."

Mr. Bennett gave a hearty chuckle, reminding Becky a bit of Uncle Jed, with his reddish-brown beard and good-natured laugh. He waited until Pa made it to the entry way, then ushered him inside. "This is where you'll sleep. We've located a cot for you, but may not have it by tonight."

The instructor turned to Becky, pointing to the one open space on the floor. "You may put his things there for now."

With a nod, she set the satchel on the designated spot on the floor. Tucking Pastor Brody's Bible under her arm, she ran her thumb over its rough, leather covering. There was something comforting in its touch in this cold, depressing room filled with empty cots and drab brown walls.

Mr. Bennett ushered Pa to the far side of the room. "Over here is a wash area, with pitcher, basin, and towels." He moved

Pa's hands over the items, identifying how they were arranged. "You'll share the room with four others. There's not much space between cots, so you'll have to learn to maneuver around pretty quickly or suffer a lot of bruises."

Pa released a hurried breath. "I can see I have my work cut out for me, even finding my way around the place."

"You'll do fine." Mr. Bennett's deep voice was reassuring. His easy nature lent well to his position as instructor for the blind. It would take a great deal of patience to teach so many sightless students.

The chatter of children grew louder as they returned downstairs. From the sitting room, Becky watched the train of younger students make their way down the hallway and outside. A white-haired man trailed behind them, helping the smaller ones along.

"Mr. Whelan." Mr. Bennett called out. He took Pa by the arm and led him toward the older man. "Joseph Hollister has arrived with his daughter."

The white-haired man tugged the children to a halt, turning toward Mr. Bennett. "Welcome. I'm Eli Whelan, founder of this facility."

Mr. Bennett guided the two men's hands together for a shake. Mr. Whelan's smile was inviting. "Where do you hail from, Mr. Hollister?"

"Miller Creek, Illinois."

Mr. Whelan nodded, eyelids lowered. "A few days' journey, I expect. Glad to have you here."

The small boy at his front tugged on the older man's hand, the same inquisitive boy Mr. Bennett had referred to as Amos. "Let's go, Mr. Whelan."

With a smile, he gave way to the young child's plea. "We'll talk later. The children are eager for their time outdoors."

Becky stared after him, watching him feel his way along the hall. She turned to Mr. Bennett, her eyes wide with question. "He's blind?"

The instructor nodded. "A few years back, Eli grew tired of being treated as an invalid. He viewed his sightlessness as a limitation, not a disability. So he hatched the idea of starting a school for blind children and petitioned the State for aid. They offered to help only if he could prove students were benefiting substantially from the program. With the help of an ophthalmologist, he selected two pupils, Elizabeth Tayler and Daniel Wilkinson. Within a year, their progress so impressed State officials that they wholeheartedly backed the program. That was three and a half years ago."

Pa crossed his arms and nodded. "Mr. Whelan sounds like one determined fellow."

"That he is. Word spread and soon others brought their children. That's when Eli realized it was a greater task than he and his housemaid, Nettie, could manage. So, in the fall of '51, he hired me as director and co-teacher. Now there are ten students...eleven counting you."

Pa's chin tipped higher, and Becky smiled to herself. To hear the accomplishments of another sightless man had obviously inspired him. Would he have the same level of determination?

Mr. Bennett clapped Pa on the shoulder. "This will be a good time to show you around, while the students are outside."

They followed the instructor across the hall to a room filled with pine desks spread in neat rows. "This is the classroom. Students have daily lessons similar to those taught in regular schools. Of course, our material and method of teaching are somewhat different."

The small classroom boasted no pictures or paintings, only a curtained window along the south wall. Such a drab atmosphere.

The director seemed to guess her thoughts. "The rooms may seem dreary, but our funds are limited and must be used for supplies and things that are absolutely necessary. Blind students won't miss wall hangings, but they would suffer from lack of teaching materials."

He picked up a book from one of the desks and opened it, revealing a series of raised dots throughout its pages. Taking Pa's finger, he traced it over the lines. "Each of these symbols represents a letter. Students are taught to recognize the symbols and learn to read with their fingertips."

Becky stared at the emblems in the book. "That's amazing."

Pa pulled his hand away. "I'm too old to figure out all that."

"Ah, but you're never too old to learn." Mr. Bennett set the book on the desk and led Pa through the room, pausing at times to let him feel his way. "It'll take you a while, but if you can picture in your mind how the rooms are arranged, you'll be moving about on your own in no time."

Down the hall, they entered a second room. "I think you'll find this room more to your liking. It's the work room where students make most of their crafts. A fellow from Massachusetts by the name of Samuel Howe designed the teaching method we follow, and one of the things it stresses most is the importance of craft skills."

Pa's expression brightened. "That's what I'm here for."

The room was filled with supplies, half-finished baskets, brooms, caned chairs, weaving, carpentry work, and spindles crafted on a lathe. All were simply made, yet many matched the quality of items sold in the mercantile store back home.

Becky ran her hand over one of the wicker baskets. "The students made these?"

Mr. Bennett leaned against the doorframe. "You'd never guess it, would you? It's amazing how quickly those who're blind develop skills to compensate for their lack of vision. By the time students leave here, our goal is for them to acquire enough skill to contribute to society."

Pa steadied himself against a table. "What do you do with the things they make?"

"We sell them to a couple of store-owners here in town. The

income is a much-needed supplement for the State aid we receive."

"Sounds like a good setup. When can I start?"

Mr. Bennett grinned, crossing one leg in front of the other. "Soon. The toughest part of being a new student is getting acclimated. The problem is, we're continually graduating and gaining new students. It's always a bit of a challenge."

He took Pa's arm and guided him to a third room containing a variety of horns and stringed instruments. "Another important part of our program is music. We require every student to learn at least one instrument. It builds confidence and is something most students truly enjoy."

The memory of Pa's fiddle awaiting them back home warmed Becky. She took a step forward, a sense of pride in her voice. "Pa plays the fiddle."

At her words, a shadow fell across his face. "You mean used to play."

"You could still play. You haven't tried." If only she'd thought to bring his fiddle along. The familiar feel of it snugged against his chin might have spurred him to try.

"I came to learn a trade, not waste time on book learnin' or music." His hardened tone sliced through Becky. She knew full well, once he made up his mind, it did no good to try to change it. Before he could succeed, he'd have to decide to try. Perhaps it was best to keep his fiddle secret a while longer. Knowing it awaited them back home might only deepen his angst.

Mr. Bennett clasped his shoulder. "Not to worry, Mr. Hollister. We'll see to it you get what you came for…and more."

Across the hall was a spacious dining room, a huge oak table at its center. Sturdy benches lined both sides of the lengthy table, with caned chairs at either end. The faint scent of sausage and egg hung in the air as they entered the detached kitchen, separated by a large, open doorway. There a heavy-set dark-skinned woman stood washing dishes, an apron tied over her calico dress.

Her coarse black hair was flecked with gray and gathered in a tight bun. She turned toward them and drew her hands from the wash basin as they approached.

"This here's Nettie. I dare say she's the heart and soul of this place."

She gave a good-natured chuckle, wiping damp hands on her apron. "Thank ya kindly, Mis'er Peter. Now, who do we have here?"

Becky tried not to stare at the jolly, dark-skinned woman. She'd never seen a—slave. But was she a slave? Missouri being a slave state, she must be. Yet Mr. Bennett didn't speak to her as a servant, nor did she act like one.

"Nettie, this is Joseph and Becky Hollister."

The hefty woman flashed a wide grin, her voice smooth and boisterous. "Joseph and Rebecca. Good Christian names. You visitin' one of the young'uns?"

"No. I'll be staying on as a student."

"You don't say?" Nettie cocked her head and turned to Mr. Bennett, the whites of her eyes growing large.

He gave a slow nod. "Joseph will be funding his stay with us."

That they had no money of their own made Becky a bit ill at ease. A hint of red stained her father's cheeks. Was he too worried where the funds would come from?

Nettie rested her hands to her hips. "Well now, I reckon it'll be refreshin' to have another grownup about the place. Will you be stayin' too, Miss Becky?"

Becky shook her head, staring down at the pine floorboards.

"She'll be staying with my sister, a few blocks from here."

Mr. Bennett cleared his throat. "I'm certain she'll visit us often."

"I looks forward to it. You come by any time, missy, ya hear?"

Becky forced a smile. "Yes, ma'am."

The floor creaked under them as they returned to the sitting room. "Well, I guess that about does it. Except for any questions you might have."

Laughter sounded outside the open window, and Becky saw a pair of young children whirling in circles.

Mr. Bennett smoothed his beard between his thumb and fore-finger, his gaze following hers. "Why don't you go have a look around, Miss Hollister, while your father and I chat?"

Pa leaned back, crossing his legs at the ankles. "Go ahead, Becky."

"All right."

Pushing open the door, she breathed in the fresh morning air. The curly-haired boy on the porch had made much progress with his caning in the short time that had lapsed. He was lean, and for his size, had delicate hands. His boyish features made him appear young, but his solid frame determined him to be about her age. She watched from a distance, amazed at how effortlessly he wove the thin strand of cane over the seat.

"You're Miss Becky, ain't ya?" he declared, without pausing from his work.

"Y-Yes." She stared at him, questioning whether he was truly blind. Long blond lashes lined his faded blue eyes. His rounded nose and full lips formed a handsome profile.

"Is your father gonna stay?" The boy's blond curls hid his eyebrows as they arched upward.

"Why, yes...but how could you...?"

The dampened cane squealed as the young man pulled it into place, his broad grin revealing a row of slightly crooked teeth. "I was listening in when Mr. Bennett was telling Mr. Whelan about you."

"Oh." Becky grinned. "You're very perceptive."

He shrugged, a smirk creeping onto his lips. "You use what you've got."

She stepped closer, intrigued by his ingenuity. His work on

the chair was near perfect. "How do you make it come out so well?"

"You mean being blind?"

Becky bit her lip. Had she offended him? "Y-you do such fine work. It must be difficult getting it just so without your sight."

He finished pulling the long strand of cane through the tiny holes along the rim of the seat. "When you've done it as long as I have, I reckon it just comes natur'l."

"How long have you been here?"

"Goin' on three years. Been here almost since the school opened. I was one of the first, outside of Elizabeth and Daniel."

As skilled as the young man was, Becky had to wonder why he remained here. Why would anyone wish to be away from home and family so long? "Aren't you eager to go home?"

He paused from his work for the first time, resting his hands on the edge of the chair. "Ain't got no home. My folks abandoned me when I was just a young'un, after I lost my sight. My kinfolk shuffled me around till I wound up here."

Becky leaned against the porch rail, swallowing down the lump in her throat. "I-I'm sorry."

He shrugged, his expression turning solemn as he resumed caning. "I reckon this is the only home I've got. Though not for long."

Not for long. What did he mean? He just said this was the only home he had. She pressed her lips together, resisting the urge to pry. Her eyes panned the wide porch, its wooden beams teeming with ivy. Her gaze drifted to the vast yard beyond, to the garden spot and the lofty trees. Away from the core of the city, it wasn't a bad place—if one had to be here. Yet with people coming and going, there could be no sense of belonging. To claim such a place as home seemed tragic. But, for the time being, her own sense of belonging was but a distant memory.

Chapter Fifteen

Matthew clenched his jaw, trying to concentrate on finding his way. But his mind kept wandering back to Becky. He could hear the steamboat whistles as he neared the riverfront. It took everything in him not to go back and make sure all was well. Until that moment, he'd not realized just how much Becky meant to him. He'd shed a piece of his heart back there. Another goodbye would prove too much.

The trip home would be a long and lonely one. He checked his pocket to be certain the folded papers were still safely tucked away. Though neither had said so in words, he sensed he and Becky had come to an understanding. In ways, the months would drag, and yet, he had a lot of soul searching to do. It wouldn't take much of a nudge to convince him it was time to settle in one place. Still, if the Lord intended for them to be together, He would make a way.

All Matthew needed now was patience.

"Would you like me to show you around?"

The boy's question took Becky by surprise. "Sure."

Scooting his chair aside, the young man rose to his feet. Tall and lanky, his haggard shirt and trousers fit snugly, as though having undergone years of wear. He sauntered over to her, his stride confident. "Name's Jimmy Bodine."

"I'm Becky Hollister." She fell in pace beside him. "Do you need help with the steps?"

Jimmy snickered. "Are you kiddin'? I know every inch of this place."

She followed him down the steps and out into the yard, amazed at the ease with which he traveled. He took her to the garden where four youths were breaking up clods of dirt and hoeing around young plants.

Jimmy crossed his arms, drawing himself up to full height. "This is our activity time. While the younger ones play, us older students work in the yard or garden."

Becky smiled at his business-like manner. Was he trying to impress her?

The dark-haired boy nearest them stopped hoeing and turned toward them. "Who's that with you, Jimmy?"

"Her name's Becky. Her father's gonna be a student here."

"Hello, Becky."

"Hello..." She struggled for a name.

"Grant," whispered Jimmy.

The boy nodded and resumed hoeing.

"Grant's my best buddy." Jimmy thinned his lips, heaving a quiet sigh. "But he's almost finished with the program, so he'll be leaving soon. *He* has a home to go to." He lowered his head, kicking at the ground with his foot.

Becky clasped her hands behind her back. She knew what it was like to leave home and to lose loved ones, but not to be entirely without a home and family. Sensing his angst, she thought it best to change the topic. "Who are the two girls out there?"

"That'd be Jenny and Angelina. Angelina's the older one. She's close to finishing too. Now Jenny's fourteen. She ain't real smart at book learnin', but she can play the piano like a mockingbird sings."

Becky watched a larger boy half-heartedly hacking at the dirt. "Who's the other boy?"

Jimmy drew up one side of his mouth, with an indifferent shrug. "Who, Stump?"

"Stump?" She brushed a strand of hair from her face and knit her brow.

"His real name's Roy, but we call him Stump 'cause most all he does is sit around doin' nothin'."

"That's cruel."

Jimmy sliced his hand through the air. "Ah, don't get your dander up. I wouldn't say it if it weren't so. He's got his mind set he can't do nothin'. When he changes his ways, we'll change ours."

"How long has he been here?"

"Only a couple months, but I think Mr. Bennett and Mr. Whelan have 'bout given up on him. He doesn't try to make friends, won't go to church, just keeps to himself."

She stared out at the over-sized boy leaning on his hoe handle. Was he as lazy as Jimmy let on, or was there something more to it? If Charlotte's snubbing had taught Becky one thing, it was that often there was some deep-seated reason for a person's actions.

Pivoting on his heels, Jimmy pumped his chin. "Come on. I'll introduce you to the younger bunch."

Becky started after him, taking quick steps to keep pace. "Why aren't you working in the garden?"

"I'm long finished with the program, so Mr. Bennett pretty much lets me go about my business, so long as I earn my keep. I help most of the time. I'm just working at caning chairs this week to fill an order for Mr. Jacobs, one of our buyers."

"You're very talented."

His pace slowed momentarily and a hint of red trickled down his face and neck. "That's the only reason I get to stick around here. The school would have a hard time making it without the money from our craft goods. And since I'm done with the program, I'd be the first to go if money runs short. Soon as I turn nineteen, I'm gone anyway."

Becky adjusted her stride to match his, disturbed at the thought of her newfound friend being sent away. "Where will you go?"

Jimmy shrugged. "Don't rightly know. But I'll get by, with the Good Lord beside me."

She stared up at him, her own faith somehow strengthened by this self-reliant young man. Someday Pa would walk just as confident and self-assured.

Laughter rang out ahead of them as Mr. Whelan led a train of young children. The lead girl clung to the man's suspenders as he zigzagged around the yard. The other four followed hand to shoulder. While most of the children seemed to enjoy the game, the raven-haired girl in back remained stone-faced, making no effort to join in the merriment.

Becky leaned closer to Jimmy. "That one little girl looks so sad." Only deep sorrow could cause the young child's anguished expression. Had she too suffered a loss?

Jimmy widened his stance, sinking his hands deeper in his pockets. "Must be Emily. She just recently lost her sight and is having a rough time accepting it. Most do at first. You'll find that with your father, if you haven't already."

"Pa's got plenty of grit. He'll manage just fi—." A bell sounded from the porch, cutting off Becky's words.

"It's craft time. Come on." Jimmy motioned her forward as students headed inside.

She followed him to the house, amazed he gave little pause

before climbing the porch steps. "You make it look so easy. I can hardly tell you're…"

"Blind?" Jimmy finished for her. "It's all right to say it. Losing your sight's nothing to be ashamed of. It doesn't cripple your hands, legs, or mind like most people think. We're no different than anybody else, if only people would stop treatin' us like we are."

Becky winced, pricked by his defensive tone. She of all people should know that. Pa was the same man inside he'd always been and didn't want to be thought of otherwise. "I-I'm sorry."

Jimmy's expression softened. "Ah, I didn't mean you. Anyway, I can't expect sighted people to understand what it's like not to see."

He was right. She couldn't. But she was trying.

He opened the door, and Becky strolled in ahead of him. "Thanks for showing me around, Jimmy."

He paused beside her. "You gonna be here a while?"

"Just for the day. Then I go to my aunt's."

His lips parted as if to speak, but then he went on.

Her eyes trailed after him. There was something intriguing about the young man. With his dignified stance and confident stride, one would never guess him a blind orphan. But what fascinated her most was that, in such a short time together, he'd accomplished what no other had since the storm—to get her mind off her own troubles and glimpse into the needs of others.

AUNT ELLEN SLUMPED in her cushioned chair by the fireplace, and threw back her head with a sigh. "By this time of night, I'm completely spent. I'm not getting any younger."

Becky rocked in the rocker, staring into the flickering flames. A month earlier she'd sat before a similar fire with her family in their cozy log home. Now here she was in a strange house with a woman she hardly knew. So much had changed. She couldn't quite wrap her mind around it.

Aunt Ellen smiled and closed her eyes. "It's nice to have someone around. Living alone has its definite drawbacks."

Becky returned a faint smile. At least her coming had brought someone happiness. Firelight danced on her aunt's face. Faint creases lined the outer edges of her gentle eyes and mouth, evidence that a smile had often lit her face. Sad she'd led such a lonely life. Had she chosen not to marry or been spurned in love?

"I just wish I could be more useful. If Pa is to stay here, he'll need money."

With a yawn, Aunt Ellen opened her eyes. "Why don't I take you with me to the sewing factory tomorrow? Mr. Billings is always in need of a good seamstress."

"I'm afraid I'm no better at sewing than I am cooking." For once, Becky regretted not having domestic skills. If it were up to her, she'd spend days with Pa at the school for the blind. But then, she needed to find some means to help pay for his training. "Would you know of any other positions?"

Aunt Ellen breathed a quiet sigh, seeming to comb her mind for ideas. A moment later, she sat forward in her chair, a slight grin lining her lips. "Say, I know just the thing. Someone at church mentioned the schoolmaster down the street is in need of an assistant. Does that sound suitable?"

Becky's stomach churned at the thought. "Possibly."

"Perfect. I'll walk you there on my way to work in the morning."

A nervous twinge pricked at Becky. To be sure, Aunt Ellen had proven more than kind, but all the kindness in the world couldn't soothe the longings in Becky's heart. She swallowed down the tightness in her throat, hoping the firelight didn't betray the moisture burning her eyes.

Her aunt fought back another yawn. "If I can't stay awake,

I'd best go to bed." She rose from the chair, glancing back at Becky. "Coming?"

Blinking back her tears, Becky clutched Pastor Brody's Bible. "I'll be along shortly. I'd like to read a bit first."

"Goodnight then."

"Goodnight." She waited until her aunt had gone, then flipped open the Bible. Skimming through the pages of the Old Testament, she reread bits of familiar stories about Joseph, Moses, and David. She tugged at her braid, leaning closer to the flickering flames of the fireplace, having forgotten the hardships each had faced. Yet in the end, God had blessed them for their faithfulness. Could she trust Him to see her through her heartache as well?

Flipping to the psalms, she ran her fingers over the verses, seeking out ones Pastor Brody had underlined.

"Some trust in chariots and some in horses, but we trust in the name of the Lord our God.

The earth is the Lord's and everything in it, the world and all who live in it.

Delight thyself in the Lord and He will give thee the desires of thy heart.

Why so downcast, O my soul? Put thy hope in God

Never will I leave thee, never will I forsake thee."

Again and again she read of God's abiding presence and peace in troubled times. With each passage, her chest tightened. How could God allow such pain? Closing the Bible, she bowed her head. *Lord, I don't understand. Why do you permit Your people to suffer?*

As she opened her eyes, a tip of paper showed from the top edge of the Bible. Odd, she hadn't noticed it before. Lifting the frayed, leather cover, she removed the folded page. She sank deeper in the upholstered chair and unfolded the note.

"Dear Becky", it began. The words sent a tingle through her.

The message was for her. She read on, imagining Pastor Brody's low voice spoke the words.

"I know in reading this that you must be drinking from the living water within these pages. Make peace with God, Becky. Hard times come to all, but the Lord warns, "He who falters in troubled times, how small is his faith." (Proverbs 24:10) Don't give in to resentment and fear. Find in Him the strength you're sure to need in the coming months."

She paused, wiping tears from her eyes. *Lord, help me trust You once again.*

She gripped the letter, her eyes soaking in the final lines.

"Know that my thoughts are with you. My prayers will cover you each day we're apart. Godspeed, dear one, until the day of your return."

"Fondly, Matthew."

"Fondly, Matthew?" She whispered aloud. Her heart raced as she retraced the message.

"Dear one", he'd called her. Did she dare hope he cared for her, or was she reading too much into his words? He was her pastor, yes, but hadn't his eyes spoken affection? Hadn't his lips kissed her hand? Hadn't his voice expressed warmth and concern beyond that of a pastor?

With a sigh, she refolded the note and slipped it beneath the leather binding. But then, what did it matter, now that he was miles away and worlds apart?

THE CAMPFIRE CRACKLED and spit as Matthew banked it for the night. No fancy restaurants or crowded streets for him this evening. Now that he was back on the Illinois prairie, he could enjoy the wide-open spaces. Though they seemed a bit lonely tonight. He couldn't help but wonder how Becky and Joseph were faring. Becky's moist eyes flashed through his mind. It had nearly broken his heart to leave her. Was she, too, thinking of him?

He spread his blanket near the fire and then lay back, staring at the stars. He'd sensed Becky's inner struggle. She blamed God for her troubles. Not unusual in situations like hers, so long as such bitter seeds didn't fester and take root in her heart.

He locked his hands together behind his head. He would pray for her each day she was away, that the Lord would soften her heart and help her accept His plans for her.

His chest tightened. Would those plans include him? After all, it wouldn't do for a pastor's wife to hold a grudge against God.

A ripple of unease coursed through him. Had she discovered the note he'd left her in his Bible? If so, could she read between the lines his growing affection for her?

Turning on his side, he let out a huff. Would that he could be with her now to help settle the questions in her mind. Yet, far better was the strength and encouragement only God could give.

He could only pray she'd seek Him.

Chapter Sixteen

BECKY SHUFFLED along behind Aunt Ellen, each step weighted with unwelcome dread. What did she know of teaching children? Especially city folks' children. She'd never even attended school herself, but had learned at home from her mother. Still, it sounded more appealing than sewing in a factory. And if Pa were to stay on, they would need the income. What would he think of her taking on a position?

She and her aunt climbed the schoolhouse steps and slipped through the open doorway. Four rows of pine desks stretched from one end to the other of the large classroom. Half hidden behind a bulky desk, a spindly man at the front poured over an open book. Aunt Ellen beckoned her forward, and grudgingly Becky complied.

At the creak of a floorboard, the man raised his head, plucking wire-rimmed spectacles from his long, hooked nose. He stood, close-set eyes perusing them from head to toe. "May I help you?"

The heels of their boots knocked against the puncheon floor, echoing in the vacant room as they made their way toward him. Pausing at his desk, Aunt Ellen flashed a pleasant smile. "I'm

Ellen Hollister, and this is my niece, Becky Hollister. Might I inquire if you're still in need of an assistant?"

"Why, yes. Do you wish to apply?"

With a soft chuckle, she stepped aside, nudging Becky forward. "Not me. My niece. She's just recently moved here and is in need of employment."

"Oh." The man raised an eyebrow, his expression sobering. He strolled to the front of his desk, scrutinizing Becky with his gaze as if she were a cow at market. "What's your age, girl?"

His nasal voice sent a cold shiver down Becky's spine. She tugged at the sleeve of her lavender dress, dropping her gaze to the floor. The hole in her worn shoe poked from beneath her skirt and she drew it back. "I'll turn eighteen this September."

"I assume you've had proper schooling?"

She gave a hard swallow. "We lived too far out to attend the town school. I was schooled at home by my ma."

He drew a hand to his chin, his pasty complexion contrasting sharply with the mop of red hair spilling over his ears. "Can you read?"

Becky bristled, lifting her head to meet his gaze. The question was an insult. Ma taught her more about life and book learning than any schoolmaster ever could. "Fluently."

He crossed his arms, leaning against his desk with a sigh. Something told Becky his decision would have been less difficult had it been her aunt applying. At last, his chin lifted. "I'd be hard-pressed to find someone else at this hour, so I'll give you a try. Class begins at eight-thirty and lets out at three-thirty. I'll expect you to be here a half-hour early and remain late whenever necessary."

"Yes sir."

He peered at her atop his rims. "If your work is satisfactory, you'll be paid at the end of each week. If not, I'll not hesitate to seek a replacement."

Becky gave a slight nod, her stomach knotting. The man was

intimidating. Obviously, she would have to prove herself. She drew a deep breath. How hard could it be to assist children?

Mr. O'Dell searched through the stack of McGuffey readers on his desk and handed her one. "The students will arrive shortly. Until that time you may look over Lesson three so that you may give assistance when needed."

"Yes, sir." Reluctantly Becky clasped the book and took a seat at the center front-row desk. How could she endure working under such a prudish man? Her only hope was to keep reminding herself it was for Pa's sake.

Aunt Ellen placed a hand on her shoulder, sympathy streaming from her hazel eyes. "I'll not finish work until around seven this evening. If you'd like, I'll meet you at the Institute for the Blind when I'm through. Do you remember the way?"

With a half-hearted nod, Becky glanced at the clock on the wall. Four o'clock couldn't come soon enough. The soft pat on her back was little comfort as her aunt swiveled and walked toward the door.

Becky opened the McGuffey reader and flipped through its pages, a wave of unease settling over her. Some of the words looked foreign. Had Mr. O'Dell given her the wrong book? This seemed too difficult for young minds to take in.

Children's voices sounded from the doorway. Rising to her feet, Becky stepped away from the desks and edged toward the windows.

What had she gotten herself into?

BECKY GLANCED at the clock on the wall above her, watching the gold pendulum sway from side to side. Five more minutes. She finished wiping down the blackboard, making sure every speck of chalk had been removed. Another glimpse at the clock. Its rhythmic ticking made her want to cuff her ears.

Two minutes. Oh, why wouldn't the hands move faster?

Mr. O'Dell sat at his desk, his back toward her. She toyed with the nub of chalk, shoving it first one way then another on the narrow shelf. At last the clock hand moved to the twelve. "It's four o'clock, Mr. O'Dell. May I go now?"

The wiry teacher peered over his shoulder. "Have you cleaned the chalkboard rags?"

Becky cringed. "No, sir."

He waved his hand in the air as if shooing away a fly. "Take them out back and clean the chalk from them. Then you may go."

Becky knitted her brows. Why hadn't he mentioned it earlier?

She snatched the rags from their spot and headed out back, resisting the urge to slam the door behind her. A cloud of chalk-dust shrouded her as she snapped the rags in the air. With a cough, she waved it away, wondering if Pa was as miserable as she was. Would he worry she hadn't come? After all, he didn't even know of her employment.

Slipping back inside, she set the rags in their place and then hurried toward the door.

She could sense Mr. O'Dell's eyes follow her through the classroom. "Slackers will not be tolerated, Miss Hollister. If you want to keep this position, I advise you to be prompt in the mornings and willing to do what I ask without question."

"Yes, sir." It was a struggle not to let annoyance seep into her voice. She closed the door behind her, a soft groan escaping her throat. The man was intolerable. Could she really handle working alongside such a tyrant for months on end?

She downed the school steps, trying to put the unpleasant thought behind her. But for the moment, a year seemed an eternity.

AT LAST, the terrain looked familiar. Matthew was pushing himself and the team, he knew, but he was eager to get back. He'd neglected his duties far too long—at least in respect to much in his congregation. And yet these past few weeks hadn't gone unrewarded. He'd watched neighbors rally together to help victims of the storm, and witnessed countless acts of kindness and generosity.

True, he'd concentrated his efforts on Joseph and Becky. And perhaps he'd been a bit selfish in his motives. Many of his actions had been by choice, although the trip to St. Louis had been at Joseph's request. Still, Matthew liked to think he'd have done the same for any of his flock in need.

He warmed inwardly. Developing a fondness for Becky had merely proven a bonus.

With a tap of the reins, the team quickened their pace. How he longed to rid himself of this awkward rig and be in the saddle again astride Gabriel. Another mile or so and he'd be at the Stanton homestead. Already he could see the outline of their cabin in the distance, a thin trail of smoke rising from their chimney.

The late afternoon sun warmed his back. This time of day, more than likely they'd offer him a night's lodging and a home-cooked meal. If so, he wouldn't disappoint. He'd tired of beef jerky and sleeping on the hard ground. A good night's rest would do him a world of good before heading off on his circuit.

Clara and the girls poured from their cabin as he pulled the team to a stop outside the Stanton home. Jed poked his head out of the barn and started toward him, a huge smile lining his lips. Coming up beside Matthew, he rubbed a hand down the horses' sweat-drenched necks. "Welcome back, pastor. How was your trip?"

Matthew hooked the reins on the corner of the wagon. "Just fine. But I'll admit it's good to be home."

Clara cocked her hands on her hips. "And Becky? How did Joseph take the news of her going?"

"Let's just say, he was less than thrilled in the beginning, but he came around."

Jed gave a soft chuckle. "She's got a mind of her own, that one."

"That she has." It was one of the things Matthew admired about her. He reached in his pocket and retrieved her letters. "She sent a note, sort of explaining things. And another for Esther."

He handed the letters to Jed who passed them along to Clara and Esther. Smiling ear to ear, Esther flitted off to the cabin with her treasure. Charlotte clutched her elbow and stared down at her feet. Was she feeling slighted? Why Becky hadn't included her, he couldn't say. The two had seemed at odds since the storm. Perhaps that was part of the reason Becky had taken such strides to leave.

Clara took a moment to glance over the note and then shook her head. "Can't blame the poor dear, wanting to be near her pa at a time like this." Raising a hand to shade her eyes from the waning sun, she peered over at Matthew. "You'll stay to supper, won't you, pastor?"

The blessed invitation he couldn't refuse. "Sure thing. Just give me a few minutes to unhitch the team and clean up."

"I'll help. And you'll stay the night." Jed clapped Matthew on the shoulder, then stooped to unhook the harness straps from the shaft.

"Much obliged." Hopping from the wagon, Matthew searched out Gabriel at the far end of the pasture. "I appreciate you looking after my horse while I was away."

"Least we could do." With a click of his cheek, Jed tugged on the bridles. The horses whinnied and shook their heads, free of their burden.

Taking hold of the horse closest to him, Matthew followed Jed to the water trough at the side of the barn. The horses dipped their muzzles in the cool water, thirsty from the long, hot journey.

Unhooking the head straps, Matthew peered over at Jed. "Would you mind returning the wagon to the livery for me tomorrow? I'd like to get started for Scottsdale first thing in the morning."

A hint of a grin lined Jed's lips. "Can't wait to get back at it, aye, preacher?"

In a sense, Jed spoke the truth. Matthew was eager to return to his ministry. Each member of his flock was as dear to him as family. Still, he couldn't shake the longing to stay in one place. "Been gone too long as it is. People have been more than patient."

"Too bad. We sort of liked having you around more."

"I've enjoyed it as well."

"Glad to hear you say that, preacher." Clearing his throat, Jed took a step forward. "There's been talk of asking you to stay on permanent with a regular Sunday church service."

"Is that so?" Matthew straightened. For weeks, he'd prayed for the Lord's direction. Was this his answer?

"Yes indeed. The town's growing. We need a full-time preacher. Give it some thought, and if you can square it away with the rest of your circuit, we'll see about fixing you up with a place to live."

"I'll do that." Matthew slipped a gloved hand down the horse's neck. What would it be like to have a home of his own? He'd been a vagabond so long, it would seem the life of luxury to stay in one place. Would he miss the freedom of roaming the prairie? He could still ride out to visit those in the far-reaching corners of the area who weren't able to make it in. What a blessing to have a roof over his head and one steady ministry.

His thoughts turned to Becky. He'd waited years to find someone to capture his heart the way she had. If he could only be certain she shared his feelings. The tender look in her eyes as they'd parted hinted she did. But would their unspoken affection withstand the months apart?

The corners of his mouth tipped upward. Jacob had waited seven years for his beloved Rachel. Surely he could wait one for Becky.

If she'd have him.

Metal clanked as Jed slid the harness from his horse's back. "I don't guess you've heard, but we've hired ourselves a new school teacher while you were away."

"Is that right?"

With a nod, Jed heaved the leather straps over his shoulder. "Starts the first of August. Pretty little gal." He nudged Matthew with his elbow, cracking a smile. "Might just be the perfect time for you to settle down."

Warmth flooded Matthew's cheeks. He hadn't the slightest interest in the new school teacher. But then, he wasn't ready to voice his intentions toward Becky either.

Sliding off the other harness, he followed Jed into the barn. "Where's she from?"

"Been working at a school in Minnesota last couple of years. Name's Sarah Prescott."

Matthew tensed, feeling the blood drain from his face. "Sarah...Prescott?"

"Ya. Do you know her?"

"I knew of one. But I doubt it's her. The girl I knew was from Indiana."

Jed lifted a brow, a twinkle in his eye. "I believe that's where this gal started out. 'Bout your age. Brown hair. Dark eyes."

Matthew gave a slow nod. Surely it couldn't be *his* Sarah.

Yet, from Jed's description, it very well could be. Tightness pricked his middle. Could his old sweetheart be taking up residence in the very town he'd been asked to minister in?

It had been four years since they'd agreed to part ways. He'd thought, then, it was for good. He drew in a breath. No matter. His feelings for Sarah were a thing of the past. His heart belonged to Becky now.

Jed's lips veered upward. "Well, now. This could be interesting."

With a shrug, Matthew forced a grin. Interesting, indeed.

Chapter Seventeen

July, 1854

BECKY LEANED her head against the windowsill, staring out into the bustling street. The schoolmaster's nasal voice droned in the background. She tuned it out, her thoughts drifting. How was Pa faring today?

Days had lapsed into weeks, with little more than frustration to show for either of them. Mr. Bennett and Mr. Whelan seemed good-natured and knowledgeable, much more interesting to listen to than Mr. O'Dell, who seemed to take great pleasure in pointing out her flaws.

Her lips curved in a slight grin. Besides, Jimmy promised to keep Pa amused. Fast friends, she and Jimmy had taken to spending time together each evening as she waited for Aunt Ellen to come for her. They often chatted beneath the sweeping branches of the oak tree out back of the building, sharing thoughts and dreams of days to come.

There, Becky described to him the miles of endless prairie grass swaying in the breeze. Her heart quickened each time she spoke of the wide array of wildflowers, trees, or animals that roamed the land she knew as home. When she closed her eyes, she could almost hear the stream rippling outside their cabin and smell the honeysuckle that lined its banks.

She breathed a quiet sigh, watching couples stroll along the busy street. Had Pastor.... Matthew made it back safely? Nearly two weeks had passed, ample time for him to return home and deliver her letters. Would he write? Twice she'd started a letter to him, only to crinkle it up. If he cared, she needed to hear it from him first.

A sudden thwack on a nearby desk jarred Becky from her reverie.

Mr. O'Dell leaned close, rapping his stick against the palm of his hand. Steely green eyes peered down at her overtop wire spectacles. His long, hooked nose flared. "Miss Hollister. Would you care to rejoin the class, or am I paying you to whittle away your time staring at passersby?"

She straightened, cheeks burning. "No, sir, I mean, yes, sir."

A chorus of giggles sounded about her. The older children had quickly picked up on her country ways, pegging her as an easy target.

"Silence." A second whack of his stick quieted the room.

Mr. O'Dell leaned against the windowsill, his pink knuckles fading to white as his bony fingers curled into fists. "Do you find my lectures boring, Miss Hollister? Perhaps you could do better."

She twisted her head from side to side, heart pounding.

The red-haired instructor's eyes narrowed. "Any more window-gazing and I'll dock you a day's wages."

Edging back, she swallowed. "Yes sir. It won't happen again."

"I expect not." His left eyebrow arched upward. "If you can't do your job, I'll find someone else who will."

"Yes, sir." She bit her lip. The thought of losing her employment was both inviting and menacing. As much as she hated to admit it, she needed this position.

With one final glare, the schoolmaster turned on his heels and strolled to the front of the room. "Please take out your McGuffey readers. We'll have silent reading the next half hour." Flipping open his pocket-watch, he gazed at it and then snapped it shut.

Becky stooped to help one of the younger children find her page, wondering how she could endure another day in this dreadful place.

THE LETTER to Becky burned in Matthew's pocket. It was time to get it sent.

He tapped his heels in Gabriel's sides, guiding him east, toward Scottsdale. Thus far, he'd had no opportunity to post the letter. For over a week now, he'd been roaming the countryside, ministering to those he'd not seen for some time and spreading the word that he'd be sending for a permanent replacement.

Before he'd left, Matthew had shared his decision to take the full-time pastor position with Jed. The whole Stanton family seemed overjoyed at the news. The Lord had opened the door, and Matthew had willingly walked through. In a matter of weeks, he'd be on his way back to Miller Creek to begin a whole new life.

A life the Lord was calling him to.

He breathed in the morning air, swaying to Gabriel's rhythmic gait. What a privilege to drink in the beauty of the vast prairie. Nothing stirred the senses like God's glorious creation. How different it was from riding through the streets of St. Louis. Becky loved the great outdoors as much as he did. How was she handling the transition?

Pulling open his vest, Matthew tucked the letter down

deeper. He must have rewritten it a dozen times to get it just so. First thing he'd do once he got to Scottsdale was stop by the post office. Letter writing wasn't the same as speaking with Becky face to face, but then a long-distance relationship had its benefits. Like Paul, in some of his letters to the churches, Matthew could be bolder in the written word than in person.

His mouth lifted. Surely by now Becky had found his note. Had she responded? He wouldn't know the answer to that until he returned to Miller Creek. Not a day passed without prayers for her and Joseph. Hopefully all was well and Joseph was making great strides with his training.

The sooner it was complete, the sooner they'd be home.

WHAT A MISERABLE WEEK. The old coot had kept her late yet again. Becky fought to catch her breath after her quick jaunt from the schoolhouse. How she missed the simplicity of home. And the people.

One person in particular.

She would never adjust to the harried pace of city life. Nor its ugliness. At least for the weekend she'd be free of Mr. O'Dell's constant scrutiny. She jiggled the coins in her pocket. Not much to show for her time and trouble. Still, it would help cover Pa's expenses, and for that she was grateful.

She bounded up the steps of the institute for the blind. With a gentle knock, she pushed through the front door. The knock was more to alert the blind students of her entering than to rally one of the workers. They'd come to expect her daily afternoon visits and rarely stopped their work to answer the door.

Peeling off her bonnet, she made her way to the craft room. The afternoon session would be nearly over by now. Sounds of spinning, caning, and carpentry poured from within as students busied themselves with their work. Becky breathed in the peacefulness of the scene. How much more pleasant the atmosphere was here than at the town school with Mr. O'Dell's constant chiding.

Roy, the large fellow Jimmy had referred to as Stump, sat slouched in the corner of the room, strumming on the tip of a reed. The mat in front of him was barely started, but already Becky could distinguish a number of mistakes. He leaned down, feeling along the floor with his hand and slid something into his pocket. A scrap of wood? What could he want with it? The boy was a bit odd, to be sure. Still, Stump seemed such a harsh nickname.

Becky's gaze fell to her father at the far end of the table, struggling to weave a strand of cane into place, his large frame looking out of place amid the children. He'd taken the news of her employment better than she'd anticipated, stating that it gave her a worthwhile way to bide her time. Little did he know how miserable she was. Nor would she tell him. He had enough burdens of his own.

Striding over, she bent to give him a peck on the cheek. "How goes it today?"

He mumbled a reply. Still struggling to complete even the simplest of tasks after two weeks' worth of attempts, his initial enthusiasm had waned, along with his spirit.

Emily, the sullen-faced little girl Becky had seen in the yard the day they'd arrived, sat across from him. In stark contrast to Roy and Pa, the young girl's nimble fingers wove wide strands of cane into a perfectly shaped basket. But, while other students chatted and worked at their leisure, Emily remained silent, intent on her weaving.

"She's very good, isn't she?" A man's low voice sounded behind Becky.

Startled, she whirled around to find Mr. Bennett. "Yes. Amazing."

He stepped up beside her, crossing his arms in front of him.

"Emily has a knack for weaving. She's been here only six weeks and has already mastered basketry."

With a nod, Becky leaned over the table. "You're doing fine work, Emily."

The young girl kept up her work, seeming oblivious to the comment. Becky turned to Mr. Bennett, wondering if Emily were deaf as well as blind.

"She heard you, but she won't speak." he mouthed softly.

He offered no explanation, and Becky didn't push for one. The girl's face carried an overwhelming sense of sorrow that echoed her own. Had she, too, lost someone dear to her? Or was it her lost eyesight she grieved?

Whatever the case, there was something tragic about her. Becky could feel it.

Pa slammed down his half-finished mat with an exasperated sigh. He leaned over, pinching the bridge of his nose. "I can't concentrate. These shadows are worse than seeing nothin' at all."

Becky slid down on the bench beside him, the angst in his voice making her heart sink. With each failed attempt, he seemed to pull deeper inside himself. Would he give up so easily? Didn't he realize going home depended on his progress? At this rate, his training would take years to complete. Home seemed but a distant memory now, a far-off dream hidden deep within.

Mr. Bennett placed a hand on Pa's shoulder, glancing down at his work. He smiled, his upturned lips partially concealed beneath his mustache and beard. "Don't be discouraged, Joseph. You're improving every day. Another week or two and you'll be ready to move on to basketry."

Pa shoved aside his less-than-perfect mat. "And where's that gonna get me? I can't make a living selling mats or baskets. Not much call for such back at Miller Creek."

Becky bit at her cheek. "Give yourself time, Pa. You've only been here a short while."

"It's a process, Joseph. You have to start simple and work

your way up to more difficult tasks. In time, you'll be ready to tackle a more suitable project." The instructor gave him a light clap on the back and moved on.

Becky handed Pa his weaving. "Please try. It's why we came."

He snatched it from her, his expression hardened. "We came for me to learn something more worthwhile than sewing reeds."

Becky bowed her head, crushed by his angry tone. In losing Ma and Melissa, had she lost him as well?

"I WARNED you he'd go through this."

Becky sighed, flattening her dress out under her as she sat beside Jimmy beneath the towering oak. "I know. But I didn't think he would take it out on me and everyone else. He's not the same. He's become harsh. Bitter."

Jimmy tugged at a blade of grass. "Your Pa's grieving the loss of his sight—something a sighted person can never fully understand, I reckon. He'll snap out of it. Eventually."

"I hope so." Jimmy couldn't know it was more than the loss of Pa's sight he grieved. As far as Becky knew, no one knew the tragic circumstances that brought them here. How she ached to speak of Ma and Melissa. Pa seemed to have stricken their names from his vocabulary, as though pressing their memories to the far recesses of his mind would erase the pain. Did he think his silence would make him forget?

Becky would never forget. At times, it seemed as though she might burst from keeping her grief pent up inside. Leaning her head against the tree, she listened to the chortle of robins and the faint whistle of a distant steamboat. The quiet evenings shared beneath the branches of the oak tree with Jimmy had become the best part of her day. A gentle breeze toyed with her hair, and she brushed a stray strand from her cheek. "Do you ever blame God?"

Jimmy creased his brow, gnawing on the grass stem. "For what?"

"For your blindness and your parents leaving?"

He gave a brief snort, emptying his mouth of the stem. "Why should I blame Him for that?"

She scuffed the heel of her tattered shoe in the dirt. "I don't know. I just figure if He's all powerful like people say, He'd be able to keep bad things from happening."

Drawing his legs to his chest, Jimmy wrapped his arms around them. "You're thinkin' of it all wrong, Beck. Scripture says, in this life we're bound to have troubles. God never promised hard times wouldn't come, only that He'd be here for us when they do."

What Jimmy said made sense, yet it didn't fully answer why God didn't intercede at times. "But how can He stand by an' watch us hurt, if He has the power to stop it?"

"I reckon He knows how to turn things around for our good." He linked his hands together behind his head and leaned against the tree. "You take my blindness and my folks leaving. I've scars from my pa whoopin' me, but I've bigger ones inside from not being wanted. Mr. Bennett an' Mr. Whelan have treated me better than my kinfolk ever did. If I hadn't been sent here, who knows what would've become of me?"

Her eyes took in his boyish features, a tinge of unease rippling through her. "But you've only a few months before you'll have to leave. What will you do then?"

With a shrug, he pursed his lips. "The Lord'll work it out, somehow."

Such simple words of faith reminded her of Matthew. He, too, saw the Lord's hand in even the bleakest of circumstances. Would she ever know such faith again?

THE FIRE POPPED and crackled as Aunt Ellen tossed another log in the fireplace.

Becky leaned back in her chair, watching Pa rock to and fro, his face ashen. She met her aunt's gaze, the discouragement in her eyes matching Becky's own.

Easing down into her upholstered chair, Aunt Ellen linked her hands together in her lap. "Well, it's certainly a treat to have you here for the weekend, Joseph. Can I get you anything?"

Pa gave a slight shake of his head and continued to rock.

Aunt Ellen raised a brow as though at a loss. "Is there anywhere you'd like to go tomorrow? Anything special you'd like to do?"

The rocking chair's steady creak remained his only answer.

Becky's chin quivered, and she fought back tears. Was it going to be like this their entire stay? Roy and Emily had been at the school several weeks longer than Pa and still made little progress—Roy refusing to try, and Emily declining to speak.

"It's been a long day. Perhaps you'll think of something in the morning." Removing the ivory combs from her hair, Aunt Ellen let her thick tresses cascade down her back.

She strolled to the bedroom, returning with a blanket and down-pillow. "I'll leave your bedding beside your chair, Joseph. Feel free to stay up as long as you wish. I'll just douse a couple of the lamps."

Becky flashed a weak smile. Her aunt was trying, that was all anyone could do.

The glow of the fire brightened against the darkened room, its amber flames lengthening and fading as Becky scooted her chair next to Pa's. Heavy silence hung between them like an unseen curtain. When had they become strangers? Her fingers skimmed the edges of Pastor Brody's Bible in her lap. "Would you like me to read to you?"

Pa shrugged, shifting his face toward her. A tear glistened in the corner of his eye, and his face held a strained expression.

Until the storm, a tear had never dampened his eye, nor had the spring left his step. Now it was as if all the fire of life had been snatched from him. Leaning forward in her chair, she placed her hand on his arm. "What's wrong, Pa?"

He turned away as if ashamed of his tears. "I'm tired's all."

There was something unsettling in his tone and a chasm between them much wider than the few inches that separated them.

He bent over and tugged at his boot, head drooped downward.

Tears stung Becky's eyes. "Please don't shut me out."

A shadow hid his face as he leaned over his empty boots. The glow of the fire faded in the stillness, casting a solemn hue over them.

Becky heaved a weary sigh. "I came so that we could be together. But right now, I feel as if we're thousands of miles apart."

He raked a hand through his hair, his strained voice finally breaking the stillness. "I-I've lost 'em, Becky. I can't picture their faces or hear their voices anymore."

There was no need to inquire who. Becky knew exactly who he meant. She, herself, found it difficult to recall her mother and sister without resurrecting images of them lying dead amid their shattered cabin. Would their memories die with them?

Pa kicked his boots aside, covering his face with his hands. "All I have is this darkness."

Becky moved toward him, tears streaming down her cheeks. His body shook under her touch as she wrapped her arms around him. The same soothing presence Becky had sensed at her loved ones' graves engulfed her. *Lord, is it You? Send your healing touch.*

With a groan, Pa lifted his hands from his face. "The years I spent memorizing every line of your ma's face, and now in a matter of weeks it's been snatched from me. As long as I had their memories, I could bear the rest. But I've not only lost my sight, I've lost everything."

"You haven't lost 'em, Pa. They're pent up inside you, same as me." Relief flooded over her as the pain festering inside her began to spill out. "Don't you see? It's not your blindness that's eating at you. It's holding in your grief. If you'd only speak of 'em now and then."

He sniffled, swiping a tear away with the back of his hand. "I can't. It hurts."

"Yes, but keeping their memories bottled inside hurts even more."

He scrubbed a hand over his face, seeming to digest her words.

Was she getting through to him? Unspoken thoughts singed her tongue, eager to voice the angst in her soul. Dare she speak what was in her heart? Her whole body trembled at the thought of voicing the truth she'd kept buried within. She drew an uneven breath. "I miss Ma and Melissa something fierce, but…I miss you even more."

His head pitched sideways, a muddled expression marring his face. "Nonsense. How could you miss me when I'm right here?"

"'Cause by shutting me out, I've lost you too." She dropped to her knees, burying her face in his lap, letting the tears flow.

Leaning over her, he kissed her hair. "I-I'm sorry. I never realized. I've been so busy grieving what I lost I forgot what I still have."

His heartfelt sobs washed over her like summer rain, soothing the emptiness inside her. Clasping his hand, she pressed it to her cheek. "Remember when you brought home that injured fawn? Ma gave you the hardest time about it. But then it was her that set its leg and cared for it those many weeks."

"Your ma had a way of sounding tough, but being soft as feather down inside."

Then he hadn't forgotten. Becky melted into his arms, all the pain of loss that for weeks had separated them now bonding them together.

"GODSPEED, PASTOR. YOU'LL BE MISSED."

Matthew circled Gabriel back to face the Laramies' cabin, lifting his hand in farewell in response to their waves. The parting was bittersweet. The family of six was his final stop prior to heading back to Miller Creek. Change was never easy. His new ministry would have its challenges and setbacks, to be sure. Still, there was a growing sense of anticipation swelling within him that couldn't be quenched.

The one aspect about heading back that had him a bit shaken was the mention of Sarah Prescott. Of course, he couldn't be sure it was her until he saw her. But something told him it was. Years ago, he'd come close to marrying the girl. But then, her true nature had emerged. Resentful of his ministry, she'd demanded more and more of his time. There'd been other instances as well. Disagreements he'd since forgotten.

They'd both been so young. Every problem had seemed larger than life. Would things have been different if he'd settled in one place back then?

Reining Gabriel westward, he pushed the thought from his mind. No sense fretting over the past. He had his future to consider.

One he hoped included Becky Hollister.

Chapter Eighteen

"WEAVING'S TRICKIER THAN I THOUGHT." Becky cocked her head to one side, holding her mat out in front of her.

Pa reached for another strand of cane, his woven mat all but complete. "How's yours coming?"

"Not bad. But yours is better." Warmth trickled through Becky as she watched him weave a final row, his fingers no longer struggling to find their place. Shades of the old Pa had begun to resurface in the week since their fireside exchange.

"Third one this week." With a grin, he laid his finished product on the table, sitting taller in his seat as he flattened it out with his hands.

Becky draped an arm over his shoulders. "I'm so proud of you."

Mr. Bennett strode over and lifted the mat from the work table. "Well done, Joseph. Your efforts have tripled this past week."

A sense of satisfaction welled within Becky. Voicing their heartaches had proven balm for their souls. Memories, once a barrier between them, now knit them together.

"You're doing so well in fact, I think we'll start you on basket weaving tomorrow."

PA GAVE A FIRM NOD. "One step closer to home."

"One step closer." With a smile, Becky brushed back a loose strand of hair. For the first time since they'd come, the return trip home seemed a bit more within reach.

Mr. Bennett gestured across the table. "In time, you'll find your niche, like Emily here. Basketry is definitely her strong suit."

The raven-haired girl across from them continued to work, her agile fingers fashioning a near flawless basket.

"Maybe she could teach Pa." Becky squatted down beside her. "Would you, Emily?"

The young girl remained ashen-faced, seemingly in a world of her own.

Becky's smile faded. The girl was impenetrable. Talent such as hers seemed ill-suited for such sorrow. What would it take to break through her silence?

Nettie appeared in the doorway, a bandanna circling her frizzed, salt-and-pepper hair. "Jimmy boy." She wrung her hands on her apron, her booming voice cutting through the chatter. "You best get out there. Mis'er Jacobs is here to pick up them there chairs o' yours."

"Yes, ma'am." Jimmy pushed aside the chair he was caning and strode toward the door.

The wood lathe's constant hum fell silent as Grant took his foot from the treadle. "I'll help."

The two boys made their way to the stack of caned chairs along the side wall. Becky could see why Jimmy had grown close to Grant. His likeable personality would be missed when he returned home. Word had it, the time would come soon. No doubt Grant's leaving would only wedge deeper the fact that

Jimmy had no place to go. Though he rarely mentioned it, Becky knew his predicament wore on him. How could it not?

Swinging her legs over the work bench, she rose to her feet, eager to meet the man who'd taken such a fancy to Jimmy's work. "I'll be back, Pa. I wanna see how Jimmy makes out."

With a nod, her father reached for another strand of cane.

Becky held the front door open for the relay of workers transporting chairs to the awaiting wagon. Within minutes, all twenty seats were secured in the back of Mr. Jacobs' wagon bed. The store-owner chatted with Jimmy as Grant and Mr. Bennett returned inside. Slight of build, Mr. Jacobs stood head to head with Jimmy. The man's thin, oval face held a good-natured smile. Thinning, strawberry blond hair combed neatly to the side helped to conceal a bare spot atop his head.

A light breeze tousled Becky's hair as she leaned against the porch railing swathed with ivy. Late spring had given way to summer, the tender leaves now fully grown, and the apple blossoms had long since withered to make room for fruit.

Straining to hear the vigorous conversation, Becky gleaned only muffled words and pleasant sounding voices. At last, the proprietor reached in his pocket, taking out a stack of bills. With a shake of Jimmy's hand, Mr. Jacobs passed him a portion of the money.

Becky smiled to herself. Her friend had worked hard to complete this order for the school's most prominent buyer. He'd done himself proud.

As Jimmy turned and started toward the school, Mr. Jacobs donned his hat and climbed aboard the wagon. There was something unsettling in Jimmy's slow, uneven pace. Instead of his usual spirited gait, he swaggered with each step, his stunned expression resembling that of an animal caught in a trap.

Becky downed the steps and touched a hand to his arm. "Jimmy, what's wrong?"

He held out the wad of bills. "He gave me a sighted person's wage, and he wants ten more chairs next month."

She glanced at the money in his hand—income which would ensure Jimmy could remain at the school a while longer. "That's wonderful."

Jimmy straightened, seeming to recover from his daze. "Course, most of the money will go to the school."

"What'll you do with the rest?"

He rolled his shoulders. "Reckon I'll hang onto it till I need it."

She tugged at his shirtsleeve. "Why not start with some new clothes? These worn-out shirt and trousers have had their day."

"What, these?" Jimmy pulled at his too-short pant legs. "Why, they've lots of wear left in 'em."

With a shake of her head, Becky looped her arm through his. There was much more to Jimmy than the clothes on his back. If only someone outside this place could catch a glimpse of his true worth.

BECKY DREDGED her bread over her plate, soaking up remnants of beef stew. She wiped her mouth, chewing the last savory bite. She had to admit, Nettie's cooking rivaled her ma's. Mr. Bennett had been right in saying the robust black woman was the heart and soul of the school. From cook to nursemaid to seamstress, Nettie took care of all the nurturing needs of the students. Her endless energy and spunk kept both students and instructors on their toes…with few exceptions.

Seated at the far end of the table, Emily picked haphazardly at her food. With a sigh, Becky leaned toward Jimmy, her hushed tone obscured by the surrounding chatter. "Is Emily always so quiet?"

He shifted his food to one side of his mouth. "Hasn't uttered a word since she got here. She's no dummy, though, you can wager on that."

"She's so gifted. It's like she funnels all her energy into her work, like she has nothing else." Perhaps she didn't. Who knew what tragedy had compelled her to silence?

"It's just her way of grieving. She and Stump choose to shut everyone out and keep to themselves. Others get angry and lash out at people—even God."

Jimmy's pointed statement nettled Becky. Hadn't she done just that—lashed out at God, blaming Him for her sorrows? Perhaps that's why she sensed a kinship with Emily, as if drawing the girl out might somehow heal her own inner wounds. "Do you know anything about her? Her family? Where she came from?"

"Not really." Jimmy swigged the last of his water, then set his empty glass on the table. "Far as I know she's never had any visitors."

Becky shifted her gaze to the large boy at the opposite end of the table. "What about Roy?"

"Stump? He's had one. Some fellow named Lon. His uncle, I think."

She watched Roy finish off a second helping of stew. "Too bad he doesn't put as much energy into his work as he does eating."

A tap on the front door quieted the mealtime chatter. Mr. Bennett excused himself and went to greet the visitor. A woman's laughter sounded in the hallway. A moment later, Mr. Bennett returned, Aunt Ellen at his side.

"It's Aunt Ellen." Becky's heart sank. Her aunt had never come this early before.

Pa's eyebrows raised in question. "So early?"

Her aunt's dress rustled as she made her way toward them. Stooping to kiss Pa's cheek, she uttered a cheery "hello".

"Everything all right?"

"Just fine." She turned to Becky. "My sewing machine is in need of repair, so they let me leave early."

Becky tugged at a loose thread on her sleeve, trying to conceal her disappointment. Not that she didn't enjoy her aunt's company, but to leave early would cheat Becky out of her time with Pa and Jimmy.

Mr. Bennett stepped up beside Aunt Ellen, his gaze locked on her face. "Have you eaten, Miss Hollister? If not, perhaps you'd join us."

She flashed a warm grin. "Why, that would be lovely. Thank you."

The unexpected invitation revitalized Becky. Perhaps she could stay a while after all.

"Bring another plate for Miss Hollister," Mr. Whelan called to Nettie.

Nettie appeared in the kitchen doorway, a smile over-spreading her round face. "Yes'r. Comin' right up." Taking a clean plate from the cupboard, she brought it to the table. "Mighty tickled ya came along, Miss Ellen. You is just the one to finish off this here stew."

Aunt Ellen's eyes sparkled as she scraped the remaining stew onto her plate. "This smells heavenly. You don't know what a treat it is not to have to go home and eat my cooking."

Nettie gave a hearty chuckle. "'Tis a pleasure to cook for someone who truly appreciates it, Miss Ellen." She cast Mr. Bennett a sideways glance, nose bent upward as she headed back to the kitchen.

"Why, thank you, Nettie." A coy grin lit Aunt Ellen's face as she dipped her spoon in the stew.

A bit flushed, Mr. Bennett took a seat beside her. "It often takes an outsider to remind us how invaluable Nettie is to us."

She poked her head through the doorway. "Mmm-hmm. An' don't you forget it."

He brushed a hand over his beard. "Nothing escapes her either."

"May we be excused?" a soprano voice called beside him.

He patted young Amos on the back. "Yes. You students may go."

A clatter of dishes and shuffling feet filled the dining room. Becky rose from the bench, eager to spend a few quiet moments outside beneath the towering oak. "Coming, Jimmy?"

"Cain't. It's my night to help with dishes." His low tone hinted of disappointment.

"Oh." Becky's mouth twisted. Each student, in turn, had the job of helping Nettie clean up after a meal.

Aunt Ellen finished a bite of stew and wiped the corners of her mouth with her napkin. "You two go on. I'll help Nettie with dishes. It's the least I can do."

"I'll not argue with that." Jimmy swiveled on the bench and stood. "Much obliged, Miss Ellen."

A gentle smile lit Aunt Ellen's face. Kindness seemed to flow through her as easily as water from a brook. Even Mr. Bennett's eyes seemed to glow with admiration.

Nodding her thanks, Becky trailed after Jimmy, pricked by her aunt's generosity. In the weeks since their arrival, not once had Becky thought to offer her help to the overworked caregiver.

Ma would be sore ashamed.

With a backward glance, Becky was stricken by the intense joy on her aunt's face. Perhaps it was time for Becky to shed her self-centeredness and, like Aunt Ellen, start giving of herself.

Chapter Nineteen

BECKY REACHED in her lunch pail and pulled out a shiny red apple. Such a treat was a rarity back at Miller Creek. Most prairie apples were cooked to applesauce or squeezed into cider. Here she could have one most any day. Aunt Ellen seemed to enjoy pampering her. It would be hard to leave her when they returned home. But not this place, this job…or Mr. O'Dell.

The sound of the students playing droned around her. It was a wonder they could find anything to be cheerful about. Unlike country schools, town schools held class nearly year around. And with an instructor like Mr. O'Dell, each day seemed to crawl at a snail's pace.

She leaned against the cottonwood tree and bit into her apple. Slipping a folded note from her pocket, she read it for the fourth or fifth time, every line a treasure.

"Dear Joseph and Becky,

Hope this finds you well. Pastor Brody delivered your note. Rest assured, Becky.

All is forgiven. Though you did give your Aunt Clara a few gray hairs. Not much news to share. Rain is scarce, but the crops are finding moisture deep down. Your cabin is sealed up tight and waiting for your return. The Lord keep you both well and safe. Let us hear from you.

Jed and Clara

Nugget sends his regards. He misses you, as do I.

Esther"

Becky smiled as she refolded the letter and slid it in her pocket. It was so good to hear news from home. Had it only been a few weeks since they'd left? It seemed an eternity. She took another bite of her apple, her mind drifting over the miles.

That they'd received her letters assured Becky that Matthew had arrived home safely. Just the thought of him stirred forgotten feelings. Her face warmed. It seemed so strange to refer to him by his given name. Why hadn't he written? Perhaps he didn't care for her after all.

The school bell sounded. With a sigh, Becky gathered up her things and brushed crumbs from her skirt. Noonings always flew by in a flash.

A cluster of young children scurried past, in a much greater hurry than Becky to resume classes. As she started up the schoolhouse steps, Mr. O'Dell peered at his open pocket watch. With a final tug on the bell rope, he cast a penetrating stare in her direction. "Hurry along, Miss Hollister. A teacher's assistant should be in ahead of students."

"Yes sir." She quickened her pace, averting her eyes as she passed him by. It seemed she could never quite please him. Either he complained of her being too slow, too distracted, or just plain ignorant of city school ways.

How she wished she could forego this awful place. Now that Pa was progressing, hopefully it would be only a matter of months before they could return to the prairie.

One thing was certain—going home couldn't come soon enough.

BECKY SAT alongside the small group of younger students in the back corner of the school building and listened to each of them read in turn from their McGuffey readers. It was the only truly enjoyable segment of the school day, free of Mr. O'Dell's scrutiny. She might even come to relish teaching, if it weren't for the instructor's reproving ways.

Much of the time, she could tune out the voices of the older children as they stood one by one and read for Mr. O'Dell. But when he called for Lena Connors to read, Becky's stomach clenched. Though gifted at ciphering and reciting, when it came to reading, the letters seemed to jumble up, causing Lena to stumble and stutter. Her attempts were always sure to garner a sharp tongue-lashing from Mr. O'Dell.

Out of the corner of her eye, Becky watched the girl slowly rise to her feet, holding the reader in both hands. "A cer-tain Pur...zian of dis...tinc...tion had for man-y ye-ars been ex...treem...ly an...kcious..."

"Stop!" Mr. O'Dell smacked his stick on the edge of his desk, silencing not only Lena, but the younger readers as well. He leaned against the front of his desk, ankles crossed, with a gnarled sneer on his face. "How old are you, Miss Connors?"

"Twelve."

"Twelve." His demeaning tone matched the look of scorn in his eyes. "And yet, each time I call on you, you read no better than a child of six."

The girl's eyes bulged as if she'd swallowed an onion. "I'm sorry. The letters just run together and get all mixed up in my head."

"Then unscramble them, you facetious girl."

Lena stared down at her feet, chin trembling. In a matter of words, the stern instructor had succeeded in again destroying any confidence the girl had bolstered. It was all Becky could to do sit by and watch.

He edged toward Lena. "Obviously, you've been dawdling away your study time."

"No, sir. I haven't."

He tapped at her book with his stick. "Then read. Fluently, as you should, or feel my strap across your hands."

Burning welled in Becky's throat as Lena struggled to find her voice. Why must he be so harsh? No child would purposely defy such a request. The girl seemed sincere in her inability. Punishment would only add shame to her predicament.

"I can't." Lena gasped, crumpling onto her seat.

The instructor's mouth grew taut. "Then hold out your hands."

Snapping her reader shut, Becky rose to her feet. Over recent weeks, she'd endured his cruel remarks and watched him incur unjust punishments on the children. Well, no more. Come what may, she couldn't sit idly by and watch this sweet young girl punished for something she had no control over. "Perhaps I could work with Lena and help her gain mastery of sounds and letters."

Mr. O'Dell glared at her. "I don't recall asking your input here, Miss Hollister. The girl's lazy, and must be punished."

"I don't believe laziness has anything to do with it." All eyes trained on her as she faced the schoolmaster in the center aisle. "The girl obviously needs individualized instruction which she hasn't received."

The instructor's eyes narrowed. "Are you suggesting I'm not doing my job properly?"

"Merely that you're misjudging the girl."

"Such insolence. You forget your place, Miss Hollister."

Sweat lined Becky's palms, and she worked to steady trembling hands. No one moved or uttered a sound. Heat rose in her cheeks. Should she yield and cower like a frightened mouse to preserve her position? To back down now would only squelch all she'd set out to accomplish.

Tears glistened in Lena's eyes, her expression a mixture of gratitude and fear—all Becky needed to sway her to hold to her convictions. She squared her shoulders, returning her gaze to Mr. O'Dell. "I only know this, sir. You'll never teach anyone by brow-beating them."

The instructor's face flamed red and his mouth pulsated as though about to erupt. He stepped toward her, talking through clenched teeth. "You may gather your things, Miss Hollister. You're discharged."

She hesitated, casting a wary glance at Lena. What would happen to the girl in Becky's absence?

Thrusting out his arm, Mr. O'Dell pointed toward the door. "Out."

With a slight nod, Becky turned to leave, haunted by the thought she'd just put an end to Pa's training.

PA SAT FORWARD in his chair. "You've been dismissed?"

Becky winced at the tension in his voice. She'd waited as far into the evening as she could to broach the issue, when most of the students had retired indoors. Soon Aunt Ellen would arrive. Would she, too, be disappointed?

Becky leaned her head against the porch rail. "I'm sorry, but I couldn't bear to stand by and see that girl punished needlessly."

Pa rubbed a hand over his face. "It's all right. We'll figure something out."

"The thing is, I truly enjoyed helping the students."

"Maybe Ellen will know of another similar position."

"Perhaps." Becky's stomach tightened. Would another place of employment be any different? She dreaded the thought of even trying. But what choice did she have? They needed the income.

Pa was too proud to accept a handout. As much as she longed to return home, even more now, she wanted Pa to have the chance to complete his training. He'd just begun to make progress. If they were forced to leave, the trip would have been for nothing.

The front door creaked opened, and Mr. Bennett stepped out onto the porch. He clasped the railing with both hands, eyes searching the street.

Heavy silence fell between them. Eventually, he and Mr. Whelan would have to be told. But for now, Becky would just as soon keep the situation private.

Mr. Bennett cleared his throat. "I...uh...couldn't help but overhear." He pointed over his shoulder at the sitting room's open window.

Becky's cheeks burned. She lowered her gaze, hoping the fading light of evening masked her embarrassment.

Pa creased his brow. "If you're worried we'll not have the funds to pay..."

"That's not my concern. In fact, I may have a solution."

Becky rested her hands on the back of Pa's chair. "What do you mean?"

Mr. Bennett turned toward them, crossing his arms over his chest. "As I'm sure you're aware, it's all Mr. Whelan, Nettie, and I can do to keep up around here. We've more students eager to come, but as things are, we're forced to decline them."

Becky's heart hammered. Was he insinuating Pa should leave so that others could come?

Pa scratched at his chin. "What are you saying?"

"Simply put, with a little extra help, we might be able to handle more students." The instructor's eyes shifted to Becky. "You've shown genuine interest in the students here, Becky.

Would you consider helping out days, in exchange for your father's continued training?"

Becky stared at him, trying to decipher if he was in earnest. "You mean teach?"

Mr. Bennett sunk his hands in his pockets. "Not the classes, per se, but if you'd be willing to learn raised lettering and some of the craft work, yes, in your own unique way, you'd be helping instruct the students...as well as sharing Nettie's load."

"But you said there was no room for me."

"As a boarder, no. You'd still need to stay nights with Ellen...uh...your aunt. But otherwise, any help you can give throughout the day would be appreciated."

Pa raked a hand through his chestnut hair, his voice hedged with uncertainty. "You sure you're not just bailing us out of a tough spot?"

"I wouldn't offer if I didn't feel she would be an asset to us." He turned his gaze back on Becky. "Does that sound agreeable?"

Not only would the arrangement allow Pa to complete his training and give them more time together, it would provide her a sense of usefulness in an atmosphere she could enjoy. It seemed too good to be true.

Her mouth tipped upward. "I'd be honored."

THE POUNDING of a mallet alerted Matthew to the new building being constructed on the outskirts of Miller Creek. The town had nearly doubled in size over the past year. That alone insured his time here would be well spent. With everything squared away at Scottsdale and Palmer, he had only to find a place to live and spread the word that he was here to stay.

He guided Gabriel through town, tipping his hat to those he passed. Most he knew, while a few faces he didn't recognize. A deep satisfaction settled over him. *The harvest is plentiful.* With the Lord's blessing, soon the church pews could be filled to the brim.

A dark-haired woman stood at the top of the schoolhouse steps. Though Matthew couldn't make out the teacher's face, her frame and mannerisms seemed strangely familiar.

His stomach churned. Could it be Sarah?

Students toting lunch tins and books spilled from within, several of them waving to him as they set off on their trek home. He smiled and nodded, bringing Gabriel to a halt outside the building. Dismounting, he scanned the street for signs of Jed and other prominent church members who'd agreed to meet with him. A glance at his pocket watch assured him he was a tad early. Surely they'd be along in a bit.

He ventured another look at the woman, but ducked his head when she glanced his way. Looping the reins over the hitching post, he tensed at the click of shoes on the steps above him.

"Matthew?" The woman's soft voice was unmistakable.

He turned, drinking in Sarah's familiar dark eyes and rich smile. The face was the same delicate oval, yet more mature, her brunette hair twisted in a loose bun instead of flowing free. "Sarah?" Then it was her. He stepped toward her, a rush of emotions coursing through him.

"My, it's been a long time. You've not changed a bit." She reached to clasp his hands. Her high-necked white shirt high-lighted her regal neck, just as her banded skirt accentuated the smallness of her waist.

He shrugged a shoulder. "A mite more saddle worn perhaps."

With a light chuckle, she released her hold on his hands. "Well, just the same, it's great to see you again."

"What brings you to Miller Creek?"

"Oh, I tired of the harsh Minnesota winters. When I saw the opening for this post, I nabbed it. Now that you're here, I'm ever so glad I did."

The intensity of her stare brought warmth to his cheeks. Had she sought him out? She couldn't have. Other than to know he pastored in the area. She seemed pleasant enough. Had she put the past to rest?

"Sounds like we'll be seeing a lot of each other. I hear you've put in for full-time ministry here."

"Yes. I'm to meet with some of the elders shortly. I hope you don't mind sharing your school building."

"Not at all. I look forward to such an arrangement." She edged closer, her gaze fastened on his.

He tugged at his shirt collar, trying to ignore the steady beat drumming in his ears. Such boldness in her gaze. Was she trying to wiggle her way back into his affections already? Well, he was wise to her.

"I see you two found each other." Engrossed in his thoughts, Matthew hadn't realized Jed had ridden up beside them.

"Yes." He cleared his throat, putting more distance between himself and Sarah.

Dismounting, Jed cast a glance in their direction. "Miss Prescott indicated you once knew each other quite well."

"Reckon we did." Matthew could only hope the heat in his cheeks wasn't registering on his face.

"Should've seen her face light up when I told her you'd be with us full time from now on."

Matthew gave a nervous laugh. The thought was almost enough to alter his plans. But then, he couldn't let himself be ramrodded out of his place of ministry. He'd simply do his best to keep his distance.

Others started to gather, and Sarah slipped on her bonnet. "Well, I'll just go collect my things and leave you gentlemen to your work." She started up the steps then turned, eyes trained on Matthew. "Now that you're here, Matthew, I hope you'll call on me from time to time. I'm eager to get reacquainted."

With a nod, he tipped his hat to her. If Becky hadn't already won his affections, he'd find such an invitation appealing. But as things were, he had no call to bolster closeness with this lady from his past.

It could only spell trouble.

As she disappeared inside the building, Jed smiled, a bit of humor in his voice. "Well now, there's a pretty prospect for a preacher looking to set up house."

Matthew knit his brow. His friend was trifling where he shouldn't. He had no qualms about associating with Sarah, so long as she didn't get any womanly notions.

Chapter Twenty

BECKY SKIRTED around the onslaught of people on her six-block trek to the Missouri Institution for the Blind. A soft breeze made the warm August morning more bearable. Lightness filtered through her, as if a terrible weight had been lifted. To be allowed to not only spend more time with Pa, but to be asked to help with the students, was indeed a blessing. In the bleakest of circumstances, she finally had a ray of sunlight to cling to. No more dreading Mr. O'Dell's tongue-lashings or potent stares. At last, her stay in the city would prove more tolerable.

How she longed to share this moment with Matthew. Despite the fact she'd not heard from him, she ached to write him. How long did it take to receive a letter across state? A week? Two? Had he sent one and it not yet arrived? Regardless, she couldn't abide waiting much longer.

The crowd thinned as she neared the building. Faint sounds of music poured from within. How nice that she'd finally get to experience the entire school day routine. In time, she'd discern how to make herself useful. But for now, she had some learning of her own to do.

A sour fiddle note split the air, followed by a choppy melody. If only Pa would be willing to try again. How he used to make his fiddle sing on long, winter evenings around the fireplace. Now the instrument lay cold and silent beneath her cousin's bed back home. Would its strings ever clip out a lively tune again? It must've been spared the storm for some reason. Perhaps Matthew would send it at her request. If nothing else, it would give her an excuse to write him.

With a wistful sigh, she knocked on the front door.

A moment later, it creaked open and Nettie smiled out at her. "Come on in, honey-child. Mis'er Peter told me you'd be a'comin'."

A travel bag rested inside the door. "Is someone leaving?"

"Sure enough. Grant's folks are t' be here shortly."

Becky twisted her mouth to one side. "How did Jimmy take the news?"

With a shake of her head, Nettie pursed her lips. "That poor child. Took it mighty hard, I fear. Made himself scarce right after he heared. Said he needed some time to his self."

If Jimmy were upset, he'd most likely take solace beneath the lofty boughs of the oak tree. Becky edged back onto the porch. "I've gotta go."

"But you only just got here, young'un. Where ya headed?"

Not taking time to answer, Becky downed the porch steps. With quick strides, she rounded the corner of the school, slowing at sight of Jimmy's familiar short pant-legs stretched out beneath the tall oak. She slid down beside him, heart-sore at his red-blotched eyes. His life had been a series of goodbyes, with no permanent home or family to call his own.

A song sparrow's sweet tune pealed overhead, loud against the faint rumblings of the city. Lifting her eyes heavenward, Becky peered through the spattering of oak leaves to a slice of blue sky above. *Lord, I don't ask this for myself, but for Jimmy's sake. Give me words to comfort my friend.*

A gentle breeze caressed her cheeks, and she turned to

Jimmy, placing a hand on his arm. "Sorry about Grant leaving. I know how close you are."

He dug his boot heel into the sod, swiping a tear from his cheek. "Never even told me he was leavin' today. Just packed up his bags and is off."

"He prob'ly couldn't bear to tell you, is all."

"If he was any sort of friend, he would've." His jaw hardened.

Becky nudged him with her shoulder. "Don't you think he knows how hard it is for you?"

With a shrug, he drew his legs to his chest.

She leaned closer, softness edging out the candor in her words. "Are you sore at him for not telling you or for leaving you behind?"

Jimmy's head drooped downward, his blond curls draped over his eyes. "Both, I reckon."

If comfort was her aim, she seemed to be failing miserably. How could she convince him she understood? She tamped down the tightness in her chest. Perhaps sharing the extent of her own loss would better help him manage his.

"It's hard saying goodbye to someone you care about. But, believe me, it's even harder not to have the chance to say goodbye." Her voice quivered, and she cleared her throat. Sharing good memories with Pa proved much easier than resurrecting the hurtful ones.

His head lifted slightly, but he gave no answer.

She drew an uneven breath, moisture gathering in her eyes. "You see, the storm that blinded Pa...killed my ma and little sister. There was no chance to say goodbye."

Jimmy straightened, the tautness of his face deepening. "Ah, Beck." He wrapped his arms around her, pulling her close. "Why didn't you tell me?"

She rested her head in the nook of his shoulder, his breath

warm against her cheek. "All this time I've been angry with God for what happened, wondering why He didn't intervene."

"Seems God often gets the blame when things go wrong. But, He's a big God…and a forgiving One."

Becky closed her eyes, dampening Jimmy's shirt with her tears. "I used to believe that, but anymore I don't know. I can't feature how a loving God could let His people suffer."

With a sigh, Jimmy leaned his chin on her head. "He may not take away the pain, but He knows how to work through it. Take Grant leaving. God knew I'd need some comfort about now, so He sent me you."

Becky blinked back moisture. Had the Lord truly sent her here? Looking back, she could see His hand at work, even in the midst of the maelstrom. The stubborn barn door that kept her from harm's way. Matthew's nearness following the storm. Doc Pruitt's skilled care and sound advice. Anger had blinded her to such blessings. "You mean, instead of dwelling on our troubles, we're to look for ways God's working through them."

"There's a blessing in every hardship, if we look hard enough."

Flecks of sunlight danced on the ground about them as a gentle breeze toyed with branches overhead. Becky dried her eyes, her wounded heart growing lighter. How was it her prayers to console Jimmy had, in turn, brought her comfort?

The sound of an approaching horse and buggy drew her attention to the street.

Jimmy loosened his hold. "That Grant's folks?"

"Looks that way."

Rising, Jimmy held out his hand. "Well, come on then. Enough sittin' around feeling sorry for ourselves. We've some well-wishing to do."

With a grin, Becky placed her hand in his. Perhaps God had a plan in them coming after all.

BECKY SET her wooden awl aside with a sigh, sliding her sheet of raised dots from her slate. Another flawed attempt. Closing her eyes, she ran her fingers over each cluster of raised dots on her paper, peeking at her letter chart when she came to one she didn't recognize. With a shake of her head, she glanced at the handful of blind students in the room. Creating the raised lettering was challenging, even for her. How could a sightless person learn it?

Emily pored over her paper, raven-black hair draped over her face. As usual, Roy slumped forward in his chair, making no attempt to fill his page. In the lax atmosphere of late summer, more seasoned students were allowed to spend a few precious weeks at home with family. Why had no one come for them?

Did they, like Jimmy, have no place to call home?

Heaviness tugged at her heart. With Jimmy's nineteenth birthday just months away, there seemed little hope of him finding a home. If only there was a way she could help. Perhaps someone from the church would take him in. But who?

Rising, she took her slate and completed page to Mr. Bennett. He scanned her work. "Very nice, Becky. You're making progress."

With a wry grin, she pointed over her shoulder with her thumb. "Little Amos over there has a better handle on it than I do."

The instructor eased back in his chair. "Give yourself time. It's only been a little over a week. By summer's end, this will be like a second language to you."

"I don't know about that."

He handed back her slate, his voice tentative. "Would you mind helping Roy with his?"

Roy was the one person she had surpassed in skill. Yet any attempts to help him had proven fruitless. It seemed a waste of time trying. Still, she couldn't let him get the notion everyone had given up on him. With a shrug, she breathed a determined huff. "I'll try."

She strode toward Roy, tightness gripping her throat. The boy's large frame was intimidating to say the least. The worst he could do was ignore her...or throw her across the room.

With a deep breath, she gave her sleeves a firm tug. "Can I help you, Roy?"

He cocked his head, but made no reply.

Becky cringed at the mass of jumbled holes and misplaced dots on his page. Even if he did let her help, would he have the gumption to improve? She squared her shoulders. "Which letter are you ready for?"

He scrunched deeper in his seat and crossed his arms in front of him. Not the response Becky was hoping for. She pressed her lips together, eyes narrowing. The boy was more bull-headed than anything. How could she make him understand she wanted to help?

Bending down, she lowered her voice. "I know you think everyone's against you, and I don't blame you for being angry. But if you don't try, you're becoming just what they say."

"But I can't see!" He shoved his desk forward, spilling his slate and stylus on the floor.

Becky blew out a puff of air. Some help she was proving. All she'd done so far is anger him. She caught Mr. Bennett's reassuring nod. Apparently, he had more faith in her than she had in herself.

Becky slid the desk back into place and pulled a chair up next to Roy. "If there's one thing I've learned since coming here, it's that blindness isn't so much a hindrance as it is an opportunity to learn new ways of doing things."

Gathering his paper and slate, she handed him the awl. "Give it a try."

Roy hesitated and then coiled his fingers around the instrument. With slow, careful punches, he formed a clumsy symbol of an R, followed by a misshapen O and Y.

"Roy. Good." Becky drew in a breath, the corners of her mouth lifting.

It was a start.

"A-MEN." Matthew peered out at the congregation at the close of his prayer. Not every seat was filled. There was room for growth, to be sure. But sprinkled among the crowd were faces of people he hadn't met. A good sign. He'd make a point to pay the newcomers a visit over the coming weeks.

He closed his Bible and ran his fingertips over its cover. He'd floundered a bit leafing through its stiff pages, yet knowing Becky held his old Bible made it well worth the trouble. A smile tugged at his lips. Was she making good use of it?

Clutching the Bible in his hand, he stepped from the pulpit. "I've been informed by the womenfolk there's to be a luncheon following next Sunday's service. I hope everyone will plan to attend."

A low hum of conversation rippled through the crowd as he made his way down the center aisle. Propping open the door, Matthew stood beside it, awaiting the line of people forming inside. As the congregation filtered past, he shook each hand with a smile. What a privilege to see so many gathered in a single place of worship.

Among the first to greet him, Jed and Clara Stanton paused beside him. Jed pumped Matthew's hand up and down, his firm grip and calloused hand hinting of hard work. "Sure is great to have you here, preacher."

"It's a blessing to be here. Thanks for putting me up this past week and for the fine victuals."

Clara reached to straighten her bonnet. "A barn's hardly much of a place to put you up."

"If a stable was good enough for the Christ-child, it's more than sufficient for me."

Jed gave a loud chuckle. "Just the same, there's a cabin right outside of town that might suit you better. The old Pratt place. Been sitting empty a couple years. The church has agreed to pay the down payment on it for you. If you wanna take a gander at it, I'd be glad to ride along."

Though the Stantons' hospitality had been first rate, the thought of his own homestead sounded appealing. "How's tomorrow morning suit you?"

With a nod, Jed clapped him on the shoulder. "Tomorrow morning it is."

Clara glanced at the swelling train of people behind them and nudged Jed forward. "We'll see you for lunch later, pastor?"

"Sure thing."

As the line pressed forward, Matthew caught a glimpse of Sarah Prescott edging closer. He'd done his best to avoid her, but he had no choice but to greet her now. Why was her presence here so disturbing? Was it the memories she resurrected? Or something more?

He braced himself as she strolled up beside him. "Wonderful sermon, Matthew." With a smile, she slid her fingers onto his. "I'd forgotten what a powerful speaker you can be."

"Thank you, Miss Prescott."

Her head tilted, and she gave his fingers a gentle squeeze. "Why so formal? I've always been Sarah to you before."

"Time has a way of—distancing people." He drew his hand away, shifting his eyes side-to-side. Anyone listening might conclude they were more familiar with each other than he cared to admit. Thankfully, those within earshot appeared engaged in conversation.

She took a step closer, voice soft. "Then I hope we'll have the chance to get reacquainted. Would you join me for lunch?"

The years had intensified her boldness. Never had Matthew been more pleased to have a viable excuse. "I'm afraid the Stantons are expecting me."

Her face pinched. "Well then, I'll expect to share a piece of my apple pie with you next Sunday."

His favorite. Had she remembered? He cleared his throat. "I'll try to do that."

"I'll look forward to it." Her fawn-like eyes held his for a moment before she moved on.

Though the tension in his shoulders lessened, a nervous twinge pricked his middle. What was he to do with this dark-eyed beauty that seemed intent on worming her way back into his heart?

Chapter Twenty-One

Becky dipped the masher in the huge pot of boiled potatoes. "Sure takes a heap of food to feed this bunch."

"More all the time, child." Nettie tapped her long-handled spoon against the side of the gravy pan, wiping sweat beads from her temples. "Thought things'd slow up a bit once Angelina and Grant left. Now, we've three new ones to take their place. Twelve students. Lord, have mercy."

"Mr. Bennett and Mr. Whelan have a hard time saying no, I think."

"Mmm hmm. You've got that right." The heavy-set woman took a head of lettuce from the icebox and plopped it on the countertop with a chuckle. "They'z softer than a couple of goose-down pillows."

A smile tugged at Becky's lips. It was that "softness" that had persuaded the instructors to go out of their way to accommodate her father. For that, she was grateful. Pouring milk onto the potatoes, Becky pumped the wooden masher. "Hope you don't mind me underfoot. As long as I'm here, I hope to make myself useful."

The woman's dark skin offset the whites of her eyes as she

stared back at Becky. "You, honey child? Why, you've been a God-send these past couple weeks. I'z tickled to have ya."

Becky sprinkled salt on the potatoes. It was good to feel needed, even if it involved cooking. Ma would be proud.

Nettie hummed as she chopped at the lettuce. There was something soothing in the poignant pitch of her voice. Becky had to admit, Nettie made kitchen work almost tolerable. Encased within the woman's blunt exterior rested a heart of gold.

Becky gave the potatoes a final stir. "How did you come to work here, Nettie?"

"Well now, me an' Mis'er Eli goes way back. My momma was slave to his folks. He an' I was like brother an' sister growin' up. Him bein' blind since birth, he never cared I was a colored child." She doubled over in laughter, slapping her hands against her thighs. "We was jus' two carefree young'uns didn't know no better."

Becky swiped her finger through the potatoes for a taste and added another pinch of salt. "So, when he started this school, he asked you to come work for him?"

Nettie's cleaver ceased chopping, and she straightened, a far off-look in her eye. "Mis'er Eli's papa freed my momma an' sister an' me jus' b'fore he died an' asked her to care for Mis'er Eli." She waved a hand in the air. "Weren't nobody standin' in line to care for no awkward blind boy."

A lump caught in Becky's throat, her thoughts turning to Jimmy. Would anyone ever be willing to open their heart to him? He so wanted a family.

Nettie resumed chopping. "When Mama passed on several years back, I took her place as Mis'er Eli's caregiver." She lifted her head, dark eyes penetrating. "Won't never leave him, neither. Mighty beholden to him an' his papa. Freedom's a grand privilege for folks like me nowadays."

Boot steps sounded outside the kitchen. Turning, Becky saw Mr. Bennett flipping through a handful of letters. He leaned against the doorframe, turning one of the letters side to side. "This one appears to have made some detours along the way. Its direction is smudged, but I can see it originated in Illinois." He arched a brow. "Does the name Matthew Brody ring a bell?"

Becky drew in a breath and dropped her masher. It took great restraint not to rush over and snatch the coveted letter from Mr. Bennett's hand. Instead, she nodded, trying to contain the smile itching to break out on her face.

She edged closer, arm outstretched. With a smile, he placed the letter in her palm. Was it real? She'd waited so long. "Nettie, could I…"

The dark-skinned woman flapped her hands at Becky. "You go on, honey child. Take all da time you needs."

Becky made her way to the sitting room, never once taking her eyes from Matthew's name penned in the corner. Sliding down in a chair, she glanced over the address. While her name remained legible, water stains had smeared much of the address beyond recognition. Multiple postmarks traced it back over three weeks.

And all this time she'd feared he'd forgotten her.

She toyed with the wax seal. Surely it wouldn't hurt to read through it herself first, then share it with Pa. Just in case it contained any…private matters. Her heart drummed faster as she pried it open and unfolded the single sheet of paper.

She swept her thumb over the greeting, drinking in each word. Such fine penmanship.

"Dear Joseph and Becky,

Sorry for not writing sooner. I had no opportunity to post a letter my first weeks back. I've thought of you many times since we parted. Our journey together remains foremost in my mind. The trip home was a lonely one indeed."

A sigh escaped Becky. Was he missing her still?

"I wanted to share with you some exciting news. For some time, I've sensed the Lord pulling me to pastor a single congregation. When I returned home, I was asked to do just that. By the time you return, I'll be settled and ministering full-time at Miller Creek. I pray this comes as welcome news."

Becky's lips turned upward in a satisfied smile. How wonderful. She would be sure to write and let him know just how pleased she was.

"I pray you're safe and holding fast to God's promises. He is near; hold onto Him. I know the weeks and months will seem long until your return, but the Lord will see you through. You are sorely missed by your kinfolk, the community, and myself.

I look forward to your safe and prompt return."

Matthew

Becky's face warmed as her gaze drifted to a second note at the bottom of the page.

"Dearest Becky,

It's my prayer that you've found peace with God within the pages of His Word. My new Bible is a bit green yet, but my thoughts turn to you each time I open its pages. It does my heart good to know my timeworn Bible lies within your reach. I hope to spend much time with you upon your return. I look forward to that day with great joy.

God bless you, dear one."

Dear one. The words were enough to convince her that his feelings held more than a mere pastor's concern. At last, she had something definite to go on, a glimpse into Matthew's heart. Tonight, she'd do her best to pen a response that would give him the same reassurance, and she would mail it at first opportunity.

She held the letter to her chest, melting down in the chair. Home never sounded so good.

"THAT ALL HE HAD TO SAY?"

Becky leaned against the porch rail, staring at the note in her hand. How could she share more with Pa without raising suspicions of why she hadn't read the entire letter? "Oh. Well, he mentions about breaking in his new Bible toward the end, but that's about it."

The familiar squealing of cane behind her stopped abruptly. "Who is this Matthew feller?" Jimmy's deeper than usual tone sounded much like a protective older brother.

"A friend." Becky fidgeted with the piece of paper, warmth flooding her face. Was she convincing?

"Sounds overly friendly to me."

Becky whirled toward Jimmy, squinting against the afternoon sun. "Why, Jimmy Bodine. I believe you're jealous."

"Ha!" He resumed his caning, mumbling under his breath.

Pa stretched out his legs, folding his arms across his chest. "No need to badger the boy. Matthew's your pastor, not your suitor."

Becky fell silent and sunk the letter deep in her pocket, suppressing a grin.

Not yet anyway.

BECKY TUGGED on Jimmy's sleeve, skidding to a halt in front of Mr. Jacobs' dry goods store. "There's one of your chairs in the front window."

With a grin, Jimmy nudged her forward. "Come on."

A bell jingled above the door as they entered. Becky paused, surveying the vast array of household items, leather goods, and elegant clothing. Such luxuries would prove a novelty back home at Miller Creek where even essentials had to be bartered for rather than bought.

Mr. Jacobs stood behind a lengthy counter, reams of fabric lining shelves along the wall behind him. A young woman in an emerald, satin dress waited as he finished bundling her purchases, her auburn hair swirled in a neat coil beneath her lace bonnet.

"Thank you, Mrs. Kelley. Come again," the storekeeper said, handing her the packages.

The woman nodded and turned toward the door. Her expression soured as her gaze fell to Jimmy and Becky. They must have looked quite a pair—a blind boy in ragged clothes and a freckle-faced girl with braided hair in a homespun dress.

The woman maneuvered past without a word. Becky clenched her jaw. She would never fit into this city's high-class standards...nor did she want to. Still, she had to admit, at times the elegant styles appealed to her. She and Pa had no money for such fancy clothes. But perhaps Aunt Ellen could show Becky the proper way to pin up her hair.

With her eighteenth birthday only weeks away, Ma would say she was far too old to wear her hair down. Her mother's words played back in Becky's mind like it was yesterday. "What young man's gonna want to court a gal that's all suntanned and wind burned with her hair floppin' in the breeze?"

She fingered the letter to Matthew in her dress pocket. Perhaps it would make her seem more mature to a certain pastor.

Mr. Jacobs stepped from behind the counter and reached to straighten the strap on his store apron, a smile breaking onto has face at sight of Jimmy. "Hey there. What brings you into town, Jimmy?"

"Becky here says I've outgrown my clothes."

The store-owner's gaze darted to Becky and back to Jimmy. "It appears she's right, son." With a spry laugh, he gave Jimmy a light slap on the back. "So, the little lady persuaded you to spend some of your hard-earned cash, aye?"

Jimmy's face darkened a shade. "I reckon so."

The storekeeper turned to Becky. "Well then, I'm beholding to you for the business, miss..."

"Becky Hollister."

"Nice to meet you, Miss Hollister."

She bobbed her head with a grin. The man was just as she'd imagined him, jovial and pleasant. Was he this friendly with all his customers, or did Jimmy hold a special place in his heart?

He rubbed his hands together. "Now. What sort of clothes were you needing, son?"

Jimmy shrugged. "Some everyday shirts and slacks. Nothin' fancy."

The store owner rolled up his sleeves and glanced at Jimmy. "Let's see. You're about my height and just a tad stouter." Mr. Jacobs' brow creased as his gaze darted around the room. He paused, eyes focused on a display at the far side of the store. "Ah. I think I've just the ones."

With quick strides, he weaved his way to the stack of shirts in the corner. He leafed through the pile and pulled out a tan, loose-fitted cotton shirt with ties at its neck. Bringing it over, he held it to Jimmy's front. "What do you think, Miss Hollister? With a pair of brown trousers, he'd make a handsome fellow."

Becky straightened her bonnet. "He would at that."

Jimmy reached in his pocket for his money. "Bundle a couple of 'em up for me, would ya?"

Mr. Jacobs cuffed him on the shoulder. "Sure thing, son." He grabbed another shirt from the display and searched through a stack of pants.

Becky meandered through the store looking over the wares. A pair of woman's black leather boots caught her eye, and she ran her forefinger down the long row of shiny, metal hooks. What she wouldn't give to own such a pair. She glanced at her feet. Charlotte's tattered hand-me-downs had begun to bust their seams. They'd been worn out when she'd gotten them. At the time, however, she'd been glad to get them.

The heavy, tan paper crinkled as the store owner packaged the stack of clothes. He paused, staring over at Becky. "You've an eye for quality, miss. Those boots are top of the line."

One look at the price posted above the boots was enough to cause her to set them back in their place. Pa could never afford such an expensive pair of shoes. "A bit too top of the line for me, I'm afraid."

He nodded toward Jimmy. "You'll have to get your rich friend here to help you out."

Becky gave a half-hearted grin. "Had a hard enough time convincing him to spend some on himself."

Mr. Jacobs chuckled as he finished tying the bundle. "Say, I've sold about a dozen of those chairs of yours."

Jimmy stood taller, edging toward the storekeeper's voice. "I oughta have the others ready by the end of the week."

"Fine. I'll pick them up Saturday." Mr. Jacobs slid the package toward Jimmy and handed him his change. "Oh, and tell Mr. Bennett I'll have a tally on that list of supplies he needs by then. Sure are a bunch of 'em. How soon will you be moving?"

Becky shared Jimmy's baffled expression. He scratched his blond waves. "What do you mean, moving?"

"Why, to the new schoolhouse." The storekeeper knit his brow, gaze shifting between Jimmy and Becky. "Didn't you know?"

They shook their heads in unison.

Cringing, the store owner raked his thinning hair to the side. "Oh, boy. I've said too much. Forget I mentioned it."

Such a comment was difficult to ignore. As soon as the door closed behind them, Becky turned to Jimmy. "Do you really think the school will move?"

"Nah. It'd take a heap of money for a new place…money we don't have."

She looped her arm through his, guiding him along the busy street. "But with the new students, the place is so crowded. And Mr. Bennett and Mr. Whelan have been gone a lot. There must be something to what Mr. Jacobs says."

"Wishful thinking's all."

She tugged him to a stop outside the post office. "Hold up a minute. I have some letters to mail." Sliding her arm from his, she moved toward the door.

"Gonna send one to that preacher fellow, huh?"

Her face warmed. "And one to my aunt and uncle."

"Uh-huh." With a slow nod, he grinned and crossed his arms.

Becky gave him a nudge. There was no fooling the young man. Even without his sight, he could read what was in her heart. How long would it be before Pa saw through her as well?

MATTHEW DISMOUNTED and stepped toward the ol' Pratt cabin. The vacant home had seen better days. Cracks in the chink, an abundance of overgrown weeds lining the yard, and a thick layer of dirt coating the porch made it less than appealing. Still, it was the perfect location, just outside of Miller Creek, within walking distance of the church.

"Well, what do you think?" Jed stepped up beside him, looping his thumbs under his suspenders.

"A little fixing up and this oughta do just fine." Matthew pushed his hat back on his head. He'd have to work at it gradually, or he'd wind up whittling away time needed to devote to his congregation.

"It's nothing fancy, mind you, but there's place for a garden, out buildings, and room to expand." The glint in Jed's eyes deepened. "I'd say what it needs most is a woman's touch."

Matthew caught his friend's quick wink and suppressed a grin. "I admit it would come in handy. I've never had need to keep house before." He crossed his arms over his chest, trying to view it through Becky's eyes. Would it be fair to ask her and Joseph to give up their new cabin and abundant acreage to live in such a ramshackle place near town?

Jed nudged him with his elbow, a grin creeping onto his lips.

"That new school teacher's a real looker. Having known her before, you may have a head start over the rest of the fellers. But I wouldn't wait too long, or I wager she'll be snatched up sure as flowers bloom in spring."

Matthew shook his head. "You don't give a fellow much time to weigh his options."

"A feller in your position hasn't time for options. A pastor needs a good wife. I say, if the fruit looks good, pluck it." Jed gave a hearty laugh.

Matthew forced a grin. Was he really in that dire need of a wife? Until recently, he'd not given much thought to such. But Jed was right. A wife could prove a great asset to a pastor. When Becky returned, he'd be twenty-five. By the time he courted her, he'd most likely be nearing twenty-six. Was it wise to wait? Would she, a farmer's daughter, be content as a pastor's wife?

Perhaps he'd let his heart run away with him. Only time would tell.

Chapter Twenty-Two

BECKY SLID Matthew's letter from the Bible and tucked her feet up under her with a sigh. Why did she bother taking it out? She'd memorized every word. Still, just seeing it sent a wave of contentment through her. She skimmed the familiar note and slipped it back under the worn, leather cover. Perhaps soon she would have another to add to it.

Dishes rattled in the kitchen as Aunt Ellen retrieved cups for tea. The quiet, uneventful evenings with her aunt, away from the bustle of the crowded blind school, proved a welcome bit of solitude. Aunt Ellen had a gift of making her feel wanted, never putting on airs.

Becky flipped open her Bible to the Psalms, for over a month now having made it her nightly routine to read one. Not only had it proven an apt way of keeping track of their days away from home, but it had provided her a source of comfort and peace.

Her hands smoothed down the pages as she began reading Psalm 40.

"I waited patiently for the Lord, and He inclined to me and heard my cry. He brought me out of the horrible pit, out of the miry clay, and set my feet upon a rock and established my goings. And He hath put a new song in my mouth, even praise unto our God."

She held her place, her mind wandering back over the past few months of her life. The words of the Psalm seemed to unfold as she recalled the fears and uncertainties that had consumed her after the death of her loved ones. For a time, she'd wallowed in self-pity, placing unwarranted blame on God. Yet, Jimmy's unwavering faith, despite his circumstances, had challenged those doubts, until she'd sought out the truth of Scripture.

"In the world ye shall have tribulation; but be of good cheer; I have overcome the world."

The passages Matthew had underlined seemed to jump out at her. Over the weeks, she'd come to realize God did care. That He'd been with them each step of the way.

"Here we are." Her aunt's soothing voice broke through her thoughts. She set the tray of teacups on the stand table next to Becky.

Setting her Bible aside, Becky added a scoop of sugar to the steamy cup. "You spoil me, Aunt Ellen."

"You're a pleasure to spoil." Sipping her tea, a smile spread over Aunt Ellen's face.

Becky stirred her tea, then set her spoon on the tray. "Can I ask you something?"

"Certainly."

"You're so pleasant to be with, so good with people, why is it you never married?"

A slight choking sound erupted from her aunt. She set her cup on its saucer and leaned back in her chair.

Becky bit her lip. "I'm sorry. I shouldn't have asked."

Aunt Ellen raised a hand to her flushed face. "No. It's only fair. You've shared your hardships with me. You deserve to know mine as well." She leaned her head against the high-backed chair, eyes glistening. "It's just...I think I'm past it, then... I suspect deep hurts never do completely leave us."

Becky gave a slow blink. "You don't have to tell me."

"I want to." She drew in a deep breath and rubbed the back of her hand. "Years ago, I met a man...Jeffrey Coates. That entire summer, we were inseparable, spending every spare moment together. It was his dream to travel west and find his fortune. He told me as soon as he had the money, we would marry and make a home for ourselves in California."

She paused, drawing in a jagged breath. "Then he got a job on a freight line in Ohio, which kept us apart months at a time. Eventually he was away more than he was here. But he kept promising someday we'd be together."

She averted her gaze, her cheeks growing taut. "Several months passed without a word. Then a telegram came, saying he'd traveled west and found a place for us near San Francisco. He asked me to forward him what money I had to help purchase it. That he would send for me. Naturally, I was thrilled and transferred the money to the bank he'd designated."

She dabbed the corners of her eyes with a handkerchief. "I waited a week, a month, six months. Nothing."

Becky blinked back tears. "Did you ever hear from him?"

Aunt Ellen shook her head. "Never. The bank said the money had been withdrawn the same day it arrived. Not only had I lost my hopes for the future, but my life's savings as well."

Becky placed a hand on her aunt's arm. "I'm sorry. I don't understand how someone could do that to you."

"Yes, well, I imagine some things aren't meant for us to understand. I just determined to keep a positive attitude and not let bitterness overtake me."

"You've succeeded. You're a wonderful person."

Smiling through her tears, Aunt Ellen patted Becky's hand. "You're very kind. The Lord has been my constant companion through the years. Oh, there have been lonely times, but He's been faithful."

A wave of calm washed through Becky. Weeks earlier those

words would have grated at her like a grinding wheel. Now, she could sense the wisdom behind them. "Do you think you'll ever marry?"

Aunt Ellen shook her head. "I'm getting too old for such nonsense. Take my advice, Becky...don't put too much confidence in a man. The Lord's the One to count on."

The words of advice churned inside Becky. Had she set her hopes too high on Matthew? After all, he'd not given her anything definite to cling to, only the touch of his hand and a few words of endearment. Nothing more. "Not every man is like Mr. Coates. Surely you'd agree there are some honorable men. Mr. Bennett, for instance."

"Perhaps. But I'm not certain I'm willing to take such a risk again."

Becky downed the last of her tea. Strange. Her troubles had made her question God. Aunt Ellen's heartache had caused her to lose faith in men. Well, Matthew was worth the risk. He was a good man. A godly man. He'd never intentionally hurt her.

Aunt Ellen stood and lifted the tray. "Anyway, I'm not lonely with you here."

A streak of sadness weighed on Becky's heart as she followed her to the kitchen. In a matter of months, they'd be leaving. Would her absence leave Aunt Ellen lonelier than ever?

MATTHEW ROLLED up his sleeves and helped load lunch tables into wagon beds. By the time they'd finished, only a handful of people remained. What a grand welcome they'd extended him. Everything from fried chicken, to biscuits and gravy, to fresh garden vegetables. Yet, the spread of food didn't compare to the outpouring of kindness the congregation had shown in helping him patch up his cabin.

The only ones missing were Becky and Joseph.

Warmth blanketed his chest. Becky should have received his letter weeks ago. He could only hope she sensed the sincerity of his words. Depending on her response, his next correspondence would only further augment his feelings for her.

"See you next Sunday, pastor," Hank Brimmer called as he climbed onto his wagon seat.

"Yes, Lord willing." Matthew lifted his hat and waved it in the air.

He sensed someone beside him and turned to find Sarah, a plate of apple pie in each hand. She tilted her head to one side, a pouty pucker on her lips. "We've not yet had our pie."

"No, we haven't." He shifted his gaze side to side. "Let me just finish helping clean up first."

Gentle hands nudged him forward. He peered over his shoulder and saw Clara Stanton standing behind him, hands on hips. "You two go on now. The rest of us can finish up."

He stiffened, still hesitating. He'd done his best to keep preoccupied, but it appeared Sarah wouldn't be put off any longer.

She pushed one of the plates at him, a smile playing on her lips. "Shall we have a seat?"

With a reluctant nod, he took the pie plate and followed her to a large oak tree at the edge of the church yard. The thin, cotton blanket spread on the ground beneath hinted she planned a comfortable stay.

Matthew lowered himself onto the blanket, his heart drumming in his chest. Something about this didn't feel right. All he could do was make the best of it and try to speed things along. Tossing his hat aside, he dug into the pie. Rich and sweet, the cinnamon apple filling almost melted in his mouth, making him forget he'd already eaten far too much.

A giggle erupted beside him. He ventured a look over at Sarah, who'd settled down across from him, dress fanned out over her feet. Her dark eyes found his, and she smiled. "I assume it meets with your approval?"

"Yes. It's very good." He dropped his gaze, shoveling in another bite. Tasty or not, what mattered was getting this over with.

"You act as though you're famished. Perhaps I should have saved back more than one piece."

"No. No. One's sufficient, I assure you." He glanced around the church yard, noting the cluster of smiling faces trained in their direction. It seemed Sarah wasn't the only one eager to see them reacquainted.

Gulping down his last bite, the pie's sweetness soured in his stomach. The two of them sharing a blanket beneath the branches of a tree could lead to only one conclusion in the minds of the congregation.

Heat rose in his cheeks. That was the last rumor he wanted to start. With a weak cough, he started to rise. "Thank you for the pie, Miss—Sarah."

She caught him by the arm. "But we've only just sat down. We've years to catch up on."

"Another time, perhaps."

She slid her hand down his sleeve. "What are you afraid of, Matthew?"

Easing back down, he gave a soft chuckle, not quite looking her in the eye. "What makes you think I'm afraid?"

"You're as nervous as a cat."

He blew out a breath. "People are prone to—assume things. As pastor, I wouldn't want to mislead them."

Lilting laughter split the still air. "Oh, Matthew. When will you allow yourself to be a man?"

He met her gaze. "Do you wish them to think there's something between us that isn't?"

"I can think of worse things." She raised a brow, placing her hand atop his. "Besides, I for one would like to take up where we left off, wouldn't you?"

The question produced a maelstrom of emotions within him. He couldn't deny her beauty or the fact he still found her attractive. But, he'd changed over the years. As had his principles. He knew now there was more to a woman than outer beauty. He clenched his jaw, pulling his hand from hers. "And where was that? Last I recall, we'd agreed to part ways."

Her lower lip protruded. "A mistake I've long regretted." She leaned closer, pressing a hand to his arm. "But we're here now. Together. Why not make a fresh start of things?"

He met her gaze, heat burning his collar. "I'm not sure that's possible."

She gave a soft chuckle. "I thought pastors were supposed to believe anything is possible."

Breaking off his stare, he donned his hat and rose to his feet. "I thank you for the pie, Miss Prescott. Good day to you."

Matthew could almost feel her pointed stare on the back of his neck as he strode away. Plainly the woman was out to win him. And though the reason for their parting remained fuzzy to him, he knew what they'd shared wasn't love in the truest form. Love was more than physical attraction. It was a melding together of two hearts into one, with God at the center. Only time would tell if he and Becky had the makings of such a relationship. He only knew he needed to hear some confirmation from her.

And soon.

Chapter Twenty-Three

"WHERE'D Mr. Bennett and Mr. Whelan go, Miss Becky?" Catherine, the newest student, cocked her head to the side, struggling to fit a reed into place. With the other students having returned from summer break, her presence marked thirteen students in all.

"I'm not sure. They didn't say." They weren't saying much about anything these days.

Jenny, older and more refined in her work, put the finishing touches on her wicker basket. "I overheard them talking about some property in town. Do you think they're planning to move the school?"

Jimmy paused from his caning. "How? We're barely scraping by as it is."

"Maybe a wealthy man donated a place," offered Jenny.

"You're dreamin'."

Becky handed Catherine another reed, deep in thought. Despite Jimmy's skepticism, something seemed amiss.

"Dreaming or not, more space would suit me." Pa tied bristles to a broom handle. Becky's mouth lifted. He'd come so far in recent weeks.

Roy sat hunkered at the far end of the room, hands probing the craft room floor. His strange habit of gathering chunks of wood was another unanswered curiosity. No wonder he'd never moved beyond mat weaving. He was much too distractible.

Standing, he brushed off his trousers, then slunk toward the doorway and out into the hall. Becky shook her head. What was the boy up to? Was he taking advantage of her being there alone —or, as Jimmy claimed, just plain lazy?

"Keep working, Catherine. I'll be back in a bit." Becky patted the young girl on the shoulder and turned to Emily. "Would you help Catherine with her mat if she needs it, Emily?"

The raven-haired girl gave a hesitant nod and kept working. Becky pursed her lips. She hadn't succeeded in breaking the girl's silence, but at least she was communicating.

Tip-toeing into the hall, Becky spied Roy making his way upstairs. She waited until he'd entered the boys' bedroom and closed the door before starting up the stairway. Heat burned her cheeks as she climbed the steps. Sneaking off to take a rest when he was supposed to be working. Perhaps Jimmy and the others had the boy pegged right after all.

Confident Roy was alone in the room, she knocked on the door. "Roy. It's Miss Becky. May I come in?"

A clunking noise sounded within, followed by silence. Prying the door open, she found Roy on his knees by his cot. She strode toward him, hands on hips. "What are you doing?"

"Nothin'." The oversized boy rose to his feet, his cheeks growing pale.

"Whatcha got under there?" Becky peered under his bed. Among his sparse belongings, she spied a wadded blanket, bulges protruding here and there.

Roy shoved the bundle farther under the mattress with the heel of his boot. "'Tain't nothin' but some wood scraps."

"I'd like to see them." She pulled the bundle from under the bed and drew back the corners of the fabric. "These aren't scraps, they're carvings."

Squatting beside him, she picked up first one piece then another. "Did you make these?"

"Maybe."

She ran her fingers over the smooth ridges of a carved boat, her eyes widening. "So this is why you gather bits of wood."

Roy slumped down on his cot. "Didn't want nobody to know."

"But why? These are really good. I bet you could sell them at Mr. Jacobs' mercantile."

He crossed his arms in front of him, jaw set. "Ain't good for nothin'. Jus' like I ain't."

Becky drew in a breath. "Nonsense. You've got real talent. I'm sure Mr. Bennett and Mr. Whelan would be happy to let you work at it during craft time if you'd only ask."

"Well, I ain't gonna. And don't you tell." He groped for the bundle and folded the edges of the blanket over to conceal his treasures.

"But this could be your chance to prove everyone wrong. To show them you are good for something."

"Let 'em think what they want." Pushing the blanket back under his bed, he laid back, locking his hands behind his head.

Becky cocked her hand on her hips with a sigh. She could be just as stubborn as him. Given time, she'd find a way to convince him.

STUDENTS CROWDED around the dinner table, vying for a spot. Late August boasted an ample supply of fresh vegetables. Nearly every meal was garnished with corn on the cob, sliced cucumbers, squash, boiled beets, or string beans from the seasoned garden. Becky filled her plate and pulled a chair up next to

Nettie's outside the kitchen. With all thirteen students back at school, there was simply no room left at the table.

Mr. Bennett stood and gripped the back of his chair. "Listen up, everyone. I have some important news."

Becky stopped in mid-bite. Judging by the look of excitement on the instructor's face, this wasn't just any announcement. She helped still the murmuring students. Maybe at last they would have an answer to their speculations.

He rubbed his hands together, a glint in his eyes. "I'm sure you'll agree we're a bit over- crowded here. Well, through the generosity of an anonymous donor and donations from area churches, we'll soon be moving to a larger building downtown. We'll have ten times the space we have now."

Nettie's "Glory be" rang out amid shouts of joy from the students.

"When?" someone called.

Mr. Bennett waited for them to quiet. "As soon as we can get the place in shape. It's been vacant a number of years, but with a little work, we should be able to move within a matter of weeks."

Becky set her plate aside, her appetite forgotten. Downtown? She'd rather liked the location here, on the outskirts of the city. Would the walk to and from Aunt Ellen's be more than she could manage?

She searched out Jimmy, noting his bewildered expression. Striding over to him, she leaned down and whispered in his ear. "Seems the rumors were true."

"Reckon so." He shrugged. "I don't mind, so long as there's a big tree out back to sit under."

A corner of Becky's mouth lifted. Of all the things Jimmy could miss, it warmed her to know how highly he valued their time together. "I'll look for one first thing."

Mr. Bennett strolled up beside her. "Oh, and Becky, there'll be room for you as well."

She straightened. "You mean I won't have to leave nights?"

He sunk his hands deeper in his pants pockets. "That's right. In fact, Eli and I would like nothing more than to consider you a house mother to the girls...for as long as you're here."

Becky took a step back. It was what she'd wished for from the beginning. To be with Pa. But could she abide living in the heart of the city? "I-I don't know what to say."

"A 'yes' will do." Mr. Bennett stroked his beard, seeming amused. "And, you may as well call me Peter."

"All right...Peter. I'd be more than happy to accept."

A knowing grin spread across Pa's face. Becky leaned over him, placing an arm around his shoulder. "You knew?"

"Since yesterday." The joy on his face spilled over into Becky. It seemed God was opening doors and blessing them more with each passing day.

"Miss Becky?" Young Amos edged toward her, his tiny hands groping the air.

"Over here, Amos."

A smile lit his face. The little fellow had taken a shine to her, it seemed. He wound his way to her. "Tell me a story, Miss Becky."

She squatted down beside him and tweaked his cheek. How could she resist the five-year-old's pleading smile and pudgy red cheeks? "All right. Can you do without me a while, Nettie? Looks like I'm spoken for."

Nettie tapped her long-handled spoon on the side of the emptied pot of beans. "You go on, honey child. Jenny and I'll finish up."

Jimmy swung his legs over the bench, fidgeting with the ties on his new shirt. "Will you be out later?"

Standing, Becky took Amos by the hand. "If Aunt Ellen doesn't come before I get there."

With a nod, Jimmy headed toward the door, looking handsome in his new clothes.

Several students had found their way to the sitting room, still chattering with excitement about the news, while others ventured outside for some fresh, night air. Settling down in a vacant chair by the fireplace, Becky scooped Amos up in her lap. Pa took a seat beside them,

She gave Amos a gentle squeeze. "What do you want to hear?"

The young boy's mouth twisted in thought, then a sudden smile lit his face. "David and Gowiath."

"Just what I would have chosen." Becky nuzzled her cheek against his dark hair. Months earlier, she'd never have dreamed to find such comfort and contentment in this place. It wasn't so bad here. The students and instructors were fast becoming like family to her.

A familiar knock sounded at the door. The smile that stretched across Peter's lips when he opened it hinted it was someone he was pleased to see. Aunt Ellen strolled in, eyes searching. "What's all the excitement about? The children are jabbering as if something wonderful has happened."

Peter's chin lifted. "We've just shared with them our purchase of a large brick building downtown."

Loosening her bonnet, Aunt Ellen let it settle onto her back. "Why, that's wonderful. Heaven knows you can use the space." Her gaze fell to Becky. "But then it may not be so convenient for us. From downtown, we'll have quite a stroll."

Becky suddenly felt ill. Until that moment, she'd not given thought to how her aunt would take the news. She'd be heart-broken without Becky's company of an evening.

"Ellen..." The depth in Pa's voice made Becky flinch. She hugged Amos tighter in her lap, venturing a glance in Aunt Ellen's direction.

Her aunt's gaze darted from one face to another. "What is it? What's wrong?"

Pa swiveled towards her. "Becky's been asked to stay on as house mother at the new school for the rest of our time here."

All the emotion drained from her aunt's face, till only a pale stunned expression remained. Her gaze flicked to Becky, then dropped. "Oh. Well…that's grand news. Just…grand." With a stiff smile, she turned to Peter. "She'll be wonderful help to you. Of course, I'll miss her and visiting all of you each evening." Her voice raised an octave as she turned away, shielding her face with her hand.

Pa sat forward in his chair. "Now, Ellen, don't get frazzled. We'll still visit on weekends."

Becky's eyes moistened. For a time, she'd helped to ease her aunt's loneliness. Now, it seemed she'd be contributing to it.

Peter reached out to Aunt Ellen, his dark eyes penetrating. "It won't be for a few weeks, not till we move. And please, feel free to visit any time. It would be my privilege to escort you whenever you wish to come."

Swiping a tear from her cheek, Aunt Ellen gave a faint grin. "Thank you…Peter."

More than mere concern streamed from Peter's eyes, stirring a glimmer of hope within Becky. Perhaps her aunt's loneliness could be eased from another willing source…if only she would allow.

MATTHEW EASED down on the bench outside the post office, the letter from Becky pressed between his fingertips. At last. She'd answered.

Breaking open the wax seal, he unfolded the note.

"Dear Matthew,

It seems so odd to refer to you by your given name. I pray you aren't offended."

A smile tugged at his lips. Not a bit.

"Your letter brought us great joy, as did the news you'll be staying long-term at Miller Creek. I so look forward to spending more time together upon our return. Pa is beginning to make progress with his training. I've been asked to help with students here, and despite my longing for home, find I enjoy it more than I thought possible. Soon I'll turn eighteen. It will be difficult to spend my birthday away from home, but Pa and I are together, and my aunt has been a true blessing. And so, for now, I am content."

Matthew pushed his hat back with his thumb. Eighteen. Such a tender age. He looked at the postmark. More than a week had lapsed since it left St. Louis. Had her birthday already passed? He'd send her a small token with his next letter.

Reading on, the next line warmed his heart.

"God has been good to us here. Each day seems a bit brighter than the one before. Rest assured, I've made peace with Him, or at least am attempting to. Thanks for entrusting your Bible to me. Each time I open it, not only do I think of you, but I find strength for each new day.

With kindest regards,

Becky"

He gave a soft sigh. She sounded much more settled and at peace than when he'd left her. If so, his prayers had been answered.

Folding the letter, he slid it in his vest pocket. It had been just the encouragement he'd needed. Rising, he eyed the mercantile with a grin. May as well stop in and check over their wares while he was in town. He needed a few items for his cabin anyway.

What was one more?

MATTHEW STEPPED from the mercantile laden with supplies. He filled his saddlebags, then leaned against the leather fender of his saddle. Reaching in his vest pocket, he took out the box that held Becky's gift. He opened the lid and ran a finger over the jeweled brooch in the shape of a cross. A symbol of faith, as well as a thing of beauty.

The perfect gift for someone dear.

"Why, Matthew. What's that you're holding?"

At the sound of Sarah's voice, he snapped the lid to the jewelry box shut and slipped it back in his pocket. With a nervous cough, he turned to face her. "I-I was just loading up supplies for my place."

The penetrating glare in her eye hinted Matthew had done little to throttle her suspicion She cocked her head to one side, seeming to let his answer slide. "Yes, I've seen that cabin of yours. It appears you have your work cut out for you."

"That I do. Still, I'm grateful to have it." He busied himself strapping his saddle bags.

She sidled up beside him. "With a little fixing up, it may even make a suitable home for a wife. Or have you given that any thought?"

Her chocolate eyes latched onto his. What was he to say? If he were truthful—that he had—she would likely take it the wrong way. It seemed wise to avoid the issue altogether.

Turning toward her, he draped an arm over Gabriel's rump. He should at least be sociable. "How are your classes going?"

Her mouth tipped upward in a smile, and she laced her hands together in front of her. "Quite well, actually. I've mastered all the children's names and am even learning who goes with which parents."

"That's a start." His muscles relaxed. If he could keep the conversation focused on her, perhaps she'd not attempt to delve deeper into his personal life. "I hear you're boarding with Miss Tuttle."

Her eyes brightened. "Yes. She's been very kind, but a bit opinionated, I'm afraid. Seems to think the mercantile is under-stocked, the mail too slow, and the church building a bit stuffy."

With a soft snicker, he slid his arm from Gabriel. "Sounds

like her." The old spinster seemed to find something wrong in any given situation.

Sarah arched a brow. "Shall I tell you what else she thinks?"

By the sparkle in her eye, Matthew wasn't so sure. Miss Tuttle had a way of prying into other people's business. He cleared his throat. "That the preacher is too long-winded?"

A vibrant giggle flew from Sarah's lips. She doubled over, brushing his sleeve with her hand. At last, she straightened and looked him in the eye. "No. That if a certain pastor doesn't pay me a visit soon, I may end up an old spinster school marm."

Heat burned his cheeks. The woman wouldn't let up. "Now, Sarah. What was between us before is…"

"I know. In the past." Her dark lashes fluttered, accentuating her penetrating stare. "But a gal has a right to hope."

With a shake of his head, he dropped his gaze and backed away. When she wasn't pressing him, Sarah could be the likable sort. Even now, he might enjoy her company on occasion. But only in friendship. Unbeknownst to her and everyone else, his affections lay elsewhere. And for the moment, he planned to keep it that way. He had no right to voice an attachment to Becky without her consent. At least until he had something more solid to go on.

Until then, he could only live in hope.

Chapter Twenty-Four

September, 1854

BECKY TILTED her head from side to side, gazing into her aunt's dresser mirror at her flaxen hair coiled in a loose bun.

Aunt Ellen pushed the final hairpin into place and smiled at her in the mirror. "Well, what do you think?"

Becky crinkled her nose. "I look so…"

"Mature. Like the young woman you are." Aunt Ellen rested her hands on Becky's shoulders, finishing her sentence for her.

Pa edged forward, feet draped over the side of Aunt Ellen's bed. "Bet you're the spittin' image of your ma."

Becky lifted a corner of her mouth in a weak grin as she peered at her profile in the mirror. With her hair fixed so, her reflection did bear a stunning resemblance to her mother. Same wheat blonde hair, ocean blue eyes, and high cheek bones. She bit at her lip, blinking back the moistness in her eyes. Her mother and sister would always hold a special place in her heart. Yet, somehow her angst at God over their passing had died away.

Perhaps it was Jimmy's ability to always see the good in things or Aunt Ellen's selfless giving that had softened her heart.

Or had it been the comforting words of Scripture coupled with Matthew's gentle prompting that had penetrated the ache in her soul? Most likely it was a blend of them all. Regardless, she had the assurance that one day she'd see Ma and Melissa again.

She swiveled in her chair to face Pa. "Ma would be pleased, wouldn't she?"

"She sure would, darlin'." He sighed, draping his leg over his opposite knee. "Hard to believe you're the age she was when we married. Seems only yesterday you were roamin' the prairie dressed in burlap and sportin' pigtails. Won't be long before I'll be losing you to some feller."

"Oh, Pa." A rush of heat singed her cheeks, thoughts of Matthew edging to the forefront of her mind. What would Pa think if he knew of their attachment? Though she had little doubt he would approve of Matthew courting her, it seemed too soon to front the issue. When the time was right, she'd know.

Pa rubbed his hands on his thighs. "May as well bring her gift, Ellen."

"All right." Aunt Ellen's muslin dress rustled as she strolled to the dining room. She returned with a bulging, wrapped package. With a broad smile, she handed it to Becky. "From your father and me."

"You didn't have to. Really." Setting it on her lap, Becky tugged at the strings that held the heavy wrapping paper in place. Her eyes widened as she unfolded the package to find a beautiful white blouse and blue tea-length skirt, along with a beige and rose plaid calico dress. She stood, holding up first one, then the other, moisture pooling in her eyes. "Oh, they're beautiful."

A smile lit Pa's face. "You like 'em?"

"I love them." She stooped to kiss him on the cheek.

"You can thank Ellen for most of it. I only bought the material. She did the choosin' and the sewin'."

Becky turned to her aunt with a smile. That she was pleased

with Becky's response was evidenced by the gleam in her eyes. Becky reached to hug her. "Thank you."

"It was my pleasure." The words were a soft whisper in Becky's ear. Her aunt clung to her like a child clinging to her favorite doll. Over a matter of months, the two of them had moved from strangers to dear friends. Becky could only pray her aunt would come to know the happiness she so deserved.

A knock at the front door drew them apart. Releasing her hold, Aunt Ellen wiped moisture from the corner of her eye. "Now who could that be on a Saturday afternoon?" She smoothed her dress and went to answer the door.

A man's deep voice intertwined with Aunt Ellen's soprano one in the front room.

"Sounds like Peter." Pa stood and made his way toward the bedroom door.

Becky laid her dresses aside and followed him from the room, holding her neck stiff, so as not to tousle her hair.

Peter stood just inside the door near Aunt Ellen, a sizable package under his arm. Her aunt's face appeared flushed, and she held a long-stemmed red rose in her hand. Was he coming to court her? Oh, if Aunt Ellen would only open her heart to him.

Pa made his way across the room. "That you Peter?"

The instructor's gaze lingered on Aunt Ellen a moment before responding. "Yes. Sorry to intrude, but I've come to deliver a gift to a young lady." He gripped the package, wrapped with ribbon, and extended it toward Becky. "Jimmy sends his regards for your birthday."

"Jimmy?" Becky knit her brow, taking hold of the weighty package.

Peter widened his stance, locking his fingers together in front of him. "I think he was a little afraid you wouldn't accept it, so I volunteered." Again his gaze flicked toward her aunt.

Setting the packet on the table, Becky loosened the ribbon. What could Jimmy give that she couldn't accept? As she lifted the box lid, an audible gasp escaped her. "High-top boots." The very ones she'd admired at the mercantile. "It must have taken most of the money he had left."

She ran a hand over the smooth leather and then shoved the box toward Peter. "He's right. I can't accept them."

Peter shrugged. "You'll have to take that up with him. I'm simply the messenger."

Lifting the lid, she took another peek at the shiny boots. "Sure are pretty."

Too bad she couldn't keep them.

"WHY DID you buy the boots, Jimmy?" Sitting cross-legged beside her friend beneath the oak tree, Becky stared at the leather boots in her hand.

Jimmy smiled a wry grin, clutching his hands behind his head. "I thought so long as I was spending money, I'd make it worth my while."

She gave him a soft nudge in the ribs with her elbow. "Be serious. You shouldn't spend your money on me. You've got your future to think of."

He shrugged. "Mr. Whelan and Mr. Bennett chipped in. They said you deserved some sort of pay for your help."

"Well, it's too much. I can't accept them." With a hesitant sigh, she set the boots in Jimmy's lap.

He caught her by the wrist and pushed the boots back into her hand, folding her fingers around them. "I want you to have 'em, Beck."

His taut mouth told her not to argue further. Did she dare keep such an expensive gift? If not, she risked hurting him. The smell of new leather drifted up to her, and she rubbed her fingers over the smooth high-top boots. "It's that important to you?"

"It is."

A hesitant grin crept onto her lips as she leaned to hug him. "You're the best, Jimmy. Thank you."

His face glowed red, and he fidgeted with the buckle on his suspenders. "Well, are you gonna try 'em on?"

Slipping her feet into the boots, she reveled in the comfort. She laced them up with a smile. "They're perfect."

MATTHEW WAVED to the Jensons as he rode away. New to the area, the young couple seemed very receptive to his visit and his invitation to attend Sunday's service. Given time, he'd call on each of his neighbors, along with his entire congregation. A more focused ministry would allow him time to get acquainted with members on a more personal level. And how better to tend his flock?

He reached to pat Gabriel's neck, then pulled back on the reins as his cabin came into view. Something moved on his porch. He squinted, trying to make out the shadowy figure. With a tap of his heels, he spurred Gabriel closer for a better view. At last, he was able to make out the image of a woman.

Sarah? He blew out a breath. She certainly was persistent. What did he have to do to ward her off?

She leaned over his rail to shake out a rug and turned toward him as he approached. With a wave of her arm, she stepped out into the yard. "There you are. Where have you been?"

Pulling Gabriel to a halt beside her, Matthew leaned forward in his saddle. "The question is, what are you doing?"

She threw a hand to her hip, tucking the rug under her other arm. "While you've been off gallivanting, I've done what I can to make this place livable."

He shrugged. "I've lived in it for days without a problem."

"Honestly, Matthew. The house was filthy. You've been here more than a week and not so much as swept it out."

"I was getting to that. Just wasn't top on my list of priorities." A weak grin crept onto his lips as he dismounted and tied Gabriel to the porch rail.

With a shake of her head, Sarah hooked her arm through his and tugged him forward. "Well, anyway, come have a look. I think you'll find it much more presentable."

He tensed. What made her think she could just come in and take over? She had no hold on him. Given opportunity, he'd set her straight on that in a hurry.

She pulled him across the threshold, a winsome smile lining her lips. "Well, what do you think?"

He loosened his arm from hers and thumbed his hat up higher on his forehead. The cluttered room he'd left behind was now tidy. Not a speck of dust marred the table or floor. A savory scent hung in the air, and a fire crackled in the fireplace. "Amazing. It hardly looks the same place."

With a giggle, she spread the rug out before the hearth, then twirled to face him. "I've a pot of stew heated for your supper. I thought, at the very least, you'd ask me to join you."

His gaze flicked to the lit candle at the table's center, a place setting on either side. He gave a hard swallow, feeling as if he'd been bamboozled. Yet, after all she'd done, how could he refuse? "I reckon that's the least I can do."

She sidled up to him. "Now that you're settled, you really should invest in more than a single tin-ware plate setting." She ran her finger along the rim of one of the off-white, ceramic plates, then gazed up at him. "Tell you what. I'll make you a present of these. Then if you have me over again, we'll be set."

"I'm not the fancy sort." Matthew shifted his feet, edging back. No doubt about it. The woman was out to ensnare him.

She tilted her head and raised a brow. "Then perhaps you can tell me what's in this fancy little box. I've been singed with curiosity all afternoon."

Matthew's stomach lurched as she strode to his stand table

and retrieved the jewelry box that housed the jeweled cross meant for Becky. Had his uninvited guest discovered the letter tucked in his Bible as well? His cheeks flamed. "It's a gift...for someone."

He reached for it, but she pulled it back with a grin. "Anyone I know?"

"Sarah, please." He held out his hand, pleading in his voice.

She stuck out her lower lip. "Can't I at least have a peek?"

He breathed a low sigh. She wasn't making this easy.

"I'll take that as a yes." With a huge smile, she popped open the lid.

"No!" Matthew reached to stop her.

A moment too late.

With a gasp, she plucked the brooch from the case and held it in her fingertips. "Oh, Matthew. It's beautiful."

"But Sarah. It wasn't intended..."

"I know. It's only meant in friendship." She pinned it to her dress, then stretched to give him a hug. "May I wear it now? It's so lovely."

Arms at his sides, Matthew's shoulders sagged. How was he going to get out of this? If he told her about Becky, she'd spill it to the entire town. He couldn't have that. He hadn't the right. Best to bide his time and explain things when her emotions weren't running so high.

MATTHEW SUNK his hands deep in his pockets, pacing outside Miss Tuttle's boarding house. He'd not slept a wink. He had to get that brooch back.

The door creaked opened, and he swiveled toward it. Miss Tuttle leaned against the door frame, her plump figure filling much of the space. The middle-aged woman swiped a stray, auburn curl from over her eye and peered out at him. "'Bout time you showed up. I'm assuming you're here to see Miss Prescott and not myself."

Matthew tipped his hat, wondering just why Miss Tuttle had been expecting him. "Yes, ma'am. There's a small matter I wish to discuss with Miss Prescott. Is she at home?"

Sarah appeared in the doorway, all smiles as Miss Tuttle moved to let her pass. The older woman gave her a decided wink and a pat on the shoulder, then slinked back inside, closing the door behind her.

"Why, Matthew. You surprise me coming so early of a morning." Sarah's smile faded. "You look awful. Haven't you slept?"

Lifting his hat, he raked a hand through his hair. She had no idea how restless his night had been. Nor the reason. His gaze fell to the jeweled brooch fastened on her dress. How should he go about this tactfully? "I need to speak with you a moment, if I may."

With a grin, she rocked back on her heals, hands clutched behind her. "

A wagon jostled behind Matthew, and he shot a glance over his shoulder. A trickle of people had begun milling about. He could sense their curious stares. Before long, the entire town would be ablaze with talk. Taking Sarah by the arm, he led her to the back side of the boarding house.

"What's come over you, Matthew?" She stared up at him, her dark eyes full of question.

His chest deflated as he forced out a breath. At a time like this, plain truth seemed the only option. "It's the brooch. There's been a misunderstanding."

She ran her fingertips over the piece of jewelry. "What's to misunderstand? I adore it. I'll make it my constant companion from now on."

The look on her face weakened Matthew's resolve. He dropped his hands to his sides with a sigh. "There are areas of my life you don't know about."

"I know all I need to." She closed the gap between them, and reached to clasp his fingers.

He drew his hand away. "No, you don't. You see, the brooch was meant…"

She placed a finger to his lips, stilling his words. "To demonstrate to a very lucky lady just how special you are."

He clenched his jaw, heat burning his cheeks. How could he explain if she kept interrupting?

With a grin, she brushed a hand down his sleeve. "Now, if I don't get going, I'll be late for class. Care to accompany me?"

He shook his head, his determination all but squelched. "I've other business to attend to."

"Well then, I'll see you later." With a quick clip, she started toward the school then called back over her shoulder. "An evening visit would be nice."

Matthew hung his head. Another failed attempt. It would be simpler to let her keep it.

But what of Becky? He had no money for another brooch. Buying a second one was out of the question. Mrs. Chaney, the owner of the merchantile, would think he'd gone mad.

He reached for the letter in his vest pocket. Becky would be expecting it. With a low sigh, he slipped it out. If he sent it without the brooch, she'd not know the difference.

Tightness gripped his chest. But he would.

Still, he hadn't the stomach to bring the issue up again with Sarah. It seemed the more he tried to temper their friendship, the more entangled their lives became. Was God trying to tell him something? Had he been wrong about Becky? They certainly made an unlikely pair—him years older and a pastor, bound to the concerns of a congregation, her, a farmer's daughter with ties to the land and her father's future to consider. No one would ever suspect.

A sudden notion shot through him. Had the brooch been misplaced for a reason? Perhaps he'd only been meant to help

Becky get back on her feet. Maybe he'd done all the Lord intended him to do.

He gripped the letter in his palm and started toward the post office.

Somehow his heart didn't agree.

BECKY FINISHED CLASPING the buttons of her new white blouse and skirt and gazed in the mirror. Was the image truly hers? With her hair up and such fine clothing, she looked almost as refined as her aunt. What would Matthew think of the change? Perhaps he would make his intentions known, now that she was a year older and looked more mature. Warmth surged through her at the thought. If only she could see him. How she longed to hear from him again. Had he received her letter? Or had it too been misdirected?

Aunt Ellen tapped on the door frame, stirring Becky from her reverie. "How's it going in here?" She stepped into the room, eyes dancing at sight of Becky. "Why, you look lovely."

Glancing down at her fine clothes, Becky suppressed a grin. "I never dreamed I'd ever wear something so grand." She lifted her eyes to meet her aunt's. "It's all the more special because you made it."

"I'm so glad. I know nothing I make could ever match your mother's handiwork, but I want you to know how glad I am you're here. You've brought this lonely woman a great deal of joy these past few months."

Tears welled in Becky's eyes. Though Ma's hand-stitched dress lacked the finery of Aunt Ellen's machine-made ones, both were a work of love to be treasured. She reached to embrace her aunt, her voice a whisper. "You've been a great comfort to me as well."

Aunt Ellen's arms tightened around her, then she straightened. With a sniffle, she wiped a tear from Becky's shoulder. "Just look at me, staining your new dress before you even wear it." She took a handkerchief from her pocket and dabbed the corners of her eyes.

"Will you two stop that sniveling in there? We'll be late for church," Pa called from the dining room.

Sharing a chuckle with her aunt, Becky drew a cleansing breath, taking a final glance in the mirror. There was healing in laughter…and in tears.

BECKY STARED past the rows of bonnets and the back of men's heads to the energetic song leader as the congregation stood and caroled "Just as I Am." She squeezed and relaxed her toes, her new boots hugging her feet tighter than her old ones. They would take some getting used to, but Jimmy's sacrifice made it well worthwhile.

Sandwiched between Pa and Jimmy, a keen sense of contentment washed over Becky, her words of praise no longer hindered. While most of the blind students were engaged in song, Roy and Emily stood expressionless, eyes downcast. At least Roy had agreed to attend. On past Sundays, they'd not been able to persuade him out of the wagon. Becky paused her singing, heaviness pressing out her joy. But then what good did it do when his heart wasn't in it?

Emily, too, remained shrouded in a world all her own. Becky bowed her head, lifting her own plea as the preacher stepped forward to offer a final prayer. *Lord, give me vision into their souls. You understand their loss and pain, as You have mine. Open their hearts to You…and to life.*

Chapter Twenty-Five

Late September, 1854

BECKY PINNED the last bed sheet to the clothesline then blew out a puff of air. "I don't know how you handled all this alone, Nettie. It's all the both of us can do to keep up."

Nettie cradled the empty clothes basket in her arms, a hoarse laugh escaping her. "Don't rightly know myself. Course there's more young'uns than b'fore you came along, but you wuz pure God-send, that's what you wuz, honey child."

Becky smiled, recalling Matthew's remark that God may have had a hand in her coming. Back then she hadn't been so sure, but now, her heart told her it was so. Grasping the pail of clothes pins, she strode with Nettie toward the school building.

A raspy cough escaped Nettie's throat, and she paused to catch her breath. She shook her head, face pinched. "Humph. Here we is workin' ourselves to death while Mis'er Peter an' Mis'er Eli gallivant around, off at that buildin' all da time. I'd of been lost without ya these past couple weeks, child. Overworked an' underpaid, that's what we is."

"Now, you know as well I they're not gallivanting. They're working hard to get that building in shape so we can move."

Nettie batted her hand through the air. "Don't mind me, young'un. I'z just blowin' off steam."

It wasn't like Nettie to be so negative. Perhaps she wasn't feeling well. Her eyes did appear red and that cough sounded tight in her chest. "With the volunteers from the church helping, Peter says we may be able to move in sometime next week."

"Then maybe things'll get back to normal…if there is such a thing 'round here." Nettie's chuckle ended in a croupy cough, and she held her chest, gasping for air.

"That cough of yours doesn't sound good." Becky touched a hand to her friend's cheek. "You're feverish."

Nettie set the clothes basket by the door and wiped her forehead with her apron. "I is a mite tuckered. Think I'll lie down a spell."

Becky held the door open for her. "I'll do my best to keep the students quiet."

Nettie gave a slight nod and lumbered inside.

Becky stared after her. Her friend looked bone weary. But, with all she did, it was a wonder she was on her feet at all. *Watch over her, Lord.*

She set the basket inside the door and headed toward the craft room. With the instructors gone, students spent their days making items to raise money for the new building. It was easier to keep them all rallied and busy in one place, seasoned students aiding newer ones.

Roy stood leaned against the wall outside the door, an unsettled look on his face. Coming up beside him, Becky placed a hand on his arm. "Did you need something, Roy?"

At her touch, he straightened and reached in his pocket. Pulling out a small object, he held it in his closed fist. "Here."

That Roy was instigating conversation of any kind was a small miracle in itself, but did he intend to give her a gift? Becky moved her hand under his. With more energy than she'd ever witnessed the boy exude, he dropped a lightweight object into her palm, then propelled himself forward.

A smile tugged at Becky's lips at sight of the wooden carving resembling a dog. Roy truly was gifted. She turned the carving over in her hand, eyes widening at the word *NUGGET* etched in tiny letters on its belly. The image of their old, yellow dog resurrected in her mind. It had been weeks since she'd thought of him. How could Roy possibly know such a detail?

"Wait." Clutching the figure in her hand, she hurried after him.

Roy jarred to a stop, his broad shoulders slumped forward. The boy was a mystery to Becky, a blend of toughness and vulnerability. She swiveled to face him. "How did you know about Nugget?"

He shrugged. "Overheard you tell Jimmy about him." Roy hung his head, his face darkening a shade. "Ain't never had nobody stick up for me b'fore. Wanted to make you somethin'."

"It's very good." Becky rubbed her thumb over the rough lettering. Somehow, it seemed she'd tapped into the deeper side of Roy, the hidden softness at his core. If only she could convince him to reveal it to the others. "Why don't I show this to Mr. Bennett? I'm sure he'd..."

"No." Roy's stern voice cut off her words.

Becky twisted her mouth to one side. How could she make him realize it was for his own good? She arched a brow. Maybe there was a way yet.

With a pronounced sigh, she slid the carving back into his large hand. "Well then, I reckon I better not keep this here Nugget dog you gave me. I'd have a hard time explaining where such a fine crafted piece came from. Sure hate to give it up, though."

"But I made it for ya."

"And I appreciate it. But I can't keep this sort of talent to myself. I'm afraid I'd give away your secret."

His jaw tensed. He shifted his feet, seeming to war within himself.

Becky held back a smile. Her plan was working. One more comment should do it. She forced sincerity into her voice. "No. Much as I hate to, I'd best give him back and let you put him in the pile with the rest."

Roy's face seemed to erupt with emotion, and a burst of air surged from his lips. He held out his open palm. "Here. Take it."

"You mean I can tell the others?"

With a shrug, he scuffed his boot against the floor. "I reckon."

Becky gripped the carving, a grin pulling at her lips. "You'll not regret it."

BECKY CURLED her legs up under her in the chair and rubbed her feet. It had been a long week and a tiring one. With Nettie ailing and having to take on extra duties, the weekend had come none too soon. The only high points had been Roy's newfound skill and Matthew's most recent letter. She slid it from her pocket and drank in each word. How exciting that he'd made a home for himself and the church pews were filling. The only part about the letter that puzzled her was his reference at the end that he hoped she liked her gift. Had he sent her something and it not yet arrived?

The fireplace logs crackled and spit as she gazed into the flickering flames. In the stillness, her mind raced back to the prairie. How she longed to return. To see Matthew again, and to make a fresh start with Pa. Still, there were things she'd miss about this place. Aunt Ellen and Jimmy. The feeling of being useful. Pa needed her, she knew. But there was something special in being used by God to meet the needs of others.

Rising, she strode to the desk and took up paper and quill. Pa and Aunt Ellen's voices droned in soft chatter behind her. If Pa suspicioned her growing fondness for Matthew, he hadn't let on, though Aunt Ellen had flashed Becky a knowing grin more than once. The way she pored over his letters, it was no wonder.

She dipped the tip of the quill in the bottle of ink, hoping Matthew didn't find her too eager writing so soon. The words began to flow, spilling out all her experiences and longings. She found she could tell him just about anything. Not like a member of his congregation, but as a friend. A very dear friend.

A firm rap on the door stilled her writing.

"Who could that be?" Aunt Ellen set down her knitting needles and rose from her chair. Her satiny dress rustled as she moved toward the door.

Peering out the window, Becky caught a glimpse of a man's brown trousers and suit jacket, similar to those worn by Peter. With only Mr. Whelan left to tend to the students it couldn't be a social call.

Aunt Ellen drew open the door and pulled a hand to her chest. "Why Peter. Another Saturday visit?"

"Not a pleasant one, I'm afraid." He removed his hat and stepped inside, voice strained. He shifted his gaze to Becky.

"Is something wrong?" Rising, she took a step toward him.

He released a heavy sigh. "I'm afraid Nettie has worsened. The doctor fears it's the influenza."

Becky clapped a hand to her mouth. The dreaded disease was known to spread like wild fire, claiming countless lives wherever it struck.

Pa's chair creaked as he leaned toward Peter. "How bad is she?"

"She's out of her head with fever. The doctor feels it best she be cared for away from the school, to avoid an epidemic."

Aunt Ellen stepped toward him, hazel eyes shining. "I'd look after her, if you'd like to bring her here."

Peter gripped the brim of his hat, returning a weak smile. "That's more than generous of you, Ellen, but her sister lives just outside of town and has agreed to take her in. I've just come from there."

Tears welled in Becky's eyes. "Will she be all right?"

"Lord willing." He drew in a long breath. "But I'm afraid Catherine and Emily have developed coughs. We feel they should be isolated from the other students. Just in case."

Concern mounted in Aunt Ellen's voice. "But where will you put everyone?"

"Our only choice is to move the rest of the students to the new school earlier than planned and leave Catherine and Emily at the present building until they recover." He turned to Becky, seeming to struggle for words. "I hate to ask it of you, Becky, but we need your help."

"What can I do?"

Peter stroked his beard. "With your father's permission, we'd like you to stay and care for Catherine and Emily."

Pa slapped his hand down on the table. "No. It's too risky. I won't have it."

Becky swept a loose strand of hair from her temple, heaviness settling over her. She had more than her own welfare to think of. If anything happened to her, who would care for Pa?

Aunt Ellen placed a steadying hand on Pa's shoulder, fixing her gaze on Peter. "It is a lot to ask."

"I know, and I'm sorry. If there was any other way..." The instructor paused, donning his hat. "Talk it over. I'll wait outside."

Becky tried to ignore the growing tension in her abdomen. What decision was there to make? These were her friends. It wouldn't be right not to help them.

"Wait." Her voice rang louder than intended.

Peter paused at the door, hope streaming from his eyes.

Becky swallowed. She'd been helpless to save Ma and Melissa. This was her chance to lend a hand to someone in need. "I'll go."

Pa shifted toward her, furrows lining his forehead. "No, Becky. I won't let you."

She knelt beside him, placing a hand on his knee. "I couldn't live with myself if I could help and didn't. Ma would've done the same."

His jaw tightened. "There's no sense in you riskin' your health. You're young. You've your whole life ahead of you."

"But I've been with Nettie, Pa. I may already be exposed."

Pa hung his head, his voice trailing in a whisper. "I lost Meg and Melissa. I can't bear to lose you too."

Tears stung her eyes, and she blinked, spilling them onto her cheeks. "It's the Lord's decision who lives or dies, not ours."

Peter took a step toward them. "I assure you, Joseph, every precaution will be taken to keep her well. I'll check in on her daily."

Becky leaned closer. "Please, Pa. Let me have the chance to help."

He reached out to her, chin quivering. She clasped his hand, sensing his inward struggle. He drew a long breath, releasing it in an audible sigh. "Promise you'll be careful."

"I will." Her heart beat faster. Months earlier, she'd sooner have turned and fled than risked her life for these people. Now, they held a piece of her heart. Live or die, it was something she needed to do.

He gave a slow nod. "Go on then, if your heart's set on it. And may the Lord keep you."

A tear slid down her cheek as she leaned to kiss him. Rising to full height, she squared her shoulders and turned to Peter. "I'll get my things."

Matthew shook hands with those exiting the church building. Widow Sally Crawford shuffled up to him, her son Josiah on her arm, both faithful as the rising sun. The white-haired woman, stood barely five-feet, yet had a heart as boundless as the prairie itself. Her aged, smiling face on the front pew each week garnered more encouragement than Matthew could say.

"Another fine sermon, young man. You'll give a mighty fine eulogy come time for my funeral." She pressed a quivering palm to his and gave a gentle squeeze.

He sandwiched her hand between his. "Let's hope that won't be anytime soon."

Out of the corner of his eye, he noticed Sarah at the bottom of the steps flanked by a group of excited young ladies. He stole a glance her way, his stomach twisting in knots at sight of them ogling the brooch. Sarah caught him staring and flashed a wide smile. He turned back to the line of greeters, trying to mask his angst. Before the day was out, she'd have the entire congregation mislead into thinking they were a twosome.

How had he gotten himself into such a fix?

Jed Stanton extended his hand, leaning in close. "I see you're not wastin' any time gettin' reacquainted with the school teacher."

Matthew's cheeks flamed. "It's not what you think. Really."

"Uh huh." With a hearty laugh, Jed nudged him with his elbow and moved on.

Clara shook her head. "Don't mind him. He's got a tendency to poke his nose where it doesn't belong."

Drawing a deep breath, Matthew nodded. It seemed best to avoid the whole topic. "Have you any news from Joseph and Becky?"

"We received a note some time ago, but nothing of late. Last we heard things seemed to be going better for Joseph."

"Yes. That's the news I've received as well."

Clara's eyes flashed. "Oh? I didn't realize you were corresponding with them."

Matthew cleared his throat. He'd have to be careful not to betray his feelings. "Just a note now and then to keep them informed of the news here at home."

Her expression lightened. "That's very kind. I haven't written to them in some time. Need to do that."

As Clara pressed forward, the tension eased from Matthew's shoulders. He pasted on a smile as the next person filed through the greeting line. What a charlatan he'd become. Keeping his feelings for one woman concealed, while another lady mistakenly wore a symbol of affection meant for the first.

It appeared matters of the soul were much less complicated than matters of the heart.

Chapter Twenty-Six

A CHILLING SCREAM pierced the night's stillness. Becky sprang up in bed, heart pounding. At the far end of the room, Emily thrashed beneath her linens. As a precaution, Peter had advised Becky to bed at a distance. She turned the lantern wick, illuminating the near empty room. Only a few small cots and a wash stand remained. Everything else had been transported to the new building.

As she made her way across the room, a second cry split the air. Catherine began to stir, and Becky quieted her with a gentle pat on the shoulder. Perching herself on the edge of Emily's bed, Becky gazed down into the young child's frightened face. She reached to push back strands of hair from the girl's forehead, beads of sweat dampening her fingertips. At her touch, Emily stiffened and clung to her.

Becky stroked the girl's hair. "Shhh. It's all right. Nothin's gonna harm you."

In time, Emily loosened her hold and sank limply onto the feather mattress. Becky dampened a cloth in the wash basin and placed it on the girl's forehead. She rubbed Emily's arm until the girl turned on her side and fell into a fitful sleep.

What seemed minutes must have been hours, for the room was lighter when Emily's cries awakened Becky again. Tears streamed down the girl's cheeks, and her head wagged from side to side. Nothing Becky tried worked to calm her. The girl's face felt aflame. With trembling hands, Becky dipped the rag in cool water and set it back on Emily's forehead. Becky bit at her lip, a sigh escaping her. Perhaps she'd been hasty in saying she'd care for the sick girls. She was no nursemaid. What if she did something wrong?

But what choice did she have? The instructors had their hands full with the other students. If only she could manage the rest of the night. Peter would be by to check on them in the morning.

Catherine's steady breathing droned behind her. At least one of them was able to rest. Becky shivered, the nippy autumn air sending a chill through her. She blinked back tears, tired muscles weighing her down. *Help me, Lord.*

THE FAINT SOUNDS of the front door creaking open and shut stirred Becky from fitful slumber. Peter.

Thank the Lord.

Leaping out of bed, she pressed the wrinkles from her calico dress. Up much of the night, she hadn't bothered to change into bed clothes. After ensuring both girls were asleep, she tip-toed from the room.

Peter met her at the bottom of the stairs, a weary expression lining his brow. "Is there any change?"

Becky slumped against the railing. "Emily's restless and feverish. I fear she has the influenza."

Peter winced and swept past her. "Any coughing?"

"Some." Becky followed him to the room. The girls' steady, rough breathing assured they were still sleeping. Becky stood at the foot of the cots as Peter felt first Catherine's forehead, then Emily's. Motioning toward the pitcher and basin, he removed the dampened rag from Emily's forehead, his voice soft yet urgent. "Get some ice. We have to get her fever down."

Hurrying to the kitchen, Becky opened the ice box and chipped off enough chunks to fill the water basin. When she returned, the instructor handed her the rag from Emily's forehead. "Wrap some of the ice in the cloth."

The urgency in his voice made Becky's hands quiver. She'd known Emily was quite sick, but was there a chance she might not make it? Quickly, Becky poured ice chips into the center of the cloth and swathed it around them, then handed it to Peter. Emily stirred but didn't wake as he rubbed it over her face and neck.

After some time, he pressed a hand to her cheek and then rose, motioning for Becky to follow. Together, they strode to the hall, heavy silence marring each step. Peter propped open his office door and gestured Becky inside. His cot and some of the furnishings had been removed. All that remained were his desk, a small library of books, and a few empty crates. With a sigh, he sat on his desk and crossed his arms over his chest. "Emily seems the worst. Sleep is the best thing, that and keeping the fever down. Keep applying ice to her face and neck, even her arms and legs."

Becky nodded, reassured by his presence. "How's Nettie?"

"Not good, I'm afraid. She needs our prayers." He offered Becky his desk chair and lifted an empty crate from the floor.

"Poor Nettie." Becky eased down in the chair, grieved to hear her friend hadn't improved. She suppressed a yawn, watching Peter pack the crate with books and supplies. If tonight was as restless as last night, she'd have plenty of time to pray. Emily's outbursts still weighed on Becky's mind. "Would fever cause Emily to cry out in the night? Twice she screamed and writhed in her cot seeming terrified."

He paused, peering into the half-filled crate. "Could be the fever. But more than likely her sickness has brought back her nightmares."

"Nightmares?"

"When she first arrived, she had them most every night." He shook his head, brow creased. "Such a shame."

"What happened?"

"From what I understand, she and her parents and little brother lived about five miles out of town. One morning, just before daybreak, the family woke to the sound of men shooting and hollering outside their cabin. Her father grabbed his rifle and went outside, but was shot down."

Becky gasped. "Why would they do such a thing?"

"Crazy drunk, I expect. They barged in on Emily and her mother and started beating them. Somehow Emily managed to slip away with her little brother. Fortunately, the men were either too senseless or lazy to follow. It's unclear whether she fell or was injured by one of the men, but somewhere along the way, she took a blow to the head."

"She lay unconscious till a fur trapper heard the little boy crying and went to investigate. He brought them in to the doctor. The boy was scared and hungry but otherwise unharmed, but Emily's injuries had rendered her blind. It was pretty iffy the first couple of days whether she would even live. She'd taken quite a beating. But as soon as she was able, she told them what had happened and gave a rough description of the fellows who'd done it."

Becky edged forward in her chair. "Did they find them?"

With a nod, Peter leaned his arm across the side of the crate on his desk. "The trapper caught up with them a couple of days later. Claims he shot them in self-defense, but there isn't a jury around that would have convicted him if he'd shot them down in cold blood. He found Emily's home burnt to the ground with her parents' bodies inside."

Gooseflesh rose on Becky's arms, and she rubbed it away. She'd suspected something tragic had happened to cause Emily to crawl into her shell, but nothing quite so severe. "She must have been devastated."

Mr. Bennett placed another book in the crate. "She kept asking for her mama and her little brother, but the doctor thought it would be too much and held off telling her until he thought she was strong enough. When he finally did tell her, it seemed to kill her spirit. She hasn't spoken since."

Becky's heart grieved for young Emily. The girl had endured the unimaginable. "Where's her brother now?"

"Some neighbors by the name of Guthrie took her and her brother in for a while. Said she clung to that young brother of hers like a doll, rocking him for hours and never saying a word. The Guthries didn't think it was healthy for either of them, so they brought her here. Claimed she was too much to handle with the boy and all."

Becky burned inwardly thinking of all the lonely months Emily had endured without a single visitor. "Why haven't they brought him to see her?"

"When Emily first arrived, they did come a couple of times, but the boy threw such a fit when it came time to leave, Mrs. Guthrie wouldn't stand for it. So, they stopped coming. Soon after, Emily took a turn for the worse."

Tears stung Becky's eyes. She blinked, sending a trail down her cheeks. Not only had Emily lost her parents and her sight, but she had also suffered a forced estrangement from her only sibling. No wonder she'd withdrawn.

"She's been here nearly eight months now, and isn't much better off than when she came. Except for her weaving. She seems to pour all her energies into her craftwork." He stared down at the filled crate. "I wish there was something more we could do for her."

Becky bowed her head. If anyone understood Emily's heartbreak, she did. A sudden thought churned inside her. "We could write to the Guthries, let them know Emily's sick. The hope of seeing her brother again might bring her around."

"You're forgetting. Mrs. Guthrie made it quite clear she wanted the boy to have no further contact with Emily."

"But she needs something to hold onto, something to give her hope. She could die without it." The firmness in Becky's voice surprised her.

He shook his head, his face sullen. "It would be false hope and simply cause more grief."

"But you say Roy's a different person since he's taken up wood carving. All he needed was a chance to be himself. Maybe all Emily needs is her brother."

With a sigh, Peter snatched up the carton of books. "It would only make things worse. It's best we leave well enough alone."

Becky sank back in her chair, wondering how things could get any worse. The girl had lost all will to live. She needed something to fight for. Without hope, Emily's chance for recovery seemed slim.

Becky clenched her jaw. She had to do something.

"Come on, Emily. You've gotta eat." Becky butted the spoonful of porridge up against Emily's mouth. The young girl pursed her lips and turned her head away. With a groan, Becky plunged the spoon into the now lukewarm bowl of porridge and wiped the smudges from Emily's mouth. For twenty minutes now she'd attempted to get the youngster to eat, and Emily hadn't so much as licked the food from her lips. If she was determined to starve herself, there was nothing Becky could do to stop her.

A raspy cough escaped Emily's throat, and she lay back on her cot, limp and pale. Six grueling days the girl had writhed with fever. Now a persistent cough rattled deep in her chest. The silence that had gripped her so long was heightened now by her sunken cheeks and pasty complexion.

With an exasperated sigh, Becky leaned back in her chair. Was she to sit by and watch this little girl die for lack of will to live?

"Miss Becky?" Catherine's tiny voice called from behind. The young girl sat perched on the edge of her bed, feet curled under her frock. Her cheeks glowed pink, making Emily's seem all the more peaked. "Will I go to the new school today?"

Becky set the bowl of porridge aside, giving Emily a reassuring pat on the arm. "I'll be back in a bit." Striding over to Catherine, she stroked the young girl's wavy, auburn hair. "Yes, sweetie. Peter will be here very soon. You can wait downstairs if you like."

A huge smile sliced across Catherine's face, and Becky gave her a warm hug. At least one of her prayers had been answered. She handed Catherine her satchel. "Hold tight to the railing. I'll be down in a few minutes."

A barky cough sounded from the opposite side of the room. Little Amos moaned in restless slumber, having fallen prey to the fever and cough three days after Catherine and Emily. Jenny, too, turned on her cot, burning with fever. Thankfully, Pa and Jimmy had remained healthy.

Becky dipped cloths in the basin of icy water and laid them across the children's foreheads. How many more would fall sick? Why she herself hadn't succumbed to the fever was beyond understanding.

She yawned and rubbed her tired neck as she eased back down in the chair next to Emily's bed. How much longer could she keep this up? Emily's eyes were closed now and her breathing labored but steady. The girl's jet black hair lay draped across her face, and Becky brushed it aside. Young Emily was giving up. She needed something to fight for—or someone.

A nervous twinge churned inside Becky as she recalled

Peter's stern warning not to interfere. She clenched her jaw in stubborn resolve. He was wrong. Emily deserved to at least have hope.

With a glance to be certain all were resting, she stepped to Peter's office. He'd left the files of those who were sick on his desk to notify the next of kin, in case they didn't pull through. Becky leafed through the files until she found Emily's. Opening it, she scanned the page of personal information. Two-thirds of the way down, she tapped her finger on the paper, a broad smile spreading over her face. Her brother's name was Stephen. Scrolling her finger further down the page, she paused on a name and address at the bottom. Taking out a blank sheet of paper, she sat down at the desk. A knot tore at her stomach as she dipped the quill in the ink bottle and wrote, "Dear Mr. and Mrs. Ben Guthrie." With a deep breath, she began spilling out her concerns and pleas.

As she penned the last stroke, the front door creaked open. She blew on the ink and skimmed the note, a tingle of excitement running through her. They'd come. They just had to. All she had to do was get it to the post office.

Peter's baritone voice sounded downstairs. Becky's heart raced as she hurried to fold the letter. The instructor couldn't know about it, not yet anyway. She sealed the letter with hot wax and fanned it dry with her hand. Sinking the letter in her pocket, she hurried to the top of the stairway.

Catherine's chipper, soprano voice sounded below. As Becky downed the stairs, Peter gave the child a pat on the back and then straightened. With a smile, he placed an arm around the young girl's shoulders. "Well, it appears you have one patient eager to leave. How are the others faring?"

Becky's gaze met his for a moment, then she stooped to fasten a missed button on Catherine's overcoat. "No better, I'm afraid. Emily refuses to eat or take her medicine." Her words poured out a bit sharper than intended.

He cleared his throat, his smile fading. "I'm sorry to hear it. I'll ask Doctor Trace to stop by again."

Becky pushed a strand of hair from her forehead. "Is Nettie any better?"

"Her fever's down, but like Emily, she's slow to recover. Only time will tell."

Becky bowed her head. She missed her friend's spry wit and spiritedness. How long could this illness drag on? It seemed weeks since she'd done anything but tend to sick children.

Catherine tugged at Peter's trousers. "Can we go now?"

Peter rubbed the back of her head, his face brightening. "Soon, Catherine, but first, Miss Becky has some visitors."

Becky's eyes widened. Having been cooped up for over a week, mention of company was balm for her soul. "Who?"

"See for yourself out on the porch. Just don't get close."

She swept past him and pushed open the door. At the far end of the porch, Pa sat forward in his chair, Aunt Ellen at his side. At sight of Becky, her aunt's face lit up, and she strode forward. "Becky. Oh, it's so good to see you."

Becky held out her arm. "Don't come any closer."

Pa swiveled toward her, mouth taut. "You sick, darlin'?"

"I'm fine. I just don't wanna take any chances." Her expression softened. "Oh, I've missed you. How's the new building?"

"The place seems huge compared to here. Don't think I'll ever find my way around." Pa crossed his legs at the ankles, looking more self-assured than Becky remembered. "How soon can you come?"

She drew in a breath of fresh air, folding her arms against the chilly October breeze. "Not till everyone's well, I'm afraid. Another week or two I expect."

"That long?" A look of disappointment cloaked her father's face.

The door creaked open behind her as Peter and Catherine stepped onto the porch. He glanced in their direction. "Why don't I take Catherine on and let you folks visit a while? I'll get her settled in and come back for you." His gaze trailed to Aunt Ellen "Just keep your distance."

A slight grin graced Aunt Ellen's lips. Peter's concern for her seemed more than mere benevolence. The slight blush in her aunt's cheeks hinted she, too, was aware of it.

Taking Catherine by the hand, Peter started with her toward the wagon.

Aunt Ellen's expression sobered as she turned her attention to Becky. "You look plumb worn out. Are you well?"

"I'm shy on sleep's all. There's always someone needing something."

Pa smacked his hand down on his knee. "I knew this wasn't a good idea. You'll run yourself ragged."

"Not much choice, Pa. Nettie's still sick. I'm needed here."

He opened his mouth as if to protest, but quieted when Aunt Ellen pressed a hand to his shoulder.

"How's Jimmy?" Becky leaned into the railing, wishing she'd thought to grab her shawl.

Pa settled back in his chair. "Struggling to adjust, like the rest of us."

Becky dipped her hand in her pocket, fingering her letter to the Guthries. Aunt Ellen was her one chance to get it mailed without arousing suspicions. "Could you mail a letter for me, Aunt Ellen?"

"Certainly. I'll ask Peter to drop by the post office on the way back."

Becky bit her lip, lifting the note from her pocket. "It's sort of a private matter...for Emily."

With an understanding nod, her aunt reached to straighten her bonnet. "I'll keep it to myself."

Becky set the letter on the railing and backed away. "I-I've another one upstairs for Matthew."

"Matthew?" Pa's stunned expression matched his uneasy tone.

"I-I mean Pastor Brody." She cringed, the words gushing out a bit too intense. How careless of her.

Pa laced his fingers together, brow creased. "You two spend a lot of time conversing back and forth for no more than he has to say. You sure you're telling all there is to tell?"

The query sent her heart pounding in her ears. "I-I...Yes, Pa." Even a slight untruth left a numb feeling in the pit of her stomach. She hadn't the right to speak otherwise, not knowing for certain Matthew's intentions.

"The girl has a right to write whom she chooses, Joseph." Becky's eyes locked on her aunt's. She knew something. Would she keep Becky's secret? If only they could speak in private.

Pa tilted his head, his expression softening. "I suppose."

With a relieved sigh, Becky backed towards the door, gesturing over her shoulder. "I'll just go check on the children and—get it."

Her heart hammered as she hurried up the stairs. Whether from her father's probing questions or betraying Peter's trust, she felt on edge. Taking a quick peek at the sleeping students, she retrieved Matthew's letter from beneath her pillow. So much had changed since she'd penned it. Yet, she'd spare him the hardships. For a week now, she'd been delayed in sending it. In that time, no gift had arrived. Hopefully, his next letter would better explain things.

A slight moan sounded from across the room. Becky pushed her thoughts aside and made her way to Emily. She leaned over to stroke the girl's raven black hair. So frail and weak. "You rest easy now, and gain your strength."

Emily's mouth stiffened, and she pushed Becky's hand away.

She was getting nowhere. Should she mention Stephen? Why not? Nothing else had worked. With her letter to Guthries nearly on its way, now was as good of time as any to see if the news would rouse her.

"You must work very hard to get well, Emily." Becky cleared her throat to steady her trembling voice. What if Peter was right? What if the Guthries refused to come?

She straightened. It was a risk she had to take. "Perhaps then Stephen can come for a visit."

At the sound of her brother's name, Emily's head gave a sudden jerk, and her face brightened.

Becky smiled, her voice gaining strength. "But he can't come until you're well, understand?"

Emily gave a slight nod.

Becky touched the girl's slender arm and pulled the covers up over her shoulders. "If I bring some fresh porridge in a bit, will you try to eat some?"

Another nod.

"Good. I'll be back soon." As she stood, Becky tamped down her excitement. It was the first sign of progress in many days. She pressed a hand to her chest and uttered a silent prayer. *Give her strength to pull through, Lord, and may the letter to the Guthries not be for nothing.*

"DEEP BREATHS NOW, EMILY." Doctor Trace moved the stethoscope along the girl's back as she breathed in and out. The older gentleman twisted his white mustache to one side, eyebrows raised.

Becky edged closer. "She's better. Isn't she?"

The doctor patted Emily on the back and coaxed her down onto her pillow. He slid the instrument from his ears and dropped it into his black, leather pouch, a twinkle in his gray eyes. "Remarkably. In fact, all your patients are much improved. You've done an exceptional job, young lady."

Becky's face warmed, and she tried to suppress the glow inside her. Wrong or right, her mention of Stephen had sparked a noticeable change in Emily.

Little Amos tugged at her skirt. "When can we go back to the new school, Miss Becky?"

She placed an arm around him, glancing at the doctor. "How soon can they be with the other students?"

"Another couple days should do." The doctor latched his bag and stood, donning his hat.

A smile spread across Becky's lips, and she gave Amos a squeeze. "Hear that?"

Amos bobbed his head up and down, a wide grin on his rounded face.

Becky drew in a long, cleansing breath. It would be so good to be back with everyone. How she'd missed Jimmy's comforting presence and quick wit.

Boot steps sounded on the stairs below. A moment later, Peter appeared in the bedroom doorway, face ghostly pale. "Doctor Trace. Come quick. It's Nettie."

Seizing his bag, the doctor rushed after him.

Fear coursed through Becky. "But you said she was improving."

Sadness marred the instructor's face as he met her stare. Without a word, he hurried the doctor downstairs and was gone.

Jenny tilted her head to one side, her face solemn. "Should we pray for her, Miss Becky?"

Becky struggled to still her quivering lips. The very thought of losing someone else dear wedged a stranglehold on her heart. Moisture clouded her eyes, and she struggled to speak. "Yes, Jenny. Let's all pray."

Chapter Twenty-Seven

"Into Thy hands we commit the spirit of Miss Nettie Cohan. Amen."

Becky shivered in the frosty air, numbed at the pastor's words. How could her vibrant, loving friend be gone? In the few short months Becky had known her, Nettie had given of herself more than most people do in a lifetime. Becky clutched her father's arm, his touch and presence a comfort to her dismal spirit.

The pastor closed his Bible and stepped aside for people to pay final respects. A flock of geese shattered the stillness, calling to each other on their journey south. Becky gazed into the cobalt sky, watching their arched formation fade into the distance. Her heart longed to soar with them, away from the pain of loss. Her throat tightened. She'd had her fill of grief over recent months.

A lofty sycamore towered overhead, its near bare branches spreading over the open grave. Giant, golden leaves spiraled downward, carpeting the ground. It was a lovely resting place. Nettie would have been pleased.

Tears stung Becky's eyes as she dropped a rose onto the

wooden casket. She leaned against her father, memories of Ma and Melissa bursting to the forefront of her mind. Now her cherished friend, too, had passed, without a farewell. Emotions too deep for words tore at her insides. It seemed unthinkable that her friend's hearty laugh and spirited ways would no longer touch their lives. Was this some cruel test from the Lord? How many more senseless deaths would she have to endure?

The meager gathering of mourners began to disperse, leaving behind only close friends and relatives. Mr. Whelan stood face downcast, weeping. His silent tears and anguished face voiced great loss of his life-long companion. The pastor clasped his arm. "Stay as long as you wish. I'll be happy to give you a ride home when you're ready."

Mr. Whelan gave a slow nod, brushing a tear from his cheek.

An aging, dark-skinned couple approached, walking arm in arm. The plain-dressed woman dabbed her eyes with a frayed handkerchief, her gaze fixed on the closed coffin. She let go of her husband's arm and whispered in Mr. Whelan's ear. He reached to embrace her, their quiet sobs intertwining. No doubt this was Nettie's sister. Same robust figure, rounded face, and gentle, chocolate eyes.

Peter led the chain of students toward the wagon, their faces solemn. Becky placed a hand on Mr. Whelan's shoulder as she and Pa passed by. At the corner of the wagon, Jimmy aided younger students into the bed, heaviness lining his brow. Becky gave his hand a gentle squeeze, and his face brightened. There was no need for words. Her touch had spoken for her.

Silence hung over the group like a dense fog as Mr. Bennett set the team of horses in motion. The steady clopping of hooves on the cobblestone street had a mesmerizing effect. The children's gloomy faces, many of whom she hadn't seen in nearly three weeks, tortured her grief-stricken heart. This wasn't the reunion she had envisioned.

Emily gave a slight cough, and Becky tugged her coat tighter around her. The young girl had made such progress in the past week. The chilly air risked a setback.

The wagon joggled to a stop before a huge brick building uptown. The smaller front yard boasted fewer trees and more pavement and building. Joy at their arrival had scattered like the newly fallen leaves that blanketed the yard. Becky helped younger students from the wagon and hurried them inside, out of the frigid morning air.

The entryway's domed, chiseled ceiling stole Becky's breath away. The unknown donor must have wealth beyond measure to make such a grand offer. She tugged at her bonnet, letting it slip to the nape of her neck as she stepped into the spacious sitting room. A crystal chandelier dangled from its center, while a huge stone fireplace decorated the north wall. A string of upholstered chairs formed an arch around the fireplace hearth.

Peter removed his hat and brushed down wavy, auburn hair. "It's a lot to take in at first glance. We're truly blessed to have it, don't you think?"

Becky gave a slight nod. Other circumstances might have warranted a more jubilant response. Instead, a cold, emptiness settled over her as she helped the younger students shed their outerwear. Hats and coats removed, the children meandered about, looking lost and troubled.

Peter struck a chord on the upright piano, resting near the curtained window. Jenny straightened, her face cocked toward the sound. "We've missed your playing, Jenny. Would you favor us with a piece?"

"I don't feel much like playing, sir," came her immediate reply.

"Come, now. It will do us all good to hear you play." Taking her by the hand, he led her to the piano bench. A moment later, her fingers were dancing over the ivory keys, her grief seemingly transposed into quiet melody. It had been weeks since Becky had heard the soft drone of music. She closed her eyes, drinking in the gentle tune. A hush fell over the children, their melancholy mood seeming to lift. There was something soothing in the sound of a well-played instrument. How wise Peter was to know just what was needed to still their troubled souls.

An ashy smell filtered out into the room, pulling Becky from her solitude. Peter was squatted by the hearth, stoking the embers in the fireplace. He fanned the hot coals until they flamed, then added logs to the swelling fire. His concern for the comfort and welfare of the children was admirable. He's been nothing but kind to her and Pa since the day they'd arrived. Aunt Ellen would do well to take notice of his fine qualities.

"That should warm us a bit." Standing, Peter rubbed his hands together. He turned to Becky, a wearied expression in his eyes. "I suppose we should get you newcomers settled in. Would you like a tour?"

Heaviness tugged at Becky's heart as she peeled off her bonnet. What pleasure would she find in it? "If you don't mind, I'd just as soon get started on dinner."

With a pronounced nod, he escorted her down the hall to the dining area and into the adjoining kitchen. Becky half expected to see Nettie prattling about. Instead, she was greeted by a cold, vacant room cluttered with unwashed dishes. Her heart sank at sight of the idle cast-iron stove, littered with food-encrusted pans.

Peter's eyes met hers, and he cringed. "I'm afraid I'm not the housekeeper Nettie was. And with the funeral and all this morning we…"

"It's all right. I'll get to it." Becky breathed a quiet sigh and rolled up her sleeves. Nettie had made such mundane tasks tolerable, even enjoyable. Tears stung Becky's eyes, and she blinked them back, refusing to tarnish her friend's memory by crying. If this was to be her lot for the duration of her stay, she would have to make the best of it, miserable or not.

MATTHEW EASED down in his caned porch chair and slid Becky's newly arrived letter from his pocket. It had been difficult to wait until he returned home to read it, but he didn't want to risk being interrupted. By Sarah, or anyone else, for that matter. Home seemed a much more suitable place to savor it. Breaking open the wax seal, he unfolded the letter. This one had taken a bit longer to arrive. He feared he'd made himself a pest to Mrs. Chaney in the post office, checking with her daily for over a week. If anyone guessed his and Becky's feelings, it would be her.

Warmth shrouded his chest as his eyes canvased the lengthy script. Becky had much to say this time. Their relationship seemed to deepen with each correspondence. He settled back in his chair, and began poring over the words.

"Dear Matthew,

Your letter filled me with such joy. It's good to hear how the Lord has blessed you with home and ministry. Although the gift you mentioned hasn't arrived, I shall watch for it daily, in eager expectation."

Gift? Matthew leaned forward, the blood draining from his cheeks. How careless of him. He'd written his last letter with every intention of sending along the brooch. When Sarah unexpectedly claimed it, he'd forgotten having mentioned it in his letter.

Becky was anticipating a gift she'd never receive.

He raked a hand through his hair. Now what was he to do?

With a sigh, he continued reading.

"Pa is doing so well now, but for his persistent refusal to take up an instrument. Oh, that he had his own fiddle in hand. Maybe that would stir him to make melody once again. I never mentioned it surviving the storm. It hardly seemed necessary. How I miss hearing him play."

Matthew lowered the page, eyebrows raised. Her father's fiddle. If Joseph having it would garner the effect Becky hoped, it would mean much more to her than any brooch. Surely Matthew could afford to send it by post.

A smile touched his lips as he read on. He loved hearing news of Jimmy, Roy, and Emily. The way Becky wrote of them, he felt almost as if he knew them. She certainly had a heart for people. Did she realize just how much the Lord was using her?

The final paragraph drew his attention. He paused, drinking in each word.

"I'm counting the months till I lay eyes on the rich, dark soil of home and our new cabin tucked within the acres of prairie grass. Though the Lord has been good to us here, and there are people I will miss, my heart longs for home, to be back in our quiet corner of the world, working the land and making a fresh start."

The words caught in his chest and a wave of uncertainty swept over him. She was so eager to return to their new cabin and homestead. And why not? All she'd ever known was the simple life of a farmer's daughter. Her spirit thrived on fresh air and the freedom of the outdoors. More than once, he'd witnessed her working alongside Joseph in the field. With his blindness, he'd rely on her now more than ever.

Matthew brushed a hand over his face. Could he ask Becky to sacrifice the person she was to become the wife of a pastor? His ministry would necessitate him living close to town. Would she grow bored and restless with him running hither and yon? Would she become frustrated when he was called upon to serve others, feeling he put his ministry ahead of her?

Like Sarah had?

The sudden remembrance stabbed at him like a knife. His

devotion to ministry had been a continual source of strife between them. Would the same prove true of Becky?

The final lines held his gaze.

"Praying the time is short until we are together once more.

Yours truly,

Becky"

His throat thickened. Was he being fair to her? To himself? Perhaps he'd best think—better yet, pray—things through more thoroughly before surrendering his heart.

Or asking her to surrender hers.

BEFORE MATTHEW HAD a chance to dismount and knock, the door to the Stanton home opened. Clara stepped out onto the porch, flanked by daughters Charlotte and Esther. "Morning, pastor. What brings you out our way?"

Matthew tipped his hat and edged forward. "I was hoping you could help me locate Joseph's fiddle. By chance did Becky leave it with you?"

"I believe so." Clara squinted up at him. "Did you need it for something?"

He cleared his throat. How could he manage this without arousing suspicions? "She mentioned in her last letter that Joseph might benefit from having it. I'd like to send it to them, if I may."

Clara's momentary pause and penetrating stare hinted she was assessing not only Matthew's words but also his intentions. Was his expression relaying more than he wanted?

"The fiddle's under our bed. Would you like me to get it?" Esther pointed over her shoulder, breaking the silence.

Clara motioned for her to go while keeping her gaze fixed on Matthew. "You hear from Becky quite often then?" Her words seemed more statement than question.

"On occasion." He rubbed a hand down Gabriel's neck. The less said at this point, the better.

"I fear I've neglected writing her and Joseph far too long." Clara's eyes softened and a slight grin touched her lips. "First chance I get, I'll have to fill them in on the goings on around here."

There seemed an underlying meaning in her words and tone that Matthew couldn't quite decipher. Just what "goings on" was she referring to?

Soft footsteps padded inside the cabin, and Esther appeared in the doorway. "Here you are," she said, handing him the fiddle.

Matthew shifted his feet, breathing a silent prayer of gratitude at her timely return. "Thank you. I'll get it off to Joseph first thing." He held the fiddle case in both hands, like a treasure. Soon the instrument would be reunited with its master—a true miracle, given what it will have gone through to reach him.

Clara gestured toward the cabin. "Jed's out tending livestock, but would you care for some coffee?"

With Clara's keen women's intuition, it wouldn't take much probing for her to get to the truth of the matter. The less opportunity he gave her to pry, the better. "Much obliged, but I need to get back." Tucking the fiddle under his arm, he tipped his hat. "See you in church Sunday. Give my regards to Jed."

"Will do," Clara called as Matthew mounted.

Laying the fiddle case across the front of the saddle, he tapped Gabriel's sides with his heels. Matthew ran his fingertips over the smooth texture of the fiddle case. Joseph would certainly be stunned by its arrival.

Would Becky be pleased?

An unsettled feeling washed over him as he rode away. Perhaps he should send only a short note along with the fiddle. Until he had a better handle on things, it seemed best not to complicate the situation further. How could he think of courting

Becky when the entire town thought he had his sights set on Sarah?

Why had she come anyway, just when he'd decided to settle here? It seemed uncanny. Was it the Lord's providence? Or Satan's way of throwing a kink in his plans? Regardless, everyone seemed convinced he and Sarah were meant to be together.

Everyone, except his heart.

Chapter Twenty-Eight

How had Nettie done it?

Becky smoothed the soft mound of biscuit dough with the wooden rolling pin. Raising the back of her flour-caked hand to her brow, she brushed away a loose wisp of hair. Up before dawn, she'd had to divide her time between the kitchen and seeing to the needs of the newer students. Tackling three flights of stairs, while preparing a meal for a crew of nearly twenty, was as taxing as being chased by a swarm of angry bees.

She cast an appreciative glance at her aunt tending the kettle of gravy on the stove. "Now I understand why Nettie was so thrilled to have my help. An extra pair of hands comes in mighty handy 'round here."

With a soft chuckle, Aunt Ellen shook her head. "With my lack of cooking skills, I'm not sure I'm an asset. I just can't seem to work the lumps out of this gravy."

"Believe me, I'm tickled just to have the company." Becky thrust the biscuit cutter into the dough repeatedly and then peeled back the excess with a sigh. "I've always done my best to avoid cooking and cleaning. Now it seems that's all I do."

Ringlets of steam swirled about Aunt Ellen, along with the

spicy scent of sausage, as she scraped the outer edges of the thickened gravy with a wooden spoon. "No doubt it's been a strain on you, without Nettie these past few days."

Becky's eyes canvassed the roomy kitchen. The familiar pine icebox and glass-paneled corner cabinet lay nestled against the far wall, remnants of the old kitchen. How tragic Nettie had no chance to enjoy them in the new setting. She'd been so excited about the move. The abundant space seemed void without her. Yet Aunt Ellen's presence helped to fill it. "If I learned anything from Nettie, it's that no job's a burden when it's shared."

Aunt Ellen tilted her head to one side. "What a lovely thought." She gave the gravy a final stir, then, taking a cloth in each hand, moved the kettle to a pad on the work table. "I only wish I could do more."

"You're very kind to volunteer your weekends." Becky leaned against the counter with a moan. "How I miss our quiet evenings at your place. Doesn't seem I've had a moment's rest since before Nettie took sick." Pushing away the thought, she arranged the limp biscuit dough in a metal pan and slid it in the cast-iron stove. The first batch had just minutes left to bake.

Aunt Ellen fanned herself with her apron, seeming to study Becky. "You look a bit peaked. You sure you're not overdoing it?"

Shoulders slumped, Becky brushed remnants of dried dough from her hands. "Peter's trying to find help, but he hasn't had any takers."

"What about the older girls? Can't they ease your load?"

Becky shrugged. "They try, but sometimes make more work in the long run. The little ones can't be trusted around the hot stove. Jenny's good help, but she's leaving soon."

Aunt Ellen pulled up a chair. "Well, you just sit and rest a spell and let me tend to things a while."

Becky hesitated before sinking onto the seat. Until this moment, she'd not given much thought to being tired. Perhaps she was overdoing it a bit. But then, she needed to keep busy. Rest gave birth to bitter thoughts. Nettie's untimely death, coupled by unwanted duties, had left her numb. She had no time to call her own anymore. Let alone time for Pa or Jimmy. Emily's disillusionment over her brother, too, weighed heavy on Becky's heart. There'd been no response from Mr. or Mrs. Guthrie. And though the young girl had recovered from her illness, she'd lost all enthusiasm, even for weaving. It seemed Peter was right. Becky had only made matters worse by interfering.

A faint burnt smell hung in the air, jerking Becky to her feet. "My biscuits." Rushing over, she snatched an oven cloth and pulled out the first pan of biscuits. With a groan, she slid them into a bread-basket, their bottoms charred and crusty.

Cringing, Aunt Ellen thrust her hands to her hips. "Lumpy gravy, overcooked biscuits, and not a soul will complain."

"Guess they realize we're all they've got." Becky leaned against the counter, rubbing a hand over the back of her neck. Why was she so tired? Every muscle in her body cried for rest.

"Indeed. They can't afford to complain." Her aunt's soft chuckle melted into a more sober tone as she turned toward Becky. "You really do look worn to a nub. Why not let me finish up? You rest a while."

"I couldn't."

Aunt Ellen pressed her hands to Becky's shoulders. "Yes, you can."

Becky twisted her mouth to one side. "I'm fine, really."

Arching a brow, Aunt Ellen swiveled Becky toward the doorway and gave her a gentle nudge. "Go."

With a hesitant sigh, Becky removed her apron and hung it on the wooden peg beside the icebox. Some fresh air might do her good at that. Donning her wrap, she traipsed through the empty dining hall and into the front room. Students were beginning to make their way down the flight of stairs. A twinge of guilt pulled at Becky, and she paused. Instead of indulging herself in a rest, she should go offer her help to some of the newer students. Still, she deserved at least a few moments of quiet to herself.

As she stepped outside, a light, south breeze eased the sting of the early November morning, but not the weightiness plaguing her every step. Her heart sank at the long line of buildings blocking the morning sun's rays. Gone were the large front lawn and apple trees of the previous school. In their place stood a lone oak tree, its branches all but bare, but for a handful of stubborn leaves unwilling to loosen their hold. Had Jimmy found a tree to sit beneath out back? She'd had little chance to explore the massive building, let alone the exterior. She drew a steadying breath. The long days and restless nights had taken a toll on her.

"Did you get booted out?"

Turning, Becky spied Jimmy seated on the steps further down, face to the wind. The corners of her mouth lifted. "Something like that."

His head bent toward her as she approached, and she pulled her shawl tighter around her shoulders. As she settled down beside him, she glanced up at the massive building towering over them. "What do you think of this place?"

Jimmy let out a huff. "I miss the smallness of the old school. I could find my way around it."

Becky took in his blond curls and youthful profile. She couldn't blame him for brooding over his loss of freedom. He'd known every inch of the old place, inside and out. She felt lost here herself. If only Jimmy had a home to go to. Then he'd be spared the confusion of learning his way around. His uncertain future weighed heavily on him, Becky knew.

She tucked her arms around her knees. "I hear you're teaching Pa how to run the wood lathe. How's he doing?"

"He's beginning to get the hang of it."

"He has a good teacher."

Jimmy shrugged, seeming to suppress a grin.

Becky leaned her head on his shoulder. "I've missed you, Jimmy."

"Have you too, Beck."

A tired smile tugged at her lips. Jimmy's friendship had come as an unexpected gift, a timely balm for her troubled soul. The young man possessed wisdom beyond his years.

Becky gazed out into the unfamiliar street, laced with horse-drawn rigs and people milling about. How her heart ached for the openness of the prairie, much like Jimmy longed for the familiarity of the old school. Winter would be setting in soon. Spring seemed ages away—as well as their return home. When the time came, would Matthew be able to find them in this new place? To be certain, she'd learn their direction and post it in her next letter.

"So, have you found us a tree out back?"

"I was waiting for you to ask."

"We've a few minutes before breakfast." She started to rise and then, light-headed, fell back, steadying herself against Jimmy. She rubbed her temples, trying to relieve the dull pain in her head.

Jimmy clasped her arm. "You all right?"

"Just a bit light-headed."

"Maybe you'd best go back inside." He helped her to her feet.

A cold sweat dampened Becky's forehead. Dark spots dulled her vision, and she closed her eyes and then blinked them open. What was happening? After all this time, was she falling prey to sickness? She pitched forward and tightened her hold on Jimmy's arm. "Jimmy, I..."

"What is it, Beck?" His muffled words echoed in her ears.

Without warning, Becky's legs gave out from under her. Then there was only darkness.

BECKY AWOKE TO A DARKENED ROOM, lantern light casting shadows on unfamiliar walls. She squeezed her eyes open and shut, trying to shake off the overpowering grogginess. Where was she, and what was this heaviness that weighted her limbs? Her gaze drifted from the dim ceiling to the chair beside her bed. There sat her father, head bowed, hands clutching hers. A groan escaped her as she shifted toward him. "Pa?"

Rousing at the sound of her voice, he leaned closer. "You all right, darlin'?"

"What happened?" She cringed, stretching tired, achy muscles.

"You passed out. Been asleep for hours."

She took a hard swallow, struggling to make sense of her muddled memory. "Now I remember. I was talking with Jimmy and then everything went black." She scanned the strange room, filled with unfamiliar furnishings. "Where am I?"

"Peter's room. He thought it best you have quiet while you rest. He'll bunk with Eli a few days while you regain your strength."

A sudden thought sent a chill through her. "Is it the influenza?"

Pa's calm shake of the head eased her fears. "Doc Trace says with all you've been through, you're just plumb worn out. Fatigue he called it. Says you're to stay in bed and rest a few days."

"But I can't…" An attempt to rise left her woozy, and she fell back on the cot.

He squeezed her hand, holding her in place. "You can, and you will. Nettie's sister, Lily, came soon as she got word. And Ellen's boss has agreed to let her have some time off. You just hunker down and rest." He reached to stroke her hair. "It's time you take care of yourself, instead of everyone else."

Her eyelids grew heavy at his touch, and she let herself relax. When she woke again, morning light filtered through the frosty windowpane, and Pa no longer sat beside her. Muffled noises sounded outside the closed door, assuring her the students were going about their daily routine. A tray with milk, fruit, and a fresh baked apple-cinnamon muffin rested on the stand near her bed. Drawing herself up to a sitting position, she placed the tray across her lap. One bite of the soft, savory muffin hinted it was Nettie's sister who'd baked them rather than Aunt Ellen. She took another bite, savoring its goodness. While she was there, Lily would prove a welcome addition.

The door creaked opened, and Aunt Ellen peered in, a pleasant smile on her lips. "Well, you're up at last."

Becky downed her mouthful of muffin with a sip of milk. "What time is it?"

"Nearly time to leave for church service."

Becky's face pinched. Until then, she hadn't given thought to her aunt being dressed in her Sunday best. "But it's Saturday."

Aunt Ellen lifted the empty tray from Becky's lap and set it on the night stand. "I'm afraid you slept much of Saturday away. It's Sunday morning."

Snugging the covers over her, Becky sank lower in the bed. "Never dreamed I could sleep so much."

"You had us all pretty worried."

"Sorry for troubling you. Pa says you've asked for time off work."

With a gentle laugh, her aunt took a seat on the edge of the bed. "Oh, it's no bother, I assure you. Helping here will be a welcome change from sitting all day at a sewing machine." The gleam in her aunt's eyes hinted of genuineness. She truly seemed to enjoy the interaction with the children and being a help. What a shame she'd never had the opportunity to enjoy a family of her own.

Becky's gaze drifted to the book in her aunt's hand, and she smiled. "Oh. I brought your Bible. I know how you enjoy reading it. I thought it might help pass the time while we're at church…unless you'd rather me stay with you."

"I'll be fine. Thank you." Taking it from her, Becky clutched it to her chest. Matthew's parting gift stirred a host of memories. The frayed Bible had been his constant companion for a good number of years. That he'd entrusted it to her meant a great deal. His winsome smile and warm touch lingered in her mind's eye.

A knock on the door broke through her thoughts. Peter poked his head in. "How's the patient?"

Laying the Bible on the bed stand, she rallied a slight smile. "Tired. Though I'm not sure why. Seems all I've done is slept."

"You just get yourself well." His gaze fell to Aunt Ellen. "In the meantime, you've a mighty fine replacement."

A shy smile accompanied Aunt Ellen's lingering stare. Becky sank back on her feather pillow, lips hinging upward. There was more between the two of them than either was willing to admit.

"Well, I'd best get the students loaded. I'll check in on you later." Peter's gaze flicked from Becky to her aunt. "Coming, Ellen?"

"I'll just be a minute."

Gripping the door handle, Peter backed from the room. As he pulled the door shut behind him, Becky couldn't hold back a smile. "No doubt about it. He's sweet on you. And maybe you're a bit taken with him as well."

Hazel eyes flashing, her aunt stood, pink staining her cheeks. "Nonsense. Why would you say such a thing?"

"I may work at a blind school, but I'm not blind." With a tired chuckle, Becky fluffed her feather pillow.

"That'll be enough of that, young lady." Even as she scolded, a faint smile crept over Aunt Ellen's lips.

Becky caught her by the arm, her expression sobering. "He's not Jeffrey. Give him a chance."

Her aunt's eyes glazed over as though, even after so many

years, her wounded heart was still tender. Leaning down, she kissed Becky's forehead. "Get some rest."

Sleep buffeted Becky off and on throughout the day, until evening shadows blanketed the room. Footsteps sounded in the hall, and she craned her neck, struggling to focus on the dimly lit doorway. Wavering between sleep and consciousness, she attempted to focus on the dark-skinned woman approaching. "Nettie?"

The woman stepped closer, out of the shadows. "No, Miss Becky. I'z her sister, Lily." The familiar tone in the woman's voice sent a shiver through Becky. Though leaner and slightly older than Nettie, the family resemblance between the two was unmistakable.

Pulling herself to a sitting position, Becky rubbed a hand over her face. "Yes. Of course. Forgive me."

"No matter." A faint smile lit the woman's face as she set the tray across Becky's lap.

She eyed the plate of ham, beans, and corn bread, the aroma stirring hunger pangs within her. "Not only do you resemble Nettie, but you share her talent for cooking."

"Thank ya kindly, Miss Becky." The aging woman chuckled, brushing back a strand of gray dappled hair. "I feels I knows ya already. Nettie talked 'bout ya all da time. Yes'm. Said you wuz pure sug'r."

Sobering, Becky stared down at the tray. "She was a good friend, so full of life. Isn't fair her being snatched away so."

Calloused fingers cupped her chin. "No need to feel sorry for Nettie, young'un. She'z right where she'd chooze to be—safe in the armz o' Jesus."

Becky met the woman's gaze. It was true. Nettie wouldn't

want pity. She'd given her entire life in service to others. Now she'd gone to her reward. "Never thought of it that way."

The woman's forehead creased as she pulled a chair up next to Becky. "'Tis only natural to miss folks taken from us sooner than we expect. Important thing iz they know the Lord."

With a slight nod, Becky lowered her gaze, letting the woman's words soak in. Most assuredly, Nettie had a heart for the Lord. Then it wasn't for Nettie's sake Becky grieved, but for herself. Was the same true of Ma and Melissa? All these long, bitter months of wishing them back. Had that, too, been for herself?

Lily pressed her chin to her neck and clasped Becky's hand. "Ain't no need to grieve, young'un. Nettie wasn't snatched from us for nothin'. Why, she's gone on ahead to welcome us home someday."

Like fresh spring water, peace settled over Becky. As caught up in her loss as she had been, such truths had long eluded her. Although the Lord had called her loved ones home sooner than she might have wished, she had every assurance of one day seeing them again.

A scuffing sound outside the doorway pulled their attention. When no one entered, Lily rose and peered out into the hallway. Muffled words ensued between her and what sounded like a male voice. A moment later, Lily stepped back into the room. "There'z a young man lurkin' about. You want I should send him in?"

Becky eased back up to a sitting position. No doubt Jimmy had come to check on her. "Jimmy? Of course."

"Tain't Jimmy. Says his name's Roy."

"Oh." Of all those Becky might have expected to pay her a visit, Roy was among the least likely. Curiosity soon edged out her disappointment. "Have him come in."

After some coaxing, Roy shuffled in, pausing just inside the doorway.

"Over here, Roy. There's a chair by the bed."

The large-framed boy worked his way over and eased down onto the chair. He shifted back and forth on the caned seat, rubbing his hands over his thighs in awkward silence.

Becky tugged at the linen sheet, struggling to find something to say. "I-I hear you're doing well with your carving."

A burst of red flared in his cheeks, and a slight smile crossed his lips.

"I'm proud of you. I'm sure everyone else is too."

Roy's mouth worked back and forth, his grin fading. Whiteness streaked his knuckles as he gripped the edge of the chair. Whatever he'd come to say was proving a real challenge. At last, like a gush of water, the words spewed from his lips. "They don't call me Stump no more."

A smile touched Becky's lips. "I'm so glad."

His chin quivered. "I...I came to thank ya."

"But it wasn't my doing. It took courage on your part."

He straightened, his words seeming to flow easier. "The pastor says we need Jesus in our hearts, but all I ever saw in people was meanness...till you, Miss Becky. I saw Jesus in you."

Becky choked back tears. "I believe that's the kindest thing anyone's ever told me, Roy. Thank you."

He took a hard swallow. "I-I want the meanness out o' my heart and have Jesus in me too. When you're able, would you help me go forward at church?"

The unexpected request washed over Becky like spring water. Somehow, in all her doubts and uncertainties, the Lord had shone through to touch this boy's hardened soul. What a blessing to know God had used her.

What else could He accomplish, if she yielded more fully to Him?

She placed a reassuring hand on Roy's arm. "There's nothing I'd like more."

A rare, toothy grin split Roy's face, shattering his rigid exterior.

Lightness filtered through Becky. If God had brought her here for no other reason, this moment was enough. She bit at her lip. Is this how Matthew felt each time he led someone to Christ? If so, no wonder he'd chosen to become a pastor.

A vivid thought pulled at her heart. She'd always fancied herself to be a farmer's wife. Was the Lord instead preparing her to be the wife of a preacher?

Chapter Twenty-Nine

"MATTH-EW!" The feminine voice held a hint of endearment, much like a bride beckoning to her husband.

Matthew tensed and pulled back on the reins. Turning, he saw Sarah motion to him from the top of the schoolhouse steps. He groaned inwardly. What was it this time? Was she going to scold him for not calling on her? Or was this simply another ploy to gain his attention?

The biting wind stung at his cheeks as he rode toward her. It seemed he couldn't come to town without her finding some excuse to detain him. Pulling Gabriel to a stop outside the school, Matthew leaned forward in his saddle. "Did you need something?"

She rocked forward on her toes, hands clasped behind her back. "Come inside. The children have something to ask you."

It wasn't the best of reasons, but one he couldn't refuse. Dismounting, he tied the reins to the hitching post, then started up the wooden steps. Sarah's dark eyes twinkled at his approach. And yet, it was the brooch fastened to her collar that drew his stare. Becky's brooch. He swallowed down the angst welling inside him. Had the fiddle made it safely to her? How he'd love to have been there to witness her reaction. Joseph's as well.

"Hurry, Matthew. It's frigid out here." Sarah rubbed her arms against the chill and followed him inside.

As he entered, his wind-burned face stung against the warmth of the wood stove. An ashy smell hinted a log had recently been added to the fire. The students arched their necks, staring back at him, faces aglow. Removing his hat, he smiled back, wondering what unknown secret they all shared.

"Come right up front." Sarah clutched his wrist and propelled him forward, fingers cold as ice. A hushed whisper fell over the group, mingling with a few girlish giggles. With a glance his way, Sarah clasped her hands prayer-like to her lips. Matthew tugged at his collar and took a deep breath. Was it warm in here, or was it merely the fact that he was the only one in the room who didn't know his purpose here?

The students quieted as Sarah raised her hand and took a step forward. "I know we're all very excited to voice our request of Pastor Brody, but we must do it in an orderly fashion." Her eyes scanned the group of children. "Alice Brimmer. Would you do the honors?"

The eleven-year-old took to her feet, a proud smile lining her lips. Her pig-tails bobbed as she glanced side to side, then settled her gaze on Matthew. "We're planning a Christmas play to put on for our folks. We'd like you to help us. And to be Joseph."

Matthew clutched his hat, a smile tugging at one corner of his mouth. "Well, now, that's a real honor, but wouldn't it be better if one of the older boys played the part?"

"No."

"We'd rather be shepherds."

"Or wise men."

Matthew held up his hand with a grin, stilling the volley of responses. "All right then. I'll be glad to help any way I can, and I'd be pleased to be your Joseph." He gave a slight bow.

An excited murmur rippled through the students. Matthew shifted his feet, calling over the noise. "By the way, who'll be our Mary? You, Alice?"

With a giggle, young Alice pointed to the front of the room. "No. Miss Prescott is."

The air dispelled from Matthew's lungs. He should have known. He could see it in her eyes each time she looked at him and on the faces of the congregation each week. Even the children. They were all convinced he and Sarah were destined for marriage nuptials.

He sensed Sarah edge closer, but resisted glancing over his shoulder at her. Like a rabbit in a snare, he'd fallen for her clever ploy. No doubt he needed to set her straight. But not today. Not in front of the children.

BECKY DREW BACK THE CURTAIN, gazing through the frosty window pane. New fallen snow blanketed the ground, transforming the yard and city street into a world of white. She squinted into brilliant sunlight, snowflakes glistening like stars in the heavens. Cold morning air sifted through the window frame, and she shivered and hugged her free arm about her.

Men and boys, wrapped in winter wear, ambled about, shoveling out storefronts and houses. Here in the city, people and buildings marred the snow's beauty. Had it snowed on the prairie? There, vast acres stretched silvery white as far as the eye could see, sprinkled with clusters of snow-laden trees. How her heart ached for the unspoiled splendor and freedom of home.

"Becky?" Pa's familiar deep voice startled her from her thought. She pivoted, letting the curtain tumble into place. He made his way to her, and eased into the chair by her bed. "How are you?"

"Eager to be on my feet again." She clamored back into bed, sliding frigid toes under still warm linens.

"Only been four days. Doc said a week."

Becky cringed, loosening her long braid. "But I feel fine."

"A couple more days won't hurt."

She slumped back against the bed frame with a sigh.

"Maybe this will help." He pulled a letter from his pocket.

A tingle rippled through her as she reached for it. Would it be from Matthew? When, if ever, would his gift arrive? Peering at the return address, a smidgen of disappointment mingled with her joy. "Uncle Jed and Aunt Clara. It's been months."

Tearing open the seal, she unfolded the page.

"Dear Joseph and Becky,

I must apologize for my neglect in not writing sooner. Busyness seems to crowd out the best of intentions. The weather has turned cold of late. Each year I seem to dread winter more. Charlotte and Esther are shooting up like spring prairie grass. Jed rides over to your place every few days, to keep an eye on things. And to retrieve Nugget, who wanders back home from time to time. Seems he's still pining away for the two of you. Comes back worn to a frazzle."

"Poor ol' feller." Pa ran a hand under his nose.

Becky clutched Roy's carved image of Nugget that dangled aside Ma's wedding ring on the ribbon around her neck. Each letter from home stirred a myriad of memories. Some welcome, others not. She licked her lips, forcing steadiness into her voice.

"We're so blessed to have Pastor Brody with us on a regular basis. The church is fuller most every week. Though, with harsh weather setting in, that's likely to change over the winter months."

Becky melted into her pillow, warmth flooding her chest. Was it a sense of pride that garnered the wide smile on her face? How she longed to hear Matthew's voice and see his winsome smile.

"Has he mentioned we've a new school teacher? Miss Sarah Prescott. She seems well liked by the students, as well as the community. You'd like her as well. But then, with her and Pastor Brody as good as…"

Tightness tore at Becky's throat, choking off her voice. She forced her eyes to focus on the word that followed.

Could it be true?

Pa leaned forward in his chair. "As good as what?"

A knot gripped Becky's middle, pressing air from her lungs. Her gaze drifted to the quilt at the foot of the bed. Had she been fooling herself these past few months, thinking he cared for her?

"Don't put too much confidence in a man, Becky." Her aunt's words rushed to the forefront of her mind, sending a tremor through Becky. Had Matthew betrayed her as Jeffrey had Aunt Ellen?

"Well, what does it say?"

Her arms fell limp at her sides, the word spilling out in a low, agonized murmur. "Betrothed." Saying it left a bitter taste in her mouth and a numbness on her heart.

"Well now, that is news." The wide grin that spread over Pa's face hinted he had little inkling of the devastation Becky harbored. "Must be quite a gal to hook Matthew."

Becky clenched her jaw. How could she have been so wrong? Releasing her hold on the letter, it sailed to the floor, her dreams plummeting with it.

A BRILLIANT MOON and spattering of stars decorated the night sky. Becky lay awake for hours, staring out the upstairs window, thoughts churning in the stillness. How could this have happened? She'd been so sure of Matthew.

Pastor Brody. May as well get used to calling him that again.

Moisture clouded her eyes, and she closed them, sending

tears streaming down her temples into her ears. How could she face him? Better yet, how could she endure seeing him alongside his future bride each week? She'd been so thrilled at the news of him taking on full-time ministry at Miller Creek. Now the very thought made her stomach reel.

Still another disappointment.

When next she opened her eyes, the white light of morning had seeped into the room. The faint sound of a fiddle being tuned droned in her head. She forced herself awake, straining to listen, but gleaned only silence. She pulled herself to a sitting position. Her crumpled pillow, stained with tears, rested against the headboard. How long had she slept? Two hours? Three at best. What did it matter? Her heartache remained.

She inhaled a jagged breath, grateful to be alone. The fallen letter lay cold and silent on the floor. Reaching for it, she reread the dreaded news. Could it be some sort of mistake? But how? Aunt Clara wouldn't make up such a tale.

With a final glance, she wadded it up and tossed it aside. Love found…and now lost.

Matthew's Bible lay atop the bed stand. Reaching for it, she ran a hand over the worn leather covering, reliving their final moments together. She couldn't have misread the affection in his dark-brown eyes or his lingering touch. Had the months apart weakened his feelings for her? If only they'd had more time.

She pulled his letters from their hiding place beneath the cover. Reading each one in turn, she could almost hear the richness of his voice. Once hidden treasures, now the tender words seemed only to mock her. With trembling hands, she unfolded the note he'd left for her to find in the Bible. Once again, she was struck by the power of the verse he'd inscribed. "He who falters in troubled times, how small is his faith." (Proverbs 24:10) And then his words of encouragement, "Find in God the strength you're sure to need."

God's strength. How right he'd been. Her own strength had waned long ago.

Below his name, in parentheses, was scribed the verse (Jeremiah 29:11). She'd not taken time to look it up before. Curious, she leafed through the Bible until she found the book of Jeremiah. Searching out the twenty-ninth chapter, she slid her finger down the page and paused at the eleventh verse. Tears stung her eyes as she read. "For I know the plans I have for you, saith the Lord, plans to prosper you, and not to harm you, to give you a future and a hope."

Pierced by the poignant words, Becky hugged her knees to her chest and buried her face in the sheet. *Lord, I don't understand all that's happened, but I believe You do love me and want the best for me. Help me let go of my hurt and trust You to make things right.*

Chapter Thirty

BECKY POURED a pitcher of steamy water into the dish pan, sensing Aunt Ellen's gaze upon her. Turning, Becky mustered a slight grin.

Apparently, it wasn't convincing, for her aunt's questioning look didn't slacken. "You've been quiet the past couple of days. Sure you haven't started back to work too soon?"

With a shake of her head, Becky shaved off a sliver of soap and swished it around in the water. Keeping busy helped take her mind off Matthew—Pastor Brody.

She took a deep breath. "Never thought I'd miss kitchen work, but it's good to be back."

"I'm glad you're well. Though I'm afraid that means I'll be headed back to the sewing factory." Aunt Ellen reached for a drying towel, eyes panning the large kitchen. "I must say, I've enjoyed helping out."

Becky filled the pan of hot water with soiled dishes, giving her aunt a sideways stare. "I believe I know a certain instructor who'd just as soon keep you here."

The slight blush of her aunt's cheeks hinted Becky's meaning hadn't been lost to her. Warding off a smile, Aunt Ellen dried more fervently. "Regardless, Mr. Billings won't take kindly to me being gone another day."

Becky glanced out the window. "If this snow doesn't let up, you may have to."

With a look outside, her aunt's mouth stiffened. "Perhaps I'd better see if Peter can take me home a bit early."

Silence fell between them, giving way to a gentle melody pouring from the front room. Becky stopped scrubbing. "Isn't Jenny due to leave today?"

"Yes. I believe so."

The corners of Becky's mouth lifted. "She must be giving the piano one final play." Jenny's lively tunes would be sorely missed.

The soapy water cooled slightly as Becky added more dishes. A fiddle's clear note chimed in with the piano, faint at first, then growing stronger. She paused, drying her hands on her apron. Her heart quickened as she recognized the tune, "Amazing Grace." Her mother's favorite. Pa had played it for her countless times before the flickering firelight on cold, wintry nights.

Aunt Ellen hummed along, reaching to put a stack of plates in the corner-cabinet. "Who's playing?"

"I—I don't know." Becky stepped toward the doorway, lured by the sound. The music grew louder as she neared the sitting room. Several children sat clustered around the upright piano, listening to the duo of instruments. Pa stood beside Jenny at the piano, his chin hugging a fiddle. Edging closer, tears welled in Becky's eyes.

A proud smile illuminated Pa's face as his bow sailed over taut strings, the notes ringing true. Becky closed her eyes, soaking in the familiar tune, and for a moment, she was back in their cabin, safe and warm with her family.

As the final note faded, silence hovered over the room, followed by enthusiastic applause. With a slight bow, Pa lowered his fiddle.

Cheeks damp with tears, Becky stepped up beside him and placed a hand on his arm. "How did you…?"

"Surprised?" Confidence oozed from him, in a way Becky hadn't witnessed for many months.

"Completely." She reached to embrace him, oblivious to the chatter around them.

Strong arms encircled her, and her father's low voice sounded in her ear. "I wanted to save it for Christmas, but with Jenny leaving, it was now or never."

Becky leaned her head against his chest. "There were days I thought I'd never hear you play again."

"Me too. Reckon I just needed the right instrument." Pa rubbed his thumb over the smooth surface of the fiddle.

Becky's gaze drifted to the instrument in his hands, noting the textured, maple body and the initials etched in its base. Her breath caught in her throat. "J.H. Why, it's your fiddle."

A subtle grin touched his lips. "Seems by some miracle, it made it through the storm."

Becky's heart raced. The miracle wasn't merely that it survived the storm, but its presence here. "Yes, but how did it get here? And when?"

"It came by post, right after you fell sick. I'd made a couple of attempts at playing the fiddles here from time to time, but it wasn't until mine arrived, I found my song."

Becky melted at his words, recalling the occasions she'd heard faint, sour fiddle notes being tuned or played. "But, who sent it? Aunt Clara?"

"No. Matthew Brody."

Matthew? The name rippled through her like a chilling breeze. He must have known such a gift would bring both her and Pa great happiness. What had prompted him to send it? Was this the gift he'd spoken of?

Hope stirred in her heart, then died away just as sudden. If not for her aunt's letter, the thoughtful deed would have touched her beyond measure. But, if Matthew's affections lay elsewhere, like Aunt Clara insinuated, it must've been sent for Pa's sake. Not hers.

Unless to appease her.

Tamping down her emotions, Becky eyed the case lying open atop the piano. "Was there a note?"

"Not so far as I know."

"I-I'll just go check to be certain." Becky took a steadying breath and strolled to the fiddle case, eager for some word, some explanation to her aunt's disturbing news.

Yet the dark lining harbored no such clarification.

In desperation, she probed the case with her hand. He must have sent something. She refused to believe he'd not be upfront with her. He was too godly of a man.

Tightness gripped her stomach. There was still the tiny compartment at the case's neck. Becky lifted the lid, heart drumming in her ears. A single folded slip of paper rested inside.

With bated breath, she clutched it between her fingertips. Such a brief note in response to her lengthy, heartfelt one. She gnawed at her lip, glancing over the three short lines.

"My gift to you.

God bless,

Matthew Brody"

She turned the paper over, hoping it held some deeper message, some insight into the mystery shrouding his feelings toward her.

Nothing.

Her heart sank. The short, impersonal note made it seem as though the long-awaited-for gift was little more than a pastor's kind gesture of friendship to patrons. Nothing tender or endearing to put her mind at ease. Could her aunt's suspicions be right?

Heart-sore, she clutched the note in her fist, determined not to let it put a damper on the occasion. Matthew's gift had breathed life back into Pa, and for that she was grateful.

If only her hopes hadn't been squelched in the process.

BECKY GAZED OUT THE WINDOW, mesmerized by the flurry of snowflakes. She toyed with Ma's wedding ring fastened on the ribbon around her neck. A bit loose for her finger, she pulled it on and off.

A sigh escaped her. Would anyone ever love her enough to place it on her finger for keeps?

The snow had deepened to several inches, emptying the street of much of its traffic.

Coming up beside her, Aunt Ellen slipped on her coat, waiting for Peter to come with the sleigh from the livery. She pulled on her gloves and peered at Becky. "Are you going to tell me what's troubling you, or must I pry it out?"

Becky dropped her gaze. "There's nothing to tell."

Aunt Ellen cleared her throat, crossing her arms in front of her. "You've been staring out that window for nearly a half-hour."

With a shrug of her shoulder, Becky turned from the window. "Guess with Christmas nearing I'm a bit homesick."

Aunt Ellen lifted Becky's chin. "Unless I miss my guess, it's more than homesickness troubling you. It's a matter of the heart."

Becky's eyes flicked to her aunt's face. "How…?"

"I've been there, remember?" Aunt Ellen looped her arm around Becky's waist, her voice softening. "I've seen the way your face lights up with each letter from your young pastor. And, forgive me, but I overheard bits of your parting conversation."

Heat flamed in Becky's cheeks. "You've known since…does Pa?"

A soft chuckle fell from her aunt's lips. "Well, if he does, it didn't come from me."

With a huff, Becky leaned against the window frame. That Aunt Ellen knew her secret was, in a way, almost a relief. Now at least she had someone to confide in. Someone who understood. "If ever I held his heart, I don't anymore."

"What do you mean?"

A couple of students wandered in and sat before the fireplace. Edging to the far side of the room, Becky slid Aunt Clara's letter from her pocket and handed it to Aunt Ellen. "Read the last paragraph."

Aunt Ellen cast a quick glance out the window, then skimmed the letter. Moisture brimmed in her hazel eyes as she met Becky's gaze. Had it revived memories of her own devastating relationship? "Oh, Becky. Has he given any indications of such in his letters?"

Becky wet her lips to still their trembling. "None. Unless you count the short, impersonal note he sent along with Pa's fiddle."

Aunt Ellen's chin lifted. Refolding the letter, she shoved it toward Becky. "Then, until you hear it from him, I wouldn't take it to heart."

"But you read what it said. He's nearly betrothed."

Aunt Ellen's brows lifted. "I read your aunt's impression. Nothing more. I only met the man a short time, but I can't believe him the sort to lead you astray."

Despite every attempt to stymie her emotions, tears welled in Becky's eyes. "But you said yourself not to put too much confidence in a man."

The jingle of a sleigh sounded outside. With a sideways glance out the window, Aunt Ellen placed a gloved hand to Becky's cheek. "There are different sorts of men. Thanks to you, I realize that now. Jeffrey was a user, who thought only of himself. Pastor Brody is a godly man, who cares for others. Your father's fiddle is evidence of that."

"Yes, but…"

Touching a finger to Becky's lips, her aunt's expression warmed. "You asked me to give Peter a chance. And I have. I'm asking the same of you with your Pastor Brody. Give him the chance to voice his intentions. Not hearsay. Pray, and if the Lord is in it, you'll know."

With a short hug, Aunt Ellen turned to go.

Edging back to the window, Becky watched Peter help her aunt into the sleigh. Becky's heart lightened as they drove away, a bright smile on both of their faces. At last, Aunt Ellen had again opened her heart to love.

Turning, Becky slid down into the upholstered chair beside the window. Could her aunt be right? Was there still a chance for her and Matthew? Given Aunt Clara's assumption, it seemed impossible.

Becky closed her eyes and bowed her head. *Lord grant me courage to accept whatever comes. To trust not only You, but Matthew. You alone know the plans You have for me. If Matthew's love for me is true, may nothing stand in its way.*

APPLAUSE VIBRATED through the packed schoolhouse. Matthew's eyes panned the crowded room. The frigid weather hadn't hindered the show of parents attending the Christmas play. If only he could persuade more of them to come for Sunday services. Intent on his observation, he nearly missed Sarah's prompt for him to take a bow. "…many thanks for his work with the scenes and his wonderful portrayal of Joseph." Stepping up beside him, she flashed a brilliant smile, clapping along with the audience.

He returned a satisfied grin and bowed to the people. Despite his reservations about partnering with Sarah, he had to admit, they'd worked well together. Still, something told him he was being coerced into more than he'd bargained for.

As the applause died away, the children dispersed into the crowd, leaving the two of them standing together. Sarah pressed her hand to his, mouthing a "thank you."

The softness of her touch brought warmth to his chest. For an instant, her dark hair faded to wheat-blonde and her chocolate eyes paled to sapphire blue, as if Becky stood at his side in Sarah's stead. Shaking off the image, he drew his hand away. What was this inward battle waging in his heart?

"You two make the perfect Joseph and Mary." He flinched at the sound of the woman's voice in front of him. Turning, he saw Mrs. Brimmer staring up at him, her gaze darting from him to Sarah.

Still lost in a haze, his throat tightened, choking off any response.

Sarah gave him an awkward stare, her smile returning. She sandwiched the older woman's hand in hers. "Why, thank you, Mrs. Brimmer. You're so very kind to say so."

As others filed by, Matthew fought to regain his composure. He pasted on a smile, feeling exposed, not only by his drafty robe costume, but by the many comments expressing the pleasure of seeing him and Sarah work so well together. It wouldn't surprise him if the whole town—Sarah included—had a date set for them to wed.

Excusing herself, Sarah wormed her way through the crowd with the grace and poise of a debutante, conversing with whomever she passed. Matthew scratched at his stubbly beard, grown at Sarah's request, for the sake of the play. She certainly knew how to make her presence known.

Jed Stanton stepped up beside him with a grin. Leaning in close, he nodded in Sarah's direction. "Quite a gal, ain't she, preacher?"

Matthew arched a brow. "She certainly is."

"Make a mighty fine pastor's wife, wouldn't ya say?"

He gave a hesitant nod, words failing him. He couldn't deny she had a way with people and beauty any man would take pride in having hang on his arm. Still, there was something about her. Something he couldn't quite put his finger on.

She glanced his way, that slight tilt to her head. Would she make the perfect match for him as everyone seemed to think? Months earlier, he'd not wanted to give her the time of day.

He'd thought only of Becky.

But now, his mind had grown muddled. Was he so easily swayed by the opinion of others? Or was he merely considering what was best for Becky? One thing was certain. He couldn't ride the fence any longer.

It was time to decipher God's will for his future.

Chapter Thirty-One

PART FOUR: NEW BEGINNINGS

January, 1855

BECKY ROSE FROM THE HARD, hickory church pew as the lanky pastor waved the congregation to their feet. Such a large gathering. How many had ventured to church in Miller Creek? Had they been bludgeoned with snow as well? A nervous twinge worked through her middle. What had Matthew spoken on today? For weeks now, she'd put off writing him, the words refusing to come. But if nothing more, she owed him a thank you for Pa's fiddle.

She stretched and pressed the creases from her dress. It was so good to be well and out and about again. Bitter winds and blinding snows had confined them to the school for much of December. Now, after weeks of waiting, Roy's day of promise had finally arrived.

Warmth flowed through Becky as she glanced up at him. The cruel nickname Stump no longer suited him. A smile had replaced his furrowed brow and drawn mouth. He stood with shoulders back, head held high, as though eager to declare his newfound faith. Becky breathed a contented sigh. At least something good had come of her journey to the city.

The church building vibrated with song as Pastor Stein led the closing hymn. Becky glanced around at the crowd of people. Drawing attention to herself had never been her strong suit. She wiped sweaty palms on her dress, then gave Roy's arm a gentle squeeze. "Ready?"

He nodded, and she took his arm, guiding him down the aisle, her petite frame dwarfed by his bulky one. Heads spun toward them as they passed, pleased and astonished expressions illuminating each face. The preacher's warm smile beckoned them forward. Becky lengthened her stride to match Roy's, careful to steer him clear of obstacles. His hand on her arm grew clammy. Was he nervous? Excited? She resisted the urge to glance up at him, but kept her eyes trained ahead of them.

As the hymn ended, Pastor Stein clasped Roy's shoulder. Releasing her hold, Becky pivoted toward the crowd, avoiding the stares of onlookers. Her blue satin skirt swished side-to-side as she hurried to her place on the back bench. She caught Peter's wide-eyed stare and suppressed a grin. At Roy's request, she'd told no one of his decision, except for a short note to his Uncle Lon, his closest relative.

Pastor Stein spoke privately with Roy and then turned to address the crowd, his tenor voice amplified in the still room. "Roy Lenard has come this morning to confess his need for a Savior and to be baptized."

Whispers and stunned expressions erupted among the blind students at the mention of Roy's name. Becky smiled to herself. Who would've dreamed this once spiteful, obstinate youth would become the humble person who stood before them? Jesus made all the difference. Would her own renewed faith bring change for her?

Holding out his Bible, Pastor Stein placed Roy's hand atop it.

"Repeat after me. I believe Jesus is the Christ, the Son of the living God, and I take Him as my Lord and Savior."

Roy echoed the preacher's words, unhindered by the room full of spectators.

"Praise the Lord." With a good-natured slap on Roy's back, Pastor Stein motioned the congregation to sit. "Now, if we could have a volunteer to help raise the pool lid, we'll have ourselves a baptism."

Boot-steps sounded on the puncheon floor from across the room. A husky, shaggy-haired man sauntered forward. Becky squinted in faint recognition. Where had she seen him? His worn clothes and rugged appearance stood out among the refined dress of the majority. Certainly she would have noticed if he'd been there before. He clasped Roy's shoulder, and the two shared a few private words that brought a smile to both faces. Standing together, it became obvious the two were acquainted.

Of course. Roy's Uncle Lon. He'd visited Roy only once in the months she'd been there. Warmth flooded over her. What an unexpected blessing.

Together Roy's uncle and Pastor Stein lifted a hinged section of the floor, revealing a hidden pool beneath. They worked to chip away a thin layer of ice from the pool of water with the heel of their boots. Becky shuddered at the thought of being plunged in the icy grave. Roy tugged off his boots and set them aside, seeming not the least bit daunted. The inconvenience left no doubt to the boy's sincerity.

As the preacher guided Roy down into the frigid water, those in the front pew scooted to make room for his uncle so that he might have the first opportunity to congratulate his nephew.

With a shiver, Pastor Stein raised his hand above his head. "I now baptize you in the name of the Father, Son, and Holy Ghost." Pressing Roy's hands over his nose, the gangly preacher lowered him into the water, stumbling forward under the weight of the bulky young man.

As he emerged, Roy gasped for air and groped for the wooden floorboards on either side of him. The congregation burst into song as Pastor Stein helped him from the pool. Though shivering from head to toe, Roy's face beamed. Another soul won to the Lord. Becky's first thought was to share the news with Matthew in a letter. How she loved telling him about the people here, of the progress various students were making, Pa's achievements, and her own renewed spirit.

But those days were over now.

She heaved a quiet sigh, gazing down at her leather boots, half hidden beneath her ankle-length skirt. If Matthew's affections had turned elsewhere, she hadn't the right to share such intimate details.

A throng of well-wishers pushed forward. Others ambled off, chattering amongst themselves, seemingly unmoved. Becky reached for the bundle of spare dry clothes Roy had brought in his tote. Even with the heat from the wood stove, the January chill had found its way inside the building. Hopefully the congregation would clear out quickly to allow him time to change out of his wet clothes.

Peter led the train of students along the outer edge of the church to await their turn to greet their rejuvenated classmate. Emily alone chose to remain seated. The girl's raven-black hair and long, dark eyelashes contrasted with her ivory complexion. Winter's chill, coupled with her recent illness, had drained the color from her cheeks.

A pang of remorse stabbed at Becky as she took a seat beside Emily. Things had turned from bad to worse for the young girl— the majority for which Becky had to claim responsibility. Each week that passed without a response from the Guthries found Emily more withdrawn and bitter. If only Becky could make it up to her somehow.

She looped her arm around the girl's bent shoulders. "Do you want me to take you to Roy?"

Emily shrank away, face puckered. Stung by the girl's rebuff, Becky sank back on the bench. Empty promises had worked to restore the young girl's health, yet it seemed every ounce of life had been sapped from her.

Becky winced. How her heart ached for the child. Perhaps she should have left well enough alone.

Still, a faint hope burned inside her, refusing to let go. She had to try again. To give up too soon would be more tragic than not trying at all. Without saying any more to Emily, she would send another letter of appeal to the Guthries.

A wave of apprehension tore through Becky. And along with it, she'd send a note to Pastor Brody.

BECKY DONNED her wrap and headed outside. The trek to the post office would be a frigid one—as well as a decisive one. A nervous pang tweaked her stomach as she fingered the letters in her pocket. With mixed emotions, she'd finally forced herself to pen the short letter to Matthew, expressing her gratitude for the fiddle. Another lengthy letter was out of the question. If he'd thrown his affections elsewhere, she'd not interfere. As dear as he'd become to her, she wouldn't allow herself to pine for him.

Or would she?

Her letter to the Guthries, too, had her on edge. Peter would scold her if he knew of her first attempt to contact them. Let alone a second. Was she deceitful in telling him she needed to mail some letters, while neglecting to mention they included one to Mr. and Mrs. Guthrie? Perhaps.

She kicked at a chunk of snow, mouth twisted to one side. But then, what harm could it do? If nothing came of it, Emily would suffer no worse heartache than she already had. But if something did come of it... Her chest warmed at the thought. She could only hope and pray.

Snowdrifts lined the city streets, creating obstacles in her path. Hugging her shawl tighter around her, Becky stepped lightly to avoid icy patches along the pavement. She snugged her bonnet close to her cheeks, the frosty morning air nipping at her skin. Horse hooves echoed through the slushy cobblestone streets as wagons and buggies carried patrons to their destinations. Even the cold hadn't hampered the flow of people. She nodded to those she met, missing the solitude of the prairie.

Even as she longed for her own home, she grieved for her displaced friends. Would Emily be forced to live out her days in an asylum? What would become of Jimmy when he had to leave? At least Becky had a home to return to.

Rounding the corner, she spied Mr. Jacobs leaning on his broom. He waved to her from his storefront across the street, and she lifted her hand in greeting.

"How's my boy, Jimmy?" he called.

"He's well. I'll let him know you inquired of him."

"Tell him to stop by sometime and that I'll soon be in need of more chairs."

"I'll do that." She paused, watching Mr. Jacobs usher a customer into the store. Such a kind man. No wonder he and Jimmy had hit it off.

A smile pulled at her lips. Why hadn't she thought of him before? Perhaps there was hope for Jimmy yet.

"YOU DON'T KNOW what you're asking, Miss Hollister."

Becky stiffened, eyes glued to the storekeeper's face. His drawn expression made her veins run cold. Had she spoken too soon? Asked too bluntly? Jimmy had so little time. She couldn't afford to be coy about his needs.

Mr. Jacobs ran a hand over his face, eyes downcast. "My

wife and I wouldn't know the first thing about taking in a blind boy."

Becky followed him to the front counter. Squaring her shoulders, she deepened her resolve. "But he thinks so highly of you, and it's plain you've a fondness for him as well."

Setting his broom aside, Mr. Jacobs smoothed his thinning, strawberry-blond hair. "The boy's a fine lad, but there's more to consider."

Becky's eyes probed his face. Did he have other obligations? Jimmy had said he had no children. Perhaps his wife disliked them or was ailing in some way. Did she dare ask? Becky pursed her lips to still her inquisitive tongue.

Mr. Jacobs leaned against the counter with a sigh, brushing soot from his apron. His eyes softened and glossed over. "My wife and I had a son, years ago. We lost him to scarlet fever when he was seven."

"I'm sorry." Becky averted her gaze to the jars of candy decorating the counter, the words catching in her throat. Given the magnitude of the couple's loss, the consoling phrase seemed inadequate.

Mr. Jacobs locked his fingers together in front of him. "When we lost our boy, it nearly killed us both. For years, we prayed for another child, but the Lord never saw fit to give us one. We're getting on in years now and have come to terms with the fact we'll never have another child."

"Then this could be your chance." She edged toward him, the intensity in her voice surprising her. Jimmy's longing for a home had wedged its way into her very core, intertwining somehow with her own happiness.

With a shake of his head, the long-faced storekeeper strolled behind the counter. "We're too set in our ways now to raise a son, least of all a blind one." Turning his back to her, he busied his hands straightening items on the shelves.

Becky bent over the oak counter, digging her fingers into the rough grain of the wood. She was not giving up so easily. "But Jimmy's nearly a grown man. He'd be a blessing, not a burden."

Mr. Jacobs dropped his hands to his sides, shoulders drooped. Was he weakening or growing weary of her nettling?

She tucked a wayward strand of hair beneath her bonnet, softening her demeanor. "All he needs is a place to call home and people who care."

Mr. Jacobs swiveled toward her, mouth open as if to speak. A jingle of the bell above the door snatched the words from his lips. Two women, engaged in lively conversation, strolled in, their satiny, hooped dresses bouncing with each step. Mr. Jacobs cast Becky a hasty glance and then turned to his customers, a rigid smile on his lips. "What can I get for you today, ladies?"

Becky stepped aside to let them pass, confident that, for now, Mr. Jacobs' answer was lost to her. With heavy steps, she strode toward the door. She'd pressed him as far as she dare. The Lord would have to do the rest.

"So, you've finally come around to my way of thinking?" Sarah's unexpected question garnered humored stares from the pair of older ladies seated closest to her and Matthew in the restaurant.

Something in her tone made Matthew bristle. He scratched at his cheek and ducked his head to shield his response. "I'm simply trying to seek the Lord's will."

A subtle grin lined Sarah's lips. She leaned closer, softening her voice. "You must feel something for me, or you wouldn't have sought out my company."

He did feel something. A kinship from the past, maybe? A sense of obligation? An outward attraction?

But not love.

He sat back in his chair, rubbing his fingertips over the linen tablecloth. His thoughts flickered to another restaurant a few months back, to a young lady much different from the one seated across from him now. Though both were beautiful, Becky's beauty was the sort that penetrated deep, to her very core.

"Favour is deceitful, and beauty is vain: but a woman that feareth the LORD, she shall be praised." King Solomon's proverb swept through Matthew's thoughts. He snickered to himself. Of all men, Solomon should know the intricacies of women.

"Matthew?"

He jerked his head up. "I'm sorry. What were you saying?"

Sarah gave an exasperated sigh and reached across the table, placing her hand atop his. "Only that I'm glad you finally took the initiative to ask me out."

The door to the restaurant veered open, ushering in a chilly draft and a somber-faced Josiah Crawford. His eyes scanned the small room, settling on Matthew. With quick strides, the brawny man started toward him. Josiah's telling expression hinted the reason for his visit. His dear mother, Sally. Her regular place on the front pew had remained empty since before Christmas, her failing health keeping her bed-bound.

Matthew straightened, pulling his hand from Sarah's. "Is it your mother?"

The man nodded, his blood-shot eyes moistening. "She's askin' for ya."

Rising, Matthew reached for his hat. "I'm sorry, Sarah. I need to go."

"But, can't we at least finish our meal?"

Given the circumstances, the question hardly deserved an answer. A woman was dying, requesting to see him one last time. He couldn't deny her that. Reaching in his pocket, he drew out a coin and laid it on the table. "Here. Order whatever you like. I'll do my best to see you home later."

Eyes narrowing, Sarah's lips stretched in a thin line

"Matthew Brody, you haven't changed one bit. Still out to save the world. When will you ever have time for me?"

Matthew's feet froze in their tracks, the old rifts between them resurrecting like an unwelcome squall. For a time, the source of their past troubles had somewhat eluded him. Now, they sprung up anew, reminding him why things hadn't worked between them. His companion knew how to gain attention and please people, but her heart lacked the genuine love and mercy of a pastor's wife. Turning, he looked her in the eyes. "I'm sorry." Then, with a nod to Josiah, he started forward.

As he pushed through the door, another truth became clear— Sarah Prescott wasn't the helpmate he wanted or needed.

Chapter Thirty-Two

THE WOOD lathe hummed as Pa pushed the foot throttle, propelling the half-finished block of walnut into steady motion. Wood shavings flung about, coating his pant legs and littering the floor beneath as he chiseled the shaft of wood into a smooth spindle. Watching from behind, Becky warmed inwardly, having slipped away from her duties to spend a few quiet moments of her own choosing. Much of her father's progress had escaped her in recent weeks, and she thrilled at his new achievement. Who cared that the piece was a mite skewed and off center?

Pa lifted his foot from the throttle, and the apparatus slowed to a stop. His face twisted into a scowl as he ran his hands along the lopsided table leg. "Crooked as a crick."

Becky leaned to give his shoulders a squeeze. "Give it time. It'll come."

With a flip of a nob, he unclamped the wood and tossed it aside. "I've grown tired of trying. I'm eager for home."

Home. The very mention of it stirred a cavalcade of longings in Becky's soul. How she yearned to stroll the miles of prairie at dusk as dew blanketed the ground or feel the warmth of the sun on her bonnetless head. With a quiet sigh, she bent to kiss his warm brow, the only balm she had for his weary soul. "You've come so far. Don't quit now."

Hurried boot steps beckoned from the hall, and an instant later, Peter appeared in the doorway. His eyes sparked as they locked onto hers, and he beckoned for her to come.

"Peter's calling. I'll be back." Stepping past piles of wood chips and cane, she strode toward the instructor. At her approach, he turned and motioned her from the room. Rarely had she seen him so agitated. What could be troubling him?

Following him out into the hall, her eyes searched his. With a straight-faced glower, he thrust out his arm, revealing a sealed letter in his hand. "This came for you today."

One glance at the name Guthrie set Becky's heart racing. At last. They'd responded. But, judging from Peter's stern demeanor, he hadn't taken kindly to her insubordination. Heat rose in her cheeks as she took the letter from him. With a tentative grin, she shifted her feet side to side, fingertips toying with the wax seal. "You're probably wondering how this came about."

"You might say that." Peter crossed his arms, brow creased, yet no harshness lined his face. He nodded toward the note. "But your explanation can wait. Let's see what they have to say."

With trembling hands, she slid her finger to break the seal and unfolded the letter. A deep breath escaped her lips as she scanned the greeting.

"Dear Miss Hollister:

Your letters have been the subject of great discussion in our household over recent weeks. I must tell you that my wife is set against our visiting Emily. Your persistence, however, has convinced me that there is something to what you say, and I am willing to bring the boy with the understanding that this visit will determine if there will be any future contact. We, too, want what's best for both children. Look for us this Friday.

Regards,

Ben A. Guthrie"

Becky clutched the letter to her chest, a wide smile spreading over her face. "They're coming!"

Shoving the note at Peter, she pressed a hand to her lips, eager for his response. He glanced over the letter, eyebrows raised. "You realize this doesn't change anything. It's obvious Mrs. Guthrie is still opposed."

"Yes, but they're coming. I've got to tell Emily." Unhindered by the instructor's skepticism, she pivoted on her heels, taking a hurried step toward the craft room.

Peter's hand on her arm jolted her to a stop. His gentle eyes edged out the firmness in his voice. "I hope you're not setting that little girl up for more heartbreak."

Becky's smile faded as she swallowed the notion. "I've prayed for this again and again. I can't see the Lord answering, only to break her heart."

His grip on her arm loosened. "Just try not to get her hopes up too high...or your own."

"Yes, sir." Turning, she attempted to squelch the joy swelling in her soul. But it refused to be deterred.

They were coming. Surely, that gave reason to hope.

BECKY WOKE JUST as the pale light of dawn began to sift through the girls' bedroom window. She winced at the sound of Emily's bitter sobs as she lay on her cot. The girl's silent tears the evening before had escalated to anguished cries throughout the night. Each whimper was like a dagger in Becky's heart. Was it not her fault the girl grieved?

She balled her hands into fists, eyes narrowing as she stared at the plaster ceiling. She wouldn't take all the blame. Mr.

Guthrie let them down. Friday had come and gone without so much as a word from him. She pitched off her covers and swung her legs over the side of the bed, rubbing tired, swollen eyes. Why had she not listened to Peter?

Others stirred in their cots, and she moved among them, divvying out a soft touch to each as she passed. The wooden floor felt cold against her feet, much like the gloom that dampened her soul. Emily buried her face in her pillow, sobbing harder as Becky sat on the edge of her bed. There was no sense trying to console her. All she'd done to gain the girl's trust had been lost.

Becky was still licking her wounds when Aunt Ellen arrived to help with Saturday breakfast. The sizzle of bacon in the skillet helped to ease the heavy silence that followed the shared dismal news.

Aunt Ellen finished setting the table and then slid an arm around Becky's waist. "You did what you thought best. No sense punishing yourself for it."

"But I gave her false hope, not once, but twice. She was better off thinking it would never happen at all."

Brushing a tear from Becky's cheek, Aunt Ellen gave her a gentle squeeze. "Offering hope to someone is never wrong. You helped stir feelings in that youngster she forgot she had. She'll come through."

"I wonder." With furious jabs, Becky transferred the cooked bacon to an awaiting platter and then placed a fresh batch in the skillet. "Peter warned me, but I was too stubborn to listen. He may never speak to me again."

"You judge him too harshly. He's a good man, you've said so yourself. He won't hold it against you."

Becky lowered her gaze, drawing her mouth to one side. "I was so sure this time. I really thought God had answered my prayers."

Her aunt's hazel eyes sparkled as she cupped Becky's face in her hands. "The Lord's ways are different than ours. He sees the whole picture, not just what we see. Who's to say He's not still at work? Have faith."

Faith? Her faith had taken a beating over recent months. Would she ever fully grasp God's plan for her? Scripture described faith as something unseen. Becky reached to hug her aunt, drinking in the warmth of her friendship. "I'll try."

A rap on the front door drew them apart. Becky knit her brow. Other than Aunt Ellen, Saturday visitors were a rarity, especially so early of a morning. "Who could that be?"

Wiping her hands on her apron, Becky hurried to the front room. A glance out the window revealed a well-dressed gentleman waiting outside. Guesses as to who he might be churned in her head. The man was more well-to-do than anyone she'd seen visit the students. The school's rich benefactor perhaps? A bill collector?

She cracked open the door and was met with a good-natured smile. "May I help you?"

The man tipped his hat, his thin mustache turning upward with his gentle smile. "Miss Hollister?"

She returned a hard blink. How would he know her name?

"Are—you—Miss Hollister?"

"Y-Yes."

His chin lifted in seeming satisfaction. "I'm Ben Guthrie."

At mention of his name, her knees threatened to buckle. Had her prayers indeed been answered? A blast of frigid air wafted in as she widened the door. Becky struggled to catch her breath, more out of astonishment than from the cold. "Please, come in, Mr. Guthrie."

He motioned behind him, and a young boy peeked around the edge of the man's trousers.

Stephen. Moisture stung Becky's eyes. The young boy's coal black hair, slim build, and shy demeanor left no doubt to his identity. But for his pudgy cheeks and smaller frame, he was an exact replica of his older sister.

Reaching for the boy's hand, Mr. Guthrie led him inside. He stripped off his hat, revealing a crown of dark hair beneath. With a glance about the vacant room, Mr. Guthrie placed his hands on the boy's shoulders. "I hope we haven't arrived too early, but I pride myself on being a man of my word."

"Not at all." Becky wanted to remind him he was indeed a day late, rather than early, but thought better of it. It would serve no purpose to express the heartache the delay had caused Emily.

"My apologizes for not being here yesterday, but..." He cleared his throat, lowering his voice as if to shield the boy from what he had to say. "I was trying to convince my wife to join us. As you can see, I failed." Unspoken tension oozed from his voice. This obviously hadn't been an easy decision.

"Well, I can't tell you how glad I am you've come." Squatting beside Stephen, she flashed him a playful grin. He was smaller than she'd imagined. Three or four at best. The boy clung to the man's trousers, his large, brown eyes staring back at her like a frightened fawn. "Emily will be so happy you're here."

At that, a wide smile lit the boy's face, and he edged forward, his tiny voice pleading. "Where's Emmy?"

Becky pressed down the giggle in her throat. Even at such tender ages, it was clear a strong sibling bond knit the two children together.

Enthralled by the young boy, she barely sensed Peter's approach. "Mr. Guthrie," he greeted, extending a hand. "It's been a long while."

The man turned and clasped the instructor's hand and then glanced down at the boy at his side. "Too long, I fear."

Stephen pulled at Mr. Guthrie's pant leg, a pout on his face. "I wanna see Emmy."

"Miss Hollister will bring her straight away." Peter placed a hand on the boy's head, nodding to Becky. If he'd been miffed at her before, his irritation seemed to have vanished.

Hiking her skirt, Becky darted up the seemingly endless flight of stairs. The aroma of bacon grew fainter with each step. Hopefully Aunt Ellen didn't mind manning the kitchen in her absence. This was one reunion she absolutely couldn't miss.

A handful of students ambled past, roused, she supposed, by unfamiliar voices. Unfortunately, Emily wasn't among them. Becky found her still on her cot, half-dressed. Finding it hard to contain her excitement, Becky rushed up beside her. "Quick, Emily, finish dressing. There's a surprise for you downstairs."

The brokenhearted girl only shrunk away, cheeks still stained with tears.

"Weeping may endure for the night, but joy cometh in the morning." The verse of Scripture rang through Becky's mind. Emily's tears would soon be ended. Praise God. The joy she craved was but a flight of stairs away. If only Becky could make her understand.

"Stephen's here. Right now, with Mr. Guthrie."

Emily's expression brightened momentarily and then died away. She flopped down on her cot, hiding her face in her pillow.

Becky breathed an exasperated sigh. The child had endured one too many disappointments. How could Becky convince her to come, short of scooping her up and carrying her? *Lord, give her courage to trust once more.*

Dropping to her knees, Becky brushed strands of hair from Emily's face. "I don't blame you for not trusting me, but you have to believe me. How else would I know he has raven black hair like his sister and calls you Emmy?"

At that, the young girl sat up and wiped her eyes. With slow, steady movements she finished dressing and made her way to the hall. Becky strolled beside her, working to hold back the tide of emotions welling inside her.

Young Stephen peered in their direction, eyes wide as

omelets. "Emmy!" In a moment, he was beside them, his short arms wrapped tight around Emily's waist.

At his touch, a huge smile transformed her face. A steady stream of tears dampened her cheeks—tears of joy, this time, rather than heartache. "Stephen." The solitary word fell from Emily's lips clear and strong, shattering the self-imposed silence she'd lived in for nine, long months.

Becky's moist eyes met Peter's and then Mr. Guthrie's. No words passed between them. None were needed. The moment was seamless. Perfect.

As Becky's gaze fell to the siblings, a sudden thought skewered her moment of bliss. One hurtle remained.

That of convincing Mrs. Guthrie.

MATTHEW RAISED a hand to Miss Tuttle's door, a sinking feeling in the pit of his stomach. It had to be done. He owed Sarah that much. When he'd returned to the restaurant, she'd been gone. Which hadn't surprised him. She wasn't the patient sort. Today marked three days since the encounter. Much too long. He needed to put this to rest.

His gentle tap produced heavy footsteps from within the two-story boarding house. The door eased open, revealing Miss Tuttle's bulky frame. With a tip of his hat, Matthew forced a smile. "Good day, Miss Tuttle. I wonder if…"

Before the words left his lips, the woman raised her staccato voice, calling over her shoulder. "Miss Prescott. Your young man is here."

The announcement left Matthew's hands clammy and his mouth dry. It seemed his host had something in common with her boarder—both were quick to cut off his words and make wrongful assumptions.

Widening the door, the woman motioned him inside. "Come on in out of the cold, preacher."

Hat in hand, he stepped into the furnished room, laden with the scent of pine. Warmth enveloped him as he eased down in the wing-back chair before the fireplace. And yet, the reason for his visit left an icy spot on his spirit.

Miss Tuttle locked her hands together over her ample middle, a wide smile spreading across her face as she stared at him. Matthew felt a little like a caged bird, something to gawk at and offer entertainment. But he wasn't in the mood to tickle the woman's flair for gossip. He'd come with words meant for Sarah's ears alone.

A rustling noise sounded from the hallway, pulling him to his feet. A moment later, Sarah appeared, clad in what looked to be her finest, an ankle-length beige dress, trimmed with white. His eyes fell to the brooch noticeably fastened to her collar. "Why, Matthew. This comes as a surprise." Her cool demeanor swept a chill through him, despite the warmth of the room.

He nodded to her, then turned to Miss Tuttle, who continued to gawk. "I'd like a few moments alone with Miss Prescott, if I may?"

With a jolt, Miss Tuttle snapped from her trance. "Certainly. I'll...ah...just busy myself elsewhere." Tossing Sarah a pronounced wink, the woman backed from the room.

Matthew waited until she was gone, then motioned Sarah to the settee. With soft strides, she crossed the room, her expression mellowing. She clasped his hand, pulling him down beside her. "Shed that scowl of yours, Matthew. If you've come to beg my forgiveness, I'll be glad to give it."

The muscles in his neck tensed as he pulled his hand free of her grasp. For once he was going to speak fully what he had to say. "I've not come merely to make amends. Though, I do wish us to part as friends."

Darkness pooled in her brown eyes, driving the merriment from them. "Part? As friends? Whatever do you mean?"

Bowing his head, Matthew released a slow breath. "There have been some wrongful assumptions about us. By you, as well as the townspeople."

A shadow fell over her face. "Such as?"

"That brooch for one." He swallowed, nodding toward the pendant on her dress. "You assumed it was for you."

Her eyes sparked, and she drew a hand to her collar. "Who else would it be for?"

Dropping his gaze, Matthew twisted his hat in his hands. "That's not important. What's important is that we come to an understanding."

Sarah threw back her shoulders. "An understanding? The entire community has come to the understanding that we belong together. You seem to be the only one ignorant to the fact."

Matthew swept a hand through his hair. "We can't live our lives to please others."

She leaned closer, voice softening. "Surely you feel something for me, or you wouldn't have asked me to dinner the other night."

"I needed to be certain."

"And now you are." More statement than question, her words reeked of cynicism.

"I'm sorry, Sarah. I once had strong feelings for you. But now, my heart belongs to someone else." There was something freeing in the declaration. For months, he'd battled within himself, trying to decipher the truth of where his devotions lay. At last, he knew.

He and Becky deserved a chance.

Sarah studied him long and hard, eyes narrowing. At last, she reached to unfasten the jeweled cross. "Well, whoever she is, she can have you. And your old brooch." With a sneer, she tossed it down on the settee and fled from the room.

With a sigh, Matthew snatched up the fallen brooch and clasped it in his palm. So much for parting as friends. He'd not meant to hurt her, but better that than suffer through a marriage of convenience. For too long, he'd listened to the voices of others and to his own doubts and misgivings. It was time to follow the Lord's leading, and determine if Becky's heart was meant for his.

But for now, he could only wait—and pray for her quick return.

Chapter Thirty-Three

BECKY LEANED against the porch rail, eyes scanning the busy street. A gentle, south breeze caressed her cheeks, its warmth hinting of the promise of spring. The mounds of snow had melted to puddles as winter gave way, and a splash of green showed in the grass below.

Emily stood statuesque at her side, jet black pigtails laced with ribbon—a bit of Aunt Ellen's early Saturday morning hand-iwork. The girl's eager lips worked back and forth. "Are they coming?"

Becky warmed at the sound of the child's tender voice and peered harder into the cluster of buggies and people further down street. "Not yet, sweetie."

At her words, Emily's shoulders drooped, and her face lost its glimmer.

"Don't worry. They'll be here." Becky placed a comforting hand on Emily's head, happily aware that now, instead of cower-ing, the girl leaned in closer. "Anyway, Stephen won't give Mr. Guthrie any peace till they come."

A slight grin crept onto Emily's lips, and her face brightened. The bond between the siblings was unmistakable. Even Mr.

Guthrie, it seemed, had developed a fondness for Emily during their weekly visits. If not for that, Becky shuddered to think how upset Peter might have been. Regardless, she would have done it all again—for Emily's sake. It was as if the young girl had emerged from a dark cocoon. To hear her speak and interact with others was reward enough. Yet there remained an unspoken longing in her soul, apparent on her face each time Stephen and Mr. Guthrie drove away.

The early morning air carried the pungent smell of the river and the murmur of distant voices. The once fearsome place had grown familiar over the months, though no more inviting. The tall buildings and hordes of people left Becky more eager than ever for the vast openness of the prairie. Her lips parted in a sigh. One day they would leave this place...and none too soon for her.

An unsettled thought pricked her resolve. Then, she would have to face Matthew and his intended. Not a thrilling prospect. And, too, it would not prove easy to leave her dear friends behind. Especially Jimmy and Aunt Ellen.

The sight of Mr. Guthrie's rig coming toward them shattered her thoughts, bringing a smile to her face. Leaning down, she gave Emily's shoulders a hug. "Here they come."

The young girl's pigtails bobbed back and forth as she straightened, her formerly pale complexion now a healthy pink.

As the buggy neared, Becky's grin faded. Someone else sat beside them in the seat. Was it a woman? Certain her eyes hadn't failed her, she strode to the door and called for Peter.

A moment later the door creaked open, and Peter sauntered onto the porch. With a silent gesture, Becky motioned him toward the approaching buggy, uncertain how Emily would take the news. The instructor's raised brows confirmed her suspicions, and he hurried into the yard.

A spark of hope rushed through Becky as the rig rolled to a stop before the school. The woman, presumable Mrs. Guthrie, sat head bowed, her sullen expression suggesting she had little desire to be there. Becky tightened her grip on Emily's hand, pulling her closer at the thought of further disappointment.

Emily scowled up at her. "What is it?"

What could Becky tell her but the truth? With a hesitant sigh, she leaned down, placing her lips close to the girl's ear. "I believe Mrs. Guthrie's with them."

Emily's face paled, and her hand grew moist in Becky's. The pain of the woman's rejection obviously still weighed heavy on the girl's heart. She seemed to battle within herself, then, all at once, her chin lifted. "Take me to them."

Becky pursed her lips, inspired by the young girl's courage. Whatever Mrs. Guthrie's reason for coming, it appeared Emily meant to meet it head on. She gave the girl's hand a gentle squeeze, and together they downed the steps and strolled toward the carriage.

Little Stephen sat sandwiched between the couple, his head jutted forward, eyes searching. When he spied Emily, he jumped to his feet, pumping Mr. Guthrie's arm. "Down, Papa, down."

With a chuckle, Mr. Guthrie hopped to the ground and caught the boy as he lunged into his arms. Mrs. Guthrie brushed something from her fur-lined cloak, making no attempt to move from the buggy seat. Adjusting her ruffled, blue bonnet, she watched the boy out of the corner of her eye, then raised a handkerchief to her red-tinged nose. Was it the chilly air, or had she been crying?

Eyes pleading, Mr. Guthrie offered her his hand. She hesitated before placing her palm in his. The tip of her bonnet barely clipped her husband's shoulder as they stood side-by-side. Chestnut hair framed her full, round face and fawn-like eyes, yet her otherwise stunning features lacked the warmth of a smile.

Peter clasped Mr. Guthrie's hand as he stepped up beside them. "Always good to see you, Ben. How are you, Mrs. Guthrie?"

"Fine, thank you," she answered stiffly, her gaze never

straying from the boy. Pulling him closer, she smoothed his hair with a sweep of her fingers.

The young boy squirmed free and made a dash toward Emily, then paused, retracing his steps. "Come see Emmy, Mama." He tugged at Mrs. Guthrie's hand, face beaming. More than likely the young boy hadn't given her a moment's peace since they'd come.

The woman gave in to the toddler's pull, venturing a few strides forward. With a silent prayer, Becky let go of Emily's hand and backed away. This moment was theirs alone.

Stephen gave Emily's waist a tight squeeze, pressing his cheek into her chest. "Mama came, Emmy."

Mrs. Guthrie's eyes brimmed with tears as she watched the siblings embrace, yet it was unclear if her emotions were fueled by compassion or regret.

Releasing her hold on her brother, Emily's expression sobered. "I…I want to thank you for looking after Stephen."

"He's a joy to have." Mrs. Guthrie wrung her hands, her gaze still not quite reaching Emily's face. "It's good to hear you talking. Mr. Guthrie tells me you're doing well here."

The young girl's face bent downward. "Much better, now that Stephen and Mr. Guthrie have been coming."

The woman's demeanor softened, and her gaze settled on Emily for the first time. "They've enjoyed their visits with you as well. Th—that's why I'm here."

A faint glimmer of a smile showed on Emily's face. "I thank you."

Dabbing the corners of her eyes with a handkerchief, Mrs. Guthrie glanced back at her husband. He gave her a tender nod, as if to spur her on. With a deep breath, she pressed forward. "It's obvious Stephen is very fond of you. It appears we've done you both a disservice keeping you apart."

A tear trickled down Emily's cheek, and Stephen wiped it away with a chubby finger. "Don't cry, Emmy."

Mrs. Guthrie seemed to falter, and her husband stepped to her side, extending a long, loving glance. "My wife and I have spoken in length about you, Emily. We want what's best for you... for all of us." Stooping down in front of the children, he gave Stephen a quick wink and placed a hand on Emily's shoulder. "What would you say about coming to live with us?"

A lump caught in Becky's throat as all eyes turned to Emily.

The girl made no reply, but stood rigid as a statue.

"Please come, Emmy." Her brother tugged at her arm, gaping up at her.

At last, she squared her shoulders, her face void of emotion. "Do you want me to come, Mrs. Guthrie?"

Becky held her breath, the air thick with anticipation. Her eyes riveted on first Emily, then Mrs. Guthrie. The pointed question demanded a straight-forward answer.

Mr. Guthrie stood, arm wrapped around his wife's shoulders. Her gaze seemed to engulf the children who stood hand in hand before her. Then, with tear-filled eyes, she knelt, cupping her hands around theirs. "I'd like it very much."

A brilliant smile transformed Emily's face, and she and her brother lunged forward into awaiting arms.

Hair rose on Becky's forearms as Mr. Guthrie stooped to embrace the threesome. What had once seemed an impossibility had at last become a reality. Lifting her eyes heavenward, she swiped a tear from her cheek. *Thank you, Lord.*

THE CALL to Peter's room came unexpectedly. That Mr. Whelan was there, too, hinted of its importance. Was this to be her reprimand for overstepping her bounds in contacting the Guthries? Becky feigned a weak smile as she took a seat across from Peter. His eyes were placid, yet held a mystique that she could not unravel.

She wiped sweaty palms on her dress. "Have I done something wrong?

Mr. Whelan leaned forward. "On the contrary. It's good news we have to share."

At that, Becky relaxed, eager to hear what they had to say.

Peter folded his hands casually in front of him on the desk, his good-natured grin reassuring. "Your father has made great progress of late. He'll soon complete his training."

Becky's heart hammered. She could almost feel the rich soil beneath her feet and smell the prairie wildflowers. "You mean we can go home?"

Peter tugged at his beard. "Your father could be ready to leave in a matter of weeks, but..."

The unfinished thought drained her enthusiasm. "But what?"

"But we're hoping you'll decide to stay." Mr. Whelan eased back in his seat, finishing his sentence for him.

Becky sat forward in her chair. There was something unsettling in his tone, like he'd closed a door on her and bolted it shut. "What do you mean?"

Peter stood, pacing the small room. "You've been a great help to us this past year, Becky. What you did for Roy and Emily was, well, nothing short of miraculous."

"It's the Lord you have to thank, not me."

Mr. Whelan tapped his cane on the wood floor. "Yes, of course. But the fact remains, you have a gift at drawing people out and restoring hope to them."

Warmth flooded her cheeks. Somehow along the way she had shifted from mere visitor to someone with a vital role in the functioning of the school. God had transformed her, allowing fears and uncertainties to swell into friendship and purpose.

Peter sat on the edge of his desk, his gaze apologetic. "We know you're eager to return home, but we'd like you to at least consider staying on with us a while."

His words produced a stranglehold on her, like an invisible hand gripping her throat. "But why?"

He heaved an audible sigh. "Nettie's passing has left us at a loss. Lily has agreed to aid in the kitchen, and I'm in hopes Ellen will continue helping weekends, but we've new students coming, and we need someone on a full-time basis who's gifted in other aspects."

Mr. Whalen cleared his throat. "We're proposing you stay on as housemother and advisor permanently."

Sinking back in her seat, Becky floundered for words. "What about Pa? What would he do?"

"He could make himself useful with his woodworking here a while. Later, the two of you could get a place nearby."

A sick feeling erupted in the pit of Becky's stomach. They seemed to have it all thought out. All these months she'd longed for nothing but home. How could they ask her to stay?

Peter leaned forward, understanding in his eyes. "We realize it would be a sacrifice, but give it some thought. Let us know when you've reached a decision."

Dark thoughts bludgeoned Becky as she left the room. In stunned silence, she rushed to the bedroom and crumpled onto her cot. Did they realize what they were asking? Home was what she and Pa had worked toward since the moment they'd arrived. Could they really expect her to give it up, just when it was within reach?

Better yet, could God?

Turning on her side, she balled her fists, heat rising in her chest. She didn't need time to think. It was asking too much of her. The answer was no.

MATTHEW PLACED another log on the fire, listening to it crackle and pop. Becky's short letter of thanks had sliced through him like a well-sharpened blade. He'd expected—no, hoped—for a much more heartwarming reaction. But then, he'd had little to say in his last communication to her, as well. Had his brief note wielded such an empty feeling in her? Long weeks had passed without any response at all. At least now he knew Joseph's fiddle had arrived safely.

Refolding the letter, he tucked it in his pocket. With a sigh, he propped a foot on the hearth and leaned his head against the mantel. His mind had been so muddled when he'd sent the note. Things were different now. The Lord had helped him see the situation much clearer. If only he could speak with Becky face to face. What he wanted to convey couldn't be expressed in a letter.

He straightened, struck by a daring thought. St. Louis wasn't so far away. Weather permitting, he could leave Monday and be there and back before the following Sunday. Surely the congregation couldn't fault him for that, after months of faithful visits to newcomers and regular attenders. After all, Joseph and Becky were still part of his flock.

A smile tugged at his lips, the weight on his heart lifting. If Becky couldn't come to him, he'd do his utmost to go to her.

Chapter Thirty-Four

BECKY HUGGED her shawl tighter to her shoulders beneath the giant oak, the early March wind nipping at her tear-dampened cheeks. Tossing aside a stray chunk of bark, she leaned her head against the tree. Sunlight filtered through its budding branches, warming her face as she lifted it heavenward. Joy over Emily's reunion seemed a distant memory now, like her prairie home so far away.

Any other time, the onset of early spring would have captivated her with its brilliant colors and new growth. But now, as the instructors' words played over in her mind, the season's treasures held little appeal. Here, hidden away on the far side of the tree, she could sulk in lone silence. To be sure, not even Pa nor Jimmy could ease her disgruntled mood. She favored herself like Jonah, brooding beneath his shriveled vine outside of Nineveh.

A shadow emerged in the grass beside her, jolting her from her self-made cocoon. "Beck?"

Jimmy's voice was sweet balm for her troubled spirit. They'd had far too little time together of late. "I'm here."

He edged forward until his foot hit against a bulging tree root. Sliding onto the ground beside her, his taut lips and furrowed brow hinted of concern. "Figured you'd be celebrating, what with Guthries claiming Emily."

"Too busy feeling sorry for myself, I reckon."

Jimmy hugged his knees to his chest. "What's galling you?"

It was impossible to keep anything from him. Why try? She drew in a breath, tightness threatening to choke off her words. "Mr. Bennett and Mr. Whelan asked me to stay on here permanent."

The corners of Jimmy's mouth lifted. "That wouldn't be all bad."

His attempt to cheer her fizzled. She lowered her gaze. "All we've wanted since Pa and I came here was to go back home. Now, that time's almost here, and they're trying to snatch it from us."

"Why wouldn't they want you to stay? With Nettie gone, they'd have been lost without you. Least you can do is to give it some thought...and prayer."

"I can't, Jimmy."

He arched a brow. "Can't, or won't?"

She leaned her head against him, eyes brimming with tears. "I don't understand. Why would God ask this of me, after all I've been through?"

"Maybe home is your Isaac."

She blinked, staining her dress with tears. "My what?"

"Your Isaac. Maybe home is the one thing God asks you to give up to prove your love for Him. You know, like Abraham did Isaac."

The familiar Bible story flashed back in a rush. God asked Abraham to sacrifice his only son, whom he loved more than life itself, in a test of faith. Yet, Abraham willingly obeyed, even to the point of raising his knife to slay Isaac. At the last moment, the Lord stopped him and provided a lamb in his stead.

She dried her eyes with her sleeve. If Jimmy was right, God

was asking her to give up what she held most dear to ensure He had first place in her heart.

But if she did, could she trust God to make things right?

ROBINS CHIRPED and scurried about as evening shadows blanketed the yard. Becky sat with Pa on the front steps, listening to the faint sound of a steamboat whistle, carried by the still night air. The mournful noise left her melancholy and longing for the drift of the water beneath her, ferrying her toward home.

The others had retreated inside, giving her opportunity to speak with Pa in private and share her heart-wrenching dilemma. His silence and bowed head spoke louder than words. Plainly he too yearned for home. It was what he'd worked towards and dreamed of. Yet, he said nothing. Why?

She touched his arm, unnerved by his quietness. "What should I do, Pa?"

He leaned forward, the amber glow of the fading sun outlining his features. "I can't answer that for you, darlin'. You've your whole life ahead of you. Mine's nearly spent. I'll stay or go whichever you deem best."

She breathed a quiet sigh. He wasn't helping. "I want to do what's right for both of us. You're hankering for home same as me, I can tell."

He reached for her, and she clasped his hand. "True. I'd love to go home, but life would be a lot harder for us there. Maybe staying here isn't such a bad option. For now."

"You're saying we should stay then?" The words coiled around her throat, choking off her voice.

"I'm saying it's up to you and the Lord to decide."

Becky bit her lip, foraging the far recesses of her mind. Apart from her own wishes, what was it the Lord wanted? "I don't know the answer."

Raising her hand to his lips, he planted a tender kiss. "Trust God, Becky. He'll make the way clear."

Like a lost child who'd found a friendly smile, she latched onto his words. The Lord had taken hold of her here as He never had before. Perhaps it was time to let go of her plans and entrust them to Him.

BECKY TURNED ON HER COT, sleeplessness hovering over her like a haze throughout the long night. She opened her eyes, faint light from the windows casting a dim glow about the room, enough to assure all were asleep.

All but her.

A weak smile crossed her lips at sight of Jenny's and Emily's empty bunks. Their dreams had been realized. Soon others would come to take their places, bringing with them a whole new set of challenges and frailties. Would she be here to encourage them along?

Becky's stomach tightened. If she stayed, at least she wouldn't have to face Matthew. Her mind raced back to the cabin their neighbors had graciously constructed in the wake of her and Pa's loss. It seemed ungrateful to let it lie vacant for years to come. If not now, how would she know when it was right to return?

Trust Me, whispered a gentle voice inside her.

"Show me how, Lord." Throwing back her covers, she sat up, tugging at her long braid. As she reached to turn the lantern dial, her hand brushed against Pastor Brody's worn Bible on the stand table. Opening to Genesis, she scanned the story of Abraham and Isaac, pausing at the point where Isaac began to question.

"And Isaac spake unto his father and said, "My father, where is the Lamb for the burnt offering?" And Abraham said, "My son, God will provide himself a lamb for a burnt offering."

Her finger scrolled through the passage as she read how God not only spared Isaac's life and provided for their needs, but blessed Abraham for his obedience. "I will bless thee, and will multiply thy seed as the stars of the heaven."

Closing the Bible, she clasped it to her chest, no longer viewing it as a treasured gift, but as a trustworthy friend. She walked to the window, gazing up into the starry sky. Thousands of glittering stars shone down on her, much the same as they had from the loft window of her cabin nearly a year earlier. It was hard to fathom that, under this same sky, her prairie home and everything she held dear were being governed by the same powerful, unseen Hand.

There was so much she still didn't understand, so many unanswered questions. Yet she was a different person than when she'd come. God had intricately woven each event, each encounter into His plan for her life to strengthen and prepare her for the next leg of the journey. How could she doubt His ways for the future, when He'd been so faithful to bring her to this point? His will now overshadowed her own. She could no longer resist and have peace.

"For I know the plans I have for you. Plans to prosper you and not to harm you." The now familiar verse rippled through her mind.

Bowing her head, she laced her fingers together. *Lord, show me Your plan. Give me the courage to obey, whatever Your will may be.*

Chapter Thirty-Five

A GENTLE BREEZE cooled Becky's face as she swept the front steps. The sound of laughter drifted from the back yard. Striding to the edge of the building, she leaned on her broom handle, watching the younger students romp. No doubt about it, she'd grown comfortable here. Domestic tasks, once dreaded and shunned, had become a means to give of herself to others. And ultimately to God.

Jimmy had been right in saying home was her Isaac. It was the one thing she'd withheld from God. The one thing she couldn't let go of. And though a part of her still yearned for the prairie, last night, for the first time, she'd yielded it to Him.

Matthew as well.

Her future now rested in God's hands. If she was needed here, she would stay, until God gave clear indication it was time to leave. He'd asked for total surrender, and she'd obeyed. She could do no more.

"Hello, Becky."

The man's smooth, baritone voice from behind was unmistakable. Becky tensed, warmth flooding through her. Had she imagined it? Swiveling, she fought to catch her breath. "Matthew. What are you doing here?"

"I had to see you." He stepped closer, his dark eyes trained on hers.

She wet her lips, taking in his handsome frame. Was he real? Even more striking than she remembered him, Becky stymied the urge to run and throw her arms around him. "How did you find us?"

He gripped his hat, a gentle smile playing on his lips. "Your return address, along with a couple of not so willing townspeople who pointed the way."

She bit at her cheek, recalling she'd never officially informed him of the move. Not after the unexpected news. "Did Pa send for you?"

"No. I came because I need to speak with you." Tenderness, meshed with uncertainty, lined his words. He edged closer, narrowing the gap between them. "Could you join me for dinner?"

She twisted the broom handle in both palms, the memory of Aunt Clara's letter washing through her. Had he come in person to break the news of his engagement? Such a notion was appreciated but hard to take. Averting her gaze, she gestured toward the students, coolness seeping into her tone. "I'm afraid we're short-handed. It's difficult for me to get away."

"Then could I meet you here later this evening?"

She worked to still the quiver in her chin. If he'd come all this way to divulge the unwelcome tidings, she'd not disappoint him. But, neither would she give him the satisfaction of seeing her cry. With a hard swallow, she lifted her eyes to his. Was the warmth streaming from them hemmed with pity?

Intent on her thoughts, Becky barely noticed a carriage roll to a stop at the front of the school. Before she could formulate her answer, Mr. Jacobs strode up beside them. With effort, she broke her stare away from Matthew's and turned to the storeowner.

Instead of his apron, he wore a fine brown suit and a ribbon tie, tufts of strawberry-blond hair lining the rim of his hat. "Mr. Jacobs."

He gave a slight bow, tipping his rounded felt hat, while exchanging a friendly nod with Matthew. "Forgive me. I don't mean to intrude."

"Go right ahead. I'm in no hurry." Matthew eased back, giving way to the storekeeper.

Still putting others ahead of himself. Matthew hadn't changed in that respect. Heat welled in Becky's cheeks. How her heart yearned to think he hadn't changed toward her either. But obviously he had.

Shaking off the thought, she forced herself to focus on Mr. Jacobs. "Have you come for more chairs?"

"Actually, I've come to see Jimmy. Is he around?"

Becky pointed over her shoulder, her gaze drifting to the woman seated on the buggy seat. A frilly bonnet hid her features. "He's out back. Would you like me to get him?"

"Don't bother. I'll see to him." He hesitated, shifting his weight from one foot to the other. "Would it be all right if my wife and I took him for a ride?"

"Yes, of course." An overpowering urge to squeal bubbled within Becky. Had her visit to the storekeeper had an affect after all?

"We'll have him back by suppertime." And, with another tip of his hat, Mr. Jacobs strode past.

Moisture pooled in Becky's eyes, all her heartfelt prayers melding into one as she watched him approach Jimmy. The two conversed a moment, then started toward the wagon together.

"It appears your prayers for your friend, Jimmy, have been answered."

Turning, Becky found Matthew stood only a few inches from her. She nodded, his nearness stealing her voice and pulling at her emotions.

His eyes swept over her face, a winsome smile pulling at his lips. "May I see you tonight then?"

She managed a slow nod. How could she refuse? She needed to hear from his own lips that he cared for someone else. But, even as she agreed, her heart resisted.

MATTHEW SWUNG his leg over Gabriel, casting a final glance at Becky as she made her way inside. It had taken all his composure not to gather her in his arms. There was no question in his mind now. The moment he'd seen her, he'd known she was meant for him. The months apart had only enhanced her beauty —matched only by the glow of compassion in her eyes for her friend. She obviously had a great love for people. And true inner beauty, befitting the wife of a pastor.

Still, he'd sensed a wall spring up between them at his request to meet. Her averted gaze and nervous fidgeting hinted of some unknown angst. While his own feelings had deepened, had hers waned?

Reining Gabriel into the busy street, he pushed away the thought. The delay offered him the chance to find a livery, and a hotel where he could bathe and shave. Best of all, he'd have time to pray more deliberately. He knew what was in his heart to say. He'd had the entire trip to formulate it in his mind. Still, he wasn't sure Becky was ready to receive it.

His time here was short-lived. He'd have to make the most of it.

BECKY'S HEART drummed in her chest as she scurried to the window and peered out at Matthew from behind the sheer, ivory curtain. Nothing could have surprised her more than to hear his deep voice call her name. Everything in her wanted to rush after him, to will him to stay and never leave her side again. But she refused to surrender to the impulse. He wasn't hers to beckon. His heart belonged to someone else now.

She watched until he faded from view and then, letting the curtain fall into place, she backed away and plopped down in a chair more confused than ever. Why had he come? What had possessed him to travel all this way just to speak with her? Just when she'd found peace, he threatened to undo it. She had half a mind not even to show when he called on her this evening. Still, she clung to that one cinder of hope that refused to be extinguished. Until he admitted to loving someone else, she couldn't let the smoldering flame within her die.

In the meantime, she needed to keep busy and spend her energies doing something useful. Rising, she made her way to the kitchen to start dinner. An hour later, Mr. Jacobs dropped Jimmy off and asked to speak privately with Peter. Becky resisted probing Jimmy about the venture until after Mr. Jacobs had gone.

"How was your ride?" she asked, pulling him aside.

"Fine."

"Fine? That's it?"

He shrugged. "Not much to tell."

Becky knit her brow. "Honestly. Getting anything out of you is like prying a turtle from its shell. Surely Mr. Jacobs had some reason he met with Mr. Bennett."

A corner of Jimmy's mouth lifted. "He wants me to help out at his store."

"You mean he offered you a job?"

"Not exactly." He hesitated, suppressing a grin. "They want me to stay with them and get more acquainted. They're clearin' out a room in back of the store for me. Said they'd come in a couple of days."

She gripped his arm. It was just the encouragement she needed about now. "Oh, Jimmy!"

"Now, don't get all fired up. Could be they decide I'm too much of a bother."

"You don't fool me, Jimmy Bodine. You're every bit as excited as I am."

Warmth flooded through her at his wide grin. If she couldn't have home herself, at least she could be happy her prayers for Jimmy were all but answered.

WITH SUPPER DISHES FINISHED, Becky bid Lily goodnight and strolled to the front room. The lilting sound of Pa's fiddle stirred her spirit. He played frequently now, with almost as much zeal as when he was sighted. Despite the heartache along with it, she couldn't deny Matthew had given them a wonderful gift in sending the instrument.

Wrapping her shawl around her shoulders, she glanced out the window. Though there was no sign of Matthew, she determined to slip outside to wait. It was best Pa not know of his visit. Learning Matthew had broken her heart would only cause Pa grief. In days to come, she'd attempt to mask her disappointment as best she could.

The March wind had stilled to a gentle breeze as she settled on the stone step. A woman's faint laughter drew her attention to the walkway out front. She caught a glimpse of Peter and Aunt Ellen ambling along the darkening street. The twilight stroll to the livery had become a nightly ritual for them. It was wonderful to see her aunt had at last opened her heart to love. She deserved such happiness.

Traffic slowed to a trickle as the sun dipped below the buildings. Lamplighters began to dot the street with light. Becky leaned forward, cupping her chin in her hand, her stomach tightening. If Matthew didn't arrive soon, she'd have no nerve left to face him.

A shadowy figure of a man appeared on the walkway further down, sending a shiver through Becky. She'd know that silhouette anywhere, the smooth stride, broad shoulders, and wide-brimmed hat. Straightening, she rose to her feet, her quivering legs threatening to land her back where she'd started. It was good they'd waited until evening. The fading light would help hide her frailties and the moisture attempting to seep into her eyes.

She had to pull herself together. Couldn't let him glimpse the hurt pent up inside her.

He jogged up the steps, a smile lining his lips. His cheerfulness flustered her. How could he be so eager to shatter her heart?

Slipping his hat from his head, Matthew stepped up beside her. "Sorry I wasn't here sooner. I had a hard time finding a hotel near the livery that wasn't filled."

"It's all right. I haven't waited long." The faint scent of witch-hazel wafted toward Becky. Even in the shadowy light, she could see his clean-shaven jaw and freshly combed hair. Had he cleaned up for her sake, or for his own, after his lengthy trip?

A couple of students filtered past on their way indoors. Matthew placed a hand on Becky's elbow, pulling her aside. "Is there a place we can talk in private?"

His nearness after so many months wasn't making this easy. She pointed several yards to their left. "Th-there's a bench over there."

Looping her arm through his, he guided her down the steps and onto the bench. The warmth of his touch set off a maelstrom of raw emotions inside Becky. The sooner this was over with, the better.

Matthew turned to face her, taking her hands in his. Moisture formed between their fingertips. Whether it was him or her perspiring, Becky couldn't be certain. But she could sense a change in him, the uneasiness in his face, his tensed jaw and furrowed brow. She nearly felt sorry for him. His discomfort, though, bolstered her courage.

He cleared his throat, clasping her fingers more firmly. "I had to come, Becky. What I have to say couldn't be said in a letter. I hope you understand, I needed to be with you when I told you."

Her chin lifted, though her voice quivered. "I appreciate you making the effort. And though I believe I already know what you have to say, I need to hear from your own lips."

He flashed a sideways grin. "Then you know that I've grown to love you, even with all these months apart."

Becky sensed the blood drain from her cheeks, her heart drumming in her ears. Had she heard him right? He loved her? "But, I heard you were all but betrothed to someone else."

Matthew's eyes flashed then narrowed. "Who told you such?"

"Aunt Clara, in her last letter."

He sat back, loosening his hold on her hands. "I should have known." With a sigh, he swiped a hand through his hair. "Believe me. There's not an ounce of truth to it."

Becky studied him, wanting to believe, and yet not fully convinced. How could her aunt be so mistaken? "Your note with Pa's fiddle was so short and vague. I feared what she said was true."

"It wasn't that." His voice softened, a slight blush staining his cheeks. "I'd begun to doubt you'd be happy as a...pastor's wife. I realized it would be a huge adjustment for you. I thought it best not to pursue things further until we'd talked."

"So you took up company with another lady?" Becky's voice quaked, her hurt mounting.

With a sigh, he leaned forward, twisting his hat in his hands. "I suppose you're due an explanation."

Becky's mood shifted from hurt to trepidation. How would

he explain away such a misunderstanding? If it were a misunderstanding.

Matthew gave a stilted cough. "You see, the school teacher they hired a few months back was an old acquaintance of mine. We were close once. She wanted to renew our relationship. I didn't. The townspeople had it in their heads we were a twosome, as did she. I set her straight before I came. I've no interest in her, I assure you."

A ray of hope sliced through Becky's angst. She'd never known Matthew to be less than completely honest. "That's all there is to it?"

"That's all."

"You're certain?"

"Very." He hesitated, then reached in his vest pocket and brought out a black felt box. Placing it in Becky's palm, he didn't quite meet her gaze. "Unless you count this. She found it by mistake and claimed it as her own. I tried to explain it was for someone else, but she's more quick to speak than listen."

Becky drew in a breath, eyeing the expensive-looking box. Whatever it was had cost Matthew dearly. Prying open the lid, she released a soft gasp. The jeweled cross was stunning and didn't give off the appearance of ever being worn. She ran her fingertips over it. "It's beautiful."

Darting him a glance out of the corner of her eye, she allowed the slightest grin to settle onto her lips. "Is this by chance the gift you'd spoken of sending?"

"The very one." His drawn expression edged out any doubt in Becky's mind of his truthfulness.

With a slight chuckle, she slid her hand into his. "Then I accept it wholeheartedly."

The light in his eyes returned, and he edged closer. "Then, am I to assume you care for me as well?"

A smile touched her lips. "You may."

He pressed her fingers to his lips, kissing them lightly. "Then may I ask your father's permission to court you?"

Becky tensed. How she longed to say yes. To shout it even. And yet, there remained a check on her spirit. She'd surrendered her future to the Lord. Was this His plan for her? Was love for this man enough to cause her to leave this place? She bowed her head. "Not just yet."

"But why not? I know it may be some time before…"

She cut off his words with a shake of her head. "They've asked me to stay here beyond when Pa finishes his training."

His tensed jaw and brief silence pulled at her heart. "Are you considering it?"

She met his gaze, her eyes brimming with tears. "I'd love nothing more than to return home. But I have to be sure it's what the Lord wants."

He draped an arm around her shoulders, pulling her to him. "Then I'll wait, until you're certain, and pray the time is short."

Becky pressed her cheek to his chest, trying to stem the flow of tears. "When will you leave?"

"Tomorrow morning, if I'm to get back before Sunday." He placed a hand under her chin, and she willed herself to meet his gaze. "But send word, and I'll be back for you."

With a slow nod, she melted into his embrace, sensing this second parting would be even more difficult than the first.

Chapter Thirty-Six

MATTHEW DISMOUNTED WITH A GROAN. The trip home had been excruciating. Even for a veteran rider, the long journey to St. Louis and back in such a short length of time had left him a bit saddle sore.

Heart sore as well.

For the most part, he'd accomplished what he'd set out to do —bare his soul and determine if Becky returned his love. Thanks to Clara Stanton, he'd bared more than intended. But at least now Becky knew where he stood. Any misunderstandings had been forgiven.

He loosened the cinch on Gabriel's saddle, mulling the situation over in his mind. How ironic that the one thing standing in the way of their future was Becky's commitment to the Lord. Not that he was displeased by that. The fact that she put God first made Matthew admire her even more. He wouldn't want anything less in a wife.

What a caring individual Becky had become. It was no wonder they wanted her to stay. Surely the Lord wouldn't initiate love between him and Becky only to call them to separate ministries. Couldn't He utilize her loving nature just as readily as the helpmate of a pastor?

Lifting the saddle from Gabriel's back, he swiveled with it toward the cabin. What a relief not to find Sarah awaiting him on the porch. Discouraging her hadn't been pleasant, but Matthew had no regrets. He'd done what was best for all concerned. He set the saddle over the porch rail, his gaze perusing the weather-worn cabin. Sarah had taught him one thing—he needed to tidy up the place and make it more suitable for a lady. Then, if and when Becky did return, perhaps she wouldn't be so hesitant to live there.

Out of respect for the Lord and love for Becky, he'd do his best to wait patiently.

But a little praying in his favor couldn't hurt.

THE PAST COUPLE of weeks had been heart-wrenching. Becky needed to talk to Jimmy. He had a way of getting to the core of the most troubling situations. Thankfully, Aunt Ellen had agreed to step in to allow Becky time to slip away for a short visit.

The bell to Mr. Jacobs' mercantile jingled as Becky opened the door and stepped inside. She scanned the store, shoulders drooping a bit when Jimmy was nowhere to be seen. Mr. Jacobs eyed her with a knowing grin as he tended to a customer. When he'd finished, he combed a hand through his thinning hair and strode toward her. "If I ventured a guess I'd say the young man you're looking for is in the stock room." With a gentle smile, he motioned to a curtained doorway.

Becky nodded her thanks, heat rising in her cheeks. Had she been so obvious? Pushing the heavy drape aside, she stepped into the hallway that led to the stock room. Ahead of her, Jimmy's muffled voice mingled with that of a woman's. Their animated conversation ended in a peal of laughter. Becky gave a slight knock at the doorframe, bringing an abrupt halt to the merriment. At sight of her, Mrs. Jacobs' expression sobered. The left half of her face drooped downward, seemingly frozen in place. She tilted her head to the side as if to hide her defect. "May I help you?"

At the woman's slurred voice, Becky dropped her gaze. "I-I've come to see Jimmy."

A spark of recognition brought Jimmy to full height. "Beck!" He stepped forward, reaching out to her.

She gave his hand a warm squeeze. "Hello, Jimmy."

Mrs. Jacobs' mouth curved into a crooked grin, though she drew a hand to her brow, shading her sagging eyelid and limp cheek. "You're Becky?"

"Yes, ma'am." With a reassuring smile, Becky met the woman's gaze. "I'm very glad to know you, Mrs. Jacobs."

The woman dropped her hand to her side, seeming to relax as she sensed Becky's acceptance. Had sensitivity to her appearance rendered her a recluse? Jimmy seemed a perfect fit for her, his blind eyes posing no threat. He would forever see her as the woman she was on the inside. "You two visit. We can finish this later, Jimmy." She strode to the doorway, giving him a pat on the back as she passed.

With a nod, Jimmy turned to Becky. "How's everything at the school?"

"Good. A bit lonelier without you, though."

He gave a lighthearted chuckle. "I've missed you too."

"Looks as though they're treating you well. Will you be staying on permanent?"

Leaning against the shelving, Jimmy sunk his hands in his pockets, lips curving in a grin. "Sounds that way."

"That's wonderful. They're good people." Becky brushed off a dusty stool and took a seat.

The room stilled, and Jimmy's smile faded. "I get the feeling you've come for more than casual chitchat."

Becky cleared her throat, folding her hands in her lap. "I did what you said, Jimmy. I surrendered going home to God. I'm willing to stay so long as I'm needed."

"Good." Jimmy gave a pronounced nod. "So, why do I sense that's not the problem?"

It was time to throw caution to the wind and let Jimmy know his suspicions regarding Matthew had been right all along. "The day Mr. Jacobs came for you, Matthew Brody showed up unexpectedly."

"Your preacher fellow?"

"Yes. Seems he's eager for me to return home." Becky tried to ignore the humored look on Jimmy's face. "Why would he come, just when I'd yielded my heart to God?"

Sobering, Jimmy propped his foot up on a box. "Do you love him?"

Heat singed Becky's cheeks. Her friend had an uncanny way of unraveling situations and getting to the crux of the matter. "Yes."

"Well, then, it could be God's giving you your answer. Maybe all He wanted was to know you were willing to stay. Maybe he's giving you back your Isaac."

Becky tensed. Could what Jimmy said be true? Could God have brought her to the point of surrender merely to reward her with what she longed for most? Hadn't He provided a lamb in place of Isaac for Abraham? "Yes, but I promised God so long as I'm needed here I'd stay."

Jimmy shrugged. "The Lord can use you in whatever way He chooses, be it here or back home as the wife of a pastor. You and He alone can decide where you're best suited."

"But how can I know?"

"Pray. When the time comes, you'll know."

Rain clouds gathered as Becky headed back. She lifted her eyes to the billowy sky, an unsettled feeling in her heart. Instead of resolving her issue, Jimmy had given her more to ponder. She couldn't speak to Pa about it. He'd already proclaimed it her decision. She'd simply have to give it time and see what transpired...and abundant prayer.

A flash of light flicked, followed by a loud crack of thunder, startling Becky from her thoughts. A horse's whinny split the air in the street. The animal bolted and slipped on the wet cobblestone. Thrown off balance, the driver pulled back on the reins, swerving to miss a cluster of people.

Large raindrops splashed down, cool against Becky's skin as they soaked through her dress. A sudden gust of wind whipped her bonnet backward, and she tugged it into place, squinting into the darkened sky. Not since the devastating storm back home had she witnessed such gray, low-lying clouds. She quickened her pace, heart pounding.

The wind blew harder, making it difficult to walk. Becky dodged the spray of people hounding their way inside stores and businesses. Another loud peal of thunder split the dark sky.

Were Pa and the other students safe indoors? The younger children would be frightened. The instructors didn't have the comforting instincts of a woman. Even with Aunt Ellen there, the students would be longing for someone they were more familiar with.

Like the day of the storm, a feeling of helplessness washed through Becky. She hiked her skirt, spurring herself into a jog. She should be with them.

The rain was coming in sheets now, making it impossible to see. She had no choice but to take shelter. Long minutes passed as she hunkered down beneath a store canopy, the sound of pouring rain her only companion. At last, it slowed and she was able to continue. Soon she could see the building up ahead. She imagined the place in disarray, students beside themselves with worry, the younger ones in tears for fear of the storm.

Drenched from head to toe, Becky made her way up the steps and pushed through the front door. Ignoring the puddle of water she left on the floor, she sloshed her way to the sitting room. Her eyes widened at sight of Aunt Ellen relaxing in an upholstered chair, a child perched happily on each knee. Many of the other students sat nearby in seeming expectation. By the open book resting in her aunt's hands, it appeared Becky had interrupted an entertaining story.

Peter tossed a log on the fire, then turned toward her, a queer expression on his face.

Feeling suddenly conspicuous, Becky peeled the drenched bonnet from her head and grinned. The peaceful scene had her wondering if there was something to what Jimmy said.

Perhaps her staying wasn't as essential as she and the instructors thought.

PETER STOOD AND "TINGED" his glass following the evening meal, a broad grin lining his lips. "Quiet, please. I have an announcement."

Becky pushed her plate aside as the room fell to silence. Peter's last announcement brought news of a new building. But he hadn't appeared half so excited then as now. What could bring such a radiant smile to his face?

He stepped to Aunt Ellen, placing his hands lightly on her shoulders. She gazed up at him, face aglow. He returned her lingering stare and then shifted his attention to the others. "I think you've all grown quite fond of Miss Ellen over recent months. Well, so have I."

Becky's heart quickened as her eyes locked on her aunt's, the blush in her cheeks speaking volumes.

Peter cleared his throat, eyes sparkling. "We wanted you all to be the first to know. Miss Ellen has consented to be my wife. We're to be wed as soon as arrangements can be made." The pair shared a quiet laugh as cheerful chatter rang out among the students.

Becky leapt to her feet at the unexpected news, a tangle of emotions welling within as she made her way to the beaming couple. Eyes brimming with tears, she leaned to embrace her aunt, holding her long and close. "I'm so happy for you."

Aunt Ellen loosened her hold, giving Becky a peck on the cheek. "I hoped you'd be pleased."

"Pleased? I'm thrilled beyond words."

Peter stepped up beside them, his expression apologetic. "I want you to know our offer still stands. You're more than welcome to stay on with us...though Ellen will be here to serve as housemother in your stead, should you wish to return home." He lifted her aunt's hand to his lips, a ready smile on his face.

Becky's gaze shifted to her aunt. "You'll live here then, among the students?"

With a sheepish grin, Aunt Ellen nodded. "I've often longed for a family. I'll have a ready-made one here I suppose."

Pa ambled up beside Becky, his voice soft amid the mounting conversation. "Seems just when you gave up on going home, the Lord had other plans."

Becky's lips parted in a teary smile. He'd done it. The Lord had made a way. How grateful she was He'd waited to reveal His plan. Without being asked to stay, never would she have known the blessing of total surrender. The Lord had given her back her Isaac.

He'd given her a way back home.

Her hand moved to the wedding band dangling from the ribbon around her neck, warmth flooding through her.

Along with someone to love.

"Pastor Brody!"

Matthew pulled back on the reins, drawn by the urgency in the postmistress's voice. The willowy woman scurried over to him, waving a telegram in her hand. "What is it, Mrs. Chaney? Not bad news, I hope."

She stopped beside him, pausing to catch her breath. "This just came for you from Becky Hollister. I thought it might be important."

His jaw tightened. Had something happened? "What does it say?"

"Just one word. COME. Does that mean anything to you?"

A smile crept onto Matthew's lips, and he fought to suppress the shout of gladness bursting inside him. "Yes, ma'am. It surely does."

"For I know the plans I have for you," declares the Lord, *"plans to prosper you and not to harm you, plans to give you hope and a future."*

Epilogue

April 9, 1855

BECKY CLUTCHED the bouquet of purple phlox, a gentle breeze toying with loose strands of hair beneath her bun. Clad in her white blouse and blue satin skirt, she stood beside Aunt Ellen as she and Peter spoke their vows beneath the towering oak. With a smile, Becky glanced over her shoulder at the small gathering of friends and students who had become like family to her. Jimmy's presence made the day all the more perfect. What a year ago had seemed so frightening and foreign had become dear and precious. She would carry this place and these people back with her, in her heart.

Her aunt's soft, airy voice drew her attention back to the eager bride and groom. Radiant in her white silk taffeta gown, fringed with pale sapphire bows, Aunt Ellen's gaze remained locked on Peter as he tenderly placed a gold band on her finger.

He stood tall, looking proud as Pastor Stein offered his final words and pronounced them man and wife. At his command, Peter touched a hand to Aunt Ellen's cheek and leaned to kiss her, sealing their bond of love.

Becky heaved a contented sigh. True love was worth the wait. How she longed for Matthew to again take her in his arms.

Pa's fiddle hummed a festive tune as the ceremony ended and everyone gathered to congratulate the happy couple. Invigorated by the merriment, Becky helped Lily slice up generous portions of the two-tiered cake.

A vague sound in the distance tugged at the recesses of Becky's mind, faint though familiar. She shook it away, divvying out the remaining cake. Nearly a week had passed since she'd sent word to Matthew. Pa assured her it was too soon, yet for days she'd kept a watchful eye on the street.

There it came again, a dog's bark, sharp and low. Craning her neck, she peered down the cobblestone street, eyes searching the mass of people and buggies. A wide smile spread over her face at sight of the canvas-covered wagon rolling toward them. There was no mistaking the big, yellow dog or the driver with the wide-brimmed hat.

Her heart swelled with joy as she ran to meet him. Matthew's chiseled jaw held a wide smile as he set the brake and hopped from the wagon. He met her in mid stride, his chocolate eyes sweeping over her face. Taking her in his arms, he pressed his lips to hers.

And in that moment, Becky knew she was home.

About the Author

Cynthia's thirst for writing began her junior year of high school, when her short-story won first place in a local college writing contest. She went on to pursue a career in writing by earning a B.A. in English/Creative Writing from U of I of Springfield, IL. Since then, Cynthia has had around 100 articles and short-stories printed in various Christian teen and adult publications.

Under this Same Sky is her debut novel and Book One in her upcoming Prairie Sky Series. Cynthia has been a finalist in both the ACFW Genesis Contest and the Olympia Contest and was named Historical/Historical Romance Category Winner in the Writers of the West (Rattler) Contest.

Cynthia counts it a blessing and privilege to be doing what the Lord has placed on her heart to do—write to inspire others. She loves to connect with readers and invites those who've been touched by her writing to contact her and to write a review of her novel on Amazon or Goodreads.

Website: http://cynthiaroemer.com/

Author's Note

Though the majority of this novel is a product of my imagination, the Missouri School for the Education of the Blind is indeed a real place that is still in existence today. As portrayed in the novel, the founder was a blind man named Eli Whalen and the first students were fourteen-year-old Elizabeth Tayler and seven-year-old Daniel Wilkinson. Jimmy Bodine, as well as all the other students, was fictional, as were Nettie and Peter Bennett. I endeavored to stay true to the time period, curriculum, and tools used in teaching the blind students, but made a few alterations in the building sites and structures.

Becky's hometown of Miller Creek, along with the other towns Matthew Brody ministered in, were fictional. St. Louis and Illinoistown (present East St. Louis) were true depictions of the towns in their day. I did extensive research to try to make them as true-to-life as possible, even down to the street names. However, that's not to say a few details may prove less than fully accurate.

I hope you enjoyed stepping back in time with me to meet Becky, Matthew, Jimmy, and the array of other characters in Under This Same Sky. I hope you'll join me for Book 2: Under Prairie Skies to read Becky's cousin Charlotte Stanton's tale of grace and redemptive love.

Also by Cynthia Roemer

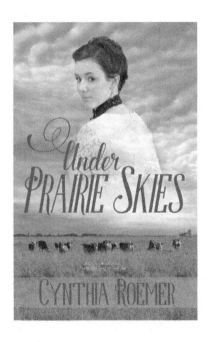

Prairie Sky Series – Book Two

~ Beyond shattered dreams lies a realm of possibilities ~

Illinois prairie ~1855

Unsettled by the news that her estranged cousin and uncle are returning home after a year away, Charlotte Stanton goes to ready their cabin and finds a handsome stranger has taken up residence. Convinced he's a squatter, she throws him off the property before learning his full identity. Little does she know, their paths were destined to cross again.

Quiet and ruggedly handsome, Chad Avery's uncanny ability to see through Charlotte's feisty exterior and expose her inner weaknesses both infuriates and intrigues her. When a tragic accident incites her family to move east, Charlotte stays behind in hopes of becoming better acquainted with the elusive cattleman. Yet Chad's unwillingness to divulge his hidden past, along with his vow not to love again, threatens to keep them apart forever.

Prairie Sky Series – Book Three

She had her life planned out ~ until he rode in

Illinois prairie ~ 1859

After four long years away, Esther Stanton returns to the prairie to care for her sister Charlotte's family following the birth of her second child. The month-long stay seems much too short as Esther becomes acquainted with her brother-in-law's new ranch hand, Stewart Brant.

When obligations compel her to return to Cincinnati and to the man her overbearing mother intends her to wed, she loses hope of ever knowing true happiness.

Still reeling from a hurtful relationship, Stew is reluctant to open his heart to Esther. But when he faces a life-threatening injury with Esther tending him, their bond deepens. Heartbroken when she leaves, he sets out after her and inadvertently stumbles across an illegal slave-trade operation, the knowledge of which puts him, as well as Esther and her family, in jeopardy.

Under Moonlit Skies is a 2020 Selah Awards finalist the Western category.